FRANKIE BOY

Rebel in Short Pants

By Frank J. Rossiter

Blessings to my new tennis friend, Helen Banner.

Frank

PSALM 118:14

Creative Force Press
Guiding Aspiring Authors to Release Their Dream

Creative Force Press
Guiding Aspiring Authors to Release Their Dream

Frankie Boy
© 2013 by Frank J. Rossiter
Revised Illustrated Edition

This title is also available as an eBook.
Visit www.CreativeForcePress.com/titles for more information.

Published by Creative Force Press
4704 Pacific Ave, Suite C, Lacey, WA 98503
www.CreativeForcePress.com

ISBN: 978-1494819422

Printed in the United States of America

DEDICATION

I dedicate this book to you,
my beautiful mother Ellen,
who loved me unconditionally.
You braved the elements
of post-war poverty
to raise eleven children,
only to die far too young.
You are always in my heart and
I think of you every single
day of my life.
I love you Mam,
Frankie Boy

ACKNOWLEDGMENT

*I want to thank my beautiful wife Bella
for making my dreams come true;
for believing in me and in my story;
for her dedication to typing, editing,
and submitting this manuscript many times
over, determined to see it through
to publication;
and also for fifty-three years of her
unconditional love!*

Liverpool, England, 1947

Upper Mann Street was dark and dismal, empty except for the lone dock worker walking briskly with hunched shoulders, cap pulled down low over his eyes, and coat collar up around his neck to keep out the winter chill. From just inside one of the four aging brick tenements, seven year old Frankie dared himself to take a peek out at the shadowy figure passing beneath the tall gas lamp.

It's gotta be the Glosher Man or Jack the Ripper, he reasoned, his small frame trembling with a mixture of fear and suspense. For a fleeting moment he contemplated running back up the stairs and into the house to safety, and then thought better of it. He was determined to find out where his mother had gone.

The boy's large brown eyes followed after the man until he disappeared beyond the wall of darkness, leaving behind the faint echo of his footsteps on the wet cobblestones. The street lamp stood alone, its halo of eerie, translucent light revealing a fine, misty rain. The sound of distant foghorns only added to the bleakness of this forlorn street.

Frankie pushed open the heavy door to the pub and stood with one eye to the crack, peering inside. He thought he recognized his mother's familiar voice, but it was impossible for him to see her through the blue haze of cigarette smoke and the crowds of people congregating near the door. He allowed the door to close again, unsure of what to do next. He sat down on the worn step and hugged his knees up to his chest, resting his chin on them. The cotton shirt and short trousers he was wearing seemed little defense against the biting wind blowing up from the river, but the boy didn't seem to be affected by it.

Three young men in their late teens sauntered by and stopped several feet away from him. They whispered to each other and glanced furtively from side to side, their hands thrust deep inside their trouser pockets. The pub door opened, sending a shaft of light spilling onto the trio. They sprang back into the shadows as a man came staggering out. He stood weaving and muttering to himself, unsure of which way to turn. Droplets of rain began to form on the peak of his cap and drip down onto his nose. He tried to wipe it with the back of his hand but lost his balance and fell against the door.

The youths emerged from the shadows. "Hey, Pops, let's give you a hand," one grinned while the other two went through his pockets. He tried to struggle free but only managed to slip on the wet pavement, pulling everyone down on top of him.

Frankie stood watching the scene with morbid fascination. Then he began to run as fast as his little legs would carry him.

***

Sunlight filtered through the early morning mist that hung like wisps of tattered shroud about the quiet street. The sound of bottles tinkled in the distance as a lone figure hurried from door to door setting bottles of milk on front steps and retrieving the empties left for him the night before. A middle-aged woman, tousled and sleepy-eyed, stood impatiently in her half-opened doorway, waiting for the milkman to reach her. Every breath she exhaled sent vapor curling into the chilly morning air.

Frankie lay in peaceful sleep with a heavy army coat pulled up to his chin. On each side of his head lay a pair of stocking feet belonging to his two older sisters, Sarah, nine, and Dorothy, ten and a half. Beside him slept his four year old baby sister, Margaret. Covering the children was an olive green army blanket and an assortment of coats thrown on top for added warmth. The small room was cold and damp from years without heat, and the only source of light was that which came through the window.

The sound of a church bell tolling in the distance caused Dorothy to stir. She opened her eyes and tried to summon enough courage to leave the warmth of the bed. Instead, she moved closer to her sister and closed her eyes, reluctant to face the cold.

"Dorothy! Are you up, girl?" Her eyes opened in response to her mother's call from the bedroom next door.

"Yes, Mam, I'm getting up!" The sound of her voice awakened Sarah, but she immediately turned over and went back to sleep. Dorothy sat up and looked down at her, wishing she wasn't the oldest and responsible for getting things going whenever her mother wasn't feeling well. Having gone to bed fully clothed, she pulled her coat from the pile on the bed and draped it around her shoulders. She tiptoed out of the room trying to keep as much of her feet off the cold linoleum as she could.

Using the last of the coal, she soon had a fire going in the cast-iron fireplace, and then stood staring dreamily at the flames, her hands thrust out to warm her fingers.

"Dorothy!" The sound of her mother's voice brought her back from her dreamlike trance.

"What, Mam?"

"Are you making a cup of tea, girl?" She reluctantly moved away from the circle of heat into the cold back kitchen.

Sitting up in bed, Kate watched as her bedroom door slowly opened. She smiled knowingly as a little curly head peeked around the door. "Come on, jump in!" she teased, as she parted the blankets to the side. Frankie ran to the bed and scampered in, curling up beside her.

"I seen a man get hurt last night, Mam."

"Well, that's what you get when you sneak out when you're supposed to be in bed!"

"But, I was looking for you, Mam."

"You can't go following me around, Frankie Boy." she said, stroking his curls with affection. "You're the man of the house now, son, so you've got to be here with your sisters." He looked up into her face to see if she had meant it. Dorothy came into the bedroom and sat down on the edge of the bed.

"There's no sugar for the tea, again," she said feeling hopeless, her gaze coming to rest on Frankie's face, as though he were somehow to blame.

"Run down to Maggie's and ask her for a cup until I go to the shops. That's a good girl."

"Oh, hey, Mam, I borrowed some from her yesterday and you never paid her back."

"Go on, girl, she knows I don't get me money until tomorrow."

Dorothy left the room with a sulky look on her face. When she came back into the bedroom, she was carrying a steaming cup of tea. Her mother looked at her tenderly and reached for it.

"Do I get one?" Frankie pleaded.

"Get your own, 'laze.' Mam, is he going to school tomorrow?"

"No, I can't send him to school looking like a scruff. I've got to get him a decent pair of trousers and a warm coat first."

Dorothy looked down at him snuggled next to his mother. "You're gonna be a dunce, lad," she said with conviction. With that she turned and walked out of the room.

The four children sat quietly on the couch, all bundled up. A small hole in the gas mantle sent little jets of flame hissing through it. The fire in the fireplace was now officially out after consuming two pairs of old shoes and a wooden shelf from the back kitchen cupboard. Kate sat at the table writing, her long dark brown hair cascading over her shoulders. When she finished she turned in her chair to face the children. Their eyes focused on her hands as she slowly folded the paper in half, then folded it again.

"Who gets to go down to Uncle Peter's for me?" she asked, making it sound like a game filled with adventure.

"I'll go, Mam," Frankie shouted without hesitation.

"No, lad. It's dark outside and you're too little to be walking 'round at night." Her gaze settled on Dorothy, but Dorothy averted her eyes by staring down at her hands clasped in her lap.

"Do this for me, girl," her mother coaxed.

"Oh, hey, Mam, I always go, and I get embarrassed asking for money all the time."

Frankie jumped up off the couch and walked over to his mother's chair. He took hold of her hand with the note in it.

"Mam, you said I was the man of the house and I wanna go."

She looked into his big brown eyes, battling the urge to protect him.

"Dorothy, walk him down the block and watch until he reaches Auntie Mary's door. Frankie, don't let her see the note; she'll have a fit. Wait until your Uncle Peter is alone before you give it to him."

With that, she stuffed the note into his pocket and pulled his coat collar up around his neck, securing it with a safety pin she extracted from her cardigan. He gave her a big smile as he turned to join his sister waiting at the front door.

Dorothy stood huddled against the entrance to the tenement, watching the small silhouette slowly disappear into the wet night. She waited just long enough to see the light from Aunt Mary's open door, then turned and ran back up the stairs into her house.

Down the street, the door opened to reveal a heavyset woman in her mid-twenties. Without hesitation, Frankie walked inside and past his bewildered aunt.

"Does your mother know you're out on a night like this?"

"Yes, Auntie Mary."

She followed him into the kitchen, muttering something to herself.

"Come over here by the fire before you catch your death of cold."
She took off his coat and settled herself into an overstuffed chair,
promptly setting him into her lap. Soon, her fingers were rummaging
through his thick curly locks in search of biddies (head lice),
destroying them between her thumbnails.

There was bread and cake still left on the table from tea time,
which Frankie hoped would be offered to him, as they sometimes
did. His three cousins, Kevin, Stewart, and Chris, were in their
typical boisterous mood, bickering over anything and everything
between them. Uncle Peter, bare from his waist up, stood at the other
end of the fireplace, lathering his face with shaving cream and
squinting to see his reflection in the mirror-like family picture on the
mantlepiece. He seemed oblivious to the fighting going on behind
him until his voice suddenly boomed out, "Sufferin' Jesus! If you
kids don't knock it off, I'm gonna give you something to scream
about. Me belt will be up your arses!"

The sudden outburst startled Frankie and he sat upright in his
aunt's lap, waiting breathlessly for what may ensue. The boys
continued their clamor, unaffected by their pending doom. Frankie
searched his uncle's face, his body tensed, waiting for the next
eruption, which he was sure would come at any second. He became
aware of his aunt's soothing voice.

"Don't worry, lad, the silly bugger just likes to hear his own
voice."

His uncle glanced sideways at him, winked, and turned back to his
shaving. "Have you had your tea yet, Frankie?" Shaving cream
spattered the picture as he spoke.

"No, Uncle Peter."

"Are you hungry then? Would you like a piece of cake?"

The boy slowly nodded yes, still a little bewildered by the sudden
change of attitude. He grabbed the cake and turning to no one in
particular, said, "I have to go home now."

"Mary, see him down the street. It's a bloody shame, your sister
letting him out on a night like this."

It was then that Frankie remembered the note in his pocket. It
didn't seem at all possible he could get it into his uncle's hands

without his aunt seeing it, too. She was sitting right there between them. But he had promised his Mam he could do it.

"Uncle Peter, can I whisper something to you?"

His uncle bent down, wiping his face with a towel. "What is it, lad?"

"Me Mam gave me a note for you and she doesn't want Auntie Mary to see it," he whispered.

"Where is it, then?" he whispered back, trying to sound secretive.

"It's in me pocket," he said, pointing to the one nearest his uncle.

"What's going on between you two?" Mary asked, her arms folded, pretending she hadn't a clue.

Peter ignored her as he read the note. He put his hand in his trouser pocket and peeled off two one pound notes and stuffed them into the boy's pocket.

"Tell your Mam this is the last bloody time, Frankie. I'm not made of money!"

With that, he turned the boy around and pushed him gently toward the door. Mary took his hand and walked him halfway down the block.

"Go on, run the rest of the way and I'll watch out for you from here. And tell your Mam she's got a bloody cheek!" she shouted as an afterthought.

Frankie stood naked in the basin of hot water on the kitchen table while his mother, with flannel in hand, gave him his weekly bath. The three girls sat around the fire pretending not to look.

"Mam, they're looking at me!"

"No, we're not!" all three sang out in unison.

"I'll send the lot of you to bed if you don't behave!"

There was silence until his penis was being washed. Margaret, the youngest, blurted out, "She's washing his teapot."

Dorothy tried to cover Margaret's mouth with her hand, but it was too late. The girls got the giggles and couldn't stop. The harder they tried, the more they giggled, until they were completely out of control. Their laughter was so contagious, Kate, herself, was hard pressed to keep from laughing. It tickled Frankie's funny bone and he began to laugh, too, wiggling his bum to accentuate his teapot even more. This evoked more laughter until the girls were rolling on the floor holding their tummies.

"Okay, show-off! That's enough of that," his mother said, covering him with a towel and lifting him out of the bowl onto the table top.

"Mam, do I get to watch them take a bath?" he quivered, as his mother dried him off vigorously.

"No, don't be silly."

"But they got to watch me."

"They weren't supposed to. Anyway, it's not the same."

"But..." Before he could finish, she covered his mouth with the towel and lifted him down onto the floor.

"That's enough of that. Go get dressed."

Suddenly, the light began to dim. "Oh, God, I don't think I have a shilling for the gas. Sarah, pass me my purse right by your head, there on the mantelpiece."

By now, the gaslight had grown so dim it was impossible for her to see inside her purse, so she emptied the contents onto the floor in front of the fire. Two pennies, a three-penny bit, and two buttons rolled out.

Dorothy, always the worrier, looked at her mother. "Mam, that's the last of the wood, too."

"Well, kids, it's too late now to do anything about it, so let's all go to bed and worry about it in the morning." She looked from one to the other, the firelight flickering across each of their young faces. "You'll be nice and warm in bed," she gently reassured them.

The bedroom door creaked open. "Come on, snot-nose, get in!" Frankie made a dash for the open space.

"Is it Christmas, Mam?"

"No, lad, why did you ask?"

"It's snowing outside. Isn't it Christmas when it snows?"

"No. Sometimes it snows before Christmas just so little boys like you can make slides and build snowmen."

Dorothy came into the room with a pained look on her face and rubbing her behind.

"What's the matter, girl?"

"I nearly froze me bum off sitting on the toilet seat."

"Here, get in beside me." Dorothy grinned with delight and climbed over to the other side of her mother. The door opened again and in came Margaret rubbing the sleep from her eyes.

"Can I get in, too, Mam?"

"Yes, ducks, come and snuggle next to me. Frankie, make room for your little sister, there's a good lad."

While everyone was giggling and wiggling, Sarah appeared in the room. "It's snowing out, Mam. Can we please stay home from school?"

"Yes, girl. Here, climb in with this giggly bunch, and I'll get up and make us a luvly cup of tea."

The first snow of the year had turned the old, decaying street into a white wonderland. Children were everywhere, squealing with delight as they chased each other with snowballs, built snowmen, or careened down long slides that glistened icily from constant use. The carnival atmosphere outside had enticed many mothers to form little groups on the tenement landings, smiling and laughing at the antics of the children on the street below.

That evening, the four children sat around a blazing fire, casting their long shadows on the wall behind them. The gaslight had gone out again, starved for a shilling in its meter. Each of the children took turns at trying to make a barking dog from a shadowy hand cast on the wall. A sharp, cracking sound came from the back kitchen area. Soon, Kate emerged holding a candle stuck on a saucer, and carrying a small cabinet door under her arm.

"Got to keep that fire going kids, because your mother's got something up her sleeve." It excited them to see her in a fighting spirit, instead of everyone going to bed feeling dejected.

"Here, Dorothy, be careful and break that door up into small pieces with the poker. I'll be back in a minute."

She returned with a tin can and a pair of heavy-duty scissors. The children surrounded her, their eyes wide with excitement as she began cutting a small hole in the side of the tin. Once the piece of tin was extracted, she snipped at it until she was satisfied it was the right shape. Next, she scraped it gently on the stone hearth until the jagged edges were smooth. Now the time had come for the big test. She placed it in the meter slot and pushed. It wouldn't go in. She pushed a little harder, but this time it stuck halfway in. The kids held their breath as she tried to pull it back out, but it wouldn't budge. She let out a long, audible sigh before attacking it again. Finally, it came loose.

"Just a little more," she promised under her breath.

Back at the hearth, she scraped off a little here and there then tried the slot again. This time it went in, lighting up the room.

"You did it, Mam, you did it!" Dorothy sang, relieved that the tension was finally over.

"Put the kettle on, girl, and we'll have a nice cup of tea before bed..."

With a huge bag of wet laundry in her arms, Kate struggled to negotiate the last of the tenement steps. When she reached her landing, she put the bag down and paused to catch her breath.

"Margaret, are you coming, girl?"

"Yes, Mam, I was playing with the kitty."

"Well, we'd better keep moving before school lets out for the dinner hour."

She glanced up at the dark clouds and wondered if she should take a chance on hanging the wash over the railings. Her friend, Abby, from along the landing, noticed her looking up at the sky.

"Looks like rain, hey, Kate?"

"It does, Abby, but what can you do? There isn't enough room to hang it all around the house."

"Do what you can and I'll take the rest in."

"Okay, girl, I'll see you after the kids go back to school."

She picked up the heavy load again and followed after Margaret, who was running along the landing.

"Open the door for your Mam, pet. Pull the string and push."

The tiny hands reached for the string hanging out of the letter box and gave it a yank. It opened with the first push.

"You're getting to be such a good helper for your Mam, aren't you?"

Dorothy came running along the landing. "Mam, Mam!"

"What is it? Is someone after you?"

Dorothy's body was trembling and her eyes were wide with fright. "The gas man! He's in the next block!"

"Get inside. Hurry!" Kate whispered, dumping the bag of wet clothing in a corner of the room and closing the curtains.

"Let's be as quiet as a mouse. Okay?"

The string on the door was pulled again and Sarah walked in. She was surprised at everyone standing there staring at her.

"Where's Frankie, Sarah?"

"Why are you whispering, Mam?"

"Keep your voice down. Where's your brother?"

"He's playing in the block. Is there something wrong?"

"Go get him. Tell him to come in right away. It's important."

She closed the door behind Sarah, and then sat down between the two kids on the couch. They waited in silence. Distant voices of children playing in the street filtered into the room. They never moved a muscle. Suddenly footsteps were heard outside the window. The latch string was pulled and the door opened. Frankie rushed in.

"Mam, there's a man outside!" Kate held her breath, her heart thumping in her chest.

"Hello, how are you today, Mrs. Hawkins?"

"I'm fine. Come on in," she said, standing slowly to her feet.

"Looks like rain, doesn't it," he said, cheerily. She backed away without looking at him. He unlocked the meter box and emptied the contents onto the table to count it. He stood staring at the strange pile for a long moment, unable to believe what he was seeing. The silence weighed heavily. Kate lit a cigarette and began coughing with her first puff. The gas man looked over to see if she was okay, then over at the four children sitting quietly on the couch.

"Well, it won't take long to count this now, will it?" he chortled, turning his attention back to the table top. He proceeded to separate the coins from the tin tokens, stacking them in neat rows. Finally, he took a little notebook and began to write in it.

"Mrs. Hawkins," he quipped, a little mischief in his voice, "seems like we came up a little short on the shillings this time." He stopped writing and picked up one of the tokens, turning it slowly between his fingers.

"Tell you what, I'll pretend I never saw these little buggers if you get rid of them and come to the gas company with twenty-four shillings by this time next week. Think you can do that?"

"Oh, yes, I will," she promised, relief showing on her face. "Soon as I get me money, I'll be right up there." She jumped to open the door for him as he finished scooping the money into a heavy black bag.

Taking one last look at the children, he headed out the door. "Bye, kids."

"Bye, mister." they chirped in unison.

"Bye, Mrs. Hawkins."

"Goodbye and thanks." He nodded his head in acceptance and went on his way.

As soon as he was gone, Dorothy jumped off the couch and ran to her mother. "Oh, Mam, wasn't he a luvly man. He wasn't upset a bit, was he?"

Kate stood staring into space. "Where in the world do I get twenty-four bob from?" she lamented.

Frankie's eyes flickered open. Dawn was just breaking, casting the room into a gloomy twilight. He stared at the ceiling, listening to an unfamiliar sound filtering through the wall next to his head. Someone coughed, and then the snoring began again. He sneaked out of bed and tiptoed to his mother's room. Slowly, he opened the door and peeked around it. Someone was in his spot next to his Mam, but there wasn't enough light to reveal who it was. He tiptoed up to the bed and peered down at the gaping mouth that vibrated, whistled and gurgled with every breath. It was Annie Flanagan, his mother's best friend from the next block. He walked out of the room feeling upset and spotted the jar of strawberry jam sitting on the table. Without hesitation, he picked it up with both hands and charged back into the bedroom, bringing the jar crashing down on the forehead of the sleeping woman. The lid popped off, spilling the jam all over her face and hair. Her eyes opened wide and her mouth stopped quivering. She was stunned into paralysis. Her hand came up to her head to feel the gooey mess. Then she stared at it dripping red. A bloodcurdling scream rose from deep within her throat. Frankie scampered out of the room and dived into his bed.

"Oh, God, Kate!" Your Frankie's just killed me! Oh, Jesus, Mary and Joseph, Kate, I'm dying." Over the screams, his mother's voice could be heard trying to calm her down. "Okay, now, Anne, get ahold of yourself. Take your hands away and let me see your head, girl."

"Kate!" she continued screaming, "I'm losing all me life's blood! I'm dying in me blood! Oh, sweet Jesus!"

"It smells like strawberries to me, girl, but let me take a look." The screaming was reduced to groaning as Anne gave way to her friend's reassuring banter and probing fingers.

"You've got a helluva cob on your head, girl, but I don't think it's bleeding. I think the sod hit you with a jar of jam!"

While his sisters sat up in bed listening to the commotion, Frankie buried himself under all the coats and blankets.

In a short while, his mother came marching into the room "Where is he!" she demanded.

"He's under there, Mam," Margaret offered, pointing to the lump in the bed.

She reached out and yanked the coats away, revealing a little body rolled up in a ball with his eyes tightly shut.

"What in the blazes do you think you're doing?" she shouted, her right arm making an exaggerated grab for him.

"Mam, I didn't mean to do it!" he implored, trying to fend off the short, quick slapping motion of his mother's hand.

"You little twerp!" she continued, latching onto one of his arms and yanking him out of the bed. "You get out there and tell Annie you're sorry! Go on, get!" She gave him a push forward. He hesitated, his little body trembling at the thought of facing Mrs. Flanagan. A whack on the backside catapulted him through the doorway and out into the kitchen.

Mrs. Flanagan stood in front of the fireplace with her back to him. She had washed up and was now combing her wet hair away from the large purple lump, with gentle strokes of the comb. She could see the boy in the mirror, approaching from behind, head bowed, hands clasped together in front of him. He stopped just short of her. She continued the slow, rhythmic motion of combing, pretending not to be aware of him, until she felt a tug on her dress.

"Annie?"

"Yes, pet." She still continued the combing motion.

"I'm real sorry I hit you." There was a long silence.

"Show him the lump, Anne," his mother retorted, her voice cold and menacing. Annie turned and squatted in front of him without speaking a word. He could see that her eyes were swollen from crying, but there was no anger in her sad looking face.

He reached out and gently touched the lump with the tips of his fingers.

"Does that hurt, Annie?" She nodded her head slowly up and down, never taking her eyes away from his.

"How come you're not mad at me?"

"Maybe it's those big brown eyes of yours. And maybe it's

because I'm bloody mad at myself for getting drunk last night," she said, straightening up and reaching for her coat hanging over the chair.

"I'm going, Kate," she called over her shoulder, as she moved toward the front door.

"I'll see you on my way to the shops, Luv," Kate called after her. "Keep a cold compress on that, do you hear?"

"Okay. Thanks." The door closed behind her.

"Go get ready for school, Frankie, before I lose me temper altogether!"

"Rags...any rags?..." the old man called out in a nasal, singsong voice, with his pushcart heaped with discarded clothing he had collected in exchange for balloons. A group of children made a dash for home, including Frankie, who hit the door on the run.

"Mam!" he called out, trying to catch his breath.

"I'm in here, son." He walked into the back kitchen where she was hand- washing some clothes in the sink.

"Can I have some rags to get a balloon?"

"You're wearing them, lad! Just throw yourself on the cart," she quipped good-naturedly.

"Oh, come on, Mam, stop messing! He's gonna be gone soon!"

"I'm serious, son, I don't have any to spare. In fact, I was just thinking of going down to see what I could find on the cart for you for school. Just look at you! You'd think nobody owned you!"

"Mam, you're just kidding, aren't you?"

"No, I'm not. You'd be surprised the things people throw away. That ragman's a crafty bleeder. He goes to the rich streets first, so he can sell the good stuff to us on Mann Street. Come on, let's see if I can get you a balloon."

By the time they reached the street, the cart was already surrounded by women picking through the clothes. One squat woman, with frizzled red hair and tobacco stained teeth, was haggling over the price of a little print dress she was holding up.

"You're a bloody robber, asking sixpence for that. I'll give you thripence and not a penny more!"

"Lady, outta the goodness of me heart, I'm gonna let you have it for fourpence, 'cause I got kids of me own, bless their cockles!"

"Only if you throw in these two pair of knickers, me old charmer," she countered.

"You're a right one, tearing at me bleedin' heart. Give me the money before I change me mind." His wrinkled face revealed a mischievous, toothless grin. For these fleeting moments, he was a king ruling over his subjects.

Katie picked out a pair of boy's dungarees, and held them at arm's length to get a better look.

"Gotta ask at least a shilling for them lass," he volunteered without looking directly at her. "Like new, they are," he added as an afterthought. She put them down quickly. A shilling was way beyond her means.

Frankie, standing beside her, tugged at her sleeve. "Mam, Mam," he pleaded in low, urgent tones, so as not to draw attention to himself.

"What is it, lad?" she said distractedly, a slight irritation showing in her voice, as she continued to search the pile.

"Mam, those dungarees, they're smashing ones. I'd give anything for them."

"That's too much money, Frankie," she said, still not looking his way.

"But Mam, I've never had long trousers and me legs hurt with the cold."

She pretended not to hear him over the women's haggling, so he continued the assault on her heart.

"And when I fall down, I scrape me knees a lot." Still no response, until a woman next to her picked up the dungarees for inspection.

"Excuse me, Theresa, I was keeping those next to me, here, until I found a shirt to go with them."

"Oh, I'm sorry, Kate, I thought you didn't want them," Theresa said, handing them back.

"Hey, mister, I'll take them for a shilling, if you throw in this shirt and a balloon."

"Jeez, you ladies are gonna have me in the poor house," he grumbled, his eyes rolling back in his head for emphasis. "Give me the shilling and call me a fool forever!"

"Mam, let me hold them."

"You'd better take care of these or I'll have your life!" she warned, thrusting the garment into the boy's arms. He squealed with delight and ran up the stairs to put them on.

It was a beautiful, clear, crisp December morning. The sun was trying its best to loosen the frost that had blanketed the street during the night. The tin can Frankie was kicking, as he meandered down the street, echoed in the stillness. A woman, bundled against the chill, hummed to herself as she swept the step in front of her door. She turned to see what all the racket was about.

"Why aren't you at school, Frankie?"

"No shoes, Mrs. McEvoy," he said, matter-of-factly, still looking at the can ahead of him.

"I shouldn't bloody wonder, the way you treat them."

"Me Mam's getting me new ones today," he volunteered, giving the can another kick, then walking after it. The string his mother had tied around the toe of his shoe broke with the last kick. The sole kerplopped now with every step he took.

Across the street were the horse stables, with half its roof blown away by the German bombing. An elderly man came out of the gate just as the boy was passing.

"Go to the shop for me, lad?"

"Okay, Mr. Thompson."

"Get me a bottle of milk and a box of matches." He pressed half a crown into the boy's palm and closed the little fingers over it for safety. "And get yourself some sweets for going," he added, a smile playing on his face.

Crossing over Northumberland Street, Frankie entered the shop on the corner. It was a little cubbyhole of a place, dark and musty smelling. A black and white cat lay sprawled out on the counter top, fast asleep. The boy reached out to pet it but jerked his hand away at the sound of a raspy voice in the darkness.

"Don't touch her!"

A tall figure of a woman emerged out of the shadows, towering over the boy with a steely glare. He took a step back, wishing he hadn't come.

"I wasn't gonna hurt it," he stammered apologetically.

"What do you want?"

He was so shaken that he couldn't remember what he came for and stood there staring at her.

"A bottle of milk, please," he blurted out, surprised that he remembered. "And two ounces of licorice all-sorts," remembering how his mother said it when she took him shopping.

She weighed the sweets on a little scale and slipped them into a paper bag, her face remaining expressionless.

"Got some money with you?" she asked coldly, placing the milk on the counter next to the bag of sweets.

The boy stuck out his hand with the half-crown in it. She took it, replacing it with some change. He grabbed the sweets and the bottle and ran out the door, happy that it was over. Halfway across the street, he tripped on the loose sole of his shoe, sending the bottle crashing onto the cobblestones and spraying him from head to toe. He stood staring down at the shattered glass, tears welling up from the ache in the pit of his stomach. He wanted to run home as fast as he could to his mother. But then he thought of Mr. Thompson waiting for him to come back. He walked slowly toward the stable, not knowing what he would say when he got there. Little sobs kept forming in his throat and his nose started running. By the time he reached the gate, he had completely abandoned himself to the feeling of hopelessness. Tears ran down his cheeks. His little body shook with uncontrollable sobs.

"My, my, what do we have here?" Mr. Thompson asked, stooping down and lifting the little chin so their eyes could meet. "So you had an accident, did you son? Well, it ain't like it's the end of the world, now, is it?" he said in a soothing tone, wiping away the tears with his thumbs. "Come on, let me show you the horses." With that, he took the boy's hand and began walking down the stable yard, humming a little tune to himself.

"I know that song, Mr. Thompson."

"You do?"

"Me Mam sings it all the time."

"Well, what is it then?" he said, happy to see the boy perking up a bit.

"Lily of the Lamplight by the Barrit Gate."

"That's it! That's it! You're a smart one. Bet you go to St. Malachey's, don't you?"

"Only been a few times and I don't like it," the boy said, shaking his head from side to side and making a sour face to emphasize his point.

"Well, for only a few times, you're doing just dandy. Hey, let me show you my favorite horse." He guided the boy into an open doorway. Inside, there were three stalls, two of which were empty. In the third stood a big chestnut mare, who, upon hearing Mr. Thompson's voice, snorted and whinnied, shaking her mane up and down and stomping a hind leg on the cement floor.

"Hey, Gertrude! Want you to meet Frankie, here. He's your neighbor from across the street." The horse turned and looked straight at the boy.

"It's like she knows what you just said, Mr. Thompson."

"Sure does, son. Smarter than a lot of people I know. Getting old now, though." His voice grew softer as he stroked her mane.

"Pull no more wagons in this life, will you, girl?" He gave her one good slap on the rump before heading out the door. The fresh air was a welcome change from the pungent odor of horse droppings and old hay. They passed by the bombed-out stalls.

"Were the horses in there when the bombs hit, Mr. Thompson?"

"Sure were, son. Your daddy was the first over to help me get them out."

The boy stiffened at the mention of his dad. No one ever talked about him. It was like he never really existed.

"Did you know me dad?"

"Sure did. Was quite the feller, tall and slim in his uniform, he was."

The boy grew quiet, trying to take it all in. Mr. Thompson opened the door to the canteen where two men sat at a wooden table drinking mugs of tea.

"Hey, Paddy, whose the little man?"

"From across the street, he is. Ran a message for me and bloody near killed himself in the bargain."

While the men talked, Frankie surveyed the room. In one corner was a huge stack of coal almost up to the ceiling. The fireplace looked like it hadn't been used in a long time, and the room was cold and damp smelling.

"How come nobody lights the fire?" he asked, as Mr. Thompson set a steaming cup of tea in front of him.

"They're in and out like blue 'arse flies around here, son. They never take the time."

The boy eyed the coal again. He had never seen so much, except down in the coal yards on Grafton Street.

It had snowed for two solid days without letting up. The street was now a blanket of crispy whiteness that sparkled under the full moon. The stars filled every inch of the sky like thousands of twinkling firelights. The street lamp cast a pale orange glow on the snow beneath it. A young couple, bundled against the bone-chilling wind, walked down the street, every step making a loud crunching sound as their feet sank into the snow. Suddenly, they stopped to listen more closely as the sound of children's voices drifted through the stillness.

> *"Christmas is coming, the goose is getting fat.*
> *Please put a penny in the old man's hat.*
> *If you haven't got a penny, an 'a penny will do.*
> *If you haven't got an 'a penny, God bless you.*
>
> *God bless the father and the missus, too.*
> *And all the little children 'round the table, too.*
> *With a pocket full of money, a belly full of beer,*
> *We wish a Merry Christmas, and a Happy New Year!"*

The couple walked on, chuckling to themselves and stealing glances at the four children singing to the closed door.

"Maybe there's nobody home," Sarah said, her voice quivering from the cold. Margaret picked at the wax dripping down the side of her candle and put it into her mouth to chew.

"Margaret, don't eat the wax, you'll get sick," Dorothy warned, sounding much like her mother would if she had said it.

"You don't get sick eating wax," Frankie chimed in, just as his candle blew out in a gust of wind. He reached over to light it again from Sarah's candle.

"Let's sing 'Silent Night,' that's a good one," Dorothy suggested, her voice trying to infuse some enthusiasm into their faltering endeavor at making money.

"Can't we go to the next door, Dorothy?" Margaret pleaded, her voice on the verge of tears.

"Now, didn't I tell me Mam not to let you come with us, Margaret, 'cause you'll spoil it? Didn't I, girl?"

"I won't say any more, honest," she pleaded, shaking her head from side to side.

"Okay, who's gonna start 'Silent Night,' "Dorothy asked, looking from one to the other. The glow from the candles' flickering light revealed pained expressions on each of their faces. Their cheeks were bright red from the biting wind and their noses were running.

"Well, someone's got to," she sighed, wetting her lips and taking a deep breath.

"*Silent night, holy night...*" slowly, with faltering coughs and clearing of throats, each one joined in, their sweet voices echoing through the deserted street.

> *'Round yon Virgin, Mother and Child,*
> *Holy Infant, so tender and mild,*
> *Sleep in heavenly peace,*
> *Sleep in heavenly peace.*"

No sooner had the song finished, when the door opened to reveal an old woman with a head of hair as white as the snow outside. Bending from the waist, she peered at the little faces in front of her trying to focus her eyes in the dim light. Suddenly, her face lit up with a surprised grin.

"Why, it's Kate Hawkins' little ones!" she exclaimed, her hands flying to her cheeks in a gesture of disbelief. "And I thought it was angels come to take me in me sleep! Such luvly singing," she prattled on, her hand reaching into her pinafore.

"Now, who's the banker outta you lot?" she queried, slipping her hand out of her pocket. The kids stood with their mouths wide open at the unexpected fuss she was dishing out.

"Er...I am, Mrs. Butterworth," Dorothy blurted out, pulling open the pocket of her mother's apron.

"Here you are, luv," she cooed, dropping some change into the opening. "And a merry Christmas to you and your Mam." When the door closed, the children turned to each other, grinning from ear to ear.

"How much was it?" Sarah asked, trying to prevent her flame from blowing out.

"Don't know until I count it, do I?" she retorted, acting like she could care less.

"But it's our money, too, Dorothy, and we wanna know now, don't we?" Frankie demanded, looking at Sarah and Margaret for support.

"Yeah, yeah, let's do it now," they both confirmed in unison.

"Okay, cry-babies. Here, hold the candle close to me pocket." Dorothy dramatically pulled out her hand, deliberately evoking a chorus of protests. Finally, she opened her fist to reveal two gleaming half crowns.

"Jesus, it's five shillings," Sarah breathed reverently.

"Five bloody bob," Dorothy confirmed, emphasizing each word with a slap on Frankie's shoulder. Frankie took up the chant, hitting Margaret on the head. Margaret grinned with delight and slapped Sarah on the back. Soon they were all slapping each other and chanting, "five bloody bob," as they moved along to the next door.

Kate could hear their high-pitched voices coming along the landing. She smiled to herself as she stirred the pot of Scouse on the fire, relieved that they sounded so happy. The latch string was pulled and the kids came in, stumbling over each other, clambering to get to their mother first.

"Mam, Mam, guess how much we made?" Dorothy challenged, her eyes bright with expectancy.

"Let me tell her," Margaret pleaded.

"Okay, okay, let's all settle down now," Kate urged. "Sarah, set the table for tea. Dorothy, light some more candles and put them around, that's a good girl."

She turned back to stirring the vegetables and minced meat in the fireplace. It had been a week since they'd turned off the gas for nonpayment, and for finding more tin pieces in the meter box. Her brother-in-law, Alvin, had promised to turn it on for her until after Christmas, but he hadn't shown his face yet.

"Bet you can't guess how much money we got for singing, Mam," Frankie teased, as they finally settled around the table.

"Mam, the Scouse tastes like smoke," Margaret chimed in, unaware of the drama being played out.

"Shut up, Margaret, Mam's thinking!" Frankie shouted.

"Well, it tastes burned," she protested again, wiping her tongue with her sleeve.

"I'm sorry, ducks. There's nothing I can do about it," Kate said, patting her on the hand. "Just eat what you can." The table grew silent.

"Go on, Mam," Dorothy whispered, nodding her head and raising her eyebrows up and down.

"Go on, what?"

"Guess."

"Why don't you just tell me?"

"Because we want you to guess. You'll never guess, Mam," Frankie chided, unable to sit still in his chair from excitement. All eyes were riveted on her face as she lapsed into deep thought.

"Two and six?" she finally blurted out.

"No! No!" they all sang out, slapping and giggling.

"One pound, seventeen shilling and threepence," Dorothy proudly announced.

They watched as their mother's face turned from amusement to astonishment. In their delight, they began laughing and banging the table exuberantly.

"And it's all for you, Mam," Dorothy concluded, pouring the money onto the table.

Kate stood looking in the mirror, dabbing the fresh lipstick with the corner of her handkerchief.

"Where you going all dolled up, Mam?" Dorothy inquired, as if she didn't already know.

"Just to the corner for an hour, pet."

"Will you bring us a bag of crisps back with you?" Sarah implored, remembering how good they tasted from the pub.

"Only if you're being good," she countered, a little preoccupied with twisting her body to get a look at the back of her legs. "Are me nylons straight?"

"Yeah," the chorus came back.

"You look smashing, Mam," Dorothy added, eying her mother with approval. "You'll have all the lads after you."

"Oh, aye, like I don't have enough bloody troubles, girl." She gave each of them a quick smile while slipping into her coat. "Now remember there's a shilling on the mantelpiece if the gas starts to go." She was glad Alvin had finally shown up and got the meter going again.

"And don't open the door to anyone," she cautioned, pulling the string in through the letter box, so it couldn't be pulled from outside. They sat listening to the click of her heels receding along the landing and down the stairs in the block. Each sat motionless for a while, lost in thought; the only sound coming from the wood crackling in the fireplace.

"I'd love to cut your hair, you know, Frankie," Dorothy sighed wistfully. "I fancy I could do a good job on it." He stared back at her, a perplexed scowl frozen on his face.

"I think you're turning funny on us, girl," he countered without changing expression.

"I'm not kidding, Frankie. Me friend, Theresa, said you look like a golliwog with your curls springing out like that."

Margaret jumped up off her chair, wanting to get things started. "Come on, Frankie," she pleaded, "Sarah and me will watch she doesn't make a mess of it, won't we, Sarah?"

Sarah nodded in agreement, not quite convinced she should play a part in it. Frankie's resolve was beginning to waiver.

"Did your friend really say that, Dorothy?" he asked, feeling a little choked up about it.

"Cross me heart and hope to die, lad."

"Okay, only a bit then, and stop when I ask you to."

Suddenly there was a carnival-like atmosphere, as the three sisters gathered around his chair.

"This is a big one," Margaret proclaimed, pulling a curl out as far as it would go, then letting it spring back. Sarah was busy securing a dish rag around his neck with a safety pin.

Kate tiptoed into the house, glad the children weren't waiting up for her. She hadn't meant to stay so long. Time had just gotten away from her, what with all the singing and storytelling of Christmases in the good old days. She was sorry that the fire had gone out. It would have felt good to warm up a bit before getting into the cold bed. She was puzzled to see things dangling from the guardrail around the fireplace and moved closer to take a look. Dozens of curls hung there to dry, each one secured by clothes pegs. Being tired, she stared at them for a second, not comprehending what this all meant. Suddenly, a moan escaped her lips and a hand went up to her mouth to muffle the sobs that were rushing to escape.

"Frankie! That's Frankie's curls!" Slowly, she walked toward the children's room, hoping somehow to find it was all a mistake. She groped in the dark, feeling one head, then another, until finally she touched his. Not one curl was left; only stubble remained. She wished she could just go to bed and curl up and sleep forever; but it was Christmas Eve and she still needed to stuff their stockings.

Frankie woke up first, aware of movement in the kitchen. His head felt cold, reminding him he now had no hair. He was bursting to go to the toilet, but the thought of freezing in the backyard made him snuggle even deeper under the covers. Then he remembered it was Christmas. He sat up scanning the room for toys. There weren't any. He spotted the stockings through the bed rail and jumped out of bed to investigate.

"Dorothy, Sarah, Margaret! Wake up!" he shouted, emptying out his stocking.

"Is me Mam up yet?" Dorothy asked nervously.

"Yeah, and she's gonna kill you for doing me hair in," he taunted, still mad at her for last night.

She pulled the covers up to her chin and watched the others examine their little mounds of sweets and fruits.

"Is there a Father Christmas, Sarah?"

"No, Margaret. I figured it out a long time ago, he was just too fat to climb down our chimneys."

"And he'd have to wash his clothes after every house, wouldn't he?" Margaret added, putting the final touch to Sarah's answer. The door opened and Kate came in.

"Isn't anyone interested in breakfast?" she asked, sitting down on the side of the bed.

"Thanks, Mam, for the sweets and stuff," Margaret said, running to give her a hug.

"Yeah, Mam," the other two called out, still sorting through their piles. She turned her attention to Dorothy.

"How come you're not up yet, young lady?"

"Don't feel good, Mam."

"I should think not. What got into you last night?"

"You're not mad at me then?"

"Too late for that, girl. Besides, it's Christmas. I've got a big fire going and lots of hot porridge. If anybody's interested."

Frankie sat watching his mother kneeling in front of the fire poking at the wood embers. She was hoping to keep enough flame going to bring the kettle to a boil. The gas man had come unexpectedly two days after Christmas, and discovered the gas had been turned back on. This time, he had unhooked the meter and carted off the whole thing.

"You didn't find any more wood today, son?" she asked without taking her gaze from the small flame. Her voice seemed to come from far away.

"No, Mam. Lots of kids go to the bombdies now, so there's nothing left."

His mother lapsed into silence again. He had brought wood home every day for weeks, searching every bombed building in the neighborhood until he found some. Today, he felt he had let her down.

"Bet there's lots of bombdies down by the docks, Mam. I could borry Lizzie's pram to pull it home in."

"No! I don't want you going down there. You might get hurt and we won't know where you are."

Steam finally started coming out of the spout. She poured the water into the teapot sitting on the hob, stirring it a few times before leaving it to steep.

"We'll have a cup, then you can go fetch your sisters from next door."

"Mam, I know where I can get some coal," he announced, matter of factly.

She finished pouring the two cups of tea before looking at him. "I don't want you bringing trouble to the door, lad. I have enough of that as it is."

"But, Mam, it won't be trouble. There's a stack of coal almost up to the ceiling and nobody wants to use it."

"Highly unlikely," she retorted. "What bloody fool wouldn't use their coal in this kind of weather? Finish your tea and go get your sister." He could tell it was useless to go on about it.

The two shadowy figures next to the stable spoke to each other in whispers.

"Scared, Stevie?"

"A bit, Frankie, are you?"

"Ready to pee me trousers," he chuckled, hoping to get Stevie to relax a little. He talked his best friend into robbing some coal with him tonight. Now, he began to wonder if he should have left his little friend out of it. Stevie said his Mam would pull his hair out by the roots if he ever brought trouble home. He could imagine Mrs. Walker doing it, too. He looked up to see how long it would take for the big cloud to cover the full moon, then glanced over at the street lamp. He had thrown a rock at it an hour ago, shattering the glass casing and the mantle. All he could see now was a little gas flame blowing in the wind. The moon was almost gone, casting the street into darkness.

"It's time, Stevie," he announced, gripping the poker a little tighter. They both moved out of the entry, staying as close to the wall as they could.

"This is the window. Keep a lookout for me."

He stuck the poker under the wire mesh and tore it away from the window frame, rolling it upward into a ball. He then hit the pane of glass with his elbow, thinking his coat would muffle the sound, but it made a loud splintering noise as the glass hit the street. They ran back into the entry at the sound of dogs barking all over the neighborhood. A door opened on the top landing and a male figure stepped out to investigate. It was too dark to see anything so he retreated back into the house and closed the door. The dogs quit barking. It was quiet again.

Katie wet her two fingers and reached over to pinch out the candle flame. Reading by candlelight was hard on her eyes, so she leaned her head back and closed them for a while. The three girls played quietly at the kitchen table, their candle getting dangerously low. Though only eight o'clock, she would have to put them to bed early again. They hated it, but what could a mother do when there's no light, no fire, and no food? No way to even boil water to make a cup of tea. She felt drained of energy. Sometimes the irresistible urge to give up would sweep over her; a longing to lay in bed and sleep forever; never to feel the pain and anguish anymore, the endless cycle of daily survival.

From somewhere deep inside of her she would always find the will to go on. Her children needed her. They trusted her to be there for them. She was their hope, their strength, and their little world was kept safe by her presence. The sound of her voice soothed their fears. Her smile assured them that things would be better tomorrow. Her thoughts turned to her son. She wished he were home by now. At the age of eight, she had seen a remarkable change in him. He seemed to have grown up overnight, from a child who needed to be with her every moment, to being fiercely independent and wanting to take care of her. In some ways, the change scared her. At other times she felt proud of him for his strength and resourcefulness and his caring ways. She remembered how proud her husband had been over having a son. He would take him everywhere with him, proud as a peacock, showing him off to everyone. The two were inseparable. How could he ever not regret turning and walking out of their lives forever, when he was such a doting, and loving father?

She could understand his leaving because of the war effort, but to never return was like a hand reaching in and squeezing her heart. The hand never relinquished its hold, the pain never subsided. She remembered the day she received the papers requesting her presence in court. Her husband was charged with bigamy. Her bright sunny day had been plunged into dark despair, her mind grappling, reasoning, sorting through precious memories, hoping to unlock the mystery that would shed some light. She had a questioning thirst just to understand, if even for a moment. On the long three-hour train ride to Yorkshire, hope had welled up in her as she watched the beautiful countryside slip by. Maybe it had been just a fling; a stupid mistake many lonely soldiers made in wartime. When he sees her he will be reminded of the four beautiful children he had left behind. It didn't take her long to realize it was not to be. He was obviously in love with the young girl, who was also pregnant with his baby.

The sound of the door latch startled her back to the present. Her son walked in, stooped over from the weight on his back. He gave her a big grin from a face black with coal dust, and ambled past her to dump the heavy load by the fire.

"And just where have you been all hours of the night, young man?" she demanded, in a tone intended to wipe the smug grin off his face.

"Mam, guess what that is?" his grin still very much in evidence. "It's coal," he reasoned, answering his own question.

She looked at him, not sure if she wanted to cry or jump up and slap him. He could see the shock on her face and searched for something to say that would make her feel better.

"Mam, it's not like me and Stevie stole it; they have lots of coal and don't even care about using it, while we sit and freeze ourselves to death every night.

"Did you say Stevie? Abby's lad?"

"Yeah, Stevie Walker got some for him Mam, too."

"My God! I'd better get down there before she crucifies the lad." She threw on a coat and headed out the door in a hurry.

The girls gathered around their brother, not quite sure if he was a fool for doing it, or their hero for being so brave.

"Can we have a fire now, Frankie?" Margaret asked, eying the sack of coal.

"Yep, you scrounge up some paper and I'll find some wood to start it."

He went into the back kitchen, but the cupboards and shelves were already gone. He tore off some of the linoleum from under the sink, knowing it burned good but may also stink up the house. By the time they had a good blaze going, Kate returned with Abby in tow.

"Frankie, tell Abby what you told me about the coal." He was glad his mother's voice wasn't threatening, but he was a bit surprised at her sudden show of interest.

"Well, the men in the stable have all this coal up to the ceiling, but Mr. Thompson says no one ever lights a fire. So it just sits there forever."

The two women whispered conspiratorially; then Kate turned back to him.

"Is the window big enough for us to climb in, son?"

He stared back at her with a perplexed look on his face. "Yes, Mam," he stammered, "but, I can do it again. I'm not scared a bit."

"No, I don't want you back in there. You and Stevie can stand outside while we pass the bags out to you. Then you must run home and stay until we get there. Do you understand?"

No, he didn't understand. This was totally out of character for his mother to be doing this and it scared him.

Kate grabbed a couple of sturdy shopping bags and headed out the door. The street was now illuminated by the full moon, and they could hear two drunks arguing outside the pub on the corner. He wanted to ask his mother to wait for cloud cover, but she seemed to have taken complete charge of the whole operation.

Kate started climbing through the window first, getting her long hair tangled in the wire mesh. For a moment, it looked like she was going to cry, but changed her mind and began threading the hair away one strand at a time. She soon freed herself and disappeared inside the dark room. Abby followed suit, banging her head and then her knee and cursing the day she was born. Soon, their nervous giggles drifted out to the boys, making them feel a little better.

There was no sound, yet Frankie sensed someone standing behind him. He turned his head slowly, and there he stood, as tall as a tree, the buttons on his black uniform shining in the moonlight. The last person in the world he expected to see was now staring down at him, a bemused look on his handsome face. The tall hat and chin strap added authority to the slender frame.

He heard Stevie gasp and take off running, but he stood frozen to the spot, his mind racing with thoughts tripping over each other. Why was this Bobby standing here? The bobbies never come down this street! Did somebody call the police? Why now, with his mother trapped inside? The officer walked past him and peered into the open window, hands clasped behind his back. He didn't seem to be in any kind of a hurry or unduly angry or upset. Frankie could hear his mother's voice calling to him.

"Frankie, are you ready, lad?" The words died on her lips as her face appeared at the window.

"Oh, God! Oh, no!" she crooned, her hand touching her mouth. The sound of a heavy bag thudded to the ground at her feet.

"What is it, Kate," Abby asked, concerned that her friend must have hurt herself and dropped the bag.

Kate turned from the window to get away from that bemused face staring back at her.

"Abby, don't look now, but there's a policeman outside."

"What the bloody hell is he doing out there?" she demanded, her voice rising in anxiety.

"I don't know, Luv, but everything will be alright, you mind my words."

"Will you ladies be coming out soon?" the Bobby called through the open window.

"We'll be out, chucks, hang on a minute," Kate called back, her voice showing signs of being under control. She appeared once again at the window, and started climbing through, faltering a little. The officer reached out and helped her to the ground. Next, Abby appeared and he helped guide her through. He stood looking at them, their hair disheveled, their frocks black from the coal dust.

"Well, get on with it then," Abby demanded, feeling naked and raw in front of him and the people now gathering on the landings.

"Why don't we take a little walk up to Essex Street station and talk about it over a nice cup of tea. How does that sound?"

Kate turned to her stricken son. "Go on up to the house and tell your sisters your Mam'll be home soon. Go on, that's a good lad." He watched the three of them walk down the street and turn the corner before running up the stairs.

The children gathered around the warm fire, staring into the flames that hissed and danced in a never ending display of movement. It was easy to become mesmerized and fall into a trance; to allow the mind free reign to travel, dream and fantasize. But no one was dreaming tonight. Their thoughts were of their mother.

"Do you think they'll keep her in jail, Dorothy?" Sarah asked, sadness in her voice.

"Of course not, silly. They don't keep mothers in jail."

"But how do you know that?"

"I just do, that's all. I am the oldest, you know. Besides, when they find out she's having a baby, they'll surely let her go home." She relished that split second it took for her words to sink into their little heads, then enjoyed seeing the expressions forming on their faces.

"How'd you know that, smarty pants?" Margaret shot back, tears welling up in her eyes for no reason she could understand.

"Me Mam told me because I was the oldest, that's why."

"But, she doesn't have a big belly or nothing." Frankie said, trying to make sense of it all.

"That's 'cause it's tiny inside her yet." With that they fell silent again. Their thoughts turned to what it would be like having a baby in the house.

The sound of a car could be heard coming up the street and stopping outside their tenement entrance. They made a dash for the window, just in time to see their mother and Abby exit the police car.

When she walked in the front door, they clapped and shouted, "You're home, Mam! You're home!" all four of them trying to hug her at the same time.

"Quiet down now, kids. It's almost midnight. Why don't we all go to bed and talk about it in the morning." She looked and sounded very tired. They let go of her and quietly made their way to bed.

The dock road was bustling with people, cars, lorries and horse-drawn wagons. An overhead railway rumbled by, sending hoards of pigeons and seagulls scattering into the steely-blue sky. The funnels of ships from every land could be seen peeking up over the tops of the warehouses, their colorful flags blowing in the March wind.

At nine years old, Frankie had felt it was time to investigate beyond his little world of Mann Street. He stood watching the myriad activity with rapt excitement. He loved the sounds, the smells and the hustle and bustle. He felt alive like never before. He had tried going to school for his mother's sake, but it hadn't worked out at all. He was so far behind the other kids there was no way for him to catch up. Most of the time he didn't have a clue as to what the teacher was even talking about. Some kids saw him fail to do the most basic things, such as spelling his own name; taunting him, as if he were some stupid kid to be ridiculed.

The last day he attended school was a nightmare for him. He vowed never to go back. He had arrived at school after the last bell and was told to report to the headmaster's office. Mr. Cogley was a small, slender man who always looked dignified in his pinstriped, three-piece suit and matching tie. A gold watch chain dangled from his waistcoat pocket. At sixty, his hair was jet black except for a slight graying at the temples. His face was smooth, with piercing dark eyes and a long slender nose. Somehow, he looked out of place here in the slums of Liverpool.

"Yes, young man. What can I do for you?" he asked, not too unkindly.

"Mr. Bullock sent me to see you sir. He said I missed the last bell."

"Ah, I see. Well, come in then, come in."

Frankie moved inside while the headmaster opened a cupboard and took out a long stick. Turning to the boy, he said, "Which hand is your writing hand?"

"Me right, Sir."

"Then you may hold out your left," he said in a monotone. He flexed the cane and swished it in a downward motion a couple of times. All this foreplay unnerved the boy and he stood there motionless.

"Your hand out, please." he repeated sternly, helping the hand up by hitting the knuckles in an upward sweep of the cane. The hand was now straight out with the palm up ready to take the punishment. The cane made a whistling sound as it sliced through the air, hitting the floor and breaking in half.

Frankie had pulled his hand away just at the last second. Mr. Cogley suddenly lost his composure and began swiping at the boy's bare legs with the broken rod.

"How dare you!" he shouted, spittle running out the corner of his mouth, and his cheeks flushing crimson.

The boy made a dash for the open door, almost falling down a flight of stairs, and fled out into the street. He didn't stop running until he reached home. His mother took one look at the large welts and marched him back to school by the hand. Mr. Cogley opened the door, looking every bit the dignified man again.

"Ah, Mrs. Hawkins, come in, come in."

"No, you come out, puddin' head, and see what you've done to this child!" she demanded, turning the boy around.

He stepped out of his office, bending to take a look. Without warning her hand crashed against the side of his head. He began spinning and clutching the air, before tumbling down the flight of stairs. He lay crumpled at the bottom, staring up at her, disbelief written all over his ashen face.

She walked down the stairs, stepped over him and stormed out into the street, without so much as a word. The boy followed right behind.

Frankie pulled the string and walked in. His mother sat at the kitchen table talking with a stranger. Their conversation stopped when he entered the room, both heads turning simultaneously.

"Where've you been, son?"

"Down the dock road, Mam. It's smashing down there. I got a ride from Mr. Butterworth on his horse and cart, and he even let me hold the reins."

"Frankie, this is Mr. Gerard from the school board."

The man cleared his throat a couple of times, like he was about to speak. He was licking at his drooping mustache in the corner of his mouth. The silence was nerve wracking.

"A cup of tea, Mr. Gerard?" Kate asked, getting up from her chair.

"No thanks, I'll be off in a moment." She sat down again.

"I'll have one, Mam."

"When the man's finished, lad."

"But, he's not saying anything."

"Hush up!"

They sat in silence while the man cleared his throat a couple more times and twiddled with the brim of his bowler hat sitting on his lap.

"Young man, going to school is the law and you have no choice in the matter. Do you understand that?" The boy looked over at his mother, but she refused to meet his gaze.

"If you don't go, your mother will have to appear in court and may even be sent to jail."

"That's not true. They never send mothers to jail, especially if they're having a baby. Isn't that right, Mam?" He was visibly shaken over the information, and needed his mother's assurance that would never happen. She shook her head.

"No, not this time, it isn't." She realized he had to hear this. He was changing too rapidly and she was losing control of his life. Many times she had sent him off to school only to have him show up at home a couple of hours later. She had even walked him to the school door and stood watching until he entered his classroom, but he managed to climb over the playground wall while out on class break.

The man glanced at his wristwatch and stood to leave. He was sure he had gotten the boy's attention and would have no need to continue further.

"Good day, Mrs. Hawkins. Good-bye, son."

Frankie sat brooding, ignoring the man completely.

"I'll make us a luvly cup of tea, lad," she said, once the door had closed; like making tea was the remedy for all their problems.

"Mam, they wouldn't put you in jail just 'cause I sagged school, would they?"

"You never know what the bleeders'll do, son. They very nearly put me away for the gas meter caper and robbing the coal from the stable. Oh, aye, the next time they see this mug, they'll have me carted off in a paddy wagon, no less." She could see his little mind trying to grasp the reality of her being in jail with all the bad people.

Frankie stood with his back to the wall, surrounded by a group of lads.

"Go on, Brian, make him fight!"

Brian was the cock of the school and liked the feeling of being in control of every kid. He wasn't sure about this kid from Mann Street because he hadn't seen him in school much. He had tried to provoke him into a confrontation before without much luck. Finally, he had said, "I'm gonna get you after school!"

Frankie suffered mental torture all afternoon, trying to devise ways of sneaking out before the others.

The girls' school on Beaufort Street had let out at the same time, and some of them stopped to witness the fight and throw in their vocal support. After pushing the boy a few times without any response, Brian turned toward the girls.

"You know he's got a hole in his kecks and his 'arse is showing," he mocked, pointing at Frankie.

"Show it to us, Bri," the girls sang out.

"Turn 'round for the girls and let them have a look," he demanded, reaching out to help matters along.

Frankie's heart was pounding like a jackhammer, his nerves all a jangle. His ears started popping from the sudden rush of blood. Everything seemed to happen in slow motion as he reached out and grabbed Brian's neck with both hands, pulling the head towards him, while thrusting his own out to meet it. His forehead went crashing into Brian's nose and mouth with a sickening thud. The girls' screams floated back to him like he was under water. Brian fell to his knees, blood oozing out from between his fingers as his hand covered his face. The crowd stood stunned and silent after the initial shock had subsided. No one was more in shock than Frankie. He couldn't believe he had done it.

Slowly, he walked away, picking up speed once he had turned the corner. Soon, he was running as fast as his legs would go, his head beginning to throb with pain.

"Hey, mister, can you give me a ride to the pier head?"

"Sagging school, are you?"

"No, me Mam's sick and she wants me auntie to come see her," he lied.

"Hop on, then. I haven't got all day."

Frankie climbed up and sat next to him. The man yanked on the reigns and the horse moved out into the traffic. They were both silent, lost in their own thoughts. The man sucked on his pipe, and pulled his cap a little lower on account of the rain that had just begun to come down in earnest.

"Horse blanket behind you, son; put it over your head before you catch your death."

The blanket stunk, but it did feel warm, especially with the wind now starting to kick up. Little whirlwinds of dust formed in the street, sucking up bits of paper and spitting them into the air. The rain turned slushy, making it difficult for the horse to walk. Its' hooves faltered on the slick cobblestones.

"Easy, girl, easy now," the man called out through clenched teeth, his pipe bobbing precariously as he spoke. The horse whinnied, snorted and shook her head from side to side against the bit that was being pulled tighter. Her hind legs suddenly buckled and for a split-second, it looked like she was going down. She regained her footing just as the heavens opened up with a torrential downpour of hailstones.

Across the street, a lorry driver lost the battle to secure the heavy tarp over his wagon-load. The wind and hail whipped it out of his hands, sending it sailing across the road. The horse reared up, front legs pawing at the air.

"Whoa, girl," the man shouted in a long drawn out wail, his knuckles white from the strain. His pipe clattered to the floorboards. Traffic screeched to a halt as the horse pranced backward and sideways, out of control, jackknifing the wagon into the middle of the street. It was pandemonium as men screamed out orders, their voices muffled amidst the wind and hail. Two burly dockers, caps askew, fought to maintain their hold on each side of the horse's bit, the strength of the horse dragging them along.

Suddenly, it was over. The hail stopped, the wind died down, and the sun came out. Within seconds, peace and calm were restored. The man looked over at the boy, hidden under the blanket.

"Are you alright, me little cocker?" he asked, a cheeky grin spreading over his rugged face. The boy could only manage a weak smile as he peeked out to look at him.

"Come on, I'll let you feed me girl for me," he said cheerily, stepping off the wagon and guiding the horse to the side of the road. Handing him the feed bag, he helped the boy guide the horse's nose into it.

"You're a man after me own heart, you are. You do that as good as meself, already."

Frankie wished he could tell his mother about all the exciting things he was experiencing, but he knew she would only worry even more. He had figured that if he stayed away from home, they couldn't hold her responsible for him not going to school; and she wouldn't have to go to jail. He hated school more than anything, and wished they'd leave him alone.

He stood on the top deck of the ferry boat watching the seagulls float on the air current, chuckling to himself at his inability to hold steady to the swaying motions of the boat. He had spent his first night away from home and survived. An accomplishment that filled him with pride and delight. But, it hadn't been easy. He had walked for hours through the darkened streets. It seemed as if every footstep behind him was a potential Jack the Ripper; every headlight, a police car combing the city in search of a lost boy. His nerves were jagged; the least sound sent him scurrying into an entry or darkened doorway to hide. On top of it all was the damp, penetrating cold that made his bones ache, drowning out the hunger pains he had felt since early afternoon. He'd tried stealing apples from a fruit cart, only to be chased down the street by a screaming woman brandishing a brush handle.

Without realizing it, he had found himself headed in the direction of home, the thought of snuggling in with his sisters suddenly reviving his sagging spirit. It had been after midnight when he finally reached Mann Street, stopping on the corner to give himself time to wrestle with his thoughts. He remembered the feeling of disappointment at how easily he had given up his dream of making it on his own. The snorting and stomping of a horse drew his attention to the stable. The stable! Why not the stable? There were horse blankets, hay to sleep on, and right across the street from his house, too!

Kate had lain in bed for hours, staring into the darkness. At times, she would drift into sleep, waking at the slightest noise or movement, listening for the string to be pulled. She had to fight off the panic whenever her thoughts turned to all the things that could happen to a nine year old out there. Calling the police was the last thing she wanted to do, feeling it would only draw attention to her inability to control him, and maybe they would even take him away.

The ferry boat shuddered spasmodically as the propeller churned the water into a broiling mass of foam. Lines were thrown out to men on the dock, who quickly tied the ropes to bollards, securing the boat to the wharf. A ramp was lowered, allowing the throngs of people to disembark. He couldn't read the large sign over the entrance, but he knew where he was.

On a clear day, he could see New Brighton from the top landing of his tenement. Now, here he was, alone among thousands of people, walking through streets filled with games, balloons, mint-rock, sand buckets and spades. He watched children on a merry-go-round and gawked at people screaming on the Big Wheel as it turned them upside-down.

Hunger was his constant companion. He found himself staring at people eating an ice cream cone, or simply drooling at the sight of chips in the familiar newspaper wrapping, his favorite food. It was time to take matters into his own hands. He remembered how successful he had been the night he stood outside the Park Palace on Mill Street, asking passersby to spare a penny to get into the pictures. He not only got in, but had enough left over to buy two ounces of sweets.

"Hey, mister, spare a penny for the ferry?"

The first man gave him a disdainful look and walked on by. The second man, holding a little girl's hand, stopped.

"Why are you begging for pennies, son?"

"I lost me money, sir, and I can't get back home."

"How much are you short?"

"Sixpence, sir, is all." The man brought a handful of change out of his trouser pocket and dropped a three-penny bit into the boy's outstretched hand. The little girl tugged at his hand.

"Daddy, that isn't sixpence! The lad said sixpence."

"Oh, yes, dear, you're absolutely right," he chuckled, bringing out the change again. As soon as they were out of sight, he ran to the chip shop and filled his empty tummy with a large bag of greasy chips.

Night was beginning to set in and he thought about heading for home. Not that it was dark in New Brighton. Everything was lit up like a Christmas tree. The crush of people paid him no mind as he walked among them. He suddenly felt lonely. Leaving home in the daytime was adventurous enough, what with all the activity going on in a bustling seaport. But nighttime found him thinking of his mother and sisters, and the way they made him feel special and important. He leaned on the promenade rail, and looked across the River Mersey at the lights twinkling all along the Liverpool skyline. He began picking out familiar landmarks, each one making his chest warm and his heart beat a little faster. The tall mill on Mill Street, the Cathedral on Parliament Street, and yes, a little hazy, but that had to be St. Malachey's bell tower on Beaufort Street, just behind his tenement block.

Tears began welling up in his eyes and he knew then that he wanted to go home tonight. He made his way to the ferry dock still crying.

"Aye, aye, what've we got here? Lost your Mam, have you?" The ticket collector squatted to get better eye contact, his face revealing genuine sympathy. "Well, then, you've gone and lost your ticket, is that it?"

"I never had one," Frankie whispered, his voice trembling with emotion.

"Never got one!" the man crooned, exaggerating his surprise. "But, how'd you make it over?" he inquired, looking befuddled and stroking his long chin with his hand.

"I bunked on when the man wasn't looking," Frankie admitted, all pretense gone now.

The man straightened himself up, his gaze never leaving the boy's face. A lady handed him tickets for her and two children and continued on by.

"Hey, missus." She turned and walked back. "Can you take the little fella and make sure he gets off okay?" She smiled and took hold of the boy's hand.

He pulled the string and walked in.

"Mam, Mam, it's Frankie, he's home!" Dorothy sang out.

The three girls got up from the table, dancing and clapping. Their show of affection was as much for seeing the end to their mother's suffering as it was for seeing their brother. Kate turned down the gas under the black pudding and baked beans, and came out of the back kitchen wiping her hands on her apron.

"Thank God, you're home, son. I couldn't have made it through another night like last night!" She pulled his head to her breast and he could smell the familiar sweetness of her body. She then pushed his head back a hand on each side of his face.

"And I wondered why I made apple tarts tonight!" she said, giving him a knowing look.

"I got the apple peels," Margaret announced proudly. "And I got the apple cores, Frankie, cause you were gone," Sarah sang out.

The day dawned bright and clear. The sun's rays filtered through the torn curtains, bathing the bedroom in a warm red glow. The racket the bin men made as they emptied the metal containers, echoed in the still morning air. Normally, Frankie would be up and out by now, especially on a day like this. The summons had arrived in the letter box three days ago, requesting mother and son to appear in "His Majesty's Court" on Dale Street. Today was the day.

He listened to his mother singing in the kitchen and wondered why she sounded so happy. He remembered the look on her face when she read the summons and how she clutched her side like it was hurting.

"It's gonna be alright, Frankie," she had promised that night, "but, you must stay in school from now on or they will take you away."

Yesterday, she had marched down to Uncle Peter's like a fearless warrior going to do battle. Hours later, she came back with a double-breasted suit and a pair of shoes from Milton's Pawn Shop.

"Try these on, lad, and let's take a look at you," she'd said in a no-nonsense voice.

"Dorothy, run down to Bridy Acheson's. She has a lad the same size as Frankie and he always looks spiffy. Tell her your Mam needs a white shirt for a few days."

Dorothy knew instinctively, that this was no time to argue about how many messages she'd run on lately. She left immediately.

"Mrs. Hawkins." The name rang hollow in the cavernous room, bouncing off the marble walls and reverberating up into the lofty, domed roof. The three of them stood and headed toward the open door, where a man greeted them with a thin-lipped smile.

"Is this the family?"

"Yes, this is me Mam," Kate said, nodding toward her mother.

Frankie was glad his grandmother wanted to come. She was a huge, stocky woman with not an ounce of fat on her. To get on the wrong side of her was begging for trouble. He had seen with his own eyes, Ninny take on three dockers outside Callahan's Pub one night. It was unbelievable how she had punched, kicked and simply mauled these men. She would have killed them but for the crowd that surged and dragged her away, kicking and screaming.

"May I see the home report, please," the judge asked, when everyone was seated. A lady got up and handed him some papers and sat down again.

Katie coughed, breaking the silence that hung over the chamber like a dead weight. She was sure they could hear her heart thumping against her rib cage. If she could have a cigarette and go to the toilet she'd feel better, but she remembered doing those things just five minutes ago. She liked the judge. He looked kind and probably had a family of his own. So he should know how things can be with kids, she reassured herself.

"Mrs. Hawkins," the judge intoned in a rich baritone voice, "things don't look too favorable on the home front. According to this report, your son is in need of some very strong guidance, and there's no father in the home to give it. You have four children and one on the way. The last thing you need is a boy who refuses to do what is right, making life more difficult than it already is, for the rest of the family."

Turning to the boy, he leaned forward in a gesture of intimate conversation.

"Frankie, it's time you learned a few facts of life, one of which is, life is not a game. It is serious business. Going to school is not your choice; it is a command by me. If I see you here one more time, I'm going to take you from your mother and let someone else discipline you. Do I make myself understood?"

Frankie sat shaking and fidgeting in his chair. He had never heard anyone speak like that before. "Yes, sir," he stammered, nodding his head, in case the judge didn't hear him clearly enough.

They stepped out into a bright, sunny afternoon and didn't stop walking until they had reached Lime Street, the hub of the city. Trolleys, taxis, horse-drawn carts, lorries, motor cars, and bicycles all converged on this one spot. Honking horns and clanging bells blared out their warnings before attempting to mow down the hordes of people daring to cross at any opening in the traffic.

"Mam, let's find a nice place and have a cup of tea before catching the tram back," Kate pleaded, pulling on Ninny's arm.

Frankie had never seen his mother so gay, even childlike in her actions. Her face was radiant and her eyes bright with laughter, as she pointed out a tea shop not far from Lewis' Department Store. A heavy load had been lifted from her sagging shoulders and with it years of stress seemed to have melted away. At twenty-nine, she was being robbed of her youthful beauty, by circumstances that were beyond her control.

Granddad Walton cursed under his breath and gave the radiogram a swift kick in the side. Ninny looked up from the newspaper.

"Oh, you dirty man. Go wash your mouth out with soap."

Granddad's small, frail body was no match for his wife. Though he walked with a cane, from wounds suffered in the First World War, she still managed to batter him many times over the years. He had become a man of few words and fewer expressions. The grandchildren loved this quiet old man and, in his heart, he loved them, too.

One day, Frankie watched with fascination, as his granddad smoked a tiny cigarette stump until it literally disappeared with his last puff. There was nothing left to put out, yet he never gave any indication that he had burned his fingers. After seeing that, Frankie enlisted the help of his cousin, Stewart, and together they walked the streets, picking up every cigarette stump they could find. They cut off both ends and took the tobacco from the middle, filling up a biscuit tin. With a penny pack of cigarette paper, they presented it to Granddad for his birthday. When he opened it, the most beautiful smile spread across his wrinkled face, and his gray mustache quivered on his lip. They had never seen him smile like that before.

He took a shine to Frankie after that, and showed the boy his secret hideaway. It was a cellar under a bombed house, full of wood he had collected on his lonely walks. Each day, he would chop just enough wood chips to fill his makeshift wheelbarrow, and sell it door to door. With the money he would buy himself a couple of pints of beer, without anyone being the wiser.

The radiogram finally crackled to life. "This is the BBC Light program..."

Kate and the children gathered around it listening to music, Winston Churchill, and a play about a horse that talked. Granddad sat next to the four-foot monster ready to give it another kick if it quit. It never did.

Ninny served kippers for tea that night, hardly a favorite with the grandchildren. But, they ate the salt fish, grateful it wasn't one of her other specialties; pig's belly, pig's feet, ox tail, ox tongue, or the granddaddy of them all; tripe, believed to be the lining of a calf's stomach. Her rough exterior and dominance over the male species belied the tenderness she exhibited toward her many grandchildren. None ever came away without getting a big, juicy kiss and a few coppers in their hand 'for sweets on the way home.'

On Saturday afternoons, Ninny would spread out the racing page of the Liverpool Echo and study it until Frankie showed up. He would be greeted with the usual mug of tea and a cheese 'butty', the bread sliced thicker than a doorstep.

"Tell Billy Button two bob each way on Lester Piggott, Frankie."

"Is Lester Piggott the horse or the jockey, Nin?"

"He's the jockey. If the horse decides to stop and take a pee, he's the one to keep it moving." She never failed to chuckle at her own little quips and it was contagious.

He would stand next to the bookie until the race was over. Ninny could always tell by his face when he walked in the door if the horse 'stopped for a pee' or 'liked smelling the horse's arse in front of him.' Then she would adjust the two pairs of glasses on her nose and get back to studying for the next race.

Frankie squatted just outside the circle of men, fascinated by the game of dice in progress. The money in the center of the circle grew and diminished with each toss of the dice. He could feel the late-morning sun warm on his back, glad that school was over for the summer. The kids had treated him better lately, but the teachers called him lazy and a dreamer for not finishing anything they had given him to do. At first he was made to stand in front of the class with a dunce's cap on, or was kept sitting at his desk long after the rest of the boys had gone home. But, none of these things had any positive results. Eventually, they gave up and left him alone.

Without warning, the group of men suddenly scattered in every direction, leaving him sitting on the ground staring at the pile of money. After the initial shock had worn off, he got up and started stuffing the money into his pockets and down his jersey, his heart pounding from the excitement. A bobby walked by but paid him no mind. The boy ran down the nearest entry, colliding with an overturned dust bin, and spilling some of the money from out of his jersey. By now, he was a bundle of nerves and decided to leave the fallen coins and keep going. He kept glancing back, relieved to find that no one was following him.

By the time he reached the safety of his block and climbed the two flights of stairs, he was totally exhausted. He yanked on the string so hard it broke in his hand. He pounded on the door, panic beginning to engulf him. He mother opened it, and managed to catch him as he fell forward.

"What in God's name is going on?" she asked, her voice trembling with emotion. "It's not the police, is it?"

"No, Mam," is all he could say as he labored to get air into his lungs. She guided him over to the couch, all the time searching his face, like she would find the answer there if she looked hard enough.

Margaret sat next to him, patting his hand, with a sympathetic look on her face. Finally, he told the whole story, at the same time emptying the money from his pockets and jersey into Margaret's lap.

Kate refused to look at the money, concerning herself more with the story being told and its possible ramifications. She opened the door and stood on the landing quietly surveying the street below. After a few minutes, she came back in.

"Did any of these men know who you were?" she asked, transferring the money from Margaret's lap into a leather bag.

"No, Mam, I don't think they even knew I was there."

"Well, in any case, you had better stick close to home. If they come looking for you we'll just give them the money back."

The afternoon dragged on. All Frankie could do was sit and wait. The noises of children playing jump rope and hop scotch drifted up from the street. He watched his mother ironing clothes, humming and singing softly to herself in a sweet, clear voice. He found himself singing along with her in his head. All the songs he knew were from listening to her and he wondered how she knew so many. Uncle Peter and Granddad were the only ones with radiograms that he knew of, and his mother never spent much time visiting.

"Mam, where'd you learn all those songs?" he finally asked.

"Oh, here and there," she said whimsically, wetting her finger and testing the flat iron.

"Yeah, but where?" he insisted.

She walked into the back kitchen and put the flat iron back on the gas flame and stood waiting for it to heat up.

"Your dad bought me a brand-spanking new radiogram when you were born, Frankie. Smashing, it was. Could get Radio Luxembourg and everything on it." Her face was animated when she came back holding the hot iron.

"What happened to it, Mam?" he asked breathlessly, warming up to any bit of information about his father and their life together. He watched the shine on her face fade into a thoughtful, faraway look, and he knew instinctively she was going to change the subject.

"Go on, Mam, you can tell me," he urged, his body slipping forward in anticipation of catching something delicate before it hit the floor.

She stopped ironing and glanced over at him. "Your dad was a terrible gambler, you know." She turned her attention back to the shirt she was ironing, unaware of the boy's eyes beckoning her to continue. He held his breath, not wanting anything to interrupt the flow of memories now flooding her mind.

"He would win big on the dogs and buy me a whole house full of new furniture and sell it all back when his luck ran out. 'Just you wait and see, Kate,' he used to say. 'I'll have it all back before you can say 'Bob's yer uncle.' Sometimes he did, too, but then it would be gone again the next week."

She looked over at the boy to see how this was affecting him. "A charmer, he was," she added, trying to lighten things up for his sake. "Just a big kid like you. Never a dull moment with him around."

"Mam, why didn't he ever come back from the war?"

She stopped ironing and stared down at the little frock spread out on the table. This was the moment she'd been dreading ever since the conversation had started.

"Lots of men never came back from the war, son, and that's just the way life is. We have to pick ourselves up and get on with it. Which reminds me, go get Dorothy. I want her to go to the chippy for me."

That night, they ate like kings. Steak and kidney pie, chips and mushy green peas. No one dared ask where the money came from for all of this.

While the kids played snakes 'n' ladders, Kate rested on the couch massaging her huge belly. "Just gas pains," she had assured the kids, not wanting them to worry and spoil the fun they were having. But, soon, it was impossible to hide. Her face was white and clammy and her hair stuck to her cheeks. Her breathing became labored until she could stand the pain no longer.

"Dorothy," she whispered through clenched teeth, "put your coat on and run 'round to your Ninny and tell her your Mam's having the baby. Hurry, now, girl, there's not much time."

Dorothy let out a little whimper as she frantically searched through the coats hanging on a nail behind the door.

"Frankie, run as fast as you can to Essex Street. Tell the policeman your Mam needs an ambulance right away. Can you do that for me?"

"You haven't seen how fast I can run when someone's after me, have you, Mam?" It was his way of assuring her the job was as good as done.

"Is there something I can do?" Sarah inquired, close to tears.

"There is, pet. Put a full kettle on to boil and fetch the bowl from under the sink. Margaret sat close to her mother, wiping her brow with a damp dish rag.

Frankie dashed through dark entries, past bombed houses, and down deserted, unlit streets, slowing down only when he reached the door of the police station.

The bobby lowered the newspaper and peeked over his gold-rimmed glasses to get a look at the intruder. The boy was out of breath but managed to blurt out, "Me Mam's having a baby, sir!"

"There's no law against that, son."

"She's having it right there on the sofa and she needs an ambulance," he insisted.

"Well now, let's see what we can do about it," he said, taking a pen from his top pocket and pushing the newspaper to one side. "Tell me your name?"

"Frankie Hawkins, sir."

"Okay, Frankie, what's your address?"

"Mann Street, sir."

"Is there a number so the ambulance knows which house to go to?"

The boy began to panic. He had never learned it. "I don't know it, but I can run fast and show them where to go," he blurted out, wishing the bobby would hurry and do something.

Finally, the officer picked up the phone and dialed. "A mother is in labor. Mann Street is all I got. Will arrive ahead of you." He hung up and grinned at the boy.

"How would you like a ride in my motor car, son?"

"Yes, sir, and I can show you where me Mam is."

"That's the whole idea," he laughed, getting to his feet and poking his head through a sliding glass window next to him.

"Be gone a bit. Got a little lady on Mann Street having a baby."

"Right you are, then, Jack," came the reply.

Frankie had never ridden in a car before and he felt strangely exhilarated as they drove through the deserted streets.

"Off you go, then," the bobby said when they had pulled up to the curb. "I'll be showing the ambulance where to go from here."

The boy jumped out and sped up the stairs and down the landing. Before he could reach the door he heard a baby crying from inside. The bed had been put in front of the fire. Kate sat up in it with a brand new baby cradled in her arms.

"Come see your new brother," his mother beckoned, as he walked in the door. The three girls sat around the edge of the bed, making faces and exaggerated cooing sounds, but the baby continued to cry. Ninny was putting the finishing touches to a stack of jam 'butties,' all the time exchanging sympathies with the baby's distress.

"Ah, God luv you. Didn't wanna be born, did you luv? Have a bloody right to complain, being born into this crazy world."

Frankie slowly approached the bed, bewildered at how fast things had changed since he had left for the police station. He touched the softness of the baby's cheek with his finger and the baby went for it, searching it out with his mouth.

"Is he hungry already, Mam?" he asked, pulling his finger away and catching hold of a tiny fist.

There was a knock on the door and Dorothy jumped up to open it.

"It's the ambulance men," she called out, opening the door wider to let them in.

"Grab a butty and off to bed with you," Ninny shouted to the children.

"Are they gonna take you away, Mam?"

"No, son, they just want to make sure everything is okay with the baby and me."

The four children sat in bed munching on their bread and jam, listening intently to the muffled sounds coming from the kitchen.

"I got to ride in a police car."

"You're a lucky thing, Frankie. What was it like?" Margaret whispered, squinting in the dark to see his face.

"Smashing, it was."

"Shh!" Dorothy said, trying to identify the latest noises. "I think they're leaving now." Soon, they heard the sound of the front door closing, and then silence.

"Don't hear the baby no more," Margaret murmured.

"Nope, me neither," Frankie confirmed, brushing the crumbs off his pillow and laying down.

"Margaret, why don't you go peek out the door," Dorothy challenged. "I'm scared Ninny might get mad at me."

"No, Dorothy, I just want to stay in bed," she said, burying herself under the covers. The kids fell silent and were soon all asleep.

Morning broke bright and clear. Dorothy lay watching the dust particles shimmer as they passed through the stream of sunlight coming through the window. The heads of two pigeons could be seen bobbing up and down, cooing and pecking playfully at each other on the window ledge outside.

Be nice to put up fresh curtains, she thought, grimacing at the tattered and threadbare one hanging there for as long as she could remember. Her gaze rested on the two dish rags stuffed into the broken window panes, discolored and grimy from a year's worth of dust filtering in from the dirty back street. The window cleaner used to do the outside with his long ladder once a week, but gave up when he couldn't collect his money. Now, they were streaked from the long winter's rain and blustery winds. She turned away, feeling a little depressed at the way things were. Her mind went back to the week before school let out for the summer. Her new-found friend, Shirley, had invited her home to spend the night and showed off her very own bedroom with pink lacy curtains and wallpaper to match. Even the counterpane and ruffled pillow were pink. She remembered making an excuse about having to be home, in case her Mam started having the baby, then ducking into the nearest entry to cry her eyes out. By the time she had reached home, she was thoroughly ashamed of herself for thinking such selfish thoughts. Now they came flooding back as she surveyed the sagging bed with heads and feet poking out of both ends.

I'm almost twelve. I should at least have me own bed, she thought, extricating herself from the mess of tangled bodies. She tiptoed out of the room into the kitchen. Ninny sat by the fire reading the Liverpool Echo, her two pairs of glasses perched precariously on the tip of her nose.

"Morning, Nin. How come you got a fire going on such a nice day?"

"Me bones are brittle, girl," she chuckled, her eyes still glued to the newspaper.

Dorothy noticed that the bed was no longer there and headed toward her mother's bedroom.

"Your Mam and the baby are in the hospital, luv. Took them away last night."

Her hand froze on the doorknob, and her eyes filled with tears.

"Only for a few days, cock," Ninny assured her, laboring to dislodge her huge frame from the tight confines of the chair. "Needs a good rest, God luv her. Go wake the other lazy buggers and I'll get some tea and toast for us."

"Can we go see her, if we promise to be good?" Dorothy pleaded, as she headed for the bedroom.

"Soon as you're washed and ready," Ninny called out from the back kitchen.

After the long ride on the top deck of the street car, the four children felt gay and carefree, skipping ahead of Nin as she labored to catch up. They meandered through the labyrinth of olive green corridors of the Smithdown Road Hospital, until they reached the ward described on the piece of paper given to them at the front desk.

The room was long and narrow with at least a dozen beds on each side of the aisle. Windows from floor to ceiling allowed the mid-morning sun to pour in, highlighting the profusion of summer flowers decorating each bedside table. Kate spotted the children first and waved her free hand in the air, while nursing the baby in the other. Her large brown eyes danced with joy at the sight of them rushing to greet her.

"Mam, you look real gorgeous," Dorothy said breathlessly, staring at the halo effect the sunlight was having on her mother's long brown hair.

"Just like an angel in white robes feeding the baby Jesus," Margaret chimed in, as she climbed up and sat next to her mother.

Frankie stood inches away, watching with fascination as the baby suckled on his mother's breast.

"Does that hurt, Mam?"

"It's a little tender, but no, it doesn't hurt."

"Did I do it when I was a baby?"

"Yes, you big boob. Wore me out, you did."

He grinned and turned away, his face flushed red. The girls laughed and pointed fingers at his red face.

"Shhh! Keep it down," Ninny cautioned, looking around at the other mothers resting. The baby stopped suckling and Kate popped her breast back into the hospital gown.

"What are you gonna name him, Mam?" Sarah asked, as all eyes focused on the sleeping, cherubic face. The baby smiled in his sleep, as if on cue, sending the kids into a fit of giggling.

"I bet little David knows you're talking about him."

"Is that his name?" Frankie asked, pulling a little fist open and checking the baby's fingers. "I like it better than mine."

"Now, now then, you were named after your dad, and he was very proud of his first-born son."

Kate could have bitten her tongue. She had said that without thinking. Now her son stared back at her with a confused and bewildered look on his face. She'd always known how impossible it would be to explain a contradiction of supreme love and total abandonment. Yet, that's what it was; an unexplainable mystery of the human heart. She changed the subject fast.

"I'm coming home tomorrow, so I want you all to be good for your Ninny, okay?"

"Okay, Mam," they all agreed, giving her a last minute hug before being rounded up by Nin.

Stevie Walker is dead, and he's never coming back. His cute little smiling face will never smile again, nor will his affecting hiccup-y laugh ever be heard again. Frankie brooded over the loss of his best friend. He didn't have many; much preferring to be a loner. But Stevie was special, so easy to be around. He had admired Frankie's tenacity and daring spirit, and followed him around whenever he was invited. Now, Frankie wished he'd have been more kind to his little friend.

Like the time they were playing in the back of Mann Street and Abby, his mother, poked her head out of the window.

"Stevie, your dad's just come home!" Stevie had stopped in his tracks, looking first to Frankie, then to his mother, and back to his friend again. Like a bolt of lightning, he was gone through the entryway.

Frankie remembered standing there alone, feeling betrayed, like someone had thrust a knife into his heart. The one special bond they had shared was shattered in an instant. They had spent many hours together, creating fantasies about how their dads had died, killing hundreds of Germans. Their fantasies had become real to them, sustaining them throughout the two years since the war had ended.

He had hated Stevie for a long time after that, refusing the sweets that were a peace offering; instead, knocking them out of his hand and crushing them on the ground. But, eventually, time healed the wound; that is, until now.

"You haven't touched a bit of it, have you, lad?" Mrs. Butterworth complained, jutting out her bottom lip to match the frown she was wearing.

"I'm not really hungry. Just had me tea," he lied, not wanting to get into a long debate about it. The sliced Spam, corned beef, biscuits and cake did look awfully good, but he felt it was wrong to enjoy a party in honor of his friend being buried that day. Mrs. Walker had gathered together all the kids Stevie's age that knew and played with him, as her last gesture to his memory; and to help the playmates come to terms with their loss, too. But, for Frankie, it worked in reverse. He had been able to block it out of his mind ever since the tragedy happened. Now the dam had broken, flooding his mind with every detail.

It had been the kind of day kids wished would last forever. The street was baking in the afternoon sun. Children were everywhere. Girls in their pretty summer dresses played skip rope, while others chose the latest craze, a spinning top with a whip. A group of boys had their usual 'footy' game going against the stable wall. A couple of boys had a rope tied to the top of the street lamp, doing Tarzan stunts to impress the girls sitting on the tenement steps. Here and there, women sat on their door steps, while others stood on the landing above, peering over the railing.

Frankie had challenged Stevie to a race that ended up at the third tenement block where his Auntie Sissie lived. The door was left open because of the heat and he walked in, leaving Stevie standing outside. He'd only had time to say hello to his auntie, who was on her hands and knees scrubbing the kitchen floor, when a loud bang resounded in the block.

(the front and back of Frankie's tenements)

"Throwing bricks off the bleeding roof again," Aunt Sissie *complained bitterly, without missing a stroke with the scrub brush. "Not a minute's peace with the sods."*

Frankie was aware of a commotion, but attributed it to the kids running wild up and down the stairs, as they usually did. Then he glanced out the open door to see grown-ups rushing by like there was trouble somewhere. He stepped outside to have a look, just in time to see two men carrying Stevie out of the block, all disjointed, his head covered in blood. He stood staring at the men running down the street, juggling the limp body between them. Then it began to dawn on him. The thud inside the block wasn't a brick hitting the pavement; it had been his friend, falling.

Slowly, he walked toward his own block. People and children everywhere were in shock, some crying openly, others leaning on each other for support, and some just standing there, transfixed, staring into space.

He felt nothing; no emotion. Not even when Stevie's mother, Abby, ran out of the block in front of him, trying to put her arm through the wrong sleeve of her coat, tears streaming down the cheeks of her anguished face. He felt nothing when his own mother ran after her to lend support, crying after Abby to wait for her to catch up. His mind became hollow, unable to retain sounds or images for more than a few seconds. He had fallen asleep on the couch afterward, waking after dark when his mother came back from the hospital. Her face looked pinched and drawn, her eyes red from crying.

"How's the baby, Dorothy?" she asked in a somber voice, settling into the big chair and slipping off her shoes.

"He's fine, Mam. You want me to make a pot of tea?"

"Yes, that's a good girl."

David started crying and Margaret stuck the dummy in the sugar and put it in his mouth. The house was quiet again. The tea was made and passed around without a word being spoken. The three girls pulled chairs next to their mother to form a semicircle around the fireplace. Frankie stayed sitting on the couch.

"Come over here," she said in a soft voice. He got up and sat on the floor next to her. She pulled his head to her lap, running her fingers through his curls. It felt soothing and he found himself drifting off to sleep again.

"Little Stevie's dead,' she announced, her voice still soft, almost melancholy. "Probably died in the block without feeling any pain." No one moved or said anything.

"Abby's gonna need me for a while until her family gets here from up north, so put yourselves to bed if I'm not back by nine. Dorothy, make the baby a bottle of tea and he should be good for the night. If he's any bother, run along and get me.

"Okay, Mam, don't you worry a bit." The children watched after her until the door closed and her footsteps receded down the landing.

The four lads sat on the Customs House wall watching the endless parade of lorries and horse-drawn carts go by, laden with goods from the ships tied up alongside the docks.

Frankie had met the three lads the day before while walking through town. He had watched Nig-Nig, a tall, muscular, black lad, distract the old lady, while Digger and Coons loaded their jerseys with apples and pears from her fruit cart.

"All I asked you, mammy, was did you have any fades! That's not being cheeky!"

"You're a bleedin' robber! I seen you with me own two eyes." Suddenly, she turned and caught a glimpse of the other two lads. "Oh, you dirty buggers! Put them back!"

The three of them took off running through the swarms of people before she could even finish her tirade. She looked over at Frankie standing close by and started yelling, "Police! Police!"

He took off, too, not wanting to explain why he was sagging school. A bobby's whistle sounded close behind, while another whistled ahead of him. He ducked into a side street, stopping only long enough to tie his shoelace, then, climbed over a brick wall into a bombed storage warehouse.

"Psst...over here, kid." The three faces grinned back at him from what used to be a window. He picked his way through a doorway whose shattered door hung precariously by one rusty hinge. Glass crunched beneath his feet as he walked.

One glance is all it took to figure Nig-Nig for the leader. Dressed in baggy pinstriped trousers held up by suspenders, a docker's cap pulled to one side, and an Air Force jacket with its wings and silver button still attached, he radiated confidence and maturity beyond his twelve years. When he smiled, which was often, he revealed a perfect row of gleaming white teeth.

Digger was quiet, almost shy, except when he was angry at something. At those times, he would become very animated, waving his arms and spitting to make his point. He was overweight and tried to hide it by wearing an overcoat, no matter what the weather. He had two buck teeth with a space between them large enough for a lorry to pass through, and a face full of red pimples, which he never ceased to play with.

In sharp contrast to Digger, Coons was a tall, slender thirteen year old, with smooth, olive brown skin and laughing blue eyes. He was dressed in a thick, navy-blue turtleneck sweater and baggy, charcoal trousers that were gathered and tied at the waist with a piece of coarse twine.

It was exhilarating sitting there on the wall with three new friends, the sun warm on his face, free to just enjoy life. He felt the surge of emotions coursing through his body at being alive amid the wonderland of activities and sounds. The smells of petrol fumes mixed with fresh horse dung baking in the warm sun intoxicated him. The sight of hoards of pigeons suddenly taking flight at the sound of a ship's horn, filled his heart with inexplicable joy, as his eyes followed their path of flight, turning and dipping, as if orchestrated by an unseen maestro.

Yesterday had been the first day of school after the summer holiday. His mother had gotten up early and made porridge for their breakfast and laid out their fresh clothes. All week long, she had raided the rag cart every time it had passed down the street, hunting and searching for just the right items, then taking her treasure home to mend, wash, and iron, working until late into the night. The girls had gotten up, pleased as punch, but Frankie felt only loss. His heart just wasn't in it.

Walking to school, he had passed by the old gray building and kept on going, his steps quickening the closer he got to the dock road. With heart pounding in his ears, his legs had taken flight at the sight of a lorry pulling away from a loading dock headed toward the pier head. Hands grasping hold of the tailgate and legs pumping faster to match the lorry's momentum, he catapulted forward until his body lay safely on the bed of the lorry. He had sat with his legs dangling over the back, feeling the fresh wind blowing through his hair, the cobblestones rushing beneath him and stretching into the distance from where he had been.

Catching a lorry had become routine, a normal part of the day's adventure. Even the train above him became a rallying cry as it slowly gained on him, eventually passing him by with a thunderous roar. The cops had become the bad guys now in his fight for freedom, so he had developed a keen awareness of them when he traveled. He had almost made a fatal mistake, laughing and making rude gestures at a bobby on a bicycle that the lorry had passed by. Suddenly, the traffic ahead began to slow down and so did the lorry. Frankie could only watch in horror as the bobby began gaining ground, pumping furiously with eyes ablaze and jaw set in a menacing scowl. Just when he had debated jumping off and making a run for it through the heavy traffic, the lorry started picking up speed again, leaving the bobby shaking his fist in the widening distance. But this incident had only added fuel to the flame of adventure now burning out of control.

Nig-Nig jumped off the wall and turned to face the others.

"Shall we depart this good place, gentlemen?" he mocked, bending gracefully at the waist and tipping his cap. Without waiting for a reply, he donned his cap on backward, hooked his thumbs into his suspenders and waddled off in an imitation of Charley Chaplin. Digger and Coons followed close behind, mimicking his walk and quacking loudly like a pair of ducks. At the end of the street, all three stopped and looked back.

"Well, are you coming, mate?" Nig-Nig shouted through cupped hands.

Frankie merely shook his head, not bothering to shout over the roar of the traffic. They stood hesitantly for a few seconds before turning and walking off, Nig-Nig with an arm around each of their shoulders. Frankie looked after them, smiling to himself at Nig-Nig's funny ways. He turned his attention to the horse drinking from a trough across the road while the driver adjusted its blinkers.

A dog, weaving through the traffic, suddenly panicked and became immobile, bobbing its head from side to side, undecided what to do next. Lorry drivers honked and cursed at it, but the dog only stood there whimpering and wagging its tail. When the traffic had come to a grinding halt, the dog slinked away, its tail between its legs.

From where he sat, perched on the Customs House wall, he could see the heart of Liverpool with the twin towers of the Liver Building rising majestically into the sky. He wondered how such a large building could have escaped the bombing raids when all around it, warehouses and factories lay in ruins. Even the little church across the street from it had taken a direct hit, leaving it just an empty shell.

It had been over three years since Victory Day, and still people were hungry and cold. Ration books were still being used. Not one building that was bombed had been torn down, except those that posed a danger. The skyline was full of charred remains, the streets full of beggars searching the dust bins for anything they could sell or eat.

For a childlike Frankie, Liverpool was a wonderful playground full of secrets ready to be explored. Hunger was a feeling that went away in time. On warm summer days such as this, he had little concern over his lack of clothing. He was extremely happy in his little world, not needing or wanting anything, except to be left alone. But thoughts of his mother kept tripping into his mind, spoiling his otherwise perfect existence.

He swung back over the wall into what was once the basement of the Customs House. All that remained were dozens of dungeon-like basement rooms with no covering over them. He found one of the few stairwells that led down into it and began to explore each room and passageway. There was enough sunlight filtering down to enable him to see quite well, but it was still kind of spooky, especially being alone. A light breeze rustled an old newspaper lying on the floor, setting his heart racing. Then a loose brick fell with a loud thud, making him whirl around, ready to make a dash for safety. He came to the room he had slept in the night before. It had been home for the three lads for most of the winter and summer months. There were plenty of horse blankets, stolen from the docks, along with tin mugs, plates, and a cast iron kettle. The place was littered with empty bean tins and moldy bread and apple cores. In the center of the floor was a makeshift fire pit with a greasy black grate laying on top.

It looked a lot better last night, he thought, remembering the flickering glow of the fire playing on each of their faces as they ate the baked beans and told funny stories late into the night.

In the light of day, everything smelled like rotten meat and looked filthy. It took him a while to find the stairs again and he took a deep breath of the fresh, warm breeze blowing in from the river. It was then that he remembered the look on his mother's face when she last tucked in his shirt and fussed with his hair...it was like she was trying to read his mind, or say something to him that would ease the pain she saw there. And he saw the pain in her face, too, and wanted to lash out at something, anything to ease the torment he felt when she was sad. He knew he was part of the problem, but he felt helpless to change what was happening to him. He wanted to go home and tell her everything was okay, but he also knew the next morning the pain would start all over again.

He wasn't afraid to go home. He had never feared his mother. It was the battle of emotions that silently raged within them that he feared the most. His loyalty and fierce instinct to protect her from pain sometimes left him drained and feeling helpless. Like the day the landlord came to the door and she hid in the bedroom.

"Tell him your Mam's not home," she whispered to him.

"Me Mam's gone to the shops, Mr. Callan," he announced, opening the door just wide enough to talk through.

"Oh, come on now, Kate, stop this messin', I know you're in there," he called out, pushing the door wider so as to be heard.

"Me Mam's not here and you'd better go," Frankie shouted, his face getting as red as a beet root. Mr. Callan wasn't about to give up that easily and pushed his way past the boy.

"Kate, girl," he called, firmly but politely, "You're five weeks past due, luv. Can't you pay just a bit toward it?"

At that, Frankie lost his temper and started kicking and pushing the man back toward the open door.

"Whoa, there, young fella, this is between your Mam and me," he protested, trying to grab the flailing hands and get things back under control. The more he tried to deflect the boy's actions, the harder the boy fought back. Kate could stand it no longer and stormed out of the bedroom with both hands swinging.

"Well, you bloody sod," she screamed, her hands slapping at the man's face. "You force yourself into my house and beat up my child, will you? Well, over my dead body!"

Mr. Callan backed out onto the landing in defeat, dumbfounded at such intense rage and warding off the blows that were coming thick and heavy.

"Now, Kate, calm down, girl, you know I meant no harm," he pleaded. When her anger was finally spent, she put her hands on her hips and leaned forward, her eyes smoldering with fire.

"Don't you ever do anything like that again. This is my house and don't you forget it."

"Aw, Kate, how long have we known each...?"

"Don't you Kate me!" At that she turned and walked back into the house, slamming the door behind her.

The story of poor Mr. Callan's encounter was told many times over in the next few days, always to the accompaniment of roaring laughter, as each scene was pantomimed in the funny Liverpool style of story-telling. Yet, Frankie still had to apologize to the man the next time they met.

By the time he reached the pier head, the sun was just starting to settle behind the Seaforth hills, leaving everything tinted red in the shimmering twilight. The bustling activity of the day was being replaced by the quiet, settling sounds of the waves lapping at the wooden pier and the creaking of ropes straining at the capstan. A lone docker rode by on a bicycle, his legs pumping slowly and rhythmically, his back bent and weary from working all day.

The ferry blew its whistle, disturbing the thick silence that hung over the water, and cast off its moorings. Frankie watched it back away, churning the water behind it like an angry sea serpent. He loved the sea passionately and dreamed of the day he would sail away to far off lands.

I bet me Mam would be proud of me then, he thought, loneliness starting to creep in, as it always did this time of day. *Better get going before it's too dark to see anything*, he thought, remembering how difficult it had been to find their quarters even in the daytime.

The dock road was deserted now as he made his way across. Flocks of pigeons had commandeered its cobblestones, hunting and pecking at the grain and corn that had fallen from ruptured sacks throughout the day. They were reluctant to let him pass and he had to shoo at them before they would open a path.

The Customs House wall looked eerie in the dying light, and more so when he climbed over it and looked into its dark caverns. For a fleeting moment he wanted to chuck it all in and go home. Then he spotted it. A flicker of light, then it was gone again. He whistled and waited, his eyes scanning the dark interior. The light appeared again, followed by a whistle.

A voice shouted back to him, "Is that you, mate?"

"Yeah, it's me, Frankie."

The light bobbed and weaved as it came closer. Soon it was close enough for the candle to illuminate the broad smile.

"Been looking out for you, mammy; where've you been?" Nig-Nig asked, putting his arm around Frankie's shoulder in a show of genuine concern and affection.

"Come on; wait 'til you see what we got into today."

Following Nig-Nig through the dark passageways was no easy matter, and he stumbled repeatedly over bricks and holes in the flooring. When they finally reached the room, it was a welcome sight. The fire cast a warm radiance over everything and the smell of cooked pork hung heavily in the air. Digger and Coons, sitting on blankets around the fire, grinned when they saw him come through the door.

"You missed all the fun, mate," Coons shouted, standing up and handing him a tin plate.

"We were legged by a copper all over town," he continued, pulling Frankie nearer to the fire where a huge, charred ham sat to one side.

"Knocked over a poor bloke's hand-cart in the bloody bargain," he laughed.

"Bleedin' plums flying everywhere. Old biddies screaming and trying to get outta the way and slipping on the plums, landing on their arses. We could hardly run, we was in stitches!"

As the story reached its climax, everyone was in fits, roaring with laughter, each trying in vain to stop laughing enough to tell his version. In the end, they gave up and laughed until the tears rolled down their faces. When the skitting and pantomiming slowed to a trickle, Frankie asked where they got such a big ham. That set off a whole new wave of laughter, with Coons lying on his back kicking his feet in the air trying to catch his breath. His foot hit the ham, sending it rolling across the dirty floor and into the wall. Nig-Nig was dying with laughter and had to jump up and run outside to relieve himself. The sound of Nig-Nig relieving himself against the outside wall set them off again. Finally, Digger got his composure back and settled down to tell the story about the ham.

"We was going down the back of Bold Street, you see, la, when we copped a bloke making out with this tart. So, we stop there for a bit and watch them. He stops kissing the bird and says, 'What do you think you're doin?' kinda snotty-like. And Nig-Nig here says, 'Hey mammy, don't get cheeky with us. We might be cops.' We closed in on him and his girl, and he starts looking sick, like. 'What's in the bag, mate?' Coons asked him. 'I'm delivering a ham to a customer. It's me job.' 'So here you stand making out with your girl and the customer is starving to death. You don't deserve the job, mate. Let's have it,' and the bloke hands it over without a fuss. That's when the copper comes outta nowhere and we start legging it!"

Frankie found himself laughing, but he couldn't help feeling sorry for the lad and his girlfriend. He was kind of glad he hadn't gone with them. He was more concerned about the ham laying in the dirt where the cockroaches would get it, than anything else at that moment. But, no one else seemed bothered by it, so he left it there. After all, it wasn't his to worry about.

***

They lay in their blankets staring at the flames, when a gust of wind rumbled down the passageway and blew in through the door opening, raising a cloud of dust and sending empty tins clattering across the floor. They pulled their blankets over their heads until the dust had settled, then resumed gazing at the fire, lost in thought.

"Hey, Frankie, what's your Mam like?" Nig-Nig asked.

"She's nice. Worries too much over me, though."

"Where's your dad?"

"Dunno. Never come back from the war."

"Then what did your Mam tell you?"

"Just that lots of dads never came home and to just get on with it."

"Wish my dad never come home," Digger interjected, sarcastically.

"Mine, neither, the bloody sod," Coons added, sitting up like the memory hurt too much to lie still for.

"You'd think he was still in the bleedin' army the way he farted and strutted 'round the house, beating the shit outta me whenever he got a hair up his arse."

"What about you, Nig-Nig?" Frankie asked, curious about this friend that was fast becoming somewhat of a hero to him.

"Didn't have a dad, neither. Don't think I ever did. Mam worked all night and slept all day. Hardly got to see her, 'til I was walking with me mates one night. There she was, under the railway bridge, talking to a bloke in a motor car. Then she got in and took off. Me mates didn't know what to do and just stood there staring at the ground. So I took off running and haven't been back since."

The story didn't sound too awfully bad to Frankie, but he felt compelled to leave it alone and not ask any more questions.

Things quieted down after this. The fire had spent its flame, leaving behind a mound of glowing embers. Suddenly a spine-tingling *woooo*...erupted from what seemed like the depths of Hell itself. Frankie's heart beat wildly, and the hair on his neck bristled. Everyone lay in shock, too petrified to move, each wondering what could have made such a sound. Frankie looked over where Nig-Nig lay, hoping for some explanation that would put him at ease. All he could see were the whites of his eyes and a row of gleaming teeth.

"Are you smiling, Nig-Nig?" he whispered, not sure what the teeth were doing.

"Are you kidding, mammy, I'm shittin' me trousers!"

Peace did finally come again and Frankie breathed a little easier, but the slightest rustle of blankets or gust of wind would trigger his eyelids to open. Not that he could see anything if something was there. The fire had gone out now and the darkness was complete.

Then, without warning, *woooo*...four bodies shot into a sitting position, like coils that had been wound too tightly. All hell broke loose as they jammed in the door frame, each clamoring to be the first one out, and certainly not wanting to be the last. Finally, with legs and arms disentangled, they made a dash down the passageway toward the stairs. In the pitch dark they had gone the wrong way and came to a dead end.

"This way," Nig-Nig shouted, his eyes wide with fright and excitement. They came to another dead end and almost fell into a huge hole. "Jesus, Jesus! Where's the bloody stairs gone, mammy?" he shouted, exasperated. "I was sure they were here!"

"I think I know," Coons gasped. They followed him to another dead end.

"I'm gonna climb the friggin' wall," Digger announced with finality. Each one searched the passageway for a portion of the wall with the most cracks and holes in it. Soon, they were all clawing their way up, inch by inch. Frankie feared he would fall back down again and the others would run away and leave him. He could hear grunts and loose brick falling to the ground, but he couldn't see a thing. The darkness enveloped him and he felt panic rising in his chest. Suddenly, a hand came out of nowhere and grabbed ahold of his wrist, pulling him to the top of the wall.

"You're the last one up, you little fart." Nig-Nig put on his usual grin before dropping over onto the dock road. They stood together under the street lamp, subdued, allowing their nerves to settle down.

"Bloody awful, if you ask me," Digger commented, rubbing his hands together and staring down at his shoes. "Wonder what it was?"

"Probably shithead coming to steal his ham back," Coons said, laughing at his own joke.

"Well, if he'd sounded that mad when we took it, we wouldn't have took it in the first place!" Nig-Nig said.

Frankie stared down the empty stretch of road, with its little beacons of light barely discernible through the mist coming off the river. He didn't want to stand and listen to any more banter. He just wanted to go home. The clock on the Liver Building said three o'clock. It would take him at least an hour and a half to walk, but at this point, he didn't much care.

By the time he reached home, he was completely exhausted. He was relieved to see the string hanging, which meant he didn't have to wake his mother up.

"Is that you, Frankie?"

"Yes, Mam, it's me."

"Put the lock on the door, lad."

"Okay, Mam, goodnight."

"Goodnight, son."

Crawling into bed with all those warm bodies was like going to heaven. He was glad he had a family to go home to. He thought about Nig-Nig, Digger, and Coons still out there somewhere, and then drifted into a deep sleep. He awakened to someone shaking him.

"It's time to get up," his mother said softly. "I've got the kettle on."

He lay there for a while after she left, wondering why she hadn't shown any anger or bitterness toward him. He was glad she hadn't, but, still, he knew he deserved something for not coming home for two days and missing school. She was a special mother and he knew it. She was the last person in the world he would want to hurt. He would do anything to see her happy, except the one thing she most wanted; and he was unable to do it.

Though the sun was shining through the window, there was an autumn chill in the air. *Another winter,* he thought, getting up slowly. The painful memories of candles, cold bodies huddled in bed for warmth, and long nights struggling to keep a fire going. She sat in front of it, holding a slice of bread dangling from a fork, close to the red coals.

"I've been worried sick over you! Where've you been?" The bread caught on fire and she quickly blew out the flame.

"I like mine burned like that, Mam."

She turned and gave it to him, spearing another slice for herself.

"That didn't answer my question."

"Mam, I wish you didn't worry over me so much. I'm almost ten now. I think that side's done, you're burning it."

She took it off the fork and turned it over.

"And I'm almost ninety! You're putting me in an early grave."

He removed the tea cozy and poured two cups, spilling some on the newspaper spread out in place of a tablecloth. They sat at the table in silence. He felt his mother's eyes on him, so he pretended to be interested in the newspaper, though he couldn't read a word.

"What's become of you," she sighed, pouring herself another cup. "You're so much like your dad, it scares me."

"Do I look like him?"

"The spitting image. Fiercely stubborn and independent, the pair of you!"

For some reason, that made him feel warm all over. His dad was not only becoming a real person, but intricately identified with

Frankie's own character.

"You realize they'll be knocking on the door any day now."

He knew it wasn't a question she was asking, but a statement of fact that he was well aware of. That's why he knew he couldn't stick around very long.

"So, where've you been staying?"

"At the Customs House on the dock road. Met a nice bunch of lads and they watch out for me, especially this black lad." He could tell his mother wasn't too impressed, so he quit talking.

He left the house when she went to the post office to collect the family allowance. As he neared the dock road from Northumberland Street, he began to wonder what he would do if the three lads had moved away from the Customs House for good.

He was preoccupied with these thoughts when, upon reaching the dock road, he spotted a lorry pulling away from the curb. Without thinking, he instinctively ran across the road to catch it. Out of the corner of his eye, he could see another lorry bearing down on him, but it was on top of him before he had time to react. He heard the screeching of brakes and deafening roar of the engine as it passed over him, coming to a stop further down the road.

He could hear screams and running feet, and voices shouting. He could hear every word that was spoken, but he couldn't open his eyes or move in any way. He felt at rest. No pain, no fear or panic, just a sweet peace, like the moment before sleep.

"The poor bugger! Never had a chance."

"Saw the whole thing, I did, ran right in front of it."

"Did someone call the ambulance?"

"Yeah, a lady in the ale house. Should be here any minute."

"Ah, such a crying, bloody shame. He's just a bit of a lad."

Frankie could make out a wailing coming from far off and growing louder until it stopped alongside him. A blanket was spread over him, but he didn't need it. He wasn't cold a bit. He felt himself being lifted up and placed on something soft, then silence.

Word traveled fast. Someone had recognized him and sent word of the accident ahead. By the time the story reached Mann Street, the lad had been 'squashed like a ripe tomato,' to 'they're still picking up the pieces.'

Once again, tragedy had brought people outside. Some in search of more information, others in need of consoling. The street and landings were full of stunned people, mourning over the loss of one of their own. Mann Street was a community of a hundred families, whose lives were knit and woven together by poverty and the hardships of war. When one suffered, they all felt the pain deeply.

They watched in silence as the police car stopped at the second block. Kate had heard the same stories that had been passed around, and was being comforted by her closest friends. Her anguished cries echoed down the street, prompting many to weep with her.

Two policemen escorted her and Abby Walker to the car and gently helped them in. When they were settled in, the driver turned to Kate.

"Mrs. Hawkins, the hospital said your son is doing just fine."

Kate stared at him in disbelief.

"What do you mean, he's doing fine?" she stammered, fighting down the urge to scream at him.

"I'm sorry, that's all the information we got when they requested us to pick you up."

She sank back into the soft leather upholstery, unable to understand. Her son was dead! Everyone in the world knew it. Did this policeman get the wrong information? Did she dare hope for the miracle he offered her only to be crushed again? The trip only took ten minutes, but to her it was interminable.

One officer guided her gently by the elbow, while Abby walked close behind. She entered the emergency room and there he was, sitting up in bed, no less. She started to cry again, but, this time, it was a cry of relief.

"Why are you crying, Mam? I'm okay, honest."

She looked over at the doctor standing at the bedside.

"He's fine. Just a concussion. He's one lucky young man. Because he wasn't expecting to be hit, he didn't tense up. He was like a piece of rubber with a lot of flexibility. When the lorry went over him, he lay between the wheels and came out untouched. It was a one in a million chance."

"Can I go home now?" Frankie pleaded, looking at his mother's tear stained face.

"We would like to keep him a little longer for observation, but we'll leave that up to you. You bring him back if he shows any side effects, like dizziness."

Kate thanked him before turning to her son.

"Come on, twerp, get your clothes on," she laughed, ruffling his curly locks. Frankie bounded out of bed and was dressed within minutes.

Walking up the street between his mother and Abby, he felt strangely aware of people stopping to stare at him. It was unnerving, as a mantle of silence descended over the length of the street. They were all witnessing an unbelievable miracle. People began moving toward them, slowly at first, as in a trance, then running, until the mass of people surrounded them; cheering and clapping and shouting their greetings and heartfelt relief. Pain and suffering was an accepted part of life to them, making joy all the sweeter when it came their way.

Frankie sat motionless, his eyes glued to the judge's face. Someone coughed behind him and scraped a chair on the marble floor. The judge glanced up momentarily, and then resumed his study of the papers in front of him, one hand adjusting the gray wig on his head.

Kate sat next to the boy, her hands constantly in motion, running her fingers round the beading on the handbag sitting on her lap, then picking at a hang nail. She felt hopelessly out of place and wished she could excuse herself and run out and keep on going until she could go no further.

The judge finally looked up; shuffling the papers into a neat pile and setting them down before him. He studied her face and saw the fear lurking behind the misty eyes and the thin, pale face, etched with premature lines. He was about to add to her suffering. He shifted his gaze to the boy's face and studied it for a moment, weighing his words carefully, in order to get the desired response.

"Do you remember our last meeting son?"

Frankie nodded his head in response, his eyes never wavering from the judge's face.

"Can you speak up so I can hear you?"

"Yes, sir."

"Then you must remember my warning about what I would do if you came before me again."

"Yes, sir."

"You haven't left me much choice have you?"

This time, Frankie pulled his eyes away and stared at his mother, hoping to find there some sort of reassurance; anything to quiet the fear beginning to creep up his spine. But, there was none.

Her face held steady, her tears flowing freely down her cheeks and into the corners of her mouth. It was a heart-wrenching sight the judge encountered daily, as he separated children from their mothers, unable to intervene.

The judge sat up and cleared his throat.

"Frankie, I'm sending you to a remand center for a period of thirty days. I hope this will get your full attention and make you realize that going to school is something you must do. There is no other choice."

He turned to Kate, who, by now, sat sobbing uncontrollably into a handkerchief.

"Mrs. Hawkins, it's a good place and they will take excellent care of him. And it's not too far. You can visit with him on a weekend."

A bailiff came over and escorted the boy to a back room that had bars on the windows. A few minutes later, his mother came in and hugged his head to her breast and stroked his curly hair.

"It'll go over fast and you'll be home in no time," she reassured him, pulling his chin up so she could look at him. "Be a good lad for me and I'll come see you when I can, okay?"

A policeman entered the room and escorted the boy out into a courtyard where a Black Mariah waited with its motor running. The van had wire mesh on the windows, but Frankie still had a good view as it passed through the heart of town. It threaded its way through the masses of people who regularly challenged motorists to a death-defying duel.

When they passed by Princess Park and Sefton Park, with its large boating lake, he could hardly stand the pain of abandonment and isolation that swept over him.

He had spent many summer days exploring the parks, making bows and arrows out of tree branches and his shoe laces. Or, sometimes, just sitting for hours on a grassy knoll watching the people boating. He felt angry that strangers had the power to take him away from his home and lock him up for no other reason than him not liking school.

All his life, he felt the fearless, unwavering protection of his mother in times of crisis or hardship. Her fragile appearance had fooled a number of people into pressing their luck, only to be crushed by her shameless attack when her children were in danger. But, today, she had been powerless to stop them from taking him away. His secure little world was collapsing and he was confused and uncertain about what it all meant.

The van passed through the gate and down a winding path to the back door of a large Victorian mansion on Menlove Avenue on the outskirts of Liverpool. He was ushered into a red flag-stoned courtyard with ivy-covered brick walls. They went through a heavy oak door that closed behind them, shutting off all sounds from the world outside.

The man in a white smock walked briskly down the corridor, forcing him to run to keep up. They entered a large, white-tiled room with a row of shower heads on one side and a row of open toilet stalls on the other. He was given a bar of lye soap and a towel and told to put his clothes in a paper bag for storage.

He waited for the man to walk away or turn his back; but, he did neither. The towering, bulky frame stood within arm's length, his shoulders hunched over, his large hands dug deep in the pockets of the white coat, jiggling a bunch of keys. The boy got the distinct impression the man was getting impatient without a word being spoken. The steel-blue eyes seemed to stare through him and beyond to something distant.

He had never undressed in front of anyone but his family before, so it was painfully embarrassing for him as he slowly shed his clothes. He wasn't sure of it, but he thought the tempo of the jiggling keys picked up a bit. Instinct told him to keep looking up from bending over to take off his trousers, flinching away just in time to avoid the full force of the blow. With trousers tangled around his ankles, he tripped and fell sprawling onto the tile floor, scraping his left elbow and wrist.

The man yanked the trousers off and lifted the boy up like a rag doll, setting him down with such force, the boy's legs buckled and he almost fell down again.

"Get under that bloody shower and be quick about it," his voice boomed out. The man's cheeks were flushed and his large bulbous nose flared.

Frankie was terrified and his hands shook uncontrollably, as he sought to turn on the shower. The water was ice cold, but he stayed under it, too afraid to move. After his shower he was given a set of underwear, gray socks, gray corduroy trousers and shirt, and a pair of slippers, all smelling strongly of mothballs.

Once again, he found himself having to run to keep up with the man. The air was full of delicious cooking odors and he realized he hadn't eaten since the tea and toast he had for breakfast. It was now five o'clock.

He was led into a brightly lit dining hall with a high, ornate ceiling and framed paintings adorning each side of the dark, oak-paneled walls. A large crystal chandelier hung over a long table where about twenty young boys sat quietly with arms folded. Their eyes followed him, as he was led past them into another dining room where children sat four to a table.

A bell rang a signal to commence eating. He kept glancing up at the boy opposite him and wondered why one eye kept staring back at him while the other was looking down. He noticed that it never blinked, either.

"What you looking at, mate?"

Frankie turned away.

"It's me glass eye that's bothering you, ain't it?"

"I didn't know it was a glass eye," he said, trying to be friendly and apologetic.

The lad went back to eating. Frankie looked over at the eye once more just to see if he could tell the difference. Pus was running from the corner of it and it made his stomach feel queasy. The lad looked up just as he looked away.

"Okay, you wanna look? Here." He popped it out of its socket and thrust it toward him. Startled, Frankie flinched backward to get away, tipping his chair too far. He went crashing to the floor. All the lads stood up to get a better look and began laughing and deriding his predicament.

He could see a pair of legs clad in black stockings, waddling speedily toward him. She grabbed one of his ears and pulled up on it until he was on his feet, and then his toes, to lessen the pain. She held on to his ear while he danced on his tiptoes, trying to keep his balance for fear she would yank it right out of his head if he let down.

"What is going on here?" she demanded, her head slowly turning to view each face with a cruel stare. His ear began to throb painfully, but she didn't let up.

"The new lad was leaning back too far, Ma Crumble, and he just lost it," the one-eyed boy volunteered.

"Sit!" she barked, and everyone scrambled to get back into their seats. She turned her full attention back to Frankie and grabbing a hold of his other ear, pulled on both of them. Her face came within inches of his and he could smell her minty breath.

"Next time you fall out of your chair, I'll make your bottom so sore you won't be able to sit for a week," she hissed. To make her point clear, she let go of his ears and gave them a short, quick slap that left them ringing. He sat down heavily, totally exhausted and humiliated.

Ma Thistlewaite, a rotund lady, came around placing a bowl of custard and jam tart in front of each lad. Her friendly blue eyes looked at him with kindness and her smile dimpled her plump, rosy red cheeks. It was the first kind face he had seen since arriving.

That night he lay awake listening to the gentle patter of the rain on the window behind his head. He felt strange having a bed all to himself. And crisp, white sheets, no less; and a pillow case on a soft pillow; and real blankets and a counterpane; and a silly, long nightshirt, like a woman's dress. And what about those underpants! He had never worn any before and wasn't sure yet if he liked them.

One person he didn't like was Ma Crumble. She was a real mean woman. And the giant who took him for his shower, Mr. Groom. Those two sure didn't like kids; well, almost.

He'd heard that Mr. Groom liked to come up behind a lad and hug him real tight and grunt and get a hard bulge in his trousers. He also liked catching lads out of bed when they weren't supposed to be, and lifting their nightshirt up to paddle their bare bottoms with his hand.

He drifted off to sleep wondering what his family was doing. He pictured them sitting around a warm fire, talking about him and missing him.

He awoke with a dull throbbing in his arm. Yellow pus was oozing from a break in the skin at the wrist; the elbow was swollen and discolored. A red line streaked up the inside of his arm to a tender lump under his armpit.

He had heard that Ma Crumble was also the nurse, so he chose not to complain and kept his long sleeves buttoned. One-eye tried to draw him into a fight a number of times, but he chose to ignore him.

By the end of the day he felt weak and nauseous. As soon as his head hit the pillow he was fast asleep. He awoke with a moan escaping his lips and thrashing wildly. His nightshirt and sheets were soaking wet. He had dreamt that Ma Crumble had cut off his arm and hung it from the dining room chandelier.

The dormitory was dark except for a faint light filtering through the door frame. He got up and stood by the window. It had stopped raining. The cobblestone street glistened under the light of a pale moon. He stood there for a long time, staring out but not seeing; shivering, but not cold. His head and arm throbbed with pain, but he was beyond caring. He felt only anger and bitterness towards the judge who put him there, and Ma Crumble and Mr. Groom for hurting him without reason. He was through letting One-eye take pokes at him, too, and he looked forward to the next encounter.

He didn't remember getting back into bed. The next thing he knew, there were bodies jumping out of bed, as Mr. Duncan went by like a man possessed, tearing bed covers away from those who dared to still be in them.

Frankie didn't move. He couldn't muster enough strength to lift himself up. Mr. Duncan stood over him with utter contempt at such an open display of disobedience.

"You're still in bed while I'm standing here?" he roared, emphasizing every word until the veins in his neck bulged out.

"I feel sick and my..." His mattress was pulled up, rolling him onto the floor before he had time to finish. The rest of the kids stood silently by the side of their beds, watching with fear and fascination and wondered if the new lad was going to survive this in one piece.

He lay on his back trying to form words to explain about his arm, but he was too weak to force them past his lips. His face felt flashes of heat while the rest of him was cold and clammy. Suddenly, his head heaved up, spewing vomit over the front of his nightshirt.

He awoke to the sound of rain again, but this time he was in a strange room. Just when he was beginning to enjoy the peaceful sound of the rain, the door swung open and Ma Crumble swaggered in with a no-nonsense look on her dour face.

"Open up." She stuck the thermometer under his tongue, then stood stiffly, with hands in the pockets of her smock and stared out the window. He couldn't remember hating anybody as much as he hated her. She showed no sympathy. She took the thermometer out and turned to read it by the light of the window.

"Does me Mam know I'm sick?"

She ignored him completely, like he had never even spoken. It wasn't until she finished checking the bandage on his wrist and elbow and poked at the tender lump under his armpit with her fingers, that she acknowledged him.

"Yes, your mother has been notified," she said flatly, and turned to leave the room.

His heart beat wildly at the news.

"Is she coming to see me?" he shouted after her, hungry for more information. But, the door closed without her saying another word. He drifted back to sleep.

Someone was shaking him and calling his name from somewhere far away. A warm hand caressed his brow. He forced heavy eyelids open and stared into his mother's face. It was the most beautiful face he had ever seen.

"Mam, you made it!"

"Yes, of course, I did, son. How are you feeling?"

He tried to sit up but fell back. Kate propped him up with a pillow. She held his bad arm and stroked the bandage with a gentle touch of her fingers, her eyes brimming with tears.

"What happened?"

Until now, he had wanted to tell her about all the cruel things they had done to him. He had fantasized seeing his mother tearing into Ma Crumble and knocking her out cold, then marching down the hall and finding Mr. Groom sitting at dinner and smashing a plate over his ugly head. He couldn't bring himself to do it. She would only worry and fret even more. She had suffered too much over him already. Besides, it was time he took care of his own problems.

"I slipped in the shower room, and didn't tell nobody about it, so it got infected."

"I brought you some sweets, your favorite kind."

"Licorice All-sorts?"

"Is there any other kind?"

They visited for an hour and then it was time to go.

"Can you bring the kids next time, Mam?"

"Yes, lad."

"And some comics?"

"Okay."

They were just bantering back and forth, not knowing quite how to say good-bye. She finally kissed his forehead and ruffled his curly locks.

"Look after yourself."

"I will, Mam." He watched after her and knew she was crying, because she wouldn't look back.

Ma Crumble checked everybody's head for lice. Frankie had to have all of his hair cut off. Mr. Carlton, the woodwork teacher, was given the job. He was a tall, slender man in his forties. Though his face was tough-looking and his voice deep and resonant, he had a soft spot for kids and often showed kindness when the lads needed it the most.

"Got a model boat in the shop that needs a lad like you to work with it. Are you interested?"

Frankie watched the curls fall into his lap and roll onto the floor.

"I guess so."

"Spotted it in a secondhand shop, I did. Got it for only three quid. No bloody masts left on it, mind you, but I could tell she used to be a beauty."

"How big is it, sir?"

"Longer than three feet, I imagine."

The curls fell like rain, but he didn't care so much anymore.

It was tea time when the haircut was finished. When he walked into the dining room, he could hear the chuckles and snide remarks and whispers. But, he kept his gaze straight ahead as he passed by the long table. He sat down in front of One-eye and gave him a cold stare. One-eye started to laugh at his bald head, and then thought better of it. He wasn't used to being intimidated in front of the other lads and sought to redeem himself.

"What are you staring at, mate?"

Frankie sensed the slight hesitation in One-eye's challenge.

"Your eye's got pus in it and it makes me sick to my stomach when I'm eating."

The dining room grew very quiet, as everyone became aware of the drama unfolding. One-eye squirmed uncomfortably under Frankie's fearless gaze.

Ma Crumble walked into the room.

"What's going on here?" she bellowed. Her eyes roamed from one table to the other, her hands on her hips and feet spread apart in a gesture of stern reprimand.

"Why isn't anybody eating?" The room erupted into the familiar din of silverware scraping on plates. She stood a moment longer, then turned and walked out.

One-eye never once looked up from eating and Frankie knew he had won his first big battle without lifting a finger. He was now the cock of the remand home. He was free to be himself without fear of being hassled or tormented by anyone; that is, except certain staff.

One day Mr. Groom gave him a hug from behind, but he wriggled free. He gave the man a contemptuous look before running to join the other lads in the activity room. Mr. Groom's face was dark and threatening whenever he saw the lad after that. Frankie knew he had to be extra careful not to be caught alone with him.

Ma Crumble and Mr. Groom were always chummy when they were together, so it came as no surprise to Frankie when she became involved. She ordered him to clean her room after supper one night. He was feeling apprehensive when he approached her door and knocked.

"Come in, it's open." She lay on a large brass bed with her head propped up with pillows, and reading a book. She wore only a short, lacy night coat that barely covered anything, except where it was tied at the middle. He looked away quickly, hoping she hadn't seen his face getting flushed.

"The dust rag is there next to the bucket. I want you to wipe everything down, starting with the fireplace and work your way around the room."

Her voice wasn't friendly, but neither was it demeaning like he had become accustomed to hearing. Still, he was filled with trepidation as he reached for the rag and began wiping the mantelpiece. He kept his eyes averted to the wall as he made his way to where she lay.

He could hear the rustle of pages being turned and an occasional squeak of bed springs as she moved her weight. He could go no further because of the bed and began to retrace his steps.

"Hey, come back here! You haven't done under the bed yet."

He froze, not wanting to face her and get embarrassed all over again. Yet, he didn't want her hollering and screaming at him, either.

He turned and dropped quickly, scurrying along on his hands and knees on the hardwood floor. In that instant, he had seen that her filmy wrap lay wide open. He lay on his belly, reaching as far as he could under the bed, his ears throbbing like his heart was right there in his head. He was shaking so bad, he lost control of his bladder and started to pee in his trousers. Now he was panic stricken.

"I've gotta go the lavatory, Ma Crumble!" he shouted up at the bed springs.

"Go on back, I'll finish up the rest."

He crawled out from the rear of the bed and walked quickly out the door.

In the woodwork shop, Mr. Carlton provided all the tools and parts needed for Frankie to work on the ship. He spent every moment of his free time sanding, staining, varnishing, building masts and sails, and connecting hundreds of miniature ropes to the rigging.

He got so caught up with the project he hadn't realized that his time was up.

"Tomorrow's the big day, son," Mr. Carlton said quietly, as he inspected the lad's latest work. Frankie stepped back to look at it from different angles. He was glad to be going home, yet kind of sad at the thought of someone else getting the pleasure of working on it and seeing it finished.

"Wish I could stay and finish it," he sighed.

"It'll be here when you get back," Mr. Carlton quipped lightheartedly, as he put his arm around the boy's shoulder. They both stood gazing at the beautiful model.

"I ain't coming back no more, sir."

"That's what they all say, son, but most eventually do."

He lay awake that night thinking about it. He had to admit he still hated school and wanted no part of it. Yet, to not go would only drag his mother through this whole thing again. He didn't want that to happen. Morning dragged into afternoon as he paced the hallway waiting for someone to come and get him. The staff just let him be, even when dinner was served and he didn't join them. Then he heard it; that unmistakable jingle on the doorbell far down the hall. And then that cough. Yes, he would know that cough anywhere.

She came into view, smiling and motioning for him to meet her. He felt all choked up and fought back the tears. No, he was not going to cry, not here, not now. He walked toward her and buried himself in her outstretched arms. He felt a bit too old to be doing this, but he would do it for her, just this once.

He watched as the teacher sauntered from desk to desk, passing out the test scores for arithmetic. He'd been back in school a whole week now, even stepping up a class because he had turned ten years old. Here he was, unable to read or write or comprehend mathematics, except for some basic addition, which he did on his fingers, and they put him in a higher class because of his age!

Humiliation was the weapon the teacher favored most in his quest to shake up the lazy rascal. He was called on a number of times to stand and read something from the blackboard. The first time he was honest and said he couldn't read it. When called on after that, he chose to just stand and say nothing and wait for the teacher to wave him to sit down.

The corrected test paper was placed in front of him without haste. The teacher hovered over the boy and stood only inches away, his thumb hooked into his waistcoat pockets, breathing down on him with a heavy sigh of discontent.

Frankie glanced at the paper. Every answer was wrong, marked with a big red x. He felt like crumpling the paper up and throwing it. Not only because of the scores, but because of the way the teacher was humiliating him and making him the focus of attention.

"Didn't study the book at all, did you? Just a stubborn lad who won't listen to anything he's told. Well, why don't you stay seated while the rest of the class goes home, because they worked very hard?" The teacher walked back to the front just as the school bell rang.

Frankie decided he'd had enough of this kind of treatment and stood to leave with the rest of the class.

"Sit down!"

He kept moving toward the door.

"I said sit down!" But, the boy's jaw was firmly set as he pushed his way through the group of lads congregating in the doorway to watch the action.

Once in the street, he began to run. Faster and faster he pushed until his legs felt like falling off and his lungs were ready to burst. He didn't slow down until he had reached his street, coming to a stop inside the block. All the tension and frustration were gone now.

He sat down on the step and watched a group of lads playing poker, wishing he had a few coppers to get in and play a hand. There was something about gambling that gave him pleasure. But his big concern for now was school.

He had tried pushing it out of his mind, but it would only creep back. He would find himself flinching with the pain and humiliation of the day's events all over again. He just didn't care anymore. If they wanted to send him away, they would have to catch him first and that wasn't going to be easy to do. He was not only quick and light-footed, he knew every alley and bombed building better than anyone, and he could climb a wall and be gone before you could blink an eye.

Now that he had made up his mind, he felt at peace with himself for the first time since leaving the remand home. He climbed the stairs two at a time and even whistled a tune walking along the landing.

Kate smiled when he walked in, glad to see him happy for a change after a whole week of quiet brooding. She walked into the back kitchen to finish cooking the Scouse and motioned for him to join her. He stepped over Margaret laying with David on the floor, while Dorothy and Sarah were busy setting the table for tea.

"How's school going?" she asked, keeping her voice down so as not to be heard by the others.

"It's not good, Mam. The teacher seems to enjoy making me feel rotten. Every chance he gets he shows me up to the class."

She turned the gas down under the kettle and put the jam tarts in the oven. "So, you're ready to sag again, is that it?"

There was no response. She had hoped her intuition was wrong when she first saw his smiling face, but his silence only confirmed her fears.

"If you don't go and they pick you up, I won't go with you to the court, do you understand that?"
He hung his head in submission.

"The doctor told me I'm going to have another baby, and I need all the help I can get from you." Her countenance betrayed her weariness. "Don't tell the others, not just yet."

"Hey, Mam, how come nuns are holy like Jesus and Mary, and batter girls for nothing?" Sarah asked as soon as everyone was seated.

"They're not holy, they're not," Dorothy assured her in no uncertain terms. "I've seen them punch girls and pull their hair and they never smile for anything. I think they're wicked, meself."

"I'm glad I don't have nuns," Margaret said, just to be part of the conversation.

"You will when you get to the big girls," Sarah shot back.

"Dorothy, go check on the tarts like a good girl."

Frankie went for a walk after tea, hoping to come up with an answer to the problem of school. It was dark outside, but the air was crisp and the sky clear and full of stars. At night, the streets looked incredibly old and decaying, especially under the iridescent combination of moonlight and gaslight. Many of the large flagstones were buckled and worn smooth with age, the cobbled streets pockmarked and filled with rain water. Except for an occasional streetcar rumbling along Mill Street, the neighborhood was free of traffic. No one owned a car in this part of the city and petrol was out of the question. If a person missed the streetcar, they usually ended up walking home.

He loved the quiet solitude and anonymity of the night, and could easily have walked for hours had he not spotted a roving gang of lads who seemed out for trouble. He dashed through a side street and hid in a doorway until they passed by, then headed for the safety of his own street. He still wasn't sure what to do about school. And how about his mother having another baby! He just didn't know why she needed another one when she had five already!

***

He woke up knowing there was no way he was going back to school. He was gone before anyone else was awake. Early dawn hung like a mystery, unable, for a few short seconds, to make up its mind whether or not to relinquish its hold on the peaceful night. Even the birds refused to sing before that magical moment had passed. He felt like he was the only one in the whole world fortunate enough to witness the birth of this glorious day. There were no rides to be had this early, but he didn't mind that. It was just good to be alive and free, and he wanted to skip and jump all the way to the pier head. Each street he walked through had its own character and personality; and he could tell just by looking whether they were friendly streets or streets of indifference. Some were quaint and narrow with their rooftops bowing gracefully to each other like old worn out friends, unable to stand erect as in bygone days. There were streets with terraced houses that stretched endlessly, all so close and tiny, with rows of chimneys standing like soldiers on guard. A child's swing hanging from a lamppost, hopscotch chalked on the pavement, goal posts painted on the brick wall, all told of happy times and friendly people.

Then there were the streets without a heart. Cold columns of gray steel doors and windows rose high above him. Their ledges and every nook and cranny were festooned with pigeon droppings. The cobbled streets were matted with layers of horse dung, along with small mounds of brown sugar, grain, and peanuts that had leaked out of holes punctured by dockers' hooks.

He shouted and clapped as he walked through the streets, sending hoards of startled pigeons skyward, their wings flapping like thunder. As he neared the pier head, the clock on the Liver Building began to chime over the sleepy city. It was six o'clock. Slowly, the world began to stir.

Stony-faced dockers appeared pedaling bicycles that rattled on the uneven cobblestones. A mummified driver guided his horse and cart through the open gate of the Albert Dock, leaving behind a trail of steaming dung.

By the time he reached Clayton's Canteen, the dock road was bustling with activity. He stopped to savor the smell of bacon cooking, and that tantalizing of all smells, toast. His mouth drooled as he crossed the busy intersection and headed toward the landing stage. He tried to envision what it would be like to be big enough to buy all the bacon 'butties' and cups of tea that you wanted.

He sat on a rusting capstan and watched the boats ferry people across the river Mersey, from Birkenhead and Wallasey to the big city to work. It was pleasant sitting there squinting into the sun. But, his tummy was empty. With all the walking he had done, he was just too hungry to think about anything but food. He knew how to put on a good begging face, but, this early in the morning? He shrugged his shoulders and smiled to himself. I can do it. He stood up and headed back in the direction of Clayton's Canteen.

He studied the faces of the two girls serving behind the counter and listened to the tone of their voices for a bit, before choosing the one who seemed the friendliest. With head tilted down and eyes peering up, he slowly approached the counter.

"Would you like for me to clean the tables off for you, miss?"

"Ah, hey, Val, would you come here and see this."

Val came over and they both leaned on the counter with their chins in their hands, staring at the lad.

"Well, God luv you. Where you from, ducks?"

"The Dingle, miss."

"Well, just look at those big, sad eyes, why don't you, Val. Are you hungry, luv? Would you like a cup of tea with toast and marmalade?"

He nodded and smiled, but the blonde girl had already turned to prepare the feast for him.

"Should I clean the tables while I'm waiting?"

"Don't be naughty," Val chastened. "Let the bloody sods sit in their own muck for a bit, cock. You just sit down and pay no mind to it."

With a full stomach, he was now ready to face the day. There was a chill in the air, a subtle reminder that winter was lurking not too far away. He checked out the Customs House for signs of life, but it was just like he had left it months ago. The town center was beginning to bustle as fruit cart vendors set out their colorful displays, stacking the empty crates behind them as a barrier from the wind whipping between the buildings. A preacher stood in the center of the square, surrounded by pigeons pecking and cooing, his voice quivering with emotion as he read aloud from the book of Revelation. Delivery vans clogged the narrow streets, making other traffic squeeze through the impossible maze at a snail's pace. Frankie stood spellbound as men flung insults at each other, cursing and threatening those who blatantly refused to budge. With fascination, his eyes and ears absorbed and savored every detail.

"Frankie, la!"

He wheeled around to see two boys darting through the shoppers toward him.

"Nig-Nig, Coons," he laughed, moving forward to greet them. "Where've you lads been?"

"Hey, mammy, let's go get us a cup of tea at Woolworth's and gab a bit," Nig-Nig said, grabbing him in a headlock and pulling him toward the shop. After they were seated, they got the giggles before settling down for a bit.

"Where's Digger?" Frankie asked, feeling like their happy meeting was somehow not quite complete. There was silence for a moment as the boys glanced at each other wondering who was going to respond to the question. "The judge sent him to a borstal for three years on the Isle of White," Coon went on. "His mam and dad told the judge to send him away 'cause he wasn't doing any good for anybody."

"What about you, mammy?" Nig-Nig asked, breaking an uncomfortable silence.

"Did a month in a remand home and tried going back to school, but it didn't work. Now I'm running again."

"Where you staying, mate?" Coons asked, hoping he would take Digger's place.

"The stables across from me house."

"Do you like it there?"

"Yeah, it's okay. Last time I slept there, though, the horse in the next stall lifted his tail over to my side and pooped on me during the night. Never even knew it until I tried to open me eyes the next morning and they were caked full of it!" Frankie ended up shouting the last part because Nig-Nig and Coons were laughing so hard and slapping the table to emphasize their pleasure.

Everyone else in the cafeteria was upset with all the commotion, prompting the pretty blonde girl to leave the safety and sanctity of her counter in order to confront the three lads.

"You are carrying on a bit, aren't you?" she said, the last word catching on the phlegm in her throat and squeaking out. She tried to clear her throat but started coughing instead. The lads stared back at her flushing, pink face as she fumbled in her apron pocket for a handkerchief, but there was none. Nig-Nig held out his serviette, but she ignored it. "You lads will be on your way then, won't you?" she said.

They rose slowly, still looking at her pretty face, flushed like a pink rose.

"We wasn't doing nothing wrong, miss, was we?" Nig-Nig persisted, enjoying her discomfort.

She smoothed the front of her apron and turned quickly, making her way back to the counter. The tickle in her throat had made her nose run and she hadn't wanted them to see it. She grabbed for a serviette and sneezed into it, sending her hair cascading forward around her face. She blew her nose and glanced up. They were still standing there looking at her.

Frankie lay under the horse blankets that night listening to the wind whistling through the cracks in the door. He could hear the sound of a tin can clattering along the street outside. The horse snorted and stomped a couple of times, sending particles of sawdust floating down into his face and hair. For some reason, just having the horse there was a comfort to him. The old wooden beams creaked and moaned under the stress, and somewhere in the darkness, water dripped from a loose tap, gurgling as it found its way into a floor drain. The straw next to his head rustled and he sat up quickly, suspecting it was a rat or a mouse. His eyes had grown accustomed to the dark, but he could only distinguish shades of black rather than shapes.

He'd climbed the gate an hour ago, feeling weary from a full day in town and the long walk back home. Now, sleep was elusive, as the night teased him with an assortment of sounds and movements. He wondered if it would have been wiser to have gone with the lads to their old train in an abandoned rail yard. At least that way he would have company at night. But, he had said no.

Here, he still felt close to his family, filling a need he had not to stray too far. He liked the idea of being able to look out the mesh window, as he had done tonight, and see his door just across the street. Sometimes he would strain, thinking he could hear his baby brother crying at night, or hear his mother coughing softly. Yes, this was much better, he thought, as he finally drifted off to sleep.

The leaden sky ripped open like a torn curtain, sending fissures of light twisting grotesquely in every direction. It was soon followed by an earsplitting sound of thunder rolling across the heavens like an angry god come to take vengeance on judgment day. A torrential rain fell, bringing the city traffic to a virtual halt and sending pedestrians fleeing in search of cover.

Kate watched awestruck through the window of the streetcar. It brought back memories of the bombing raids of 1940. The wail of sirens, the scurry of feet, the deserted streets, the sound of thunder, the sky pierced with light, and most of all, the feeling of helpless terror. She was young then, only twenty-one years old, and very much in love.

Her husband, Frank, had been called up, leaving her with two small children and one on the way. Their life together had been an exciting, but rocky, roller coaster ride from the very start. She chuckled as she remembered her mother chasing him down Wolf Street with a frying pan poised over her head, shouting, "You dirty bleeder! If I ever get me hands on yer puddin' face, I'll mark you for life!" She would, too, and he knew it. A saner man would have no problem giving up the prize when confronted by a woman weighing in at sixteen stone and wielding a heavy weapon. But, not Frank! He would always find a way to see his dark-haired, seventeen year old beauty. He would climb over the backyard wall and shimmy up the drainpipe and knock on her bedroom window, just for a kiss. Then slide down again and run like hell knowing her mother might, at any moment, spring from out of nowhere and cook his goose.

"Mam, Mam, I think this is our stop," Frankie said, pulling on her coat sleeve and standing up. "Oh, I'm sorry son, I didn't mean to daydream and leave you all alone."

They stepped off the tram and she tried to take hold of his hand, but he pulled away because his hand was clammy. They walked in silence to the courthouse door and stepped inside.

As soon as she received word he was back, Ma Crumble grabbed the comb and scissors and headed for the shower room. He had just stepped out of the shower and started to dry himself off when she came through the door dragging a chair with her.

"Come on, sit down and be quick about it, I don't have all day."

Although he wasn't quite finished, he wrapped the towel around his middle and sat in the chair. Goose bumps popped out all over his wet body, and he shivered as the curls tickled his skin and fell in a heap in his lap. It was over within minutes.

"Wash yourself off and clean up this mess before you come upstairs." Her voice was flat and her face expressionless as she retreated with the chair.

He ran his hand over his head and was shocked at how close she had cut it. He felt an inner rage. She was robbing him of his dignity and making him feel worthless, dirty, and ugly! But, he felt helpless to retaliate.

There were only a few familiar faces left from his last visit and they must have gotten the word out to the other lads not to mess with him. It was a relief to walk into the dining room without feeling humiliated, even though everyone knew the reason for such a short haircut. He picked at his Yorkshire pudding, while his mind drifted back over the last day's events.

He'd awakened early that morning and looked through the stable window, surprised to see a bobby standing outside his door. His mother opened it and the bobby took his tall hat off and put it under his arm as he stepped inside. Frankie's first inclination was to run, but then he hesitated. He'd been running for three weeks now, and he was tired and worn out from constantly looking over his shoulder. Even the headmaster, Mr. Coggley, had formed a group of older lads to chase him down whenever he was spotted in the area. It had produced some terrific chases that had sometimes lasted all day long, covering half of the city's streets, docks and warehouses. But, he'd never gotten caught, even though it had been close a few times.

Some of the lads were happy for the chance to be out of school, but they had no heart for catching the poor lad. Others felt exhilarated and important, like they were in hot pursuit of a wild animal that needed to be locked away. Every bobby he saw now gave chase, which was exciting at first, dodging and weaving through crowds of shoppers, scurrying across roads filled with cars and trams blasting their horns at him. But, by day's end, he would be frazzled and emotionally drained.

He'd waited for the policeman to leave before climbing over the gate and going home. His mother was pouring herself a cup of tea when he entered. She glanced at him and then back to the tea, putting a spoon of sugar in it and some milk. He could tell she'd been crying.

"Is there any more in the pot, Mam?"

"Yes, help yourself," she said, in quiet resignation, pulling a straight-backed chair closer to the fire. She stared at the flames until he sat down in front of her then turned to him

with a long, determined look. He could see the reflection of the flames dancing in her misty, hazel eyes, and a slight flare to the nostrils of her long, finely chiseled nose. He braced for the worst.

"Where do you think this is all gonna end?" she demanded, her voice firm, yet conciliatory. They stared at each other. She, searching his inner soul for answers; he, longing in his heart to be at peace with her.

"Take a good look at yourself, Frankie. You look like a lost dog without a home. You're gonna die out there; running, stealing, sleeping God knows where. Think of what it's doing to me, worrying and fretting every day, afraid that every knock on the door is bringing news you're either hurt or lying dead somewhere." He had to look away from those eyes brimming with tears. They were silent for a while.

"You must've seen the policeman leave?" He nodded in response. "They want you in court this afternoon or they're coming for me."

It was like a bomb exploding in his head.

"Why they wanna pick on you for, all the time? Why don't they just leave you alone!" he shouted, knocking the chair over as he stood up.

"Don't you dare go near that door! You're not going anywhere! I'm your mother and they hold me responsible; so I want you in that back kitchen and give yourself a good scrub down."

The sleepy-eyed girls came out of the bedroom wondering what the shouting was all about. When he saw what it was doing to the family, he resigned himself to going to court with her.

Ma Thistlewaite came around with a silver bowl and a large

spoon, asking for anyone who wanted seconds of custard to raise their hand. While dishing it out, she noticed Frankie's plate was barely touched. She sat down in the empty chair next to him putting the big bowl in her lap.

"You don't like my cooking?" she asked in exaggerated disappointment.

He looked over at her and couldn't help but smile. Her face was like an angel, full of loving kindness that washed over him and made him feel good again.

"I just wasn't hungry, Ma Thistlewaite." She rose from the chair with a big sigh and patted his shoulder knowingly, before resuming dishing out the custard.

Because it was a short-term facility, emphasis wasn't placed on classroom learning, but on handcrafts like leather work, making wallets and footballs, or woodwork, where boys could whittle and chip away industriously. For Frankie, it was the ship. He was taken by surprise when Mr. Carlton gave him a key and asked him to unlock a cupboard and get out some tools. He opened the doors and saw the ship sitting majestically on the shelf. He grinned over at the teacher, then reached in and took it out, setting it on the bench it had occupied before.

"Wouldn't let a soul touch it after you left, lad. Just figured you'd be back to finish the job." Frankie fought back the tears.

Four days before he was to be released, the governor of the house came by to view the finished ship. He'd heard about it for some time, but was obviously unprepared for such a magnificent display. His portly frame arched back in surprise when Mr. Carlton removed the covering, then leaned forward to inspect and admire the very delicate and intricate detail more closely.

"My, my," he repeated over and over, as he circled the table with his face only inches from the ship. Finally, he straightened up and turned to the six lads in a semicircle.

"And which one of you is responsible for doing this?" he asked, peering over his gold-rimmed spectacles and squinting at each face, like he was trying to guess which one by their expressions. He did, too. His gaze settled on Frankie.

"You're the rascal, aren't you?" he smiled, beckoning the boy over to join him. Frankie moved forward, his face flushed and trembling a little. He had never been singled out before except for being bad. Now, here was the governor of the house, himself, putting his arm around his shoulder and beaming with delight.

"Young man, I would like to put this on display outside my office, for all my guests to see and admire, if that's okay with you."

Frankie looked over at Mr. Carlton who was smiling and nodding his head in his direction. "That's alright with me, sir. I'm glad you like it."

"It's beautiful and it will always belong to the house, in recognition of all the boys who pass through here.

When his mother came to take him home, he asked if she could see the ship on display. The governor came out to greet her as she stood in the carpeted hallway, tears of pride trickling down her cheeks.

Old Tessy opened her back door just wide enough to allow Frankie to speak to her.

"Four jars of Ovaltine, Tess, two bob a piece."

She knew that was half the price the shops were charging, but still she shook her head.

"No, I don't want them, that's too much."

He'd been coming here two or three times a week and he was tired of the way she haggled over everything. Maybe after today I won't come here no more, he thought.

"Okay, one an' six, then, Tess."

She still hesitated, wondering if she could get him to go lower. She knew there were others on the street who bought from him, so she figured she'd better grab them at that price or chance him storming away like he'd done the last time.

"I'll give you five bob for the lot," she announced, opening her purse like the deal had been settled. She couldn't resist the chance to squeeze that last shilling out, if possible.

"No, Tess, that'll be six bob for the bloody lot or I ain't coming back no more."

He felt good having said it, but he hoped she wouldn't shut the door in his face. His other customers hadn't cared for Ovaltine. She gave him the money and a dirty look to go with it.

He climbed the stairs two at a time and went into the house. Dorothy screwed up her face at the sight of him.

"You're getting to be a real scruff, lad. People are talking."

"Oh, yeah, well, let them. I'm a hard-working man, girl, and I'm bound to get a little dirty." With that, he plunked two half-crowns down in front of his mother, who was sitting reading the Echo. He'd done this quite a few times lately, but she wasn't fully convinced he'd been working.

"So, tell us about this work, son," she said, laying the newspaper down on her lap. He walked into the back kitchen like he was putting the kettle on, but he was really stalling for time. He could have kicked himself for not being prepared for such a question.

"Anybody else wanna cup?" he hollered out.

"No, we just had one," Dorothy called back. Their eyes followed him as he came back and sat sipping his tea.

"Oh, yeah, you wanted to know what I do. Well, I stand outside Tate and Lyle, you see, 'til a driver needs a hand to load his wagon." He'd actually heard lads say they did that, so it wasn't too far-fetched.

"I don't believe him, do you, Mam?" Dorothy said, in her proper little mother voice.

"Well, t'would be a shame if he did work hard all day, and his own family didn't believe him. So maybe it's best we give him the benefit of the doubt." Dorothy could see why he got away with so much. She was always defending him.

Frankie's hand felt under the heavy tarp, his fingers prying open the seam in one of the paper bags. He pinched its contents and brought it out and up to his nose to smell. Peering into the darkness, he could make out the shadowy figure of Nig-Nig searching another wagon load.

"Psst, Nig-Nig. I've hit the big one." he whispered, excitement mounting in his voice. He looked across the deserted street at the David Lewis, where the lorry drivers were eating a meal or catching a few winks before heading out.

"What is it, mammy?"

"Tea! Can you believe it? Tea!"

Next to tobacco, tea was the most sought after item and by far the easiest to sell. They heard a foot crunch the gravel somewhere in the parking lot and stood motionless, staring at each other. Maybe it was Coons, left his lookout post to come check on them? There were no more noises for the next few minutes.

"Let's grab what we can and get the hell outta here," Nig-Nig whispered, tearing open the bag and stuffing packages of tea down his jersey. Frankie followed suit. Suddenly, they heard the noise again, even closer this time. Once again, they froze to the spot, their ears fine-tuned to the slightest sound. Nig-Nig slowly squatted down to take a peek under the wagons. Without warning, beams of light from police torches raked the darkness, as uniformed officers came running from both ends of the parking lot, converging on the spot where Frankie stood immobilized. Nig-Nig escaped by crawling underneath the wagons until he reached the street, and then took off running. By the time the police spotted him and gave chase, he was safely lost in the maze of dark streets and entryways.

They put Frankie, with his jersey still stuffed with tea, in the back seat of a police car and drove to the Cheapside Police Station. He felt drained of energy. After questioning him for about an hour, they left him alone to drink the cup of tea they had given him. He stretched out on the hard wooden bench, proud he hadn't snitched on his two friends, yet, ashamed to have been the only one caught.

Kate had just tucked David into bed with a warm bottle of tea when the knock came at the door. She knew by the type of knock that it was the police, and remained standing in the dark bedroom, wishing she could just climb in with the baby and go to sleep. She heard Dorothy jump up from the floor and run to open the front door.

"Mam, there's a policeman at the door." Reluctantly, she left the solitude of the bedroom. "Would you like to come in, officer? Girls, pick up the game and go sit down on the couch, that's good children."

Even with his tall bobby's hat off, he still had to stoop to enter. He grinned at the three girls sitting quietly on the couch, which made them giggle and fidget nervously. Kate offered him a chair, but he chose to remain standing.

"I'm from Essex Street, meself, Mrs. Hawkins. They're holding your son, Frankie, downtown at Cheapside. There's no hurry. Just whenever you can get there."

"What did he do this time, officer?"

"Caught stealing, is all I know. They'll most likely tell you everything when you get there."

She thanked him and closed the door behind him, wondering how she was going to get downtown this hour of the night. The streetcar quit running after eleven and it was almost half past that now. She arranged the fire guard around the hearth and reached for her coat hanging on the nail.

"Dorothy, don't put any more coal on, do you hear me, girl?"

"Yes, Mam."

"And don't answer the door for nobody, do you hear?"

"Yes, Mam."

Dorothy knew the scenario by heart. She watched as her mother pulled the string in, put the lock on, overlapped the curtains to prevent anyone peeking in, and checked the fire guard one more time, just like she always did. All done while she buttoned her coat, tied her scarf, and located her handbag hidden in a drawer. She took one more long look around the kitchen for peace of mind, then kissed each of the girls and left.

Mary's always good for a taxi at a time like this, she thought, picking her way cautiously down the dark steps inside the block. The smell of urine and dog poop assailed her nostrils and she vowed to scrub the block out the first chance she got.

After four hours in the police precinct, Frankie was happy to see his mother's face, but not his Auntie Mary's. While his mother spoke with the sergeant, his aunt marched over to the lad and glared down at him.

"There's something drastically wrong with you," she said, poking a finger in his chest. "You oughta have your head examined, dragging your poor Mam into all this caper. You'll put her in an early grave, you will."

Mary had spent her last two shillings on a taxi to get them to the police station. Now, they had to walk the two miles home in the drizzling rain. Kate complained of her bunions and took off her high-heeled shoes and walked in her stocking feet. Mary squealed with delight at the sight of her sister marching unabashedly through puddles of rain water. But, it didn't take long before she, too, decided to take off her shoes and join in this merry little game of romping through the puddles.

Frankie could only look on in wide-eyed wonder, as these two grownups now began to splash and kick water on each other, then chase each other screaming down the quiet streets, with their shoes scooped full of water ready to throw. He was glad there was nobody around to witness it.

The last part kept ringing in his head...*until you are fifteen years of age.*

Kate's body jerked as though a knife had suddenly been thrust into her heart. She'd expected three to six months to teach him a lesson, but almost five years was incomprehensible. That was his whole childhood.

Frankie sat motionless, staring down at the white marble floor. It was like the time when his friend, Stevie, died. He felt nothing, no emotion, no feeling. A veil had descended, protecting him from the onslaught of pain and agony that threatened to sweep over him and crush his spirit forever. He was aware of his mother sobbing next to him, but he, himself, was empty of tears.

In the holding room, she spoke to him in soft, reassuring tones, all the time playing with his long curls. Her voice felt soothing to him, but the words she spoke floated away and were lost. He was glad when they came to separate them.

He leaned his head against the cold paneling of the Black Mariah and closed his eyes. The droning of the engine and the sound of tires meeting the wet roadway lulled him to sleep.

The back door opened and Mr. Groom grinned at him, shaking his head with mirth. The lad knew what was expected of him and did it mechanically, bagging his street clothes, bathing, and cleaning up after himself. Mr. Groom never took his eyes off him, but to the lad, it was as if the man wasn't even there. He expected chicken legs to waddle in at any moment, brandishing a pair of scissors, but she never did.

From somewhere inside the far reaches of his mind, he could hear a voice calling to him. His eyelids fluttered open in reflex to his shoulder being shaken vigorously by a strong, firm hand. It took him a few seconds to clear the sleep from his mind before he could focus on the face in front of him. It was the face of a stranger with a thick, reddish-brown mustache. The sunken cheeks gave the face a sinister appearance in the semi-darkness of the dormitory.

"Are you awake, son?" the man inquired in a raspy voice. Frankie found himself in a state of trepidation and managed only a nod. The stranger pulled himself erect and donned a floppy hat on his balding head.

"Let's hurry now, we've got a very long way to travel," he concluded, before turning and melting into the darkness.

He eased himself out from between the warm covers and stood looking out the window, shivering slightly in his nightshirt and bare feet. It had rained all night. Now, it was just a fine mist that blew against the window pane, forming droplets that shimmered in the light of the street lamp, before coursing their way down to the bottom of the window sill.

In six months, his mother had come to visit him less and less as time went by, making every visit more precious. He found himself running as fast as he could after every visit just to catch a glimpse of her crossing the street to get on the tram car. Then he would stand staring out of the window long after she'd gone, turning away only after the aching and loneliness had subsided. Now, he was about to be moved to a more permanent place hundreds of miles away, where, he knew, she could never afford to go. This was his last good-bye and she didn't even know he was leaving.

He heard soft footsteps approach from behind, and turned from the window to face the stranger.

"How come you're not ready to go, son?" the man said, bewildered at the lad's lack of cooperation and reticence.

Frankie chose not to answer, turning instead to the bag they'd given him the night before containing his own clothing. As he opened the bag, a pungent, acrid odor assailed his nostrils. His clothes were damp and mildewed, and when he put them on, they didn't fit him anymore. He felt frustrated and angry at everything, especially at this stranger standing in front of him hurrying him along, and who was about to take him far away from home.

The city was still sleeping when the car headed out the gate and down Menlove Avenue towards town. The only sound was the methodical thump, thump of the windshield wipers and the swishing sound the tires made on the wet road. A faint light began spreading across the heavy sky, ushering in a new day. He leaned his head back on the soft leather seat and watched the city slowly awakening.

Here and there a figure stood with coat collar up and cap pulled forward, waiting for the first bus of the morning to come along and take him to work. A milkman guided his horse-drawn cart to the curb and blew on his fingertips, before jumping off and grabbing for the cold bottles to make a delivery. The car passed within inches of a man on a bicycle, spraying him with rainwater from the ruts in the road. Frankie had witnessed the city waking up many times before, but this morning, knowing he would not see it again for many years, he wanted to capture every detail. He felt the driver glance over at him a few times, but no words passed between them until they were through the Mersey Tunnel and into Birkenhead.

"If you need to pee, now's the time to do it," the driver warned, pulling the car to a stop alongside a quiet country road and getting out. He chose to stay in the car. He had contemplated making a run for it earlier and changed his mind because of what it would do to his mother. Now the man had given him one last chance and he didn't want to trust himself to get out while still being this close to Liverpool.

By early afternoon, the sun had come out, lighting up the beautiful lush countryside with its patchwork of gently rolling fields that stretched as far as the eye could see. They passed through picturesque villages of thatched-roof Tudor cottages, whose roads were merely one-lane carriage paths, unchanged for centuries. Here and there, old limestone church steeples dotted the escarpment, their ancient gravestones blackened and crumbling under the weight of time.

The car stopped frequently to allow small herds of sheep or cattle to cross the road. The farmers, their faces ruddy and somber, tipped their hats in a gesture of courtesy, but refused to be pressured into moving any faster. To Frankie, it was a whole new world he'd never known existed. Beneath the sadness at being torn away from home, a new feeling of adventure began to stir within him. A glimmer of hope sprang to life that sent shivers through his body, forcing him to smile for the first time in many days. *Maybe it won't be so bad*, he thought to himself, feeling strange at the sudden change in his outlook.

It was just before sunset when the house came into view. The red-brick mansion stood majestically on a hill, like a mighty fortress guarding the farms and small villages that spread out beneath it. The car wound its way along a driveway festooned with freshly dug flower beds that budded with the promise of spring. Birds flew from the weeping willow trees, startled by the sudden churning of wheels on the gravel path. When the car came to a stop, they both sat for a moment bathed in the quiet serenity of the countryside. The large oak door opened and a young man dressed like a priest, greeted them with a smile and a handshake.

"Welcome to Saint Gilbert's, Mr. Bloomfield. I'm Brother Gerard. I hope you'll stay and join us for tea before heading back." His voice had a pleasant Irish lilt to it. Turning, he ruffled the boy's tousled locks.

St. Gilbert's Boys' School, Hartlebury, Worcs.

"And you, dear lad, will take a nice bath and change into some fresh clothing. How does that sound?" Frankie nodded, feeling out of place and out of sorts.

The house was more like a king's palace than a boys' reform school. Rich tapestries and large gold-framed paintings of Bible characters hung on pale-blue walls. From the high, ornate ceiling hung a beautiful chandelier whose crystals danced and sparkled. Soft light reflected through a stained-glass window. The oak floor shone like a pool of still water. A large oak staircase spiraled upward, its hand-carved rail also polished to a high gloss. A deep hush pervaded the house that made you want to whisper when you spoke.

Brother Gerard led the way up four flights of stairs to the top floor. There, Frankie was shown into a ten-bed dormitory where a stack of neatly folded clothes lay on the bed closest to the window. He was amazed at how orderly and clean the room looked. The dark-brown linoleum, like the floors in the foyer and reception room, was polished to a high gloss. The light-green walls looked freshly painted without a mark anywhere. Every bed was made perfectly uniform, with slippers peeking from beneath the counterpane of each one. Even the large bathroom, which catered to four dormitories on that floor, was spotlessly clean.

After showering, he dressed in his khaki uniform and stood for a moment gazing out the window at the breathtaking view of the Worcestershire countryside now bathed in twilight. When he entered the dining hall, the noise level dropped to a murmur as over a hundred lads turned to look in his direction. He fought back the fear of intimidation rising within him, remembering how much better and freer life was once he'd stood his ground and refused to be pushed around. Like everything else in the big house, the dining area looked bright and cheerful; each of the tables, seating four, had a white linen table cloth on it. He sat and ate in silence. When the meal was over, everyone stood and bowed their heads while a staff led them in prayer. Then they filed out and headed down to the school yard.

To Frankie, it seemed unnatural to see so many lads behaving so well with only one staff supervising. He stood under the floodlight and watched as the youths formed little groups that began walking slowly around the yard, talking and laughing with each other as they went. The night air was chilly and he wished he had a coat. Homesickness suddenly began to creep back in and he felt weary from the long day of travel. He was glad when the whistle blew and they marched back to the big house to wash up for bed.

That night, sleep eluded him. He tossed and turned, his mind refusing to relinquish a nagging suspicion that all was not well here. Why was everything so beautiful and shining? Everything so proper and in perfect order? Why hadn't he seen any of the raucous behavior usually attributed to large gatherings of youth, like a push or a shove, or even a high-spirited shout once in a while? So far, all he'd witnessed was the most well-behaved group of lads he'd ever seen, which made him very uneasy and distrustful. Amid the high-pitched chirping of the crickets, his mind finally gave in to the overwhelming desire for sleep.

With one sweep of Brother Cuthbert's hand, Frankie's bedding lay in a heap at his feet.

"Robert, show our new guest how to make up his bed."

Robert Troak was a small, unpretentious blonde boy, whose blue eyes and handsome, delicate face looked startled at the sound of his name being called.

"Yes, Bro," he called back, springing into action while the rest of the lads stood quietly at their beds until it was finished.

After breakfast, everyone dispersed throughout the big house to begin their one-hour cleaning detail before school. Frankie was taken to a staff bathroom by an older student, Brian Bartlett.

"This is yours, Frankie."

"Looks to me like its clean already," Frankie said, surveying the scene with a puzzled expression on his face.

Brian glanced around to make sure they were alone, then pulled the lad closer, in confidence. "Look, mate, they'll beat the shit outta you if you cop an attitude. If you don't believe me, just still be standing there, when they come to check on the job."

He watched after Brian until he disappeared into the vicinity of the dining hall. Everywhere he looked, there were lads on their hands and knees, polishing, waxing, buffing and cleaning, with very little talking among them. He began to suspect that fear was the motivating force that moved everyone here; though, he had to admit, he hadn't seen anything to be fearful about. He wasn't to wait much longer.

After Chapel on Sunday morning, he sought out Robert Troak and together they sauntered around the yard.

"What's going on, Robert? Everybody seems so quiet today."

"It's like this every Sunday. Have you met the headmaster yet?"

"No, but I saw him from a distance the other day."

He remembered it clearly. The flowing black robes billowed in the wind, as he teased his Alsatian dog into a menacing, snapping posture by stalking it in a crouched position. Threatened, the dog suddenly lunged forward catching his master's hand and drawing blood. Intentionally, the headmaster turned to look at Frankie, who'd been watching. His eyes were penetrating and cold and his lips curled into a cruel grimace. Without warning, his fist shot out and Frankie heard a sickening thud. The huge dog keeled over, whimpering and pawing at its snout. His attacker leaned over him, flexing his fist to get circulation back into it.

"So, what about the headmaster?" he went on, trying to push the memory of that awful scene from his mind.

"You see, on Sundays, he comes down and holds an assembly." Robert stopped talking so Frankie looked over at him.

"Well, go on. What about the assembly?"

Robert was physically shaken up and continued with some difficulty.

"He's like a madman. I've never been so afraid in my whole life," he blurted out, a touch of indignation beneath the quivering voice.

"How long have you been here, Robert?"

"Almost three weeks."

"Maybe it's not so scary all the time. Maybe he's got bad days and good days."

"No. Once you've felt the fear, then you'll know it's his way of doing business."

Frankie felt sorry for him and wondered why anyone would want to put a nice kid like him in such a place as Saint Gilbert's.

Rows of chairs, about six abreast, were set up in the activity room for the assembly. Frankie noticed a definite avoidance of the aisle seats, as lads scrambled over each other trying to get to the comfort and security of the middle sections. When they were all seated, the room took on a strange silence as each one became reflective about his past week's performance.

Even before Frankie saw him, he knew the headmaster was there, standing in the back of the room. Not one head turned or dared to steal a glance backward. Bodies began to squirm and fidget in their seats as fear swept over the room like an invisible tidal wave. Frankie felt the fear begin to grow in the pit of his stomach, too.

With head bowed and shoulders slightly hunched over, the headmaster made his way slowly toward the front of the assembly, then turned to face his captive audience. Though he couldn't have been much more than five and a half feet tall, his presence emanated power. His head was small, with black close-cropped hair. Deep lines were etched into the leathery face. Frankie remembered those cold blue eyes, even more menacing now as they raked each face unmercifully. He pursed his thick lips, and then pulled them back to form a sinister grin, while picking at his nose and rolling the contents between the knobby fingers of his right hand.

It was obvious he relished the hold he had over them. The sight and smell of their fear fed the flame of contempt. Slowly, with calculated steps he entered the middle aisle. His hands were now clasped behind his back, and his eyes stared straight ahead.

The room grew deathly silent as the tensions mounted with every step he took. Frankie could not remember ever feeling so many emotions ebbing and flowing at one time, causing him to feel sick to his stomach.

The headmaster stopped and turned his head slowly to his right and stared at a lad three seats from the aisle. Time stood still. He gave a slight jerk of his head, indicating for the boy to move out into the aisle in front of him. The lad's face took on a sickly pallor and his eyes brimmed with tears as he stood shakily to his feet.

The headmaster leaned to within inches of the boy's face. The lad tried to look away, but the madman pinched the flesh of his cheek and twisted it until the head came back to face him. The tears now flowed freely.

"Ah, tears, Mr. Kelly!" he mocked. "Would they happen to be tears of repentance?" The lad couldn't reply even if he wanted to. The headmaster now had a hold of both cheeks and was twisting the flesh in opposite directions, making the lad's mouth all contorted.

"Yes, Mr. Kelly, I had a complaint about your very poor vocabulary toward Miss Weatherby yesterday. She works very hard in the kitchen and will be shown every respect, is that clear?"

The last words hissed out of his mouth while his nostrils flared in a show of angry indignation. At the same time as he let go of the lad's cheeks, he pushed him in the direction of his seat, sending him sprawling backward and into the laps of the nearest group of boys. Chairs and bodies went flying in every direction. In seconds, order was restored and he resumed his intimidating stroll up the aisle to the back of the room.

Like a cat, he sprang into action, this time grabbing a fistful of shirtfront and yanking a lad off his seat, pinning him against the back wall.

"Graham, the next time you're caught wandering around in your nightshirt, I'll leather your backside so bad you won't sit down for a week!"

For over an hour the tirade continued. Like an actor, his demeanor changed with each encounter. There was no way of telling what he would do next, or how he would go about doing it, or to whom. It was physical and mental torture, in order to manipulate and control a large number of boys with a minimum amount of effort. Fear is a good motivating force; terror works even better.

After what seemed like an eternity, the assembly came to an end and the lads filed outside in silence, their spirits broken down. It was some time before anyone felt good enough to play or run in the yard. It was even longer before laughter was heard.

Frankie found himself a quiet spot to sit and let his nerves unwind. *How am I ever gonna survive four years of this?* He thought to himself. *Maybe I'll just keep to meself and stay away from trouble.* That was his simple, heartfelt solution to the problem, but it was not to be.

Only two days later, his greatest fear came upon him. The boys in his dormitory were in good spirits, swapping comics, playing pranks on each other, or just sitting at each other's beds visiting before lights out. John Ryder, being a little over-rambunctious, kicked at Frankie as he walked by in his nightshirt. The foot caught him in a very sensitive area between his legs, sending him into excruciating pain. He turned and leapt on John, knocking him to the floor, then sat on him and pounded away at his face while John screamed for help.

After the initial shock, some of the boys pulled him off, just as Brother Leo came running into the room. He immediately grabbed each of them by an ear and began twisting until they danced and winced in pain.

"I want both of you to report to the headmaster's office right now, and be quick about it," he shouted, propelling them toward the door.

"But, Bro, it was an accident," Frankie pleaded, dreading the thought of facing the headmaster.

"You'd better get moving, Hawkins, before I lose it with you," Brother Leo shot back.

He backed into the hallway with a sinking feeling in the pit of his stomach. He would have done anything to avoid this. He felt like he was going to his death. By the time they reached the bottom of the stairs, he was in a state of panic.

"Hey, John, hold up a bit," he called out in a strained whisper.

"What's your bloody hurry, anyway?"

John stopped and turned to look back at him. In the dim light of the hallway Frankie could see the glazed look in his eyes, and knew they were both feeling the strain.

"I feel like doing a run," Frankie said, leaning his back against the cool wall.

"In your nightshirt, mate? You wouldn't half get far now, would you."

"Just keep on running and running," he repeated to himself, like he hadn't heard a word John had said.

They crossed over the large foyer area with its huge staircase and chandelier. Even in the dim light, everything sparkled and shone. The air was heavy with the smell of wax and polished wood. He glanced over at the front door not twenty feet away. Though there were no barred windows or locked doors, the fear of what lay in store for anyone who ran, kept them in mental chains more restrictive than the real thing.

Since the headmaster's arrival at Saint Gilbert's, he had enjoyed a measure of fame and notoriety in having the least escapes of any school in Great Britain. He carried this distinction with pride. Frankie had heard the story of how he had personally hunted down the last three lads who did a run together. They were flogged for days, their screams reverberating through the big house for all to hear.

John knocked on the office door and a voice told them to come in. When they entered, the dog got to its feet and began a low, deep growl that made the lads back away.

"Sit!" the headmaster commanded, without bothering to look up. The dog made a couple of turns and lay down on a rug, panting heavily with its pink tongue hanging to one side of its huge jaw. As usual, he was in no hurry. He continued writing while the two boys stood at attention in their nightshirts. Finally, he looked up over his spectacles, then down again without moving his head.

"Go on."

Frankie glanced at John who was in obvious distress and unable to talk.

"Brother Leo sent us here for fighting, sir."

The headmaster gave no indication he had heard and continued writing. Frankie stared at the bent head and deformed hands in front of him and hated the man who dared dress in a holy robe.

The headmaster got up from his desk and moved toward him.

"Oh, yes, I know. You're from the big, bad city of Liverpool and you're out to prove just how tough you are!"

The statement caught Frankie off guard and made him back away as the man loomed closer.

"Afraid of me, though, aren't you?" he taunted.

He opened a drawer and took out a pair of flimsy black nylon shorts and threw them at his feet. "Here, put them on."

While he obeyed, the headmaster reached into a cupboard and withdrew a long birch cane, bending and testing it for flexibility. Frankie forced himself not to be afraid. He could hear the swishing sound the cane made as it sliced through the air, setting his bottom on fire with repeated blows. His resistance to show his pain infuriated the headmaster even more and he began to flail at the bare legs, dropping the lad to his knees. Still, no sound escaped his lips.

"Get out! Get out!" he hissed.

Frankie let the shorts fall to the floor. Half-way down the hall, he heard the sickening sound of cane hitting flesh, followed by cries that shattered the stillness of the big house.

Spring finally arrived, bringing with it a wondrous profusion of color. The air smelled fresh and slightly scented from the breeze that blew through the apple blossoms at the bottom of the garden. The days grew longer and warmer, giving the boys more time after school to ready the cricket pitches for summer, or go for long walks with Mr. Whittle, Frankie's favorite teacher.

This tall, thin man, with sunken cheeks and piercing blue eyes, had a passion for the outdoors and constantly challenged the lads to marathon walks that would leave them exhausted, while he himself thrived with youthful vigor.

By the time the apples, pears and plums littered the country lanes, the lads were only too happy to follow after him. On Saturdays, the whole school dressed up in their tweed suits and striped ties, and marched two abreast to the Stourport Cinema five miles away. It was there that Frankie fell in love for the first time.

Across the aisle from him a girl kept looking his way like she wanted eye contact, but he was too shy to accommodate her. It was only after she reached across to deposit some sweets into his lap did he manage a weak smile her way. When the lights came on and they stood to leave, he stole a quick glance and was smitten by her beauty. She saw him look at her and beamed a smile back that made him feel warm all over. From then on, he lived only for Saturdays, when they could pass their little love notes to each other in the darkened cinema.

When he reached for the sweets she offered, it was the touch of her soft hand he desired the most. It lasted through most of the summer, making the lad feel alive and carefree like never before. Then one Saturday, she didn't come.

"She could be sick, right, Robert?" he contended to his friend on the long walk back. Robert nodded in agreement. He had helped compose each of the love notes and even written them out for him, because Frankie could neither read nor write.

It seemed like Saturday would never arrive. Then there was, what seemed to Frankie that day, the endless walk to Stourport that drove him crazy with anxiety, not to mention what it did to Robert who had to endure the never-ending *What-ifs...?* By the time the lights dimmed, he knew she wasn't coming. Not that day, not ever again. He tore the love notes into small pieces, letting them slip from his fingers to the floor.

***

Frankie closed the book and sat in contemplative silence, his right hand abstractedly caressing the book's glossy cover, as though he were smoothing out some imaginary wrinkles. For the past few weeks he had been traveling on an amazing journey, while reading "Down the Amazon with Oleanders," as the Spanish Conquistador and his army hacked their way through the merciless jungle that never seemed to end. He was there with them as their numbers slowly dwindled, weary men, one by one falling victim to the cruel ravages of malaria and dysentery.

For the first time in his life, he could feel the pain and suffering of others through the written word. He found himself caught up in their struggle for survival, as though they were real people to him. It both excited and saddened him.

He looked around at the twenty-four other boys in his class; each one lost in his own little world of mystery and adventure.

"Hawkins, what is it that you need?"

"Nothing, sir, just finished me book, is all," he said quietly.

Mr. Williams' round, expressive face, with its inquisitive blue eyes and distinctive mutton chop sideburns, broke into a big, satisfied grin. He leaned back in his chair and ran his hands over his bald pate, clasping them behind his head.

"Class! Please put away your books!" When the room was quiet again, he beckoned Frankie to stand to his feet.

"It wasn't too long ago that this young man couldn't read anything much beyond his name. Today he finished reading his first book. Let's all give him a big round of applause!"

Summer was ablaze with color, the air filled with the smell of burning leaves and tree branches. Everywhere, there were lads mowing, trimming, raking and weeding, their lively voices echoing in the valley. Frankie sat on a fallen log, intoxicated with the pungent aroma of freshly dug earth and cut grass and watched the smoke from the fire curl lazily into the clear, blue sky. Robins fluttered from tree branch to earth and back again, with juicy worms wiggling in their little beaks. He gazed at the gently sloping landscape spread out before him like a feast on a king's banquet table, and pondered whether it was right that he should love this place so much. That this place that had brought him so much pain and humiliation, should now, three years later, be his strength and nourishment, was ironic, to say the least.

He spotted Mr. Whittle digging at the bottom of the garden; his wispy, graying hair disheveled and matted around his wet face, his pitted army shirt unbuttoned and blowing in the light breeze. He was a good man and fair in his dealings with the lads, though Frankie shuddered at the memory of the incident with Whittle only last winter.

It had been one of those mornings when everything was white with frost. The boys were huddled in small groups in the yard, trying hard to stay warm and stomping their feet to keep their circulation going. Brother Leo had no heart at all for the lads, so they waited for Whittle to come on duty, hoping he would allow them into the activity room where it was toasty warm. He was the only staff who ever did. A sigh of relief could be heard when he finally showed up and everyone waited patiently for the signal.

"Let's line up," he shouted through cupped hands, the icy wind carrying his words away.

They formed the usual four rows, two abreast and stood looking at him, their eyes pleading for mercy. His eyes gleamed back with mischief and he had a sly grin on his face that made everybody hold their breath in anticipation.

"We're going for a nice walk and I want you all to stay close and not get strung out along the road."

In the midst of the stunned silence, Frankie shouted, "F--- you, Whittle!" He hadn't meant to say it so loud, but the words just seemed to hang out there in the silence. Every head turned to stare at him in disbelief, then to the front to catch Whittle's reaction. Whittle's eyes were wide with shock.

"Hawkins, kindly step to the front here."

His heart palpitated madly, as he stepped out of the line and walked forward. Before he even came to a stop, Whittle's hand shot out and gave the lad a stinging slap across the cheek and bridge of his nose. He felt something warm trickle from his nose and into his mouth.

"Bastard!"

A part of him felt ashamed to be openly challenging Mr. Whittle in such a blatant way and putting his favorite teacher on the spot. Yet, a part of him felt exhilaration at finally standing his ground after years of submission to the many kinds of abuse perpetrated in the name of discipline.

He stared defiantly into the deep-set eyes and winced as he felt the back of the same hand connect with his other cheek, making his eyes water from the sting.

"Bastard!"

He could feel the adrenaline coursing through his veins now and knew no amount of punishment could ever make him retreat. He set his jaw for the next blow, which didn't come. Mr. Whittle hesitated, unsure of what to do next with this blatant disregard for authority. He could tell by the look on the lad's face that he was willing to take a beating rather than submit. He grabbed him by the arm and marched him into the recreation hall and slammed him up against the wall.

"What the hell are you trying to do, Hawkins, making a fool of me out there? Well, you'd better wise up or you'll find yourself walking to the headmaster's office."

Whittle wished he hadn't said that. He'd always prided himself on his ability to take care of any situation that might arise without the help of threats or fear tactics. He pulled a handkerchief out of his back pocket and handed it to the lad.

"Here, wipe the blood off your face and go get back in line." His voice was heavy with resignation.

For Frankie, it was a hollow victory. He'd won his battle with the best staff, rather than with one of the worst.

"Hey, Hawkins, how about getting some work done!"

The warm sun had almost put him to sleep. He looked down the hill at Whittle waving a spade in the air and trying to get his attention, a big grin on his craggy face. They had grown to respect each other since the incident. He waved back at Whittle like he was full of nonsense, but he got up anyway and began to dig some more.

"Keep your right up, Marley! Up, man! Protect the chin at all times!" Brother Hubert hollered.

Frankie feigned a left jab to the face, then hooked it with lightning speed into Marley's solar plexus. Marley winced with pain and dropped his gloves in a reflex response. Frankie came over the top with a punishing right to the side of the head, dropping him to the floor.

Brother Hubert jumped into the ring to check the lad out. "Are you okay, son?"

Marley nodded and grabbed the ropes to stand, but fell back, his eyes still rolling in his head. Hubert glanced over at Frankie, who was in the process of taking off his gloves.

"Don't take them off just yet."

The tone of his voice told Frankie there was trouble brewing. Ever since he'd put the gloves on for the first time two years ago, he'd known he was a natural boxer. He loved the sport and trained diligently every chance he got. Now, almost fifteen, with a lean, muscular body, his skills in the ring were far superior to any of the other lads on the boxing team. He tried hard not to be too cocky or overconfident, so he was puzzled when his trainer, Brother Hubert, began putting him down in front of his peers. He tried helping Marley out of the ring, but Hubert brushed him aside.

"He's okay, let him be. You wanna go a couple of rounds with me?"

Frankie searched the brother's face, trying to figure out where he was coming from.

Why is he out to get me? He wondered, not liking the look on Hubert's face. The rest of the lads stood watching as Hubert pulled the gloves on then thrust them forward for someone to tie.

Frankie felt strange standing toe to toe with a grown man. He wasn't sure he could take a punch at him, even if it was done in sport. He knew he was about to be taught a lesson.

Amazingly, he got through the first round without getting injured. Those jabs and punches Hubert threw really hurt, and Frankie fought most of the time just protecting himself. Between rounds he looked over at Hubert, who was laughing at something, and felt anger building up inside of him. The bell rang and Hubert came out wide open, thinking the lad would just go on the defensive again. Frankie's right caught him flush on the nose, snapping his head back and sending blood spurting in every direction. Hubert's mouth fell open and his eyes blinked in rapid succession as he tried to grapple with what had just taken place. Frankie stared back at the shocked expression and noticed the knees that were beginning to buckle.

Oh, God, I've knocked him out! He thought, his body unable to make up its mind whether to move forward to help, or get the hell away from there. He hesitated just a little too long. Brother Hubert was on top of him, wrestling him to the floor and raining blows to the boy's head.

"You little devil, you!" he fumed. "You need to be taught a lesson you'll never forget."

Frankie rolled himself into a tight ball, protecting his head with his gloved hands and forearms, and waited until the initial onslaught of anger subsided.

"Get up! Get up!" Hubert yelled, as he straddled the boy and began pulling off his boxing gloves in order to get a better hold on the boy's body. He reached for the only exposed part of the head, which was the back of the neck, and yanked him to his feet by the hair. Frankie winced with pain, but still protected his face, as Hubert tried to slap him with his free hand.

"You miserable little devil!" he taunted, pushing the boy backward with rapid shoves to the chest. "Go get dressed and get out of my sight."

Frankie took off the gloves for the last time. He was never allowed to box again.

Frankie awoke at the break of dawn and his stomach immediately began churning with nervous anticipation.

So this is it, he mused, gently massaging his belly to relieve the knots that began forming like little fists. *I'm going home.* He glanced over at Robert in the next bed and was surprised to see him laying on his side staring back at him, the covers pulled up to his chin.

"How long have you been awake, Robert?"

"A while." His voice was barely audible.

He turned to stare up at the ceiling rather than let Robert see him with misty eyes.

"You'll be getting out yourself in four months. It'll go over real fast, just you wait and see."

Morning light began to spread across the room. Bodies stirred. Deep in the bowels of the big house the faint sounds of kitchen preparation could be heard.

"I don't think I'll go down for breakfast, Robert."

"That's right, isn't it?" he exclaimed, resting his head on an elbow. "You can do whatever you feel like today."

The smallest deviation from the normal routine was quite a big deal to the lads whose lives were regimented every moment of every day.

"Yeah, it's gonna be different every day forever," he giggled, swinging his pillow and hitting Robert's grinning face.

"What's the first thing you're going to do when you get home?"

"Kiss the best looking girl I can find."

"No, come on, get serious, for once."

Frankie made like he was really thinking hard. "Kiss me Mam, and then kiss the best looking girl I can find!"

"You sound like a sex-starved maniac, Hawkins," Robert shot

back, throwing Frankie's pillow at his head and missing. "They'd better lock you up for good."

"Hey, Hawkins, kiss one for me while you're at it," Jonesey called out from across the room.

"Yeah, Jonesey, I'll kiss the ugliest one I can find just for you," he laughed.

By now, everyone was awake and sitting up, wanting to live vicariously through his first day of freedom.

"Load up on fish'n'chips tonight. I love fish'n'chips."

"I'm dying to see a new picture called 'Shane,' do you think you'll go see it?"

Footsteps could be heard coming up the stairs and along the corridor, sending the lads skittering back down in repose. Brother Leo appeared in the doorway, his hands clasped behind his back. He sauntered slowly toward Frankie sitting up in his bed.

"So, this is the big day you've been waiting for," he said dreamily, his head bobbing back and forth like it was attached to a rubber band.

"Yes, Bro, this is my big day," he said, bobbing his in imitation, a big smile on his face.

"Well, then, good luck and God bless."

They shook hands. He clapped once and everybody but Frankie jumped out of bed and stood at attention.

When they were gone and he was finally alone, he felt bewildered, almost melancholy. He stood for a while staring out of the window at what was shaping up to be a beautiful morning. He watched as the shadows of fluffy, white clouds moved over the tops of the lush, green fields towards the horizon. His eyes followed the familiar garden path that wound its way from the big yard, through the pine grove, and into the playing fields that held four football pitches and a number of cricket layouts.

God, I'm gonna miss all that, he thought, remembering the thrill he got when his name first appeared on the list of the first string football team. He even scored the winning goal that day. And the endless summer days of cricket and the boundless energy of the track and field teams practicing for the regionals in Kidderminster town. The whole school turned out for that one, piling into chartered buses that shook with the merry laughter of youth tasting freedom.

He turned away from the window feeling a little foolish for crying.

Jeez, Hawkins, what's gotten into you, he thought out loud. *You've spent the past four years, dreaming about this moment, and here you are mooning and slobbering all over the place!*

He began to dress in the new outfit they'd given him the night before. Chuckling nervously to himself, he slipped into his first pair of long trousers in over four years. When he finished dressing, he stood staring at his reflection in the full-length mirror, amazed at the transformation.

He remembered the little boy that had first entered a lifetime ago. The mop of curly, disheveled hair was more manageable now that he kept it cut short. His face was the face of a young man, ready to take on the world, the jaw strong and firm. He straightened his tie and buttoned his gray tweed jacket before taking one last look around the dormitory.

Walking through the big house, he could smell the strong odor of fresh wax. The headmaster came out of his office just as Frankie got to it.

"Well, then, are we ready to go?"

"Yes, sir."

"Got everything that's yours?"

He nodded and lifted up the paper sack for the headmaster to see.

"Then, let's do it."

He shaded his eyes from the glare of the sun, scanning the campus and yard for signs of life. There was no one around.

"Come on, son, hop in the van and let's get going. Trains don't wait for anyone."

It's not supposed to end this way, he thought, as he climbed into the van and settled into the front seat. *Not one person to say good-bye, not even Robert, my best friend.*

As the van pulled away from the front door, he heard prayer in unison coming from the school building. *Classes are over,* he thought, hoping the headmaster would drive just a little bit slower. The bell rang and the metal doors sprang open, spilling lads out into the play yard.

Robert was one of the first out, waving both arms madly in the direction of the receding van. Suddenly, everyone in the yard began to wave as Frankie craned his neck to get one last look.

Standing on the quaint little platform of the Hartlebury train station, he watched the van disappear over the crest of a hill. A trace of a breeze smelled as fresh as the beautiful, lush countryside that surrounded him.

I'm free, he thought, marveling at his aloneness. *Free to go anywhere I please, any time I please.* He smiled, drinking in the reality of it. He could hear the faint rumble of the approaching train that was coming to take him home. This was the dream he had dreamt many, many times.

* * *

The train passed over the Runcorn Bridge that spanned the estuary of the River Mersey. The long journey was almost over. Frankie's heart began to beat more rapidly now as the thought of meeting his mother again became more real with each passing second. He wiped the palms of his hands on his jacket and took a couple of deep breaths to relieve some of the tension.

My family, they'll be all grown up like me now, he thought, incredulously. *Dorothy will be eighteen! Sarah, she'll be almost seventeen, and little Margaret, twelve. God! I'm not gonna know them at all!* he pondered, standing and staring out the window at the Liverpool skyline in the distance. *How will I feel about all those familiar places I loved as a child? Will I feel the same? Will the sounds, the smells, the people be the same? And will it all come rushing back to me?*

The scenery was changing fast now. Row after row of tightly-packed, terraced housed came into view, blackened and aged by a million chimneys and smokestacks spewing coal dust into the air. Backyards were strewn with debris and alleys covered with graffiti. He began to feel uneasy. His memories of the city had all been through the eyes of an adventurous child. Now he was seeing it for the first time through the eyes of a young man. *It'll take a little getting used to*, he thought, waving back at two dirty-faced children sitting on a wall that ran alongside the railroad track. *I've lived in another world too long.* He took off his tie and opened the small sliding window and threw it out.

The train slowed to a crawl as it entered the cavernous expanse of Lime Street Station. He began to scan the faces of the crowd on the platform, in hopes he could spot someone he knew.

"Frankie, over here, lad!"

It was Uncle Alvin waving wildly in his direction.

"Bleedin' hell, I almost didn't recognize you," he shouted, grabbing him by the shoulders and planting a big kiss on his cheek.

"You're looking like a man, now. Your Mam's gonna go mad when she sees the cut of you."

"Is she okay, Uncle Alvin?"

"Yeah, she's smashing, Frankie, a bag of nerves waiting for you to come home, though. Come on, let's grab a taxi."

As the taxi moved nearer to home, he began to recognize the familiar streets and landmarks that triggered a flood of childhood memories. Soon, he was recognizing faces among the crowds of shoppers that overflowed the sidewalks. Then the taxi turned into the most familiar street of all, with the four huge tenement blocks and the horse stables, just the way he remembered them.

As the taxi pulled up to the curb, children ran from everywhere to gather around it, wondering who it was that was rich enough to ride in a taxi. He got out and walked up the tenement steps, his whole body shaking with nervous anticipation, his breathing coming in short, labored gasps. He walked down the landing and stopped at the window and looked in.

She's the most beautiful person in the whole world, he thought, biting his lower lip to keep back the tears that threatened to break loose. He watched as her delicate fingers put the finishing touches to a tray of sandwiches. She looked smaller than he remembered her, and a little thinner, too. Her long, dark hair was now streaked with gray. He'd suppressed his emotions for so long, he hadn't fully realized until now how much he'd missed this special person in his life.

She must have sensed someone looking at her and turned her head slowly toward the window. She tried to blink the tears away in order to get a better look.

"My God, it is! It's my little boy," she murmured, her lower lip trembling at the realization that her little boy was gone forever. They just stood there crying neither one making a move to open the door.

When Dorothy and Sarah came home from work and saw their big brother, they screamed with delight and flung their arms around him, almost wrestling him to the floor.

"He's luvly, Mam, isn't he?" Dorothy swooned, stepping back to get a better perspective.

"You always were a little soft, girl," he laughed, throwing a small couch cushion at her head.

"Oh, hey, listen to the posh way he talks," Sarah said good-naturedly. Margaret sat quietly by his side on the couch, her eyes never leaving his face.

It's like looking at the face of a stranger, she thought, the memory of a younger brother still very much alive inside her mind. She was almost afraid to speak to him and was on the verge of getting up, when he turned and put an arm around her shoulder and pulled her closer to him.

"You sure look cute and all grown up, Margaret. I bet you've got a lot of lads running after you."

"Hundreds, Frankie. Falling over each other to get to me, they are."

"She's a bloody liar, Frankie. She's got none," David teased, sticking his tongue out at her for kicking him in the leg.

Daisy and Allen, the two youngest, sat cross-legged on the floor in front of their new-found brother, giggling at the antics of David and Margaret.

That night, everybody gathered around a blazing fire until way into the wee hours of the morning, telling stories, laughing at funny memories, and just sharing whatever came to mind.

"What did you think about me Mam getting married again?" Dorothy asked, once their mother had retired to bed.

Frankie remembered the letter his mother had written him about it. It had left him feeling betrayed by her allowing another man into the house.

"It took a little getting used to. What's he like?"

"Ah, he's not a bad sort, is he Dorothy?" Sarah confessed, her voice revealing a touch of sympathy for this poor soul that had inadvertently wandered into a hornet's nest.

"Oh, go on, Sarah, he's old enough to be her father," Dorothy retorted, her facial expression clearly showing disdain for this intruder.

"Besides, he's never here for her," she continued, her voice getting louder.

"Dorothy, keep your voice down, girl. He's a seaman and me Mam knew that when she married him," Sarah reasoned.

Frankie could see this was a touchy topic and tried changing the subject.

"How long have we had electricity?"

"Been over a year now, Frankie," Margaret volunteered, obviously relieved at the change of topic.

"Ever since Dorothy and Sarah went to work at Higson's Bottling Company, we've been doing smashing, even got us a second-hand radiogram."

The fire was dying down and there were no more calls to put the kettle on. Frankie broke the silence as everybody stared into the dying embers.

"I'll sleep on the couch so I can be up bright and early to look for a job."

"Billy Miller's got an advert in his shop window for a butcher's boy."

"Thanks, Margaret, I'll try it first thing. Good night."

"Do you live close by, that's the thing? Don't want none of this coming in late every morning."

Frankie watched the ash on Billy Miller's cigarette grow longer and more precarious.

"I live on Mann Street, only three streets away."

Miller stopped boning the lamb shank and reached for his cigarette, but it was too late. The ash dropped off and disappeared into the fresh cut he'd made in the lamb. He made a feeble attempt to wipe it with a bloody rag that was tucked under his apron string.

"How does two pound seven a week sound?"

The cigarette smoke curled relentlessly upward past the half-moon spectacles and into his eyes, causing him to tilt his head back and squint at the lad through the blue haze.

"That sounds okay to me, Mr. Miller. When do you want me to start?"

"Start in the morning at eight."

"Hey, Harry, come out here and meet the new boy," he hollered, taking a cleaver and sending it thudding into the lamb bone.

An old man, tall and stocky, came sauntering out from the back room wiping his hands on his blood-spattered apron. He also held a cigarette bobbing between his lips. Frankie shook the huge hand that was offered him and smiled back at eyes that seemed to dance with mischievous merriment.

"Watch out you don't get crazy like us, son. Glad to have you aboard."

His days were filled with making sausages, delivering meat by bicycle to customers throughout the city, and placing bets on the horses for Billy and Harry. His evenings, though, were a mixed bag of loneliness and uncertainty as he walked aimlessly through the streets. The four years at Saint Gilbert's had changed him more deeply than he'd realized, but he wasn't sure in what ways. All he knew was he wasn't fitting back in. People remembered him, but they didn't know him; not any more. In some strange way, he didn't care. He was becoming less tolerant and more critical of the old, crumbling, decaying city; and it hurt. It hurt because it felt like all his memories of childhood were being destroyed.

After a few weeks, Billy entrusted him with the keys to the shop. In return for setting up the window display and putting down fresh sawdust each morning, Billy promised him a nice leg of lamb for his Mam every Saturday.

One morning, a tiny shriveled up old lady came knocking at the shop door.

"Not open yet, Mrs. Corcoran," Frankie shouted.

"I know that, luv. I just wanna talk to you," she squeaked through the letter box opening.

He opened the door and let her inside.

"You can make a few bob for yourself, you know, ducks, just like the lad before you."

He stared down at this cheeky little lady with the face like a wrinkled prune.

"How do I do that, Mrs. Corcoran?"

"It's easy," she said, flashing him a toothless grin while retying her soiled scarf under her scrawny chin. "First thing every morning, you put a few chops and things together and run them over to me house on the next street, and I'll pop a few bob into your pocket."

"My God, Mrs. Corcoran! I couldn't do that to Mr. Miller. He's been good to me."

"Oh, he knows you're gonna fiddle a little bit," she said, turning and shuffling toward the door. "So long as you don't get too greedy, he'll turn a blind eye. I'll check back with you again, luv."

He closed the door behind her and leaned his back against it. Out of the two pounds seven, he was giving his mother one pound ten, leaving himself less than a quid for cigarettes and the pictures on the weekend. He thought about the smart-looking Teddy Boy suit he wanted to buy with the velvet cuffs and half-moon pockets that was fast becoming the rage.

No, forget it, he heard himself say, as memories of the reform school flashed through his mind. *It isn't worth it.*

Next morning she was back, cackling through the letter box.

"Hey, sonny, just a few pork chops and a little minced meat, luv." She dropped something through the letter box and shuffled away past the window.

His hand trembled when he reached to pick up the envelope from the floor. Inside was a ten shilling note and the lady's address.

The first morning, he nervously prepared a small package for delivery. The second morning went a little smoother, though he was sure Miller could see the guilt written all over his face. The third morning was the clincher. In his haste to get the deed done and over with, he inadvertently left the door unlocked. While separating a rack of lamb with a cleaver, he heard the door creak open behind him and his head spun around to see who it was. A wave of cold fear swept over him as he stared into the face of a bobby.

My God, he thought, *It's really happening. I'm going back to jail!*

"Good morning, young fella. How's the new job coming along?"

The blood was thundering in Frankie's ears, but he managed a weak grin.

"Not bad, thank you, sir. Quite good, really," he stammered.

"Good. Glad to hear it." His eyes roamed the whole shop before turning toward the door.

"Well, I'll be getting along. Have a good day."

Then the dam broke. Anger, rage, fear, frustration, all came pouring out as he ran screaming into the back room still holding onto the rack of lamb. *Why, you bloody fool, you*! He cried, flinging the chops at the wall. *Why'd you let a little old lady talk you into this whole bloody mess, I ask you?* But, he knew it wasn't the little old lady. Each day that went by found him a little less confident, a little less sure of who he was and where he wanted to go.

Throughout the summer of 1955, he found himself being drawn more and more to the sea. He sat alone for hours after work, watching the ships ply their way up and down the Mersey River. He grew restless, impatient for the day when he would be sixteen and old enough to join the British Merchant Navy.

"Mam, I want to go away to sea."

Kate didn't respond to his words right away.

"You want a cup, son?" she asked, stirring the pot and putting the lid back on.

"Yeah, okay, Mam. Did you hear me?"

"Yes, I heard you alright. I'm just thinking about it." She passed him the cup of tea and a spoon to put his own sugar in.

"I've seen it coming for a while now, lad. Ever since you came home from the school you've been acting sort of different."

He grew silent for a bit, searching for words that would explain exactly what it was he was feeling.

"Mam, I honestly didn't know how I was gonna feel. I was excited to be coming home. But when I got here, I felt strange, like I didn't belong."

"But, you haven't been home very long, son. Give yourself some time."

"But, that's part of the trouble. I don't like the way I'm changing."

She stirred her second cup of tea in a slow, rhythmic manner, her eyes focused on his troubled face.

"You'll never be happy here again will you, son? You've tasted something more."

He got up and turned to look out the front window. Children were playing rounders in the street below and their voices drifted up whenever the ball was hit and one of them ran around the bases.

"I loved it here as a child. What's happening to me?"

"You've grown up, that's all." She stood up and began clearing the dishes off the table.

"You know you've got to be sixteen, don't you?"

He turned to look at her.

"No, I can go any time the Norwegian shipping office has an opening."

She stood motionless, the cup and saucer rattling a little in her hands.

"I see."

"Mam, you know I can take care of myself, don't you?"

"Yes, I know that, son, but that doesn't mean I won't worry about you."

He smiled for the first time since their talk began.

"You mean it's okay then?"

"Yes, it's okay. I can't imagine what it would be like trying to stop you."

The five lads stood in a circle outside the Norwegian Consul, puffing on cigarettes and debating whose turn it was to go up and check on the job situation.

"I went first yesterday, remember, mate, and the old bloke stared at me like I'm from Mars or something!" Tim protested.

"Okay, you go this time, Davy," Fred instructed, while slicking

Davy's hair down and straightening his tie for him.

"I'm packing it in after today," Tim confessed. "The buggers in there don't seem to like us much."

Davy was only gone a few minutes. "That's it then, lads! They'll have nothing to do with us, thinking we're Teddy Boys."

"Well, did you tell them we weren't?" Frankie asked, not wanting to give up so easily.

"You go tell them and see if they believe you, looking like that," Davy shot back.

"Let's go get a cup of tea at Lewis'."

"I think I'll head on home," Frankie said, digging his hands into his pockets and spitting his cigarette stump into the gutter. He made a dash for the tram that was pulling away, but the doors closed just as he got there. The four lads whistled and clapped at him good naturedly before they swaggered off down Harrison Street.

While waiting for the streetcar, he lit up another Woodbine and leaned against the lamp post to study his reflection in the shop window. He loved his pale-blue suit with its black velvet rolled collar and matching velvet half-moon pockets. He remembered the day he walked into Burton's to be measured for it.

"Don't forget, the jacket has to be fingertip length and the trousers tight around the ankles."

The man had smiled back at him knowingly.

"Yes, son, I'm quite familiar with the Edwardian look of the Teddy Boys. You're gonna look real smart by the time I'm through with you." And he was right. With the white silk shirt and lace tie to complete the look, Frankie strutted around like a peacock, inviting all the girls to turn their heads in his direction.

Being identified as a Teddy Boy was exciting and heady stuff. Almost overnight, thousands began stepping out from the shadows of their parent's authority to become identified with this youth movement. The drab uniform of poverty was being replaced by this smart and stylish dress suit. As young lads became more confident and outspoken about things that affected their lives, grownups began losing control. Slowly, though, things began to unravel, as angry youth began roaming the streets in gangs, causing fights and scaring people. The newspapers began to hail all Teddy Boys as a menace to society, and employers all over the city began closing their doors to anyone who looked like a Teddy Boy.

Frankie had noticed a definite change in people's attitudes toward him. Even strangers now gave him a wide berth or moved to a different seat, if he happened to sit next to them on a streetcar or in a cafe'.

By the time he got home from town he knew exactly what he had to do. He changed into an old pair of dungarees and a turtleneck sweater and handed the beautiful suit to his mother.

"Here, Mam. You can use it for the pawn shop or sell it for what you can get."

Milton's Pawn Shop

Kate felt sad seeing her son give up this treasure, but she could see in his face a settled peace about it. He had made up his mind what was more important to him at this time in his life.

"I bet I don't come back without a job," he said, flashing her a confident smile.

She took the suit and watched after him, hoping he would get what he wanted; sad that it would mean saying good-bye again.

Frankie woke to the sound of engines throbbing rhythmically, deep within the bowels of the ship. He lay there tingling all over with excitement and anticipation. He lit up a Woodbine and inhaled deeply, propping his head up with a pillow. The early morning sun cast a pale orange ball on the cabin wall as it shone through the porthole. He watched the reflection dip to the floor then rise to the ceiling with each sway of the ship.

He turned and looked at the bunk beneath him, then lay back again. *Good. The old man's gone*, he thought, remembering the strong smell of stale alcohol that had assailed him when he entered the cabin to go to bed. The man had snored so loudly, it had become impossible for Frankie to sleep for much of the night. He finished the cigarette, swung his legs over the side and climbed down. His stomach felt a little queasy with the constant swaying of the ship and the stale smell that still lingered in the tiny cabin. He opened the porthole and gulped in the fresh sea air.

My God, he whispered in astonishment, as his eyes scanned the vast, empty horizon for signs of land. His hands trembled as he rushed to get his legs into his dungarees. When he stepped out on deck, he flung up his hands and screamed with pleasure as the wind spattered him with a fine mist of sea spray.

"This is it!" he shouted. "I'm really at sea! I really made it!"

He leaned against the rail and stared out at the vast expanse of sea and white caps that sparkled in the sun, and thought of how close he had come to giving up the dream.

> *At the Norwegian Consul's office, he'd been met with stone-faced indifference.*
> *"No, I'm sorry," the pinched face had said, "we're*

not hiring any more young people from Liverpool;
too many problems with them."
Frankie had stared back at him incredulously, not
wanting it to be true.
"Sir," he pleaded, "that's why I wanna get away
from here. I don't need any problems, either."
The little man had given him a hard look.
"Haven't I seen you dressed as a Teddy Boy not two
days ago?"
It was then he made up his mind to pop in and show
his face every morning and afternoon, until they
relented and gave him a job. By the fifth day, though,
his resolve had begun to weaken considerably to
where he'd felt that this may very well be his last
shot.
"Ha, this is the young man I was telling you about,"
old pinched face said to another man, upon seeing
him again.
The tall blonde had grinned at the lad while holding
out his hand to shake.
"I'm glad to make your acquaintance, son. You're a
very persistent young man. Now, how long will it take
for you to pack your bags and get yourself a
passport?"

Standing there leaning over the rail made Frankie's stomach heave, so he made his way mid-ship to the galley area and mess hall.

"Hey, Frankie! Come and sit down with me," Ginger shouted, pointing to a seat across from him. Ginger was the only other Englishman, and they hit it off as soon as they'd met yesterday.

"You look a little green around the gills, there, Scouse. Are you up to eating bacon and eggs?"

Just the mere mention of greasy food made him gag.

"No, I'm not feeling too good right now. Maybe I'd better go lay down for a bit."

Ginger nodded his carrot head knowingly.

"Eat plenty of crackers and dry bread," he called out, as Frankie made his way back over the swaying deck.

Before he could reach aft where his cabin was, his stomach erupted, heaving its contents up and through his mouth like it was shot from a cannon. The wind whipped it back into his face and hair before he could make it to the ship's rail to lean over. Each time he tried leaving the rail, he would have to make a mad dash back again to heave some more.

"I'm dying, Ginger," he mumbled, as his friend helped him away from the rail and headed toward the cabin.

"Boy, do I know how it feels, Scouse. I was seasick for a whole week my first time out." Frankie looked at him through bloodshot eyes.

"A whole week! I'd rather die first!"

"There were times when I wished I had," Ginger laughed. "Felt like the whole lining of my stomach was being ripped out."

It seemed only minutes had passed since his eyes had closed in a fitful sleep. Now, someone was shaking him awake.

"You're on watch, English. It's time to rise."

Frankie's mouth felt dry with a horrible taste in it. He felt too weak to speak, so he nodded his head in hopes it would be sufficient to get whoever was leaning over him to leave. It didn't. He opened his eyes slowly and tried to focus on the face in front of him.

"I'm sick, Norsky, can't you see that?" he whispered through parched lips. "Just leave me alone."

After a slight hesitation, the young seaman nodded in sympathy and glanced at his watch.

"I hope you can make it in twenty minutes. The second engineer isn't very nice. I've seen him drag drunken men out of their bunks and put them to work.

Frankie peered through heavy lids and raised himself up on his elbows.

"Is that what you think? I'm drunk?"

"No, no, I'm sure you're sick," he reassured him, a little surprised at the display of anger and defiance. "Just want you to be aware of the situation, that's all."

Frankie eased himself back down onto the pillow, his whole head throbbing with pain from his outburst.

"Thanks, I'll try to make it."

The ship began pitching and swaying more ominously now, as the wind whipped up, forcing the sea-swells to form into large waves. He staggered out on deck just as a squall blew in, drenching him with icy rain that stung his face and hands.

"Jesus Christ," he mumbled, blinking his eyes rapidly in order to see where he was going.

"This is crazy!" He planted one foot in front of the other, as his cold hands gripped the rail to steady himself, but it still felt too dangerous for him to move. The steel deck was slick and waves washed over it, as the bow and stern dipped and heaved alternately in the steadily increasing swells. He was glad no one was out on deck to witness this poor show of his manhood.

Suddenly, the deck lurched and tilted, sending his feet sliding out from under him. He clutched wildly at the rail but his fingers had grown numb with cold and it slipped out of his grasp. He slid freely on his stomach, his fingertips digging into the steel deck to try to slow down his movement, but it was in vain. Like a rubber ball, he bounced off the bulkhead and into a coil of rope before the ship righted itself and, for a moment, gave him time to stand and gather his wits about him.

"I'm bloody good and mad now," he shouted into the wind. He glanced across the open deck to mid-ship and took a deep breath, bracing himself for the struggle ahead. By the time he reached mid-ship, he was totally exhausted and his rib cage ached. He opened the steel door to the engine room and a blast of hot air hit him in the face. The roar of engines was deafening as he secured the door behind him and made his way along a catwalk and down a deep stairwell.

My God! It's like going into the pit of Hell, he thought, ducking under jets of hissing steam and vapor coming at him from different directions. The deeper he descended, the more deafening the noise became. That, along with the stifling heat, brought back the severe headache and queasy stomach, forgotten temporarily in the struggle to survive up on deck.

The second engineer stood up and glanced at his watch when he caught sight of Frankie on the last tier of steps.

"You're late," he shouted, holding out his hand.

"Sorry, sir. I'll try to do better," he promised, taking the hand and shaking it firmly.

"Can't hear you if you don't speak up," the second shouted back. The lad nodded his understanding. He was in no mood to get into a shouting match.

The second turned his attention to a fireman who was reading a myriad of gauges about ten feet away.

"Carl," he bellowed, "come over here."

Carl sauntered over, wiping his hands with a greasy rag and

grinning at the sight of the boy.

"I see you made it in one piece!"

Frankie stared back at him, a puzzled look on his face.

"We were ready to run out and rescue you for a while up top, there," he shouted, planting his fists on his waist and laughing at the thought of it. Frankie could feel his face turn beet red.

"Take him around, Carl, and show him what to do," the second shouted, inches from Carl's ear. Carl nodded, still laughing to himself, and waved the lad to follow after him. They passed by the three huge pistons that filled up most of the cavernous engine room and who's thrusting up and down created most of the noise and vibrations within the ship. They were an awesome sight to behold.

"They're what turns the shaft that turns the propeller," Carl shouted, as he pointed along the huge shaft that disappeared into a narrow passageway. "Every moving part along its path must be oiled and checked every hour or the friction will cause it to break down or catch on fire."

Frankie crawled on his hands and knees into the narrow passageway close behind Carl, and followed the shaft to the end. He felt claustrophobic in the cramped and darkened confines of the tunnel, and wondered why in the world he ever thought going away to sea would be fun and adventurous. So far, all he'd experienced was constant nausea from seasickness, a top bunk in a tiny cabin occupied by an old drunk, and a job that buried him deep within the bowels of a creaking old ship that sounded like it was about to explode and sink at any moment.

For the next four days, the lad felt sure he was going to die. He couldn't keep any food down and gave up eating all together. It left him weak and in need of attention, especially while on the job. Many times, he found himself slipping on the narrow, steel catwalks that formed bridges high over boilers and bilge pumps, or had the oil can torn from his hand and chewed up by a machine he was servicing. Once, he lay down inside the narrow tunnel 'just for a moment,' and fell asleep for hours, while all available hands searched the ship looking for him.

On the fifth day out, he awoke to the sound of silence. The ship was dead in the water. The only sound he could hear was the gentle lapping of waves against the sides of the ship. He also became aware of a ravenous hunger and leapt out of his bunk feeling better than he'd felt since boarding the SS *Basra*. The bottom bunk was empty, as it had been for the past few days. He wondered if he should say something, in case the old man had fallen overboard or lay dying someplace.

Looking out of the open porthole, he could almost reach out and touch the lush grass that stretched from the water's edge up to the top of the gentle sloping hills. Houses painted pastel greens, blues, and yellows dotted the beautiful landscape. This was Norway; land of the midnight sun. He dressed quickly and stepped out into the morning sunlight. The view of the Fjords was breathtaking.

"Hey, Scouse, had breakfast yet?"

Frankie looked toward mid-ship where Ginger was waving madly for him to come join him. "Haven't seen you in ages. Where've you been hiding out?" he inquired, when they'd sat down facing each other.

"Mostly working and sleeping off the damn seasickness is about all I could manage until now."

"When it's over, it's gone for good," Ginger said, pouring two large mugs of thick, black coffee and handing one to him.

"You don't really expect me to drink that, do you?"

Ginger laughed his infectious laugh. "You'd better get used to it. There ain't no tea on board this ship, mate."

Frankie liked this open, freckle-faced lad with the strong jaw and friendly eyes. His stocky six-foot frame made him seem older than his nineteen years.

"What're you all smiles about now?" Ginger asked, breaking into a grin of his own.

"I was just remembering the look on the faces of those two Norwegians the night they sat at our table and talked bad about us, remember?"

"Oh, shit, yeah. They'll never live that down, will they? Went white as a ghost when I stood up and spoke perfect Norwegian back to them."

The ship shuddered and sprang to life, followed soon after by a belch of black smoke and a whistle from the red and white smokestack. They both stood up and walked outside to watch the ship maneuver itself for the two-day trip through the fjord, then out into the cold, Arctic waters of the North Sea, and the Russian port of Arkhangelsk.

In the weeks that followed, Frankie had successfully established himself as the 'hard-nosed, hard-headed young Englishman from

Liverpool, who loved to pick a fight.' But, the lad saw things differently. He felt because he was not yet sixteen, most of the ship's crew had begun treating him much like they would a cabin boy, and played practical jokes on him for their own amusement. One day, he decided it was time to fight back. If they didn't want to treat him with respect as a man, then he would force them to fight whenever they showed him disrespect.

Sitting down for coffee one morning, minding his own business, he heard the cook call him from the open galley.

"Hey, English. You work down below, don't you?"

"Yeah, that's right, Hans," Frankie called back. He had this strange feeling that something was in the wind. Maybe it was Hans' tone of voice, or the way the four deck hands sat close together at the other table talking in hushed tones and glancing up at him.

"Can you run down and ask the second for a bucket of steam for the galley?"

"Sure, Hans." He got up and headed for the engine room knowing exactly what he wanted to do. The second engineer watched him fill a bucket with water.

"Finished your coffee break already?"

"No, Sec, not quite yet."

The second watched the lad ascend the steps wondering what in the world he needed a bucket of water for. Frankie walked into the mess hall and passed the deck hands, who craned over each other, curious to see what ended up in the bucket. When he stepped into the galley, Hans turned his back to the lad for fear he would crack up with laughter if he saw his face.

"Hey, Hans, the sec said he didn't have any steam to spare just yet."

"Okay, English, thanks for trying." Hans called over his shoulder, while pretending to be busy in the sink.

Frankie could see his shoulders shaking from silent laughter. "Oh, by the way, Hans, the second sent this up for you instead."

Hans turned his head, curious to see what he was talking about. A gasp escaped his gaping mouth just at the instant the water cascaded over him, sending him staggering back against the sink. Frankie calmly exited the galley amidst a tirade of Norwegian and English expletives and threats of food poisoning.

The older, more mature men gave the lad a wide berth and ignored his anti-social behavior, but not the younger and stronger ones. This was their ship and English was an unwelcome guest who'd better get his act together. But the lad refused to be put down any more and ended up fighting each one of them at various times. His early street fighting and boxing skills gave him the winning edge, and eventually, he was left alone and shunned, by all except Ginger. He seemed to tolerate the lad's tough exterior in hopes he would eventually mature and settle down.

When the ship reached Arkhangelsk, Frankie and Ginger leaned against the ship's rail, pensively watching the activity going on at dockside. The sky was heavy, casting a gloomy pall over the area. Frankie pulled his balaclava up over his nose, but his eyes still watered from the stinging, icy wind that penetrated his duffel coat and woolen jersey. He tried forcing his teeth together to stop them from chattering and stomped his feet to get the circulation going again.

"You know something, Ginger? I don't see a bird anywhere! Not even one lousy seagull! Don't you think that's strange?"

Ginger raised his eyebrows like he was taking a look for himself; then continued gazing at something on the wharf.

"See those soldiers guarding the gangway? Well, they're all Russian women!"

They both fell silent as Frankie studied the soldiers more closely.

"How can you tell?" he finally said.

"Cause they're too ugly to be men," he laughed.

"Ginger, you're full of shit."

"All kidding aside, though, they are women."

"Are you going ashore later?"

"Not with you, I ain't. You're liable to get me shot with your bad temper."

"I promise I won't do anything stupid."

They were silent again, watching the soldiers parade back and forth on the dock, their rifles slung behind them.

"They'll only allow us to visit the seaman's mission, you know."

Frankie looked over at Ginger to see if this was going to be another one of his jokes.

"I'm not kidding you," he said, with more conviction in his voice this time. "You follow one road to the mission only, and the same road back. Any deviation and you can end up getting shot or sent to a labor camp." He looked into Frankie's face and saw only mischief in those big brown eyes. "I ain't going with you. No way," he said, shaking his head and making his way toward the mess hall to get himself a mug of steaming, black coffee.

Frankie lit up a Camel cigarette and watched after his one and only friend. *Guess I'll just have to go by myself, then,* he thought, taking a deep drag and slowly exhaling it.

He picked his way cautiously down the icy gangway and was met by one of the soldiers on guard. *By god, it is a woman,* he thought. Only the eyes moved, as she searched his face, then the face on the passport. When she was satisfied it was the same person, she pointed him in the direction of the mission one mile away. He pulled the collar of his duffel coat up around his neck and dug his hands deep into its pockets. The weather had turned even nastier now that evening was approaching.

The road was no more than a wide path that had deep ruts and holes filled with muddy rainwater. It was like walking through a ghost town, except there was no town. A few dismal looking houses lined each side of the road and an old abandoned picture house advertising '*Gone With the Wind.'* He shivered with the cold and the eeriness of it all. There wasn't a soul to be seen anywhere, not even a cat or a dog. No cars, no bicycles, nothing but empty streets and an incessant, howling wind.

He finally spotted the mission ahead and ran the last few yards, banging hard on the weather-beaten door and dancing a little jig while he waited. A woman opened the door and he rushed inside without looking at her, glad to get in out of the cold. He was surprised at how warm and cozy it was inside. Couples sat on couches around a huge log fire, while others danced to American records or just stood around talking and eating refreshments from the buffet table.

"Can I take your coat, please?"

"Oh, yeah, thanks." He turned toward the woman and began taking off his coat. *Jeez*, he thought, blinking his eyes in disbelief. *She's very pretty*. He handed her his coat and watched her slim figure as she disappeared into another room. *Definitely not Russian*, he mused, remembering the stocky soldiers, dockside.

She came back and pointed to a couch. "Would you like to sit and talk?"

This whole experience was doing him in. It wasn't anything like he'd expected. He sat down and looked her straight in the face.

"Tell me, where's all the fat ladies with hob-nail boots I expected would be here tonight?"

Her eyebrows arched in a questioning look, while her dark, slightly oriental eyes searched his face. She knew only a few sentences in English and she'd used most of them already.

"Just trying to make conversation," he assured her, patting her hand. "It was just a joke."

"Find it for me in the book," she said, placing a red book on his lap.

"No, no, you won't find that in any book," he chuckled, opening it anyway, and glancing at its contents.

"Hey, this is fantastic! Look, I say to you, 'I'm very pleased to make your acquaintance,' and you read the Russian across from it and know exactly what I just said. Here, go ahead and read it."

She read it and looked up coyly and gave him a big smile. He could feel warmth begin to creep into his face and neck and looked quickly away. She saw his discomfort and glanced through the book for something easy to say to him.

"What is your name, sir?" she asked, pronouncing every word slowly, while holding up the book. He laughed out loud at the way she was doing things and also to release some of the tension he was feeling being this close to her and smelling her fragrance.

"I'm Frankie Hawkins, and I'm crazy about you," he chuckled, getting up his nerve to have some fun with her.

"Frankie, ah, Frankie Hawkins!" she exclaimed.

"How come you make everything sound so cute?" he asked, taking one of her delicate hands in both of his. She pulled away and quickly searched the room with eyes that were full of fear, then turned back to him, shaking her head slowly from side to side. She could tell she was losing him again and reached out to touch his hand.

"Would you like to dance, Frankie Hawkins?"

He'd never been much for dancing, but the idea of holding her close was enough reason to give it a try. He could feel her body, warm and soft beneath the black silk dress and his heart began to thump more loudly against his ribs. He pulled away slightly so she wouldn't be aware of the pounding in his chest, but she gently pulled him close again. That simple act set off his whole nervous system. His knees got so weak they began to bang into hers.

Johnny Ray had better quit walkin' in the rain, soon, he thought, as his hands got clammy and perspiration beads began breaking out on his forehead.

"Hey, there, you never told me your name yet, did you?" he blurted out; hoping it would distract her enough she wouldn't detect the fast deterioration of his bodily functions. She looked at him with an angelic face and never said a word.

"Me, Frankie Hawkins," he said, pointing a finger to his chest. "You?"

She laid her head against his cheek and whispered, "Elanya," in his ear.

He could feel her breath, like a feather, brush his neck lightly in response. He wanted to kiss those soft, ripe lips so badly he could taste them. He plied her with questions from the book just so he could watch her lips move and hear her sweet voice. He figured the only way he would get to kiss her was if she agreed to walk him back to the ship. But, she kept saying it was not permissible. Whenever they weren't dancing, they would sit and just stare at each other, trying to communicate with their eyes, what they were feeling inside.

It was time to go and Elanya helped him with his duffel coat. While he buttoned, she pulled his collar up, touching his neck lightly with her fingers. It was no accident. She told him so when he looked into those black velvet eyes. He gave her hand one last squeeze before heading out the door.

Large snowflakes were falling now, laying down a thick carpet of white that crunched beneath his boots as he walked. There weren't many street lights in the area and those that he passed only gave off a very weak glow. The snow brightened things up a little bit.

Suddenly, he stopped and listened. Nothing but silence. He adjusted the balaclava over his mouth and continued walking. He stopped once again and looked behind him. The snow was like a thick curtain now and he wasn't able to see very far, but there was definitely someone out there. The hair on his neck bristled as he began to realize just how vulnerable he was in the middle of this desolate, God-forsaken land. Then he heard it, muffled, but unmistakable.

"Frankie Hawkins!" Like a mirage, she appeared out of the snow, waving a mittened hand, her breath vaporizing out of her mouth in short bursts. He stood looking at this glorious person wrapped in a blanket of fur from head to toe, and blinked his eyes in disbelief.

"Elanya, what's going on? What..." She put a finger to his lips and turned her head to indicate someone following her. He grabbed her arm and walked her quickly in the direction of the ship. There was no way of getting her past the guards at the dock gate and no way to elude whoever it was following, because of their footprints in the snow. He wanted so badly to spend some time with her, but he just didn't know what to do about it.

A short distance from the gate, he spotted the old picture house and pulled Elanya into the darkened doorway and kissed her. At first, her body stiffened, uncertain of how to respond to this sudden show of affection, then her lips softened and became moist and inviting.

Footsteps could be heard coming down the road. They stopped kissing and looked toward the sound, their hearts pounding and their breath coming in short, labored gasps. The silhouette of a soldier appeared out of the snow and stood for a moment peering over at the darkened doorway.

"Go back to your ship," he ordered, nodding his head in the direction of the gate. As they stepped out of the shadows, Frankie squeezed her hand one last time before turning and walking away. He wondered if he would ever see Elanya again.

The ship, deeply laden in the water with its cargo of cut timber, picked its way cautiously through a sea of ice floes. In the distance, dark, ominous clouds gathered along the horizon and the wind began kicking up white caps. A storm watch was put into effect, and men swarmed the decks securing anything that moved. Frankie sensed when he got up that morning this was not going to be just a normal day.

By the time he got dressed and up on deck, waves were already pouring over the side. He stood there timing the waves and the roll of the ship before taking off at a dead run across the open deck. Half-way across, the ship heaved, as if being raised by a giant hand, then shook violently when the propeller came up out of the water and ran free. The ship then plunged headlong into a trough, causing the next wave to completely submerge it in cascading water.

He felt the tremendous pull of the wave but somehow managed to hold onto a derrick that held one of the lifeboats. He opened the steel door to the mess hall and joined a dozen deck hands drinking coffee and talking in hushed tones. He sat studying each face for a while before heading for the engine room. It was hard to stand, let alone walk. Now the ship pitched wildly to one side and shook and vibrated until it righted itself, then pitched over to the other side.

He stood on the catwalk, staring down into the belly of the ship, his knuckles white from holding on to the steel rail on each side of him. Hell had broken loose in the engine room. Ruptured pipes were spewing steam and hot water everywhere. Men, their uniforms soaked, worked feverishly from one emergency to another. He began his slow descent, wondering if he would ever get to see his family again. The second engineer called for him to help out with a bilge pump that had blown a gasket.

Twelve hours later the storm began to subside and everyone in the engine room breathed a little easier.

"Hey, English, how about bringing down a pot of coffee and anything else Hans may want to throw in," the second hollered.

Frankie jumped at the chance to get up top and see what the world looked like. He stepped out on deck and felt the cool night air on his flushed face. *I'm alive,* he marveled, looking up the the heavens. "Alive!"

The ship limped into Haugesund, Norway, battered and bruised, her engines in need of repair. Frankie and Ginger took a whole day off to explore and enjoy this winter wonderland. It was so different from the bleak, desolate country of Russia. The town was full of life and the people looked happy and healthy. Horse-drawn sleds were a common sight on the streets of this small seaport town. When night fell, the lights from the shop windows and street lamps cast a warm glow on the snow.

"Just like a photo on a Christmas card," Frankie said to Ginger, without taking his eyes from the scene outside. "Everything looks so neat and clean. Picture perfect; like you'd see in a storybook or a film."

"Are you going to order something, Scouse, or just sit there drooling all night?"

"Why don't you go ahead and order for me, seeing as you can read that Norwegian stuff. Anything but fish, please. We get enough of that on the ship."

"Did you know two beautiful girls have been staring at you for the past ten minutes and all you've done is stare out the window?"

"Oh, sure, tell me more," Frankie said, looking around the restaurant in an exaggerated fashion. Suddenly his eyes got real wide.

"Is that them?" he whispered. "The table closest to the door?"

"Yeah, the blondes. Hey, look at you blushing. And all the time I thought you were a lady killer."

"What do we do now? Invite them over? Yeah, that's it. Why don't you do that? You speak the lingo."

"Hey, don't give me that crap, Frankie. I never met a Norwegian yet who couldn't speak English. Invite them yourself."

While the waitress was taking their order, he glanced over there again. Sure enough, the girls were whispering to each other and staring right at him with flirtatious blue eyes. *It's now or never*, he thought, getting up out of his chair.

"I ordered you some steak and chips, Scouse."

"Yeah, that's good, thanks," he said, as he moved toward the girls. His heart began to race and his legs were having a hard time bending at the knees. He hadn't formulated what he was going to say and he was already standing there in front of them.

"Excuse me, ladies. Do you speak English?"

The girls looked at each other and giggled nervously.

"Yes, I do," one of them finally said. "Are you an English boy?"

"Yeah, how did you know?"

"It's your hair and your face. You look very English."

"Well, then. I'm Frankie and my friend over there is Ginger. We'd love to have you sit at our table."

"I'm Bridgette and this is my friend, Elsa. Elsa, would you like to join them?"

She nodded quickly and said, "Yes," with a beautiful, friendly smile.

All through the meal he tried to make up his mind which one he liked best, but he couldn't. Both girls were very beautiful and each had a uniquely sweet personality. When they finally got up to leave, it was Bridgette who put her arm in his, so the choice was made for him.

Once outside, Bridgette tilted her head back and began catching the large snowflakes that passed within easy reach of her outstretched tongue. He watched in fascination as she moved gracefully from one snowflake to another, all the time emitting little squeals of delight.

A horse-drawn sled, its little bells tinkling, passed within a few feet, spraying both of them with slushy snow. While he was busy wiping off his dungarees, Bridgette shaped a snowball and hurled it in his direction. He looked up just in time to see it coming, but not in time to duck. It splattered on his forehead and dribbled down his shocked face.

"Bridgette, you nasty lady," he shouted after the fleeing figure. "I thought you were a nice person when I met you."

Ginger and Elsa had witnessed the episode and stood laughing at Bridgette's attempt to flee the scene of the crime. She stumbled and sprawled face down in the snow, then scampered to get back up, only to slip again. She lay still for a moment trying to catch her breath, then turned her head slowly until her eyes met his. He stood over her, a snowball in each hand, grinning broadly.

"Please, don't!" she begged coyly.

"What a pathetic looking face," he laughed, dropping the snowballs on her head, and then reaching to help her get up. She grabbed his hands and pulled him down on top of her, kissing him full on the lips. Her mouth was moist and warm, sending ripples of pleasure coursing through his body. He tried to extricate himself, but she held him tightly around the neck with both arms.

She's trying to do me in the middle of the street, he panicked, prying her arms apart and getting to his feet. He looked around for Ginger, but he and Elsa were nowhere in sight. In fact, the whole street was becoming deserted now, and many of the storefronts began turning off their lights, casting the street into a pale gloom.

Bridgette put an arm through his and snuggled her face into his shoulder.

"Are you angry at me?"

"No, I'm not angry at you. What made you think that?"

"The way you jumped up." Her voice was so soothing and childlike, he found himself at a loss to explain the desire she'd created in him.

"Well, Bridgette, maybe it's not such a good idea to kiss like that in the middle of a public street. You know what I mean?"

"But, in Norway, it's not such a bad thing." She looked up at him to see his reaction. He could smell the fragrance of her hair as it brushed against his chin. He reached out with his free hand and stroked it gently.

"If you kissed a lad like that in Liverpool, there'd be a lot more than kissing going on in the street. They're a bad lot over there, you know." She chuckled into his sleeve, amused by the way he said it.

They walked in silence toward the water, the snow swirling and dancing around them in an endless ebb and flow. The wind came off the river more bitingly here. He could feel Bridgette squeeze tighter on his arm for warmth.

"Hey, take me on your ship," she said excitedly, tugging on his arm to emphasize her eagerness for him to respond favorably to it.

The ship was a short distance away and his eyes scanned the deck looking for signs of life. Except for the occasional porthole light, the ship sat, forlorn and abandoned, in a gloom of white powder.

That's not a bad idea, he thought, his body shivering with a mixture of pleasure and cold feet. Normally, there would be a watch on the gangway. But, here in dry-dock, it didn't seem to apply.

"Yeah, okay," he whispered, a slight quiver in his voice from the nervous tension beginning to build in the pit of his stomach. He envied Ginger's air of maturity. Whenever he tried to emulate him, though, he felt foolish and frustrated. By the time they climbed aboard and entered his cabin his nerves had begun to unravel.

"Bridgette, you'll be okay in here. I gotta go to the toilet. I'll be right back, okay?" She smiled back at him, like this was the most natural thing in the world.

God, how does she do it, he thought, closing the cabin door and tiptoeing down the dark passageway.

"Ginger! Ginger, are you there, lad?" He switched on Ginger's light, but the cabin was empty. He ran up the stairs and out onto the deck, unsure what he should do next. The cold air felt good on his clammy body. He moved to the rail and took a deep breath and waited for the pulse to quit pounding in his head. The snow was falling so heavily it was impossible to see more than a few feet ahead. From out of nowhere, a figure emerged and headed straight for the gangway.

"Ginger, is that you?" Ginger looked up, his red hair and beard matted with snow.

"Yeah, what is it, mate?"

He didn't answer until Ginger climbed the gangway and stepped on deck.

"She's here! She's in my cabin right now!" he said, excitedly.

"Yeah, okay! So what, may I ask, are you standing out here freezing your arse off for?"

Suddenly, he felt stupid. He wasn't a bit sure why he was standing out on deck.

"Well, I was kinda waiting for you. You know...er...I don't know what to do with her!"

Ginger looked back, incredulous.

"You big dummy! What do you mean, you don't know what to do with her?" he shouted, thumping Frankie on the chest a couple of times.

"What makes you think she wants any more than to be your friend? These are very friendly, outgoing people. Not like your Liverpool girls back home."

He hung his head a little, his face flushed with embarrassment and humiliation.

"Why don't you go down to her," Ginger suggested, his voice a little more conciliatory and understanding.

"It's getting late and she may be ready for you to walk her home."

He nodded his head. "Yeah, you're probably right. I'll see you in the morning."

When he entered the cabin, he found Bridgette fast asleep in his bunk, her clothing neatly folded on the floor beside her.

Frankie lay on his bunk in a dreamlike trance, enjoying the deep rhythmic throb of the ship's engines that lulled his mind to rest. It had been more than a week since he last saw Bridgette, but she was in his thoughts every waking moment. He relived their three days together over and over in his mind, recapturing her whimsical smile, the purity in her laughter, and the childlike innocence in her gestures and demeanor.

There was a knock on the cabin door. Ginger opened it without waiting to be invited.

"Still thinking about her, ain't you?"

Frankie didn't answer. He was reluctant to reveal his intimate thoughts about Bridgette to anyone, including his best friend.

"I'm fixing to leave this old tub when we get to Scotland," Ginger added.

"Frankie's eyes never left his face. Ginger nonchalantly settled himself down on the narrow bench and leaned his head against the steel bulkhead. Frankie sat up and lit a cigarette.

"Yeah, thought it was time to settle down and tie the old knot," he intoned, more for the benefit of his own ears than those of his friend.

"Come on, for Christ's sake, Ginger. Quit pulling me bleedin' leg! You never mentioned having a girl before."

"Hey, calm down! What are you getting all fired up about?"

"Oh, come on mate, give me a break, will you? This lot hates my guts and you know it. You're the only friend I got."

"And whose bloody fault is it?" Ginger shot back as he stood to his feet. "You're forever going around proving how tough you are, never stopping to realize that they have feelings, too! This is their ship, you know! You act like they owe you something for being here. I tried teaching you Norwegian so you could communicate better and show an interest in them. But, no. You wouldn't have it. So, here you are, with one friend in the world, and you're still blaming them for it."

Frankie was stunned into silence. He never realized his friend felt that way about him. "Thanks, Ginger. It's nice to know whose side you're on."

They stared at each other in silence. Even the throb of the engines seemed to recede into the distance, leaving the cabin in a timeless vacuum. Eternity passed before Ginger finally turned and opened the door, slamming it behind him.

Frankie stood watching his friend walk down the gangway and stop briefly at dockside to adjust the kip bag on his shoulder. *If he looks back, I'll wave*, he promised himself. *That I'll do, for sure.*

They hadn't spoken or seen each other for two days now. It didn't seem quite right. He couldn't bring himself to be the first to give in, always hoping that, somehow, Ginger would make the first gesture. Now, it was almost too late. He watched as the tousled red head bent forward to pick up the suitcase with his free hand.

Now, Ginger, look back now, mate, he inwardly pleaded, as he gripped the guardrail and began to shake it. But, Ginger wasn't aware of him standing there. He headed for the street that would take him through the dock gate. Frankie knew if he shouted out loud, his friend would still be able to hear him and turn around. His pride wouldn't let him do it. Ginger passed through the gate. He was gone.

After Ginger left, Frankie felt more empty and alone than he'd ever felt in his entire life. Crew members passed him by without speaking or acknowledging him in any way. He took to eating in his cabin and reading a lot.

He lay on his bunk and let his mind wander through the docks and warehouses of his childhood. Once again, he was running through the cobbled streets of Liverpool or riding on horse-drawn carts or bunking on the ferry across the Mersey River to New Brighton.

It was at these times that he began to feel a deeper understanding and appreciation of his mother's love. As he recounted the endless bitter winters she suffered through, he marveled at the tenacity of this frail, yet resourceful woman. He also came to recognize the enormous pain he, himself, must have inflicted upon her. He longed to see her again to let her know, that even when he was at his worst, he had always loved her.

The journey to South America was an unusually rough one, with gale force winds whipping the sea into an angry, foaming mass of water that buffeted the ship relentlessly for over a week. The old ship creaked and groaned so loud, it became impossible to sleep for more than a couple of hours. Midway through the storm crew members began to collapse from exhaustion. As usual, the engine room became a disaster area with bilge pumps breaking down, one after another, allowing water to rise to dangerously high levels. All hands were ordered to form a bucket brigade to keep the water level from reaching the boilers. The engineers worked feverishly to get the pumps working again.

"I swear on my mother, this is gonna be my last bloody trip!" Frankie shouted in exasperation.

Carl, the fireman, passed another bucket of water to him and looked him straight in the eye.

"It may very well be the last trip for all of us, English. We are in serious trouble if this storm continues."

"Did you have to say it like that, Carl?" Frankie lamented. He'd been so preoccupied with work and being fatigued, he hadn't given much thought to the possibility of the old tub going under. Only those who have endured such a harrowing and lengthy ordeal could possibly understand the depth of relief and gratitude one felt for having survived it. The initial reaction is much like a spiritual euphoria, when men greet each other in quiet whispers, or sit alone in silent repose, heads slightly bend, somewhat like a Buddhist monk, reflecting upon the inner sanctums of his soul. Then, after everyone is sick of doing the Chinese shuffle, all hell breaks loose and it's party time. The booze flows, the raunchiest jokes make a comeback, and the female anatomy is once again the main topic of conversation over a game of poker.

The day after the storm abated, Frankie was summoned to the second engineer's cabin.

"Sit down, son. Would you care for some coffee?"

"Yes, sir, I would, thanks." he lied. He hated coffee, unless it had at least six heaping spoons of sugar in it.

While the engineer was busy with the coffee, he studied his surroundings. Except for the two portholes, which were draped with heavy curtains, the impression was, not of a cabin, but more like a room in a plush hotel or stately home.

"You did a fine job during the storm."

"Thank you, sir. I do me best work when me life depends on it!"

"Don't we all!" the engineer chuckled. He set two cups on the coffee table and eased himself into a chair opposite the lad. After a long and uncomfortable silence, the engineer finally spoke.

"Son, I want to be honest with you. The crew doesn't like you much." The engineer waited for the boy's reaction. Except for a slight tightening of the jaw muscles, there wasn't any. There was another long silence. The engineer chose a Sherlock Holmes-looking pipe from an assortment hanging on a pipe rack and began stuffing it with tobacco from a pouch.

I sure could use a 'ciggy' right now, Frankie thought, as a sweet aroma began to fill the cabin.

"I did some checking around before I asked you here tonight. You send half of your money home each month, and it's not for yourself, is it?"

"Me, sir? No, sir. I think you got me mixed up with somebody else. I don't have much money on the books."

Up until now, Frankie had concentrated his gaze on the untouched cup of black coffee in front of him. He now turned and fixed his gaze on the engineer.

"No, sir, it's not for me. It's not a big deal. She needs the money and I send it. Kind of like the man of the house."

The engineer leaned forward, pulling the pipe from between his teeth.

"Oh, but it is a big deal. It tells me a lot about you. Behind that wall of indifference is a nice young man with a good heart." He paused to see if any of this was sinking in, then settled back and resumed sucking on his pipe.

"You know, you ought to lighten up a little. Give people a chance to know you."

Frankie sensed the little chat was over and stood to leave. "I guess I can try a bit harder, sir."

"That's my boy," the engineer exclaimed. He stood, putting an arm around the boy's shoulder and guiding him to the door.

It wasn't long after his encounter with the second engineer that Carl, the fireman, began making overtures of friendship toward him. Carl was in his mid-thirties, short and stocky with no neck to speak of. His huge head just sat there right between his shoulders, giving him the appearance of having a humped back. He was the ugliest man Frankie had ever seen, with a wrinkled, flat face like an English bulldog. To top it off, his teeth were all spacey and tobacco-stained.

Hey, English! Wanna see a picture of my wife?" Carl hollered over the roar of the engines.

"Yeah, wait'll I wash off my hands, Carl. Won't be a mo'." He put the grease can away wondering what kind of girl would let Carl kiss her, let alone marry him.

"Carl, you're pulling me leg, lad. This is a photo of a film star or something," he shouted, with genuine admiration showing through his wide-eyed stare.

Carl chuckled. "You really think she's nice?"

"Nice! She's fantastic!"

By the time the ship reached the coast of Trinidad, Carl had managed to take Frankie through the basic steps of the job of a fireman. The array of gauges and valves were mind-boggling, not to mention the fierce heat the oil-burning furnaces generated. Within minutes of entering the fire room, Frankie's clothing was soaked from perspiration.

"Don't much like it in here, Carl. Kind of hard to breathe, like I'm suffocating already."

"Yeah, but after a while you don't even notice it," Carl mumbled, letting go of a mouthful of tobacco juice and watching it sizzle into a brown stain on the furnace wall.

Toward mid-afternoon, Carl began to nod off to sleep in a chair.

"Hey, Carl, why don't you go topside and grab yourself a cup of coffee and some fresh air." Carl squinted up at the wall of gauges, then closed his eyelids again.

"I mean it," he insisted. "I've watched you all day and I think I can handle it easy enough."

He took time to think about it before finally easing himself up out of the chair. He stood inches from Frankie's face and looked at him long and hard.

"So, you think you got it all figured out in a day, hey?"

"Come on. All I said was I think I can handle it for a bit."

Carl nodded a few times, then turned abruptly and headed out the steel door.

"Won't be gone long," he shouted over his shoulder.

Frankie stood there all alone. He sensed the awesome power and responsibility that had just been given him, if only for a few moments, and trembled slightly. *Piece of cake, this*, he reassured himself, eyeballing each gauge as he paced the floor. *Not bad, not bad. Might even offer me the job if Carl ever quits. Yeah, that'd be something to write home about. 'How's your lad doing, Kate?' he mimicked. 'He's a fireman now, girl. Very important job, it is.'*

He glanced up at the gauges again and stopped dead in his tracks. Number three boiler was getting too hot, sending the gauge creeping up toward the danger zone.

"That was awful fast!" he exclaimed, rushing to adjust the amount of oil feeding number three furnace. He stepped back and held his breath, waiting for the indicator to start dropping back, but it didn't!

"Another half turn'll do it, that's it," he muttered, through parched lips. Panic began to creep up his legs and into his torso. He stepped back once again and waited for the latest adjustment to take effect. For a split second, the indicator stalled and quivered slightly, then continued its slow ascent toward the red Danger area.

"Oh, my God! I bet I'm turning the wrong valve!" he shrieked, his mind trying desperately to remember the steps Carl had shown him to follow. He clutched at another valve and gave it a full turn, then watched as the indicator slowly made its way into the Danger zone! In total panic he began closing off all the valves that fed oil to the four furnaces. He was aware of running feet and turned to see the first engineer bursting through the open door, followed by the second engineer and Carl close behind. The last thing he remembered before being pushed aside was the stark terror on Carl's ugly face.

He climbed the three flights of steps like there was a ball and chain tied to each ankle. There was no place to hide. No place to run. He stood on deck with the rest of the crew, watching the funnel spew ugly black smoke into a clear blue sky.

"I almost blew up the ship..."

To compensate for his feelings of embarrassment, he became more hostile toward those who challenged his sense of worth. He was finally beaten badly by the boson, the head of the deck hands, who broke his nose and fractured his jaw.

It was early Spring when the ship reached the coast of Holland. Frankie stood on deck watching the lights of the city of Amsterdam shimmer in the evening mist. For him, the long journey was finally over. He was going home. A few crew members made it a point to shake his hand and wish him luck; though they had never associated much after the fire room incident; Carl was one of them.

He swung the kip bag over his shoulder, headed down the gangway and never looked back.

The train chugged slowly into Lime Street Station, its hissing steam and screeching wheels sending hoards of pigeons scurrying high into their lofty perches.

"Taxi, son, taxi?"

Frankie shook his head and walked out into the noonday sun. The sheer joy of being home overwhelmed him and he stood for a moment fighting back the tears. Just a short year ago he couldn't wait to leave. Now, it filled him with such happiness he could hardly contain it. Every sound, every smell, every sight, brought exciting childhood memories flooding back.

He jumped the 82 bus and climbed to the top deck to get a good view of the city and its sea of people. Once again, as had happened before on his homecoming, joy began to turn into sadness, as the bus neared Toxteth where he lived. This was truly the forgotten part of the city. How else could one explain why dozens of bombed out buildings were still left standing, as though the war had just ended instead of twelve years ago?

His smile came back, along with the butterflies in his stomach, when he finally turned onto Mann Street and saw the four huge tenement blocks.

Should've warned me Mam I was coming, he thought as he neared the block. "Hello, Mrs. Rainey. Nice day, eh?"

The woman scrubbing her front step looked up and furrowed her brow until it dawned on her who was walking down the street. "Thought me eyes were playing bleedin' tricks on me, lad," she hollered after him. "You're the spit of your dad."

He hit the stairs two at a time, his smile growing wider with every step. By the time he pulled the string on the door, he felt like he was about to explode from pent-up emotions. His mother sat at the table eating dinner with her children when the door opened behind her. Dorothy sat directly facing the door in animated conversation when, suddenly, her voice trailed off into a whisper.

"Mam, you'll never guess who's standing behind you!"

Kate, with her fork almost to her mouth, looked across at her daughter's wide-eyed stare, afraid to turn around.

"It's our Frankie, Mam, Frankie's back!" Margaret shouted, scooting her chair out and running toward him. Kate got up slowly and turned around to face him.

"You shouldn't do this to me, lad! The ol' ticker can't take it anymore," she pleaded, her voice trembling with emotion.

He could see she was genuinely upset and reached out to give her a big hug.

"Ah, I'm sorry, Mam. I thought it would be fun to surprise you for a change. You know I wouldn't hurt you for the world, now would I?" he assured her lightheartedly, one arm around her shoulder in a gentle squeeze.

She managed a weak smile and slapped him playfully on the cheek.

"You big ape! Next time I'll punch your lights out!" she warned, feigning a swing to his jaw with a bony fist. "Now, are you hungry?"

"Starving to death, Mam."

He awoke before dawn and lay still for a while, listening to the faint ticking of the clock on the mantelpiece. For the moment, he was content to luxuriate in the sensations of being home. Here he felt safe. Threatened by no one and loved by all. Loved for no other reason than for who he was. A son and a brother made to feel important, a vital part of their lives and happiness. The joy on their faces needed no words. He was surely missed, and he missed them, too, more than he'd realized. Yes, he wanted to lie basking in the afterglow of adoration for a little while longer; just long enough to erase the memories of his long and lonely journey.

His mother's coughing startled him; then the quiet settled in again. Something about her disquieted him. The sparkle was no longer there in her eyes. Her once beautiful face was now pale and drawn. Her slender frame a little too thin to be healthy. When he'd voiced his observations to his older sisters, they'd both discounted it with a laugh.

"She'll outlive us all, Frankie. She's as strong as an ox," Dorothy quipped, looking at Sarah to confirm it.

"Yeah, that's right, lad. Should see her when she gets a couple of Brown 'n' Bitters down her in the pub. Dance all bleedin' night, she will." Sarah had danced a little jig to mimic her mother, pulling her dress up above the knees in the French can-can fashion.

The morning light began to filter through the curtains. He got up from the couch and dressed quietly, being careful not to wake anybody up. Once outside, he pulled his coat collar up in response to the crispness of the spring air, and began walking in the direction of the dock road.

A feeling of expectancy came over him and his face flushed with a warm rush of excited pleasure. He felt giddy and fought back the urge to laugh out loud and run as fast as he could through the quiet streets. The small boy inside of him struggled to be set free to explore once again, this enchanted land that had captivated his heart and mind and spirit so long ago.

By the time he reached the dock road, it began to dawn on him that something was amiss. It was too quiet. He stood in the middle of the street and looked down its great expanse and saw nothing. No lorries, no horses, no bikes, not one person walking anywhere. Never had he seen such a vibrant part of the city so utterly deserted, not even on a Sunday or a holiday.

He walked slowly toward the dock gates and pushed on one of its huge doors. It creaked open to reveal an empty loading yard littered with broken packing crates and empty oil drums. Tall weeds and moss grew between the cobblestones and up the sides of the warehouses. Inside the warehouses he found the same story, empty and strewn with rubbish. Dead pigeons lay half-eaten by rats that scurried off into the darkened corners when he approached. He walked through one dock after another for over a mile, hoping to find some sign of normalcy, but there was no relief.

Something inside of him was dying. He had come to recapture a moment in time, only to find, like his youth, it had been snatched away. He sat on a rusting capstan and watched a boy fishing in the murky water. The tousled head of hair and knee britches with the hole in the rear end were somewhat reminiscent of himself at that age.

"Catch anything?"

The lad glanced over at him, a little startled at finding someone watching him.

"Not yet, haven't been long at it."

"Don't eat them, do you?"

"Not likely, mister, just throw the buggers back, like"

He smiled at the 'mister' bit. That name was reserved for grown men. *Do I look that old already?* he wondered, getting up off the capstan and heading for the gate.

"Hey, mister, got any spare coppers on you?"

He turned to look at the lad.

"Sagging school, aren't you?"

The lad's face got sheepish and he turned away from Frankie's gaze.

"Yeah, I hate school," he mumbled somewhat to himself. He reeled in his line and whipped it far out into the river. "Don't hurt nobody. I just wanna be fishin' right here by meself."

"I think I know the feeling, mate. Two bob do it?" The boy reached out and took the money.

"Thanks, mister. You from 'round here?"

"No, not anymore," he answered wistfully.

He was glad to find his mother home alone. She'd built a nice fire that made the kitchen warm and cozy. The aroma of apple tarts baking in the oven filled the small room, reminding him he hadn't eaten all morning.

"You look nice today, Mam." He watched her face break into a big smile.

"Well, thank you, kind sir. And what have you been up to this morning?"

"Went for a walk through the dock area. Why is everything shut down?"

"Dockers did themselves in, son. Kept going out on strike 'til the shipping companies got fed up with it and moved out. How about a cuppa?"

"Sounds good. Are the tarts done, yet?"

"Just be a minute."

"But, what happens to all those men?"

She'd disappeared into the back kitchen and didn't answer until she reappeared holding a piping hot apple tart and a pot of tea.

"The sods are made up. They collect their dole money and hang out in the pub all day pretending to feel sorry for themselves. Ought to line 'em up and shoot the bloody lot of 'em." Frankie laughed out loud. He'd never heard her talk this way about anything before.

"So, what're your plans, son?" Her voice took on a more personal intimate tone when she spoke to him.

"Not sure yet, Mam. Just enjoy being home for a while. After that, I don't know. Why were you so easy on me?" The words jumped out of his mouth without any process of thought beforehand. He wondered where in the world the thought even came from. His mother flinched as if a bee had suddenly buzzed her too closely, and set her cup down slowly.

"You think I was?" Her voice was subdued, almost melancholy now. "I thought about that a lot over the years. What mother wouldn't. But, I still don't know the answer. Ever since you were a little boy, you stuck close to me, wanting to ease my pain, be my little helper. So, it was easy to keep you home from school and make excuses why you couldn't go. Who knows, maybe I needed your comfort." She stopped talking, but her eyes continued in silence; as though she were reviewing something from the past that would shed more light on her wounded thoughts.

"Even when you were thieving, it was always to help me out, not 'cause you were bad. So, you see, Frankie, it wasn't an easy thing to get mad at you, knowing why you did. Though, Lord knows, I wanted to knock your block off a few times." She paused again with that far-away look in her eyes, while her finger traced the rim of the cup in a slow rhythmic movement.

"By the time I woke up to what was really happening to you, it was too late. You'd become very independent in your ways. The few times I did try to put my foot down, we both hurt and you'd stay away. I just had to let you go and hope for the best." She paused and looked straight at him, and he knew she was finished. He reached over and squeezed her hand.

"You did a luvly job by me, Mam. You were always there when I needed you."

"You're only after another piece of my apple tart, I can tell."

He laughed at the funny face she put on.

"You wha', girl? You make the worst tarts in the whole bloody world, but I'll have another, just so I don't hurt your feelings."

Frankie spent some of the most precious moments with his family as they gathered each evening around a blazing coal fire, reminiscing about the good ol' days of their childhood. It was magical how some of the most heart-rending experiences now became hilarious in the telling. Tears flowed, but they were tears from too much laughing.

Kate, their mother, laughed the hardest. She had a funny bone that, once touched, was impossible to control, and it was infectious. It was good for him to see her this way, too. It made him realize that if she could find such humor in her own dreadful experiences, then she would surely survive without him worrying about her.

He sat alone on a grassy knoll overlooking the beautiful and tranquil lake in Sefton Park. His eyes followed a pair of swans moving gracefully through a maze of lily pads and bulrushes. The sun danced and sparkled on the ripples they had left in their wake.

A young woman pushing an empty pram stopped to enjoy the serene setting, causing the little toddler who was following close behind to bump into her and topple over. The child's pathetic cry pierced the stillness, sending the swans skittering across the lake out of harm's way.

She picked up the child and held it to her breast, soothing the head with gentle strokes until the child lay silent. Her eyes suddenly caught sight of Frankie watching her and she smiled at him. Before he had a chance to respond in kind, she had turned to put the child back into the pram.

That beautiful, winsome smile had ignited something deep within him, throwing his perfect morning all out of kilter. He watched after her as she continued her slow, rhythmic walk.

"I hope the baby's okay," he blurted out in desperation. *God, I wish I hadn't done that,* he thought, half hoping she hadn't heard him. She stopped and turned to look in his direction, a smile, slightly less visible this time, playing around her eyes and mouth.

"Yes, she's fine now, thanks."

Did he detect a slight quiver in her voice? An unspoken message in her eyes? Or was she just a friendly person being polite to a stranger? He didn't want to make the wrong assumption and ruin her day by being too aggressive. But, wouldn't it be worth testing her just a little further before she was gone forever? He couldn't bring himself to make a move and could only watch as she made her way along the lake path. He sat for a long while staring into the distance, his mind lost in a fog of uncertainty as to what his next move should be. He felt angry and a little frustrated at himself for allowing this beautiful stranger to steal his heart so completely and then watch her slip away from him while he stood by helplessly.

A black Labrador retriever bounded out of nowhere and began to circle him, sniffing and wagging its tail within inches of his distraught face. He was about to give it a swift kick in the rear end when the dog suddenly began to shake like crazy, sending a spray of water all over him. He jumped up in shock and began throwing rocks at the fleeing dog. When his anger was finally spent, he sauntered slowly toward the ornate gates of the park and out onto the busy street of Aigburth Road. For a week after their initial encounter, he waited faithfully by the lake each morning, hoping for a chance to see her again. She never came.

He stood at the top of the stairwell, waiting for his eyes to adjust to the gloom of the old Victorian building. From behind the frosted glass door came the rhythmic clatter of a typewriter. Frankie adjusted his tie and ran his fingers through his hair before opening the door. It was time to find out if his notoriety from the last ship had preceded him. The smell of fresh brewed coffee tried in vain to mask the pungent odor of stale tobacco smoke and old wax. A small, thin man looked up from his typewriter and removed the pipe from between his teeth.

"Yes, can I help you?"

He reached into his pocket and withdrew his seaman's papers and passport. "Looking for a ship out, sir."

The man drummed nervously on the counter top while scrutinizing the papers in front of him. Finally, he looked up.

"Can you be ready to leave in the morning?"

Frankie stared back at him, unable to speak.

"Ah, I can see that's too short a notice for you, hey?"

"No, that's fine, sir. I'm ready to go."

Once outside, he leaned his back against the wall and lit up a Woodbine. Leaving the security and familiarity of home was never an easy thing, yet to stay was unthinkable. Though his heart never ceased to pine after the rich and colorful memories of his childhood, his head now told him it was dead and time to get on with the future. And the future wasn't here. No, not here. For some inexplicable reason, Liverpool left him cold. The whole city seemed to live under a cloud of depression sucking away at the fabric of the human spirit and leaving its people content with mediocrity. Here, a child's dreams and a youth's aspirations do not survive much beyond the teenage years. The pubs and betting shops are full of grown children without a sense of purpose who sold their dreams long ago without knowing the dream's true value. And their children follow suit, believing what they see their parents do must be the dream.

Frankie refused to believe that this was his destiny. Though he was full of trepidation about the unknown, he was much more fearful of staying where that spark of light, that precarious candle flame, would be extinguished forever, and forever regret his weakness.

The pub was raucous. Bodies were packed so tightly together it was a challenge getting enough room to bend an elbow to take a drink. Everybody was talking at once, which left absolutely no one listening, not even to the poor cowboy who was singing his heart out while he plunked away on an old guitar. And, why the telly was on competing with this din was anybody's guess.

Frankie took time to look around at the familiar faces of those who had come to celebrate his pending voyage. Uncles, aunts, cousins and, of course, his own family. To most of them the local pub was as vital to their well-being as eating and breathing. It was a lifeline to each other, a communal meeting place where local gossip was exchanged and old worn out stories were infused with new life and expanded upon.

Liverpool people are gifted storytellers with a great sense of humor and colorful self-expression. Frankie found himself laughing so hard at some of their antics, he would sometimes miss half the story line before he could control himself. It wasn't difficult to understand how the local pub could become a haven from the bleak reality of the outside world. Here, it was always possible to catch a good story to lighten the heavy load.

He caught his mother looking at him from across the room. He smiled back to reassure her all was well. She never returned the smile. Only a short while ago, she'd been laughing at something. Now, her eyes held a melancholy, far-away look that his smile couldn't reach.

The *SS Free State* turned out to be a beautiful, sleek-looking oil tanker, at least twice the size of Frankie's last ship.

From the moment he stepped on board, he felt at home. When he entered the single-berth cabin, he was really impressed. The bulkhead and floor looked freshly painted. On one side of the room stood a modern chest of drawers and a writing desk with a lamp, while a larger than normal bunk lined the other side. He dropped his kip bag and fell exhausted onto the bunk and lit a cigarette. He felt troubled, but couldn't understand why. Why had his mother gotten up so early to see him off? Why the lingering look when he whispered good bye, like she hadn't quite comprehended the meaning of the words?

"I won't be gone long, Mam. Maybe a year at the most," he'd said, trying to sound lighthearted. He'd wanted to give her a hug, but feared that would upset the fragile balance of emotions that seemed to emanate from her.

A knock on the cabin door startled him back to the present. When he opened it, four young lads stood grinning back at him.

"Blimey, mate, you don't half look like you've seen a ghost," the first one chortled, stepping gingerly inside and giving the cabin the once over.

"Hey, this ain't bad! How do you rate a single berth?" The others followed after him and Frankie closed the door.

"Is this some kind of joke? You're not all English, are you?"

"Well, if you wanna call these three Londoners English that's up to you. Meself, I can't understand a bleeding word they say. Always talk like they got a dollop of mush stuffed in their gob. By the way, I'm Ron, from the great port city of Liverpool on the Mersey. Scotty Road, to be exact."

Frankie managed a smile, as he shook the hand that was offered to him.

"I'm Frankie from the Dingle area, Ron. Were you lads expecting me?"

"Yep! Told us this morning another Englishman was due on board. I was hoping it was one of me own kind, like, and not another bleedin' foreigner, like these lot." The three Londoners sat in a row on the bunk bed puffing away on American cigarettes, their backs leaning against the bulkhead.

"It doesn't take long to realize Ron's problem, Frankie," the smallest of the three challenged, in mock seriousness. "You see, his mum didn't know she was having him and just thought she was having gas pains and sat on the lavatory and out he came. So, right from the start, he's had this strange perception of the world around him!" Everyone was cracking up so bad, they were coughing and sputtering on the smoke trapped in their lungs.

"Brian, are you suggesting I was born from a big fart!?" Ron shot back, trying in vain to contain his own laughter. Brian eased his small frame off the bunk and flipped his cigarette butt through the open porthole.

"This your first trip, Frankie?"

"No, Bri. Did about a year on a small cargo ship, mostly to Russia, Norway and South America. It was an old tramp steamer. Leaked so badly, I thought I was a goner a couple of times. How about you lads?" The cabin suddenly became very quiet.

"First time for each of us," Brian answered with a look of

consternation beginning to creep into his boyishly handsome face. "You mean it gets really bad?"

"You better believe it does. It ain't your ferry ride across the River Thames or the Mersey, you know. I've been in storms that lasted for days, with twenty to thirty foot waves crashing over the deck and pounding the ship relentlessly, day and night 'til you think the ship can't possibly take it anymore. Pipes bursting all over the place, rivets popping out of steel plating, water seeping in from everywhere 'til the bilge pumps can't handle it, and start breaking down, one by one. Men working around the clock, dropping like flies from sheer exhaustion, and seasickness! God, you just wanna die, it's so bad."

Brian eased a pack of Chesterfield's out of his shirt pocket, as though he were in a trance, and offered them around.

"Blimey, he makes it sound like we'll never get back home again, don't he?"

No one bothered to answer his remark. Each seemed lost in his own little world. Chad, who had spoken very little since entering the cabin, stood slowly to his feet and walked over and peered out the open porthole. The cool sea breeze ruffled his dark wavy hair.

"This is my first real job since leaving school two years ago," he said in a reflective and somewhat melancholy voice. He paused long enough to take a deep breath of the fresh air and slowly exhale it before continuing.

"Searched everywhere, I did, but no bloke would take me on. After a bit, I couldn't think of a bloody reason to get up in the morning, like, why bother?" Again, he paused, glancing over his shoulder, then turned back to the window.

"Me and the old man got into it just about every day. Round and round we'd go, like a broken record. 'Lazy, shiftless, good for nothing bum,' he'd call me. After a while, I began to believe him. Mum would throw me a few coppers on the sly, like, so I could take me bird to see a flick and grab a pint afterward, but I knew it was her way of getting me out of the house to save the peace." He turned to face the four lads and delivered a heartfelt chuckle.

"This is it, mates. Sink or swim, there's no going back for me. Whatever lies ahead has to be a damn sight better than what I left behind."

At that moment, as if orchestrated by an unseen hand, the ship's whistle gave three long blasts. The cabin vibrated as the ship's huge turbine engines came to life.

"Could use a cup of tea right now," Frankie grinned. Four faces grinned back at him. "Last one to the mess hall stinks!"

Life on board settled into a routine. Up at seven, breakfast at seven thirty, work by eight. Brian and Chad were part of the deck crew while Frankie, Ron and Shaun worked together in the engine room. Evenings and weekends they'd gather in Frankie's cabin to play poker for packs of cigarettes, or just sit around talking about family and friends and each other's' dreams for the future. Not since the days of Nig-Nig, Coons and Digger did Frankie feel such an intimate, integral part of a group as he did with these four lads. There were times when they abandoned all pretense of being grownups, choosing instead to run wild all over the ship, playing tick or blind mans' bluff or even hide 'n' seek. With all the screaming and running going on up and down stairs and through passageways, the Norwegian crew were surprisingly polite about the whole thing, even finding their behavior amusing and referring to them as the 'crazy five.' But the honeymoon with some of the crew took an unexpected turn for the worse when Ron found himself infatuated with the only female on board.

Working in the officers' quarters, the small, petite Scandinavian blonde with round blue eyes and a capricious smile, was seldom seen by the crew. Over a game of poker, Frankie felt compelled to broach the subject.

"Ron, you've gotta be careful, messing with another man's girl. It spells nothing but trouble." Ron glanced over his cards, surprise showing in his thin face at this sudden turn of events. For a moment, it seemed like he was going to say something, and then changed his mind. His eyes dropped back to the cards in his hand.

"I'll take two," he said in a monotone, flipping the cards on the table.

"Ron, Frankie's right. The carpenter's not gonna sit by while you make a fool of him. He's too proud for that," Brian cautioned.

"Hey, knock it off!" Ron shouted, slapping the rest of his cards on the table. "What's this? Pick on Ron night?"

"No, Ron, it isn't!" Frankie shot back, his voice less conciliatory now, as memories of his last ship came flooding back. "These men will band together and make life miserable for all of us if they think we're messing them around!"

Ron got up and began pacing the floor with a hurt look on his face. Suddenly, he stopped in mid-stride.

"Christina don't belong to nobody. If she chooses to be friends with me, then she's got that right. The hell with the carpenter!" He stormed out, slamming the door behind him.

By mid-August, the ship had reached the Great Lakes of North America and Canada. Frankie made his way topside and stood on deck, watching the ship glide slowly through the narrow channel. Soft music from a radio below deck drifted up and hung suspended in the stillness of the morning air. On each side of the ship the land stretched like an emerald carpet to the distant mountains clothed in tall pines. A flock of geese circled overhead in perfect formation until, one by one, they peeled away and glided in for a landing on a nearby lake.

"God, can you believe this is for real?" he whispered breathlessly, while stepping over Chad's supine body to stand next to the rail. Chad opened his eyes and leaned on one elbow to stare at Frankie's back.

"What do you see, Scouse?"

He didn't answer right away. When he did, his voice sounded far away, almost mystical.

"I see a beautiful country out there, Chad, like you see in a dream. Wild and beautiful." Another flock of geese came in for landing, sending ripples of silver sunlight dancing along the crest of the waves they created.

"I'd pack my bag and be on my way in a minute, if it was possible."

"Yeah, well, it's a tad bit far from home for my taste."

Chad lay back on the mattress and lit a cigarette. "How come you didn't sleep on deck with us last night?"

Frankie turned to face him and nodded toward Ron's sleeping figure.

"He's acting strange lately, and so are some of the crew. I think it's best if we try keeping a low profile for a while 'til things work themselves through."

Chad took a drag of his cigarette and exhaled slowly, like a man in deep thought.

"But, if the shit does hit the fan, we'll stick together, won't we?"

"Yeah, but let's make sure we're not the ones doing the pushing." He looked at his watch. "Blimey! We're gonna be late for breakfast. Let's wake this lazy lot up."

When the five of them walked into the mess hall, the room became very quiet. A large group, which included the carpenter, sat at a table in the far corner of the room, speaking in low tones so as not to be overheard. Ron stood glaring over in their direction before joining the others.

"I wonder what that lot's whispering about?" he queried in a mocking voice loud enough for everyone in the room to hear. He scraped his chair back as a show of disdain, and sat down and began drumming his fingers nervously on the table. The chef poked his head through the serving hatch.

"Sorry, Englishmen. Breakfast was over with ten minutes ago. No more serving."

Frankie's body tensed in anticipation for what he was sure would follow. Except for the ticking of the large wall clock and the muffled droning of the ship's engines, the room was now plunged into a sickening silence. He searched each tense face around the table before finally settling on Ron's stony gaze. He shook his head slowly from side to side, without taking his eyes off of him.

"Not here, Ron, not now," he cautioned soothingly. "There'll be a right time, you'll see." He watched as Ron's jaw muscles slowly relaxed and his eyes began to lose some of their intensity.

The full moon hung suspended from a cloudless sky, casting a silver twilight over the gentle swells of Lake Michigan. Frankie stood motionless, staring out at the wake left by the ship's propeller. He was glad for the peace and solitude and a chance to refresh his mind and sagging spirit. He sensed someone behind him and glanced over his shoulder. She stood barely three feet away, a demure expression playing on her small round face.

"I'm sorry if I startled you," she whispered.

"No, no, Christina, you didn't," he lied, turning his body around to face her and leaning his back against the rail for support. She looked much younger and smaller close up. Her light summer dress billowed in the warm breeze, causing it to hug her lithe frame and outline the contours of her breasts and thighs in the moonlight. He ran his tongue over his lips, half wishing she would turn and go away, yet wishing he could just reach out and grab her and kiss those inviting lips. He glanced away feeling a little uncomfortable, like somehow she could read his thoughts.

"You must be Frankie, Ron's friend from Liverpool."

"Yeah, that's me," he said, managing a weak grin. "What brings you out this time of night?"

She moved to the rail next to him, brushing back golden strands of hair from her face with gentle strokes of her hand.

"Probably for the same reason as you. Do you think there's going to be trouble?" Her face turned to within inches of his, sending his heart thumping wildly against his rib cage. The scent of her perfume only added fuel to his already confused state of mind.

"Yeah, I'm sure of it," he stammered. "Thought it was gonna be this morning, like, in the mess hall, but it'll happen. It's just a matter of time."

There was a long silence, as both stared into the white foam directly beneath them.

"Do you think it's wrong of me to have more than one friend?" She made the question sound so innocent, he found himself at a loss to explain.

"I guess it depends on what kind of friendship you got in mind. You could be friends with the whole crew, if that's all there was to it. But, men don't see it that way." He paused to take a deep breath and turned to face her.

"I saw you tonight and thought about nothing but my own desire; that's how you make me feel. That's not the kind of friendships your boyfriend wants you to have, right? So, that's why he's mad at Ron or anyone else. He knows what men are after, and he don't wanna share you, because you're special to him."

She laughed for the first time and slapped him lightly on the shoulder, as though admonishing a small child.

"You men are all crazy, like little boys, always looking for new toys to play with." She became reflective again. "Do you think Ron and I are more than friends?"

"Yeah, I think so. It may have started out innocently enough, but the way Ron is acting lately, I'd venture to say he's in love with you."

"I like Ron a lot, but I'm not in love with him."

"What about the carpenter?"

She thought about it for a long moment.

"We're just good friends, at least, that's the way I feel."

"Maybe it's time you let them know how you feel, before someone gets hurt." He tried to keep his tone as gentle as possible. A long silence followed before she spoke again.

"We'll be in Detroit by morning. Do you plan on going ashore?"

"Sure, I do! This is my first trip to America and I'm looking forward to seeing as much of it as possible. Are we very far from Hollywood?"

She laughed out loud and patted his hand holding the rail. "Yes, Frankie, a long way. Good night. I'm going to bed." He watched after her, as she melted into the shadows.

As the ship eased its great bulk slowly toward the dock, the early morning mist began to rise like a delicate veil, allowing the sun's rays to filter through, bathing the city in a warm, red glow. Frankie had been up before dawn, eager to get his first glimpse of America. He knew very little about the country. Yet, for some inexplicable reason, the name *America* left him slightly trembling with a mixture of excitement and pleasure. *Maybe it's all the films I bunked in to see at the Palace*, he thought, chuckling to himself at the vivid memory of a fearless little waif standing outside the pictures begging passersby for spare coppers to get in.

Ron, Brian, Chad and Shaun joined him at the rail and stood pensively watching the longshoremen working feverishly to secure the ship to the wharf. Brian was the first to break the silence.

"Let's stick close together when we go ashore, okay? I've heard America's full of gangsters."

"Oh, sure, Brian, and while we're at it, let's keep an eye out for Indians, too," Ron teased, shaking his head and rolling his eyes in disbelief.

"Okay, then, why do you think cops carry guns around with them all the time?"

"I don't know, Bri. What are you getting so worked up for all of a sudden?"

"I just don't want us getting separated, that's all."

Chad put an arm around his shoulder.

"It's okay, Bri, we'll all watch out for each other. We're gonna have a lot of fun. Right, lads?"

Ron stepped back a pace. "Whoa, there, wait just a minute. If you see me latching on to a nice piece of fluff, I'm gone. And don't nobody come looking for me!"

"We wouldn't dream of spoiling your love life, Ron," Frankie laughed, slapping him playfully alongside the head. "What girl's gonna go for you, anyway, you're so darn ugly."

As soon as the gangway was in place, the five of them ran down it like rats abandoning a sinking ship. The day couldn't have been more perfect. A warm summer sun shone from a blue, cloudless sky and the air smelled of fresh lilac. The long trek toward town gave the lads a chance to admire the endless variety of fancy American cars that paraded past them on the broad, tree-lined boulevard. A sleek red Chevrolet with its top down and radio blasting out rock'n'roll music, pulled to the curb just ahead of them, drawing them to it like a magnet.

"Hey, mister, you mind if we look at it a bit?" Shaun asked, his hand already caressing the contours of the chrome around the bonnet.

The man, in his mid-twenties and dressed in a cowboy outfit and wearing sun glasses, pulled his Stetson down low over his eyes and leaned his head back to rest.

"Sure, go ahead, help yourselves," he smiled, stretching out his legs to reveal a pair of beautiful, hand-crafted leather boots. "Where you guys from, anyway?"

"England."

"England! Man, you're a long way from home. I take it you don't have cars like this over there."

"Nope!" Shaun said emphatically. "Wouldn't fit on the bleedin' road. It's too big."

The cowboy laughed out loud and sat upright. "Tell you what. Jump in and I'll take you for a spin."

The lads looked at each other for a few seconds, then suddenly there was a mad scramble to get the door open and bag the front seat.

"By the way, Hank's the name." He shook each hand as they gave their names, then took off like a shot out of a cannon, squealing the tires on the road and sending up a plume of smoke. Frankie sat between Hank and Shaun, wondering if they would come out of this in one piece. Hank turned the radio up louder and began singing along. "Ever hear of Elvis Presley?"

The music was so loud, it was impossible to carry on a conversation, so each of them just shook their head in response.

"Great voice. Really knows how to sing a mean song. You do have radios in England, don't you?"

"Yeah, but it's not anything like this," Frankie shouted, not wanting to go into detail.

"Man, I couldn't live without my music."

When they reached the center of town, he slowed to a crawl and turned the radio down. The late morning sun felt good on Frankie's face and he began to relax and enjoy the luxury of cruising the streets and getting a good look at the people swarming the sidewalks.

"Are all Americans rich, Hank?"

Hank gave Frankie a quizzical glance, then took a closer look at the crowds of people.

"Yeah, I guess you can say that. This is the greatest country in the world. You can be just about anything you put your mind to being, if you're willing to work hard enough for it. Yep, I'd say the sky's the limit here, man."

They passed by a small group of black men standing outside a pool hall in animated conversation. "Take the Nigra's over there," he continued. "They're rich too, only they don't know it. Sure beats the hell out of climbing trees after coconuts now, don't it?" He laughed and slapped his leg a few times and turned to see what kind of reaction he was getting from the back seat. Nobody had a clue as to what he was talking about and they sat staring back at him with blank expressions.

"Er, you can drop us off anywhere along here, mate," Ron said, cracking a sick smile just to be polite.

"Yeah, hey, thanks a lot for the ride," Frankie intoned, trying hard to end the relationship on a positive note.

"Pleasure's all mine, guys. Don't take any wooden nickels."

"What the hell was he talking about, 'don't take any wooden nickels?'" Brian shouted, throwing up his hands in confusion. They stood watching the car until it was swallowed up in heavy traffic.

"That was some strange Yank," Shaun said, as he began to sniff the air. "Do I smell fried onions?"

They followed the aroma to a hot dog stand and gathered around it.

"How much are your sausages, mister?"

A huge man with a tiny baseball cap perched on top of his large head, peered at one face then another, trying to figure out which planet these kids had come from

"They ain't sausages," he bellowed sarcastically, wiping his mouth with the back of his hand. "They're hot dogs and it'll cost ya two bits a piece."

The lads looked at each other then back at the man.

"Two bits of what?" Brian asked.

"A quarter, man, just like this here." He laid a silver coin on the counter top.

"Looks just like a shilling, don't it? Shaun mused, picking it up to have a closer look. Brian dug in his pocket and laid out a dollar bill.

"How many do we get for that?"

"Four."

He laid down another dollar. "We'll take five with onions."

"Onions cost extra."

"Shit, I don't care! Just give us the hot dogs before we starve to death!"

They walked until they found a bench in the shade outside of a barber shop and sat down to eat their hot dogs.

A spry little black man, dressed in baggy bib overalls and shirtless, without a shirt, came out of the barbershop and stood facing them.

His thin frame rocked from side to side like he was about to break into a tap dance.

"No, no, no..." he repeated over and over, all the time stroking the salt and pepper stubble on his chin like a man perplexed.

"Maybe we're sitting on his bench and he wants us to move," Frankie whispered to Ron, who was staring back with rapt attention at the craggy ebony face that seemed full of mischief.

"Man, a meaner bunch of dudes I never did see. You all gonna kill the chicks for sure, but, man, them shoes just ain't gonna cut it!"

They each looked down at their shoes then back at the face that was beginning to break into a big toothy grin.

"I never understood a word he said, did you, Frankie?"

"No, Ron. Something about killing chickens with our shoes."

"What's the first thing the ladies notice when they walk by slick looking dudes like you all?" he teased, pantomiming a woman's walk with one hand on his hip. "Where you all from, anyway?"

"England," Chad shouted.

"England! Man, I'm gonna give those shoes a shine even the sweet lady in the palace would be mighty proud to see. Come on, follow me."

By this time, he had completely won them over with his charm and they eagerly followed him into the barbershop.

They emerged an hour later, each sporting a new haircut and a fancy shine on their shoes that reflected the brightness of the noonday sun outside. The little black man stood in the doorway chuckling softly to himself as he looked after them.

"Watch out for them ladies now, you hear?" They turned and grinned back at him and waved one last time.

"Smashing little bloke, ain't he," Chad said, as he stopped to admire his reflection in a shop window. They all decided to stop then and have another look at themselves. Brian pulled his shirt collar up around his neck and gave himself a mean look.

"You know, with Yankee clothes and a pair of sunglasses, I bet I could pass for James Dean."

Ron glanced sideways at him with a pained expression on his face.

"The man only gave you a haircut, Bri, not a face job."

Brian acted like he hadn't even heard. "You like the way the Yanks dress, don't you, Frankie? You and me can do some shopping together."

"Yeah, sure we can, Bri. And we'll buy us some nifty sunglasses, too. There ain't no reason why we shouldn't look like cool dudes and kill as many chicks as we can before we leave this place." They headed down the crowded street laughing at Frankie's feeble attempt at putting on an American accent.

"You almost sounded like the little darky in the shop," Shaun screamed, slapping him hard on the back and leaning an arm on his shoulder.

"You really like it here, don't you, Scouse?"

"Yeah, I like it a lot, Shaun. There's a kind of wild untamed spirit about America that's refreshing; makes me feel alive and wanting more. Kind of like when you're a child and you wake up on Christmas morning not expecting much; then, there, all around your bed, is a bunch of shiny new toys, more than you ever dreamed, and you get up and look out the window and the sun is shining and everything is covered with a blanket of pure white snow; and you run into the kitchen and there's your mam sitting next to a blazing fire with a stack of toast and a steaming pot of tea sitting on the table just waiting for you to get up; and you're caught between the magical moment of staying there in that cozy room with your mam or running free outside in the new world of snow." He finished with a shout of pure delight, surprising Shaun with his childlike exuberance and depth of feeling.

"You got it bad, don't you?! Was that a true story about Christmas and all?"

"Yeah, lots of times, mate. Back then the world seemed so pure and full of adventure, I thought I would burst from excitement." He stopped talking long enough to take in a sweeping view of the wide boulevard with its bright neon lights and scores of healthy looking, suntanned bodies. "I'd give anything to be a part of this. It's like discovering a whole new world."

By the time he and Shaun caught up with the other three, Brian was engaged in conversation with a police officer.

"Can you at least take it out so we can see it up close?"

The cop stood with arms folded and leaned up against his patrol car. He shook his head from side to side, a smile playing at the corners of his mouth.

"Sorry, gents. The only time I take it out is when I'm ready to use it."

"Did you ever kill anybody with it?" Chad asked, squatting down to get a closer look at the revolver. The cop answered with a good-natured laugh and adjusted his hat so it sat further back on his head in a more casual manner. The radio in the patrol car crackled to life a few times, but his handsome face remained relaxed and friendly.

"Tell me, what do English officers use if they don't carry firearms?"

"They carry Billy clubs," Brian answered.

"What if they're confronted with a gun?"

"They run like hell, I guess, just like the rest of us would."

The cop laughed again and turned to get into his patrol car. Brian leaned in the open window, an earnest look stealing over his boyish face.

"Tell me, officer, are there gangsters still in America?"

The cop put his sunglasses on and glanced at himself in the rear-view mirror before turning his head slowly, thoughtfully, toward the five faces full of youthful wonderment.

"Dead! All dead. Killed every last one of 'em off a long time ago." He gave them a cool smile. "You guys enjoy yourselves."

Frankie stood alone outside the arcade, watching the last of the sun melt behind the city skyline. Weariness crept into his body and he leaned against the wall and lit up a cigarette. The day had been one long adventure with so much to see and so many new things to experience.

With the night came a different feeling, one he was all too familiar with; a sense of not belonging, of not being a part of anything; a stranger estranged from the world around him. Except for an occasional glance, people passed him by as though he were not there. The night belonged to them. They were familiar with it and with each other. Fancy cars, making their nightly pilgrimage to the sacred strip, filled the avenue with music and laughter and shouts of greeting to each other, sometimes bringing traffic to a complete halt when friends decided to share the latest news in passing.

Brian came out of the arcade holding onto a bottle of *Coca Cola* and stood next to him. "Did you try this stuff, Frankie?"

He glanced at the bottle and shook his head.

"You ought to try it, it's great! Are you okay?"

"Yeah, I'm fine, just a little tired, I guess. Don't you think it's time you took them sunglasses off?"

Brian took them off and immediately put them back on.

"Everything looks so much better through these, especially the neon lights."

"Yeah, but you look like a bleedin' gangster. You'll have the cops coming to cart you away."

Brian took them off and put them in his pocket. They were silent for a while, both absorbed in watching the carnival-like activity going on in the street.

"Think you'll ever see anything like this in England, Frankie?"

"No, Not England or any place else in the whole wide world. This is pure American."

Two attractive young women walked by and Brian whistled after them. They glanced back for a second but kept on going.

"Brian, what are you doing? With all these good looking Yanks with their fast cars and fancy clothes, no woman's gonna go for dudes like us."

Brian looked hard into his face. "Hey, Scouse, what's gotten into you? You've been chatting up chicks all day long and having a laugh with it, so why suddenly ain't we good enough for them?"

Frankie couldn't help but grin back at the cheeky face in front of him. "Because, you dumb little Cockney, it's party time for them and we ain't got nothing to party with. We're skint, remember? We spent all our money on Yankee clothes so we could look cool, remember? And, besides that, we're all too young to even get into the bars."

A police car sped by with its lights flashing and sirens blaring, forcing the traffic to make a path for it.

"I'm ready to head back to the ship. See if the others wanna go."

Brian went into the arcade and returned shaking his head.

"Want me to walk back with you?"

"If you'd sooner stay, that's fine with me."

Brian listened to another police siren coming from the other direction.

"No, I think I'm ready to go."

"Probably after someone wearing sunglasses," Frankie quipped, as they headed out. "Sure glad you took 'em off!"

36

Frankie leaned back on his pillow and closed his eyes, allowing the book he was reading to slip from his hand and fall to the floor. The gentle rocking motion of the ship and rhythmic throbbing of the engines lulled his mind like a drug. It would have been easy to let go and drift away, but the tantalizing thought that she may be up there waiting, kept him from giving in to it.

He dressed quickly and climbed the stairs two at a time, his heart pounding in his chest. With trembling hands, he opened the steel door and stepped out into the night. The cool sea air felt good on his face as he stood probing the darkness. She stood with her back to him, her soft, golden hair dancing in the wind. Twice before she'd appeared, seemingly out of nowhere, staying only minutes before stealing away again like a thief in the night. He moved slowly toward her, stopping only inches away. The smell of her perfume sent ripples of pleasure coursing through his entire body as he leaned into her, pinning her gently against the rail. He felt her body stiffen, but she made no move to get away.

"I thought you would never come," she whispered, her voice trembling like a small child.

"I don't remember us making a date, Christine, do you?" He pressed into her a little more and kissed her neck.

"You always come at this time."

"Now, how did you know that, Christina, if you've only seen me a few times?" he teased, peeling her blouse away from her shoulders and kissing the nape of her neck. She laughed nervously, but didn't answer.

"I bet you've been spying on me like a bad little girl, Christina," he chided, gathering her hair in his hand and pulling on it playfully. "Am I right?"

She shook herself free and turned to face him, her blue eyes searching for something beyond.

"Can we go someplace else; the lifeboat, maybe?" She moistened her lips with her tongue and reached for his hand, just about the way he had envisioned it in his fantasy.

***

He could hear footsteps running down the stairs and along the passageway. Instinctively, he glanced toward the door, just as Ron burst through with Brian, Shaun and Chad following close behind.

"The carpenter, he's gone mad!" Ron shouted, searching around for something he could use as a weapon.

Frankie jumped out of his bunk and locked the door. "If I'm gonna die, I don't want it to be in my underwear! What the hell's going on, anyway?"

Before anyone could answer, the door began to vibrate from the heavy pounding.

"Englishmen, come out for me to kill you, you sons of bitches," the carpenter roared, slamming his body against the door.

Frankie pulled on his jeans and reached for his heavy boots.

"I think it's time we knocked this lad's head off, don't you mates?"

The pounding suddenly stopped and footsteps began to retreat down the passageway, amid garbled shouts and curses. They sat around quietly watching Frankie pace the floor like a caged animal. He stopped to stare out the porthole for a minute before turning to face them.

"There's no way we can stay here like this," he announced tersely, his voice angry but controlled. "If we do, we're gonna look like losers to the rest of the crew, and they'll be more than happy to treat us that way. Personally, I'd sooner be dead than be thought of as a coward to this lot."

Brian looked like he was about to say something, but changed his mind.

"What is it, Bri?"

"Well, I was just kind of thinking they've been drinking a lot and maybe by tomorrow...," he shrugged his shoulders without finishing.

"Maybe by tomorrow they'll be okay and everything will be back to normal, is that what you wanted to say? Well, let me fill you in on a little secret. Tomorrow won't be normal because it hasn't been normal around here for a long time. The carpenter's got a lot of pride, but he's also a coward; otherwise, he wouldn't have waited 'til he was drunk to have a go at us."

"So what are you trying to tell us, Frankie? Go up there and get our faces rearranged just to prove we're not cowards?" Shaun said testily.

"Yeah, something like that," Frankie shot back, giving Shaun a scathing look.

Ron stood to his feet. "He's right. Tomorrow I won't feel worth shit if I don't show them I've got some balls."

"I'm in, too," Brian said, raising his eyebrows and looking from one to the other like he was daring them to make light of it.

Chad got up slowly. "I guess you can count me in."

All eyes turned to Shaun now, who was sitting on the bunk bed shaking his head in disgust.

"Yeah, yeah, okay, but next time Ron goes sniffing at that girl's knickers you can count me out!"

"Yeah, Ron, shame on you," Frankie prodded, as he led the way out the door.

The carpenter had just stepped out of the mess hall into the passageway when the lads came into view. He was immediately joined by a group of his friends who stood behind him in stony silence, watching the lads approaching.

"Look dead serious," Frankie whispered over his shoulder.

Suddenly, the boson's huge frame came out of the open doorway of the mess hall, cutting the two groups off from each other, stopping Frankie in his tracks.

"There'll be no fighting aboard this ship, so you boys just turn yourselves around and go on back," he said sternly. He set his feet apart and placed his hands on his hips in a challenging, unmovable posture.

For a fleeting moment, Frankie had the urge to do just that, but he forced himself to stand his ground. He didn't want it to look like he was eager to give up without some semblance of a struggle. He could see the carpenter's face over the boson's shoulder and gave him a look of contempt.

"If he messes with us one more time, he's gonna get it when he least expects it, and no one will be around to save him."

"Now, I won't tell you again," the boson bellowed, waving a massive arm in a sweeping motion. "Get back, before I throw the lot of you off the ship and be done with it!"

Frankie gave the carpenter a long, stinging stare for good measure before turning to head for his cabin.

"For a minute there, I thought you were gonna go toe to toe with the boson," Ron laughed, his body free-falling onto Frankie's bunk in a mock faint. "Scared the daylights outta me, you did!"

"Me, too," Brian quipped, as he nervously offered his pack of cigarettes around.

"Did you see the look on the carpenter's face? He kept blinking his eyes like he couldn't believe what was happening."

"Yeah, like he was blinking back the bleedin' tears," Ron interjected sarcastically.

"I bet we've heard the last of Mighty Mouse, hey, Frankie?"

Frankie sat on the floor with his back against the bunk bed watching the smoke from his cigarette curl lazily up to the ceiling. He smiled, but chose to remain silent with his own thoughts. He had felt the fear no less than they had, and he hated it. He wished he was half as fearless as they thought he was.

It was a relief to the lads when the coast of England finally came into view. The ship had become nothing more than a psychological battleground now, which was far more demeaning than any physical confrontation. Crew members refused to acknowledge them in any way, silently removing themselves whenever the lads entered the mess hall for meals or coffee breaks.

Down below, Frankie, Ron and Shaun had been handed the mammoth task of hand-painting the whole engine room, while up on top, Brian and Chad spent endless days chipping and scraping the decks on their hands and knees. It was all a conspiracy to force the lads to give up the ship in England.

To get even, the five had broken into the storage room in the middle of the night and stolen all their precious coffee, dumping it into the ocean. For the Norwegians to go without their thick, black coffee for a few minutes, let alone days, was nothing short of a reason to mutiny. Yet, there was no way to prove who had done it, though there wasn't any doubt, either.

Frankie glanced at his watch while Ron pushed the door of the pub open and stood craning his neck to see over the crowded room.

"Can't see a bleedin' thing with all the ciggy smoke, Frankie."

"Well, go inside and have a gander, then," he urged, giving Ron's back a light push. "And hurry up about it, it's after nine already and the pubs close at ten."

Ron disappeared inside while Frankie scanned the narrow cobblestone street both ways, looking for signs of the other three. A light fog mixed with a fine misty rain left the old brick buildings glistening like black coal. A warm thrill ran through his body at the thought of how close to home he was standing there. But, he knew it wasn't to be. At least, not yet. He smiled at the incongruity of life. To his family, he was off sailing to some exotic, faraway lands with tropical palm trees and hidden treasures, while in reality, he stood less than a hundred miles from home, shivering in the damp cold of Newcastle, broke and looking for some cheap tart to have fun with.

Ron returned and stood silently with his hands dug deep inside his trouser pockets, a look of resignation written on his narrow face.

"Nothing doing, hey, Ron?"

"Yeah, there's three in there, but you've gotta be pretty hard up or pretty drunk."

They could hear the other lads' voices echoing through the quiet street before they appeared out of the fog.

"Any luck?" Frankie shouted. They didn't answer until they got up closer.

"Nah, nothing." Brian said disdainfully, spitting into the gutter. "But, we had a bit of a laugh with a couple of prostitutes trying to shag us for a fiver. Anything in here?"

"Put a sack over their heads and you're on." His cigarette bobbed between his lips as he spoke.

"All kidding aside, Ron, what are they like," Brian insisted, knowing time was running out for them to find any girls.

"Well, one looked like she did the hundred yard dash smack into the back of a bus; one looked like the back of a bus; and the other looked like the bus driver."

"The hell with it, let's go in and have some fun with them," Frankie laughed, reaching for the door.

The pub was typical of most pubs in England, with its high ceiling and old oak-carved paneling, blistered and unpainted from years of neglect. Windows and mirrors were steamed up from the body heat of people packed in like sardines and the incessant cigarette smoke that had no escape route, except through the door whenever it was opened.

Frankie gagged on the foul smelling air as he led the way through the maze of bodies, all the time searching for the three women sitting alone. The girls, all in their late teens, stopped talking to each other when they spotted him heading for their table.

"Hi, would you ladies mind if we joined you?"

The three just sat staring up at him in wide-eyed wonder, their mouths hung open like little birds waiting to be fed their daily morsels. With not a word spoken, they scooted closer together without taking their eyes off the five faces that now ringed the table. There was no way five more bodies could fit into that booth, but somehow, they managed to do it.

Gloria, her plump face flushed crimson, kept staring at Frankie with large puppy dog eyes.

She's definitely ugly, he thought, remembering Ron's vivid description. He turned his head to get a better look at the other two, but Gloria tapped lightly on his shoulder.

"At first, I thought you were Americans, but you're not, are you?"

"No, but we just came from America," he grinned, pulling out a pack of Chesterfield's and offering her one. "Bought all our gear over there."

"Is it nice in America?"

"Smashin', it is. Everybody drives fancy cars and eats in restaurants. They don't worry about money like us."

"Wouldn't it be luvly to live like that?"

The barmaid interrupted them, filling the round table with pints of beer and bottles of pale ale for the women.

"How long before you close, luv?" Shaun asked.

The waitress glanced up at the big clock. "A little more than half an hour."

"Then you'd better bring us another round right away."

They kept the drinks coming as fast as the barmaid could deliver them, until the final bell rang out for last orders. There was so much beer on the table, the lads began stacking them on top of each other to make room for more. Frankie's vision began to blur, as he watched Gloria's double chin bob up and down, trying to engage him in conversation. He felt sorry for her, but he'd lost interest in anything she had to say.

With a shaky hand he reached for his pint. His movement created a domino effect, as one pint after another toppled into each other, spilling the foamy substance across the table and into the laps of the three girls, who were caught totally by surprise. In his haste to stem the tide, he lunged forward with both arms extended in a futile effort to round up the wayward glasses. His sudden movement tipped the table up, pinning the girls to their seats. They could only watch in horror now, as everything on the table slid toward them, splashing like a tidal wave off of their buxom breasts and into their faces and hair. The lads were packed in so tightly, they landed in a heap on the floor, in an attempt to flee, all the time laughing hysterically at Frankie's predicament. He didn't know if he should laugh with them or run like hell for the door.

Every face in the pub was now riveted on him. Once again he felt his old enemy, fear, begin to crawl up his back.

"What the @%*... are you all looking at?" he shouted, while taking a defiant stance and raking the room with a fiery glare. Most people went back to minding their own business except one young man sitting next to a beautiful woman.

"Hey, let's knock off the language, okay?"

Frankie took it as a challenge and pushed past his mates, the alcohol and adrenaline rushing to his head, blinding him to any attempt at reason. He stopped barely two feet away and gave the man a cold, menacing look.

"What did you say?"

The man began to squirm uncomfortably in his seat but he refused to back down.

"I don't like that kind of language in front of my girl," he repeated, a little less sure of himself now.

Frankie steadied himself and hauled back his clenched fist, letting it fly with all the force he could muster. The handsome face of the stranger looked horrified as the fist whizzed past his chin. Like a dream in slow motion, Frankie could see his fist heading for the beautiful face of the girl, but he was powerless to stop it. He heard the sickening sound of bone cracking as his fist exploded on the side of her jaw. She made a feeble attempt to cry out but the sound died on her lips. The force of the blow sent her reeling sideways onto the bench seat; she rolled like a rag doll under the table and onto the floor.

Silence spread throughout the room as everybody slowly stood to their feet. The music coming from the jukebox sounded discordant and warped in Frankie's ears, as he fought down the panic that was beginning to engulf him. He stood alone and helpless in the sea of faces that now pressed into him, raining blows to his head and torso, driving him to his knees. Suddenly, he was beyond pain. He drifted in and out of a dream-like state, detached from the body that was being kicked and pummeled. A pair of rough hands yanked him to his feet again and forced him to stand, while he wobbled on rubbery legs. A hard slap to his cheek sent his head reeling. From somewhere far off he heard a familiar voice shout, "Hey, officer, don't hit him anymore; he's been hurt enough!"

"It's Brian," he thought, relieved. He tried to open his eyes but they were swollen shut.

"Is this your friend?"

"Yes, sir."

"Then you'd better get him the hell away from here before I end up killing the bastard for what he did to the young lady!"

The barmaid got close enough to whisper in Brian's ear. "Don't take him out the front, there's a gang laying in wait. If you follow me, I'll show you through the back entry."

He took Frankie by the arm and guided him through the dark passageway and out into a courtyard filled with crates of empty bottles.

"Stay to the left and close the gate after you, luvie."

The thick fog was a godsend as the two picked their way through a labyrinth of odor-filled back streets. They never spoke a word until they were safely on board ship and into Frankie's cabin. He was sober now and winced with pain. It would be weeks before the black eyes, split lip, the broken nose and rib, not to mention all the cuts and bruises, healed. But, right now he wanted to know where the other three lads were while the fighting was going on.

* * *

The huge tanker sliced through the thick fog like a silent ghost, the mournful cry of its foghorns echoing in the vast emptiness of the unseen world beyond the veil.

Frankie stepped out on deck and closed the steel door behind him, cursing softly at the unrelenting fog and piercing wind that had ravaged his spirit and kept everyone a prisoner for more than a week now. He finished buttoning his heavy duffel coat and leaned his head back against the cold steel, allowing the effects of the champagne to caress his mind and dull the misery that threatened to erupt into rage at the slightest provocation. The search for an elusive dream, a life full of adventure and fulfillment, had left him wondering if there ever was such a life, or did it exist only in the mind to keep the soul from shriveling up and dying. He made his way toward the steep staircase, pausing to light a cigarette before taking the steps two at a time. He stood on the bridge clutching the rail until the dizziness subsided, then walked slowly toward the lone figure standing vigil amid the swirling fog, like an apparition in a timeless dream.

"Excuse me, sir." He waited for the silhouette to turn and acknowledge him before going on, but there was no response. He flicked his cigarette over the side and pulled the collar up around his neck. "Thought I'd visit with Brian, me mate, for a bit, seeing it's Christmas Eve and all," he reasoned, his voice revealing a slight agitation at being ignored.

The officer turned slowly to face him, his chin buried deep within the folds of the neck scarf, his heavy-lidded eyes barely perceptible beneath the peak of his cap.

"I don't like distractions on a night like this," he said tersely, his thick Scandinavian accent resonant in the frigid air. He kept his gaze firmly fixed on the young face, but the boy stood his ground, a fierce look of defiance emanating from his eyes and finely chiseled jaw line.

The officer was well aware of the boy's reputation as a trouble-maker and it would have been easy to dismiss him from the bridge, but he hesitated to do so.

"Don't stay too long," he muttered with resignation, turning back to his lonely vigil.

The wheelhouse was in darkness except for the blue instrument lights reflecting up into Brian's face. He was startled by his friend's unexpected appearance.

"Well, look at you, Scouse! Come to cheer me up, have you?"

"Who in their bloody right mind can sleep peacefully knowing you're the one driving this thing," Frankie chided, pushing him to one side and taking over the wheel.

"Give me a heading for Liverpool. The bastards won't know what hit them 'til they wake up and find themselves staring at the Liver Birds at the Pier Head."

Since the pub fight in Newcastle, he had become like a big brother to Brian and less trusting of the other three. The only problem was Frankie's uncanny ability to find trouble wherever he went, and now Brian was never far behind.

"You're a blinkin' head case, you know that?" Brian laughed, taking back the wheel.

"Hey, you dummy! Who do you think untied a police launch in Trinidad and threw rocks at it as it drifted out to sea!"

"Yeah, but I was drunk," he protested. "Besides, I never did anything like that in my whole life 'til I met you!"

"Are you sorry you did it, Bri?" he teased, "come on, 'fess up."

Brian chuckled. "It was bloody wild, I tell you. Enjoyed every minute of it!"

The bleating of the foghorns silenced them for a while, lost in their own thoughts.

"What was Christmas like for you, Frankie?"

"Gotta go back a long way for that. Wasn't much more than ten when I left home." He was thoughtful for a moment before continuing. *"I remember one Christmas Eve we were huddled around a dying fire listening to the wind whistle through the cracks around the door and rattling the windows. Man, it was cold! The gas was turned off and there was only one candle left, so me Mam told us all to go to bed. We could tell she didn't have anything for us. No sweets, no apples, nothing for our stockings. She had that empty look in her face that we'd come to know so well. I slept with me three sisters in those days and I don't know who started sobbing first, but pretty soon we were all sobbing and trying to muffle the sounds in the blanket. It was terrible. Not for us, mind you, but we were crying for me Mam. Well, I'll tell you, Bri. The next morning we got up, it was like Father Christmas had really been there. There was stuff all around our bed. Snakes'n'ladders, Tiddly Winks, story books, sweets, chocolate; it was unbelievable! Come to find out me Uncle Alvin had come home from the navy that night and shared all his kids' stuff with us."*

Brian found himself blinking back the tears. "Jeez, Scouse, I thought you came to cheer me up, for Chris' sake." He wiped his nose on his sleeve. "Where was your dad in all this?"

"The hell if I know," he lied, "Didn't make it home after the war was over." He'd known for some time now that his dad had abandoned them. It was easier to perpetuate the myth of his childhood rather than try coming to terms with the truth or explain it to others.

"On top of all that, it snowed that morning, can you imagine that? Snow on Christmas Day!" He tried to end the story on a positive note for Brian's sake, but Brian wasn't fooled. He could almost feel the hurt himself.

Toward midnight, the last of the crew began to head for the door, leaving the five lads in sole possession of the mess hall and singing a sorry rendition of 'Maggie May,' a seafaring ballad about a famous Liverpool prostitute who took advantage of lonely sailors. When they finished singing, all five heads turned simultaneously to take in the empty tables, some with glasses of champagne still sitting untouched.

"Do you suppose we ran them off?" Ron asked, the concerned look on his face masking his real need to laugh out loud.

"They were decorating the Christmas tree, last I know," Shaun said, getting up from the table to take a closer look. "I think they finished the job; it looks smashing to me."

Chad filled his glass with champagne and set the bottle down with a loud thud, drawing everyone's attention to him.

"Quiet, lads, quiet!" Chad has an announcement to make," Frankie shouted in mock respect, even though everyone was already quiet. Chad slumped lower in his chair and looked around at each face, debating whether to speak his mind or keep it to himself. Frankie reached out and plucked an ornament from the tree, setting it in the center of the table where it began to roll back and forth with each sway of the ship.

"So, let us in on it, Chad. What's on your mind?"

Before he could answer, the ornament rolled off the table and shattered on the floor, sending everyone but Chad into a fit of laughter. When it was quiet again, he took a deep breath and sat up straight.

"Yeah, I think we ran them off tonight, but ain't that just like us lately."

He waited for Frankie to finish grabbing for another ornament and set it on the table before continuing.

"Well, we did go on a bit. 'Maggie May' was bad enough the first time around, but four times! Christ, that's enough to put a damper on anyone's Christmas spirit."

The second ornament hit the deck but this time nobody laughed.

"So you think the crew's got it in for us, hey, Chad? Well, that don't bother me none," Frankie stated flatly. He turned and pulled another ball off the tree.

"Hey, Bri, bet a pack of ciggies this one takes off on your end."

"You got a bet there, Scouse," Brian shouted with glee. Everyone but Chad got into the game now, making side bets and cheering the ball on, like it was a horse race. By two a.m., they had consumed every drop of champagne in the mess hall and broken every ornament on the tree. Frankie was the last to shuffle out the door. He took one long look behind him like he was seeing the chaos from someone else's perspective, shook his head and slowly closed the door.

38

The familiar street appeared stark and foreboding beneath the translucent pallor of a full moon. An evil presence emanated through the darkened windows and lurked like a sinister apparition within the sunken cavity of every doorway. Frankie stood motionless, breathless, his eyes searching the desolation for a sign of life, but there was none. He was alone among the silent tombs. Panic began to rise within him like a tidal wave, threatening to drown him in a sea of despair. This isn't for real, he breathed. It just can't be. The hair on his neck bristled with fearful expectancy and his body trembled under the weight of hopelessness. He wanted to withdraw within himself and shut out the desolation of terror that raged within and around him, but it was impossible to do. He closed his eyes and welcomed death if it would come quickly, painlessly, like a light being turned off.

"Run!"

"No! I can't outrun it!"

"Yes, you can! You can run so fast the wind will carry you up like a bird away from it all!"

Suddenly, his memory flooded with the sensations of flying. Yes, I can fly! I've done it before, I know it! A glimmer of hope wavered like a candle in a breeze.

Oh, God, will I be able to run fast enough to take off and fly before I'm caught from behind? His legs began to move involuntarily, slowly at first, then faster and faster. The pounding of his heart was like a jackhammer in his throat, cutting off his air supply. Like a hunted animal sensing the moment of his demise, Frankie lunged forward with every muscle screaming for release and waited for the sensation of his feet leaving the ground. He cried out in desperation, Now! Now! but his legs faltered. His feet became leaden and he struggled to put one foot in front of the other. It was as if some mysterious force was pushing against him. He dropped to his hands and knees and clawed at the wet cobblestones in a last desperate effort to get away. There was no escape now, only the sensation of waiting for the darkness to be complete.

Brian went flying across the room.

"My God, Frankie! What in the world's gotten into you?" he protested, picking himself up off the floor and rubbing the side of his head. "You're getting crazier by the minute!"

Frankie raised himself up on his elbows and gave him a blank stare.

"What's happening, Bri? What the hell were you doing laying on my floor?"

"I touched your shoulder to wake you up and you exploded on me!"

Slowly, he lowered his head back onto the pillow, trying hard not to disturb the hangover that was threatening to erupt. "Sorry, mate. I had a bad nightmare."

He tried to shut out the dream, but there was something morbidly fascinating about it that drew him back to nibble at its edges. He began to chuckle to himself.

"Know what it's like to fly like a bird?"

"Well, you'd better know how to fly, Scouse, because the captain wants us all in his office in an hour."

He sat himself down on the side of the bed. Frankie gave him a suspicious look.

"You're not kidding, are you?"

"Nope, and the crew is ready for the kill."

"The hell with the crew. I wanna know what the captain wants. Bet it was that mess we left last night."

"Oh, so you do remember," Brian said coyly, getting up and

heading for the door. "We'll meet on deck when you're ready."

He showered and shaved and picked out the best shirt from the dirty laundry basket. He forced down his anxiety, not wanting to display any fear, especially in the captain's presence. The morning air felt crisp when he stepped out on deck. The fog had finally given way to a cold, blue sky.

"Hey, Scouse, over here."

"What a motley looking lot you are," he laughed, joining them at the rail. "Anyone know where the captain hangs out?"

"Yeah, that's easy," Shaun said. "Just follow the blood stains, it'll lead you right to his door."

"Don't be morbid on Christmas Day," Chad shot back.

"Hope the captain remembers that when he's chewing us out," Ron stated wryly.

All five puffed away on their cigarettes like it was going to be their last, then one by one they flicked them over the side and headed for the officers' quarters. They walked single file down the narrow carpeted hallway, slowing only for a longer glance at the beautifully framed paintings adorning each side of the hall.

"Go ahead and knock, Chad," Ron whispered, when they'd piled up at the end door. Chad hesitated.

"Well, go on! He's only a man with a dick and balls, just like us."

They covered their mouths to stifle the nervous laughter that was threatening to get out of control. Finally, Ron gave the door a couple of hard knocks.

"It's open, come on in."

The captain was truly a commanding presence. He stood over six feet tall with broad shoulders and a narrow waist. The starched, white uniform contrasted with the deep tan on his handsome face. His light blue eyes were warm and friendly as he beckoned the lads closer. He positioned himself in front of the large oak desk, settling on the edge of it in order to seem less intimidating. The lads lined up in front of him, aware of their own shabbiness in such elegant surroundings.

"So, you're the five young Englishmen."

It wasn't exactly an indictment, but the lads squirmed a little under the steady gaze.

"I've been following your adventures for the past six months now and found much of it quite amusing, though a little disconcerting at times. Do any of you know why you're here this morning?"

They glanced furtively at each other.

"Yes, sir. We wrecked the mess hall last night and didn't clean it up," Frankie said, trying his hardest to sound apologetic.

"We also destroyed the Christmas tree, sir," Chad added, his voice repentant.

"Yes, son, you're quite correct but that isn't all you destroyed. You also destroyed the Christmas spirit for everyone on board this ship and that's a crime I'm not eager to forgive or overlook."

His words had a stinging, acrimonious ring to them as he stood to his full height and reached for an official looking document laying on top of his desk. The lads stole quick, nervous glances at each other as the realization began to dawn on them that this was no mere slap on the wrist situation. The heavy silence reminded Frankie of his earlier experiences as a child waiting for the judgment that would crush his spirit. When the captain commenced to speak again, he directed his full attention toward Frankie and Brian, completely ignoring the other three.

"In a few days we will be arriving in the United States' port city of Baltimore where you, Mr. Hawkins, and you, Mr. Chadsworth, will be put ashore. I believe this decision to be in the best interest of my ship and also an opportunity for the other young men to make some positive changes in the way they conduct themselves."

Frankie stood staring back in total shock and disbelief, as the captain handed them signed documents of release.

"The American government will only grant a thirty day stay, so be sure to keep in close touch with the Norwegian shipping office. Do you understand that?"

Frankie felt an overwhelming sense of guilt and responsibility for getting Brian into this predicament and wanted desperately to set the record straight.

"Sir, if you don't mind, I think you've gotten Brian here all wrong..." Brian cut him off before he could continue.

"Hey, I'm going with you, Scouse, so let's hang it up and get out of here."

The captain nodded in agreement. "That will be all, gentlemen. Thank you for coming."

Back in Frankie's cabin, they sat pensively smoking one cigarette after another, struggling to come to terms with their pending separation and the uncertain future that lay ahead. After an interminable silence, Ron could stand it no longer.

"Anyone for a game of poker?"

His less than enthusiastic challenge failed to arouse any interest, but it did help break the silence.

"Should be a bloody law against dropping kids off in a strange country," Shaun complained bitterly, kicking at the wall for emphasis.

"Yeah, especially in America," Chad added. "It's like a war zone out there, everybody running around with guns and switchblade knives. Do you know I read somewhere that a bloke gets killed every five minutes in America, can you believe it?"

The concerned look on Brian's face prompted Frankie to jump in and take control of the situation.

"That's a bunch of rubbish, Chad, and you know it. Did we experience anything like that in Detroit? No, we had a great time, didn't we. But what did we see? We seen young lads like us driving nice cars and enjoying life. How many lads in England have ever driven a car, let alone own one! None that we know of, right? We're so used to poverty, we think it's normal, but it isn't. Now, me and Bri, we might even decide to stay in America, right, Bri?"

"That's right, Scouse!" he agreed, beaming. "It's gonna be great, I can feel it." He looked around to see how the others were taking it. The beam faded.

"You're both gonna end up in jail if you keep talking that way," Ron warned, shaking his head in disbelief.

"Yeah, but they'll have to find us first and that won't be easy to do in New York City!"

The train made a wide, sweeping loop and suddenly the New York skyline burst into view like a blurry, majestic aberration, shimmering in the late afternoon sun. They both stood in silence for a long time, totally captivated by its awesome beauty.

"Can you believe it? Can you believe we're really here?" Brian breathed reverently.

"Yeah, it's like a dream, only it's for real. We're going to live in New York City in America!" They turned away from the window and faced each other, astonishment dancing in their eyes at the revelation. Slowly, their faces broke into big grins and Brian punched Frankie in the chest.

"You're crazy, Scouse!"

"I know it. And, now you're crazy, too, you little Cockney!"

When they stepped off the train in Grand Central Station, they were immediately swept along by a surging mass of humanity and deposited unceremoniously onto the sidewalk outside.

The noise and congestion on the wide avenue was unbelievable. Limousines, taxi cabs, delivery trucks, buses, all inching along in one massive gridlock, the discordant sounds of their blaring horns reverberating up the canyons of granite. After watching the frenzied activity of American life for a while, the two lads turned and headed for the Empire State Building, clutching battered suitcases and thirty-seven dollars between them. They wanted to stand on top of the tallest building in the world, and there, to dream the impossible dream.

When they emerged from the New York subway station on the southernmost tip of Manhattan Island, their excited chatter faltered, then stopped altogether as they surveyed their surroundings in the dying embers of twilight.

The Seamen's Mission was a grim, weather-beaten fortress surrounded by crumbling warehouses and vacant lots that were strewn with an assortment of garbage. Frankie took a deep breath and cast a wary eye toward a group of shabby-looking men loitering outside the Mission entrance passing a bottle of wine between them. He pulled his shoulders back and put on a look of defiance before proceeding, his heart thumping wildly.

Where in the hell did our beautiful New York suddenly disappear to, he wondered, stepping over broken bottles and glancing behind to make sure Brian was close by. Across the highway, the Staten Island Ferry blew its horn, sending a plume of black, acrid smoke into the chilly air. The watery eyes and craggy stubbled faces followed the two lads in mute silence as they walked between them and into the Mission's front entrance. The gloomy atmosphere of the once elegant reception area did little to dispel the growing feeling of uneasiness creeping, like icy fingers, up Frankie's back. When they approached the desk, a stoop-shouldered old man brushed the newspaper he'd been reading to one side and gave them a weary smile.

"Now, then, what can I do for you two young men?" His voice was surprisingly pleasant and held the slightest hint of a Scottish brogue.

"Me and my mate, here, would like a room right next to each other," Frankie announced, setting down his suitcase on the threadbare carpet and reaching for his wallet.

"The best I can give you, son, is three rooms apart on the same floor." Frankie looked at Brian for his reaction.

"Well, go ahead, Scouse. I don't want you breathing down my neck all the time, anyway. The separation will do us good," he laughed good-naturedly.

"Okay, see if I care when I hear bloodcurdling screams in the middle of the night. I'll just roll over and go back to sleep."

"That's fair enough, then, isn't it?" Brian retorted.

The old man cleared his throat. "That will be two-fifty a night each or Fifteen dollars if you're staying a full week." Frankie paid for a week, leaving them less than seven dollars to survive on.

The rickety elevator managed to squeak and vibrate them to the third floor where they stepped cautiously into a long, dimly-lit hallway reeking of stale tobacco and body odor. As they made their way surreptitiously down the hall, they stole quick glances into open doors. Each room was little more than a cubicle with a narrow cast-iron bed and a cheap wooden table and chair. The bare light bulb dangling from each ceiling was so dim it cast the room and its' occupant in a colorless gloom. A large black man stood in his open doorway watching the lads coming up the hall. When they were abreast of him his thick lips parted into a toothless grin.

"Hi, I'm Joe," his voice boomed.

They each gave him a perfunctory nod, and kept on walking. Frankie came to his door first, and stood waiting until Brian was safely inside with his door closed. He glanced back down the hall before entering his own room. Joe was still there, grin and all.

He fell on the bed totally exhausted in mind and body, and lay spaced out listening to the bed springs complaining, before drifting into a fitful sleep. He awakened with a start, his mind clawing away at the cobwebs in a desperate effort to identify the intrusion, but there was only silence and darkness. Easing himself off the bed to avoid offending the bed springs again, he turned on the light and looked at his watch. It was seven-thirty. *Still early enough to catch a subway train and get back to the city*, he thought, excitement beginning to surge through his weary body. *Yeah, anywhere on earth would be better than this hell hole.*

When he pulled open his door he almost died of shock. The massive black frame of Joe's body stood there with that same grin plastered all over his ugly face.

"Came to invite ya over for a drink, a nightcap," he announced in a secret whisper, his eyes glancing from side to side to make sure they were alone.

Frankie's mind raced with the instinct of a threatened wildcat, causing every nerve and muscle to throb with the readiness to fight for survival.

"No, I don't need no drink. What I do need is for you to get away from my door," he stated in a firm, controlled voice, calculated to grab Joe's attention without provoking a confrontation. Joe hesitated, stung by this unexpected show of cold indifference, then slowly backed away to allow the lad to step out into the hallway and close his door.

"That nigger's one spooky dude," he hissed, when Brian let him in. "He was standing right there with that stupid grin plastered on his face when I opened my door. Scared the living shit outta me. I bet he's been standing out there listening to me sleeping and drooling at the mouth. In fact, I bet it was his heavy breathing that woke me up in the first place."

"Hey, calm down there, Scouse. Maybe you're getting all worked up for nothing. Maybe he just wants to be your friend."

"And maybe you're full of shit, Bri. Come on, let's get something to eat and go to the pictures."

When they passed by Joe's door, it was closed.

"Probably in there sulking," Frankie whispered, laughing.

Times Square, with its dazzling display of neon lights and endless procession of happy, boisterous people, was just the thing they needed after the discouraging blight of the Mission's environment. With a renewed sense of wonder and fascination, they picked their way through the tightly packed bodies until they spotted a small Italian restaurant that advertised a spaghetti dinner and garlic French bread for ninety-five cents. From their window seat they watched enraptured by the strange, colorful world outside.

"Think it's like this every night, Scouse?"

"Sure beats me. Wouldn't surprise me a bit, though. Seems like everything the Yanks do is bigger than life." The waitress placed a huge mound of spaghetti in front of each of them.

"See what I mean?" he laughed, "That would feed my whole family back in Liverpool!"

"Do you ever get homesick?"

"Sometimes, mostly at night when I can't sleep. Not so much for Liverpool any more, but for my family; me mam, especially. How about you, Bri?"

"No, I was lonely at home; didn't have many friends to speak of. Mum was okay, I guess, but my step-dad spent most of his time in the pub. That was just as well, though, 'cause he could be a real pain when he wasn't sleeping off a drunk."

The revelry outside was picking up momentum now as police on horseback rode the perimeter of the crowd barking orders through a bull horn.

"Something strange going on out there that I can't quite put me finger on," Frankie mused, without taking his eyes from the scene. "People ain't moving or nothing, like they're all waiting for something to happen."

"Do you really think it's possible for us to stay in America, or are we just kidding ourselves?"

Frankie turned from the window, surprise showing in his face at the serious tone and directness of Brian's question.

"I don't honestly know. Sometimes I wonder about that, too, especially back there at the Mission." His voice was low. He wanted to appear strong for Brian's sake, but he could see now that it wasn't being fair to him. They were heading down a blind alley without a workable plan on how to survive. He was afraid, too, but it would hurt too much to admit it.

"We have a month to work it out before we become fugitives, right? If things aren't looking good, we ship out knowing we gave it our best shot."

Brian was thoughtful for a minute before he spoke again.

"We're skint now, and we know we can't work legally, so how do we go about paying the rent for another three weeks and eat every day?"

"Hey, you're looking at a master survivor," Frankie beamed, throwing open his arms in a gesture of daring bravado. "Wanna go to the pictures?"

Brian cracked a lame smile. "I think you're nuts."

"Yeah, that's what you keep telling me," he laughed, as both cleaned off their plates with the last piece of garlic bread, and headed out the door.

Police were busy setting up barricades to stem the flow of traffic into the area, while mounted police began the delicate process of extricating those cars that were caught in the milieu of gyrating kamikazes roaming the street in full battle cry.

When they emerged from the movie theater two hours later, Times Square resembled a world that had gone completely mad. It was now a sea of screaming, chanting, waving bodies, as far as the eye could see. A cacophony of sound from thousands of noisemakers rent the chilly air. It was pandemonium at its best. Slowly, like a dim light being turned up, it began to dawn on Frankie what this was all about. He turned toward Brian who had a sheepish grin on his face and was nodding his head slowly.

"It's true, ain't it? It's New Year's Eve and we didn't even know it!"

"Trust the Yanks to pull a stunt like this," Frankie said, shaking his head in disbelief. "Leave it to the Americans!"

A chorus of voices began a countdown. "Ten, nine, eight...," the noisemakers began to diminish in intensity as more voices joined in the count. "Seven, six, five..." Suddenly, all other sounds ceased as an electrifying crescendo of voices rose in unison to finish the countdown. "Four, three, two, ONE!"

Distant canon boomed a final farewell to the last heartbeat of 1958, as confetti rained down from above. The whole place erupted into an orgy of sound and motion. People embraced each other in a wild show of affection and shouts of "Happy New Year!" Suddenly, the sound of melancholy voices singing *Auld Lang Syne* began to drift like a cloud over the square, stilling the tumult like some magical wand. Some began to weep, while others clung to each other in reflective silence. The singing swelled like a lamenting choir of angels before ending in an outpouring of jubilation.

"What a way to end our first day in America, Bri!"

"Fantastic, ain't it! Did you bag any kisses out there?"

"Yeah, a few, what about you?"

"I didn't do too badly," Brian grinned, puckering up his lips.

Frankie awakened early and tiptoed down the hallway carrying his little bag of toiletries and a towel slung over his shoulder. He peered under the door of each stall just to make sure he was alone, and stood at the crusty window watching the dawn of a new year break over the Hudson River. He could imagine his mother's face when she read the letter he'd sent her yesterday. Her mouth would quiver first, followed by the quiet tears and a good nose blow into her hanky. Then she'd slip the letter into her apron pocket to be read again at a later time.

While sitting on the toilet, he sensed rather than heard someone enter the bathroom. His eyes glanced upward just in time to catch a glimpse of a head disappear from over his stall. He yanked up his pants and tore open the door, only to find the bathroom empty. He shook with anger as he glanced down both ends of the hallway. There was no one anywhere.

"Some sleazy, slimy cockroach was peeking over the stall at me taking a quiet sit, can you believe it?" he shouted, his eyes ablaze with indignation.

Brian had been in a deep sleep when Frankie banged on his door, so his head was still foggy.

"A cockroach?"

"No, not a cockroach, a slimy queer!"

Brian scratched his shaggy mane and sat up in bed. "Did you get a good look at him?"

"No, he was gone in a flash."

"Maybe it was old black Joe."

"No, this one was white, that much I know. Dark, curly hair and weasel eyes."

"Sounds like the one who peeked at me yesterday."

"What? And you didn't tell me?"

"Yeah, mousy face, dark curly hair, bushy eyebrows, and a long, pointy nose."

"Great. I want you to point him out to me next time you see him. Stand guard for me while I take a shower, okay? Then we'll go down and grab some breakfast."

"I thought we were skint!"

"We are, so now we've gotta do some fast talking or starve to death."

The lobby was deserted except for the desk clerk, sleeping soundly with his chair tipped against the wall. The gaunt frame looked pathetic sitting there with arms folded and chin resting on his chest. A knit cap was pulled down low, almost obscuring the sunken eye sockets. Little tufts of hair stuck out from the base of the cap, giving his thin colorless face a clownish appearance.

"Looks like death warmed over," Brian whispered. "The poor bleeder looks like he's on his way out, don't he. Be a shame to wake him."

"Yeah, it would. But, if we don't get some food down us soon, we're gonna look just like him."

Frankie tapped lightly on the desk.

"Excuse me, sir."

His quiet voice elicited absolutely no response at all, so he leaned further over the desk to get a little closer to his subject.

"Excuse me, sir."

Slowly, the head rose off the chest and the face broke into a pained expression as the man's heavy eyelids raised, then halted at half-mast. For a few moments, the glazed eyes held steady, then the head fell forward again onto the chest, quivered a couple of times, then lay still.

"Blimey, I think he's a goner," Brian said, concern evident in his voice.

"No, he's just sleeping off a drunk. Come on, let's get outta here."

It was cold enough inside the Mission, but when they stepped outside, the icy wind blowing off the Hudson River took them completely by surprise. They stood there shivering, undecided whether to go back inside or brave the cold and keep on going. A layer of white frost covered everything in sight, including an old man lying in a fetal position alongside the Mission wall. Brian stooped over to see if he was dead and almost got an empty wine bottle shoved in his face. Frankie couldn't help laughing at the startled look on his face.

"Knock it off, Scouse. It wasn't that funny."

"Sorry, Bri, honest. It just came out, like." He put an arm around his shoulder and they walked off into the cold morning. Three blocks from the Mission, they stopped to peer longingly through the window of a small, cozy-looking coffee shop.

"Oh, don't it look good in there," Frankie remarked, massaging the tips of his fingers and stomping his feet to get some feeling back into them.

"Think he'd mind too much if we just went in and sat for a bit?" Brian asked, referring to the large, balding man standing behind the counter.

"Wouldn't hurt to ask, would it, seeing the place is empty and all," Frankie said, pushing the door open and stepping inside.

"Be right with ya," the man shouted as he reached to turn down the volume on the television set. He grabbed for a coffee pot and two mugs and made his way toward them.

"Sit anywhere you like," he reassured them when he caught their concerned look.

"Got no money, mister. Just came in from the cold," Frankie blurted out. There was a moment's hesitation in the man's stride before he continued on to the table next to the window.

"This is as good a place as any, don't you think?"

They sat down slowly, their eyes sheepishly avoiding his gaze as he filled the two mugs with steaming, black coffee.

"Freeze your tail off in a hurry," he continued, finishing the pouring and glancing out the frosted window. "You guys from around here?"

"We're staying at the Seaman's Mission, but we're both from England," Brian said, reaching for a mug and wrapping his cold hands around it.

"Damn, you're a long way from home. How about some of my famous pancakes?" He saw the quizzical look on their faces.

"Never ate pancakes for breakfast?" They both shook their heads.

"Man, are you in for a real treat."

He returned carrying a plate stacked high with thick, spongy pancakes and two empty plates. "Just eat what you can."

"Thanks, mister. Soon as we get a job, we'll be back to pay you," Frankie said.

"Don't give it another thought. By the way, Gene's the name." They shook hands.

Frankie sat propped up on the bed, staring vacantly at the ugly green wall directly in front of him. An unlit Camel cigarette dangled loosely from the corner of his mouth. He ignored the craving sensation in his body to light it, knowing all too well the agony he would face if there was nothing to smoke when he got up in the morning.

Brian sat at the small, wooden table composing his first letter home since coming to America. Whenever he shifted his weight, the chair would creak unmercifully in the small, quiet confines of the room.

"One more squeak outta that chair, Bri, and I swear it's going through that window!"

Brian flashed an impertinent little grin and went back to writing.

"Almost finished now, so hang on a bit!"

"What do you find to write home about, anyway? That we're starving to death in a flea-bitten, queer-infested hotel surrounded by dying winos?"

"Hell, no! I'm telling them about our little trips to Brooklyn and the Bronx last week and how we laughed and had a smashin' time walking our feet off."

"Oh, good. We wouldn't wanna give them the wrong impression now, would we?"

This was their fourth week at the mission and they were now forced to share the one room, taking turns sleeping on the floor. Graying socks and underwear they'd washed by hand, hung like stiff pieces of cardboard across the bed frame and chair. Because of the coldness of the room, they seldom went to bed without being fully clothed, including wearing wool cap and jacket. Their shabby appearance now differed very little from the homeless people they encountered every day on the street. Their survival now depended on whether they were picked from a pool of men willing to do scab labor for little more than the price of a meal. Today was not their day.

A light tapping on the door brought Brian's head up with a snap. The air grew thick with expectant silence. More light tapping was followed soon after by the sound of feet shuffling back down the hallway. Without a word passing between them, Brian went back to writing and Frankie lit his cigarette, inhaling deeply until he could feel the tension in his body slowly melt away. Like a vulture, Joe was circling closer, bolder, hoping to capture the boys at their weakest moment.

Frankie suddenly swung his legs over the side of the bed. "Let's go out and roll us a queer tonight."

The challenge sounded so corny, Brian started to laugh.

"No, I mean it. All we've had to take from Joe and those 'peek-a-boo's' in the bathroom got me thinking. It's time for a little pay back! What do you say about it?"

Brian still looked amused, but he wasn't laughing any more.

"You can't go around rolling queers like you would a drunk. They're not exactly helpless, you know. Look at Joe, for instance. Can you imagine rolling him? He'd kill both of us with one hand behind his back."

"Nobody's saying we'd pick on a guy like him! We'll find us a little fairy with no balls for a fight."

Brian stood to his feet and began pacing the floor. "You're crazy, Scouse, I keep telling you that."

"Yeah, I know. But, we're also out on our little buns if we don't come up with another two-fifty by noon tomorrow, not to mention the fact that we haven't eaten a thing since the stale doughnut this morning."

Brian kept pacing with a concerned look on his face.

"Bri, I swear, nobody's gonna get hurt in all this. We'll scare the hell out of him and run with the money, that's it."

He finally stopped in front of him.

"And where are we supposed to do all this? Not in this place."

"No, not here. We'll head for Times Square, that's where all the action is, anyway."

"What are we gonna use for the subway?"

"We'll walk, Bri. It won't take us much more than an hour if we move fast."

They tried tiptoeing past Joe's closed door, but a squeak in the floor boards gave them away. The door flew open and a massive black hairy arm extended out, revealing an assortment of gold wrist watches clear up to the elbow.

"Come in, come on in and take your pick." he blubbered, his eyes wide like as excited child.

"You nearly gave us a heart attack, Joe," Frankie protested. "No, we don't need no watch, we both got one."

They turned and walked casually down the hallway and past the elevator, hitting the stairs two at a time.

"Did you see the look on his face, Scouse?"

"Sure as hell did."

When they reached the corner of Forty-second and Ninth Avenue, they made a run for cover beneath the canopy of a penny arcade. A misty rain had fallen steadily all evening, leaving them soaking wet and helpless to ward off the chill that was in the air. They had come to Times Square many times over the past month. Its bright lights and happy people never failed to weave their magic on them and make them feel alive and glad to be in America. But, tonight, it felt strange and indifferent, like somehow they had worn out their welcome and didn't belong here anymore.

"What a great picture we'd make for the family back home. If only they could see us now," Frankie interjected. Brian rolled his eyes upward and blew on his hands.

"Who would ever believe it? You and me standing in the middle of New York like two drowned rats, waiting to be picked up by some strange queer."

"How to succeed in New York in only four weeks. We could write a book about it and make a fortune."

They began to laugh at themselves like a couple of fools, and for a little while it helped to lessen their discouragement. In fact, it felt so good they soon became delirious with laughter. Just about the time they were ready to give up and head back to the Mission, a small fragile-looking man in his late thirties headed straight for them.

This is it, Frankie thought, giving the man the once over. Short and skinny, just the way I envisioned. His heart pounded out of a mixture of fear and excitement.

"Hi, are you boys from around here?" His syrupy voice made Frankie cringe. He looked away, feeling disgusted with the idea of talking to him.

Brian wasn't prepared to take the lead, either, and stumbled badly. "Er, yeah, kind of from around here, I mean, we've been here for a bit, yeah."

"You sound...are you really English? You do sound English," he said, nodding his head with a pleased look on his face. He turned to look at Frankie.

"I would imagine you are, too. You certainly look English, what with all that gorgeous curly hair and all."

Now Frankie felt nauseated. The thought had never crossed his mind that in order to sucker the guy into believing they were available, there would have to be some kind of friendly dialogue between them. He cleared his throat a couple of times and shifted his weight from one foot to the other. "Yeah, I'm English, too."

"That's nice. That's real nice," he crooned. "Would you boys be interested in joining me for a drink?"

"Yeah, sure, that sounds good, don't it, Bri?"

They stood nodding at each other, looking totally unconvincing.

"Good, that settles it. I'm Gordon. My friends call me Gordy for short."

Frankie barely touched the limp hand that was offered him. Gordon seemed oblivious to the disdainful look. Instead, he grew more animated as he twirled around to flag down a taxi.

"You'll just love Greenwich Village."

Frankie settled into the soft leather seat and stared abstractly out the car window, leaving Brian to contend with Gordon's incessant chatter about life in the Village.

Within a few miles of Times Square, the taxi began a slow cruise through an old section of the city inhabited by a strange assortment of people dressed like character actors out of an old nineteenth century play. The festive sounds of music and boisterous laughter percolated out onto the busy streets from crowded coffee houses and bars that were interspersed with quaint storefronts and cramped apartments. This was the world of the Bohemians Frankie had heard about, but he was in no mood to enjoy any of it right now. His wet clothing irritated his skin as he stepped out of the warm interior of the taxi and followed after Gordon and Brian down a flight of stairs. The Cellar was cozy but crammed with people all shouting at each other in order to be heard.

"Don't look so disgusted, Scouse," Brian quipped, when Gordon left them alone to talk with a man further down the bar. "This is all your idea, remember."

"Yeah, I know. I didn't count on all this crap first."

Brian spotted Gordon and his friend staring over at them in animated conversation. "Quick, smile back at them like we're having a good time," he said, his face breaking into a cheeky grin.

Frankie's grin was more like a pitiful grimace. "We're being looked over like a couple of cheap tarts," he hissed, through clenched teeth, while still maintaining the grin.

Gordon sauntered back and ordered another round of drinks.

"Got a friend over there who'd like to meet you guys."

Frankie bristled at the suggestion.

"Not this time, Gordy," he heard himself say. "It's time we got outta these wet clothes, though, before we catch a case of pneumonia."

Gordon's eyes lit up at the suggestion and he gulped down his drink.

"My place isn't far from here; it'll only take us a few minutes to walk there."

He led the way up a steep flight of slippery, wooden stairs to the back door of his apartment. They passed through a small kitchenette and dining nook to a room with a large, king-sized bed in it. The open floor plan gave the small apartment the appearance of being larger than it really was.

They both watched in stunned silence, as Gordon stripped off his clothes and jumped into bed without so much as a word being spoken. Frankie quickly retrieved a carving knife he had spotted on their way through the kitchen and casually walked up to the side of the bed where Gordon lay. He grabbed him by the throat with his left hand and held the knife inches from his face.

"Don't make a move and you won't get hurt."

A horrible look of fear lay frozen on Gordon's face as he stared at the knife through glazed, unblinking eyes.

"Brian, get his wallet. He stuck it in the top drawer under the window."

There was no sound or movement from behind, so Frankie took a quick glance over his shoulder. Brian stood transfixed with his mouth partly open, his eyes staring blankly at Frankie's back.

"The top drawer, hurry, we ain't got much time!" he commanded.

Gordon made an unexpected lunge for the knife, but Frankie

pulled it away, giving him a hard slap across the mouth with his left hand. He tried to grab Gordon's throat again, but he squirmed his head away and grabbed Frankie's right wrist with both hands and began to wrestle for the knife.

Oh, my God, this is getting outta hand, he thought, doubling his left fist and exploding it into the man's right temple. For a fleeting moment, he loosened his hold on Frankie's wrist, but immediately grabbed onto it again. Now it was Frankie's turn to panic. The knife was only meant to be a scare tactic, so there would be no need to use physical force, but Gordon was fighting for his life and doing a good job of it.

"I got it, I got it. Let's get outta here!" Brian pleaded, not realizing Frankie was desperately trying to get away, but couldn't.

Gordon started to scream, "Larry, help me! Larry, Larry, help!"

He sent another left into Gordon's open mouth, but it had no effect. Gordon was in a frenzied fight for survival, and he was fighting will all his might. He yanked with all the strength he could muster to get his arm free, but only managed to pull Gordon right out of the bed and onto the floor.

"Brian, get moving, get out the door," he shouted, over the incessant screams of Gordon calling for Larry to come rescue him.

After what seemed like an eternity, he reached the open door that Brian had disappeared through, dragging Gordon along with him. Gordon slammed the door shut with his shoulder and leaned his body against it, cutting off his escape. Frankie dropped the knife on the floor in order to use both hands to wrestle him away from the door, but he lunged down for the knife. Frankie brought his knee up with a sharp jerk, catching Gordon high on the forehead, sending him staggering backward out of control. He hit a chair and toppled over against the table. Frankie pulled the door open, almost colliding with the next door neighbor coming to help his friend. He pushed with both hands into the man's chest and sent him reeling backward into the open doorway of the man's apartment, then skipped and slid his way down the stairs, holding onto the banister with both hands until his feet hit the bottom.

Brian stood trembling a block away, his mind incapable of making a decision whether to keep on running or go on back and help his mate. He was afraid of what he might find if he went back there.

"Run, Brian, you should've kept on going, you dumb shit!" Frankie shouted, as he ran toward him, taking great gulps of air into his open mouth. They were running side by side now, zigzagging from one street to another.

"You didn't use the knife, did you?"

"Hell, no! The stupid bleeder tried to do me in with it!"

Their breathing was too labored to keep up the banter, so they fell silent, each listening to the sound of their own footsteps bouncing off the wet ground and echoing ahead of them into the deserted streets. Whenever they heard the sound of a car or saw headlights approaching they would take the nearest cross street to get out of the way. There was no doubt in Frankie's mind the police were out scouring the city in search of them. They were lost. Nothing looked familiar to them now. In their haste to put distance between them and the crime scene, they had lost all sense of direction. By pure luck, they happened onto a subway entrance and descended into it, glad to find cover away from the exposure of the open streets.

The platform was deserted, silent, except for the sound of their labored breathing. Frankie glanced at his watch, then up at the stairs, expecting any second to see a rush of uniforms descend with guns drawn. It was one fifteen and no way of knowing if there was a train due or even running this late at night. Brian stood with his hands in his jacket, hugging his body against the cold, staring across the track. A distant rumble could be heard coming from the dark interior of the tunnel; or was it just a car passing somewhere overhead? Frankie glanced at the stairs again; his ears straining to identify the sound. The platform began to vibrate gently beneath his feet. Another anxious glance at the stairs, then at the tunnel where a faint light began to penetrate the darkness.

"Thank God, it's a train; we're gonna make it."

The rumble became more distinct, the vibrations more acute as a searchlight burst through the final stretch of the tunnel.

"Hurry, please hurry," he urged, as the train thundered into view, sending carriages flashing past his face at a decreasing speed. When it came to a stop, he gave one last glance in the direction of the stairs before stepping on board. They sat slumped down in the seat, their heads resting against the window in back of them. Brian had his eyes closed. Frankie stared up at the ceiling, lost in a tangled web of memories. He couldn't shake off the image of Gordon's face; the terror in those bulging eyes, the thin lips, pulled back and frozen in a horrible grimace.

How could I have done that to another human being? He felt the panic Gordon must have felt, and felt the shame of it wash over him. *But, why was he so stupid as to fight me with a knife only inches from his face? He was brave, that's it. Very brave! He was fighting for his life because he had no idea I never intended to use it. God, was he brave! What would I have done if it was me laying there? I don't know. I honestly don't know. And I thought he was a wimp. Probably beat the shit outta me without the knife.*

He looked at Brian's handsome young face, more peaceful now than when they first came aboard. *Just a nice kid until he met me. Now he's an accessory to armed robbery. He shuddered to think they could end up in an American jail.*

"We'll sign up first thing in the morning," he sighed. "It's time we shipped out."

Brian opened his eyes and glanced sideways at him, nodding his head in slow affirmation.

"How much money did we end up with?"

Brian dug into his coat pocket and produced a crumpled five dollar bill and two ones. Frankie stared at the money, an incredulous expression mirrored on his face.

"I nearly killed a man for seven lousy dollars!"

It was late afternoon when Frankie arrived back at the Mission. He stood waiting for the elevator, still angry over the raw deal he'd just gotten. *Three dollars for a whole day's work*, he thought, spitting into the cylinder ashtray sitting next to the elevator doors. *The fat little Jew. No wonder they got a bad name.*

"I only pay for time you work on the load," the man had said.

"Yeah, but the load happened to be in New Jersey, mister, and that's a two-hour ride each way!"

"Don't pay out good money for sitting on your ass in my truck and taking a joyride, son."

The moment he stepped off the elevator, he sensed something was amiss. Joe stood half-way out of his doorway wringing his hands in nervous anticipation, a glassy faraway look in his eyes.

"He's gone," he announced in a breathless whisper. "Packed up and left over an hour ago."

Frankie stood with a blank look on his face, trying to figure out what the hell he was talking about.

"Your friend, he's gone. He moved out," Joe reiterated, trying hard to conceal his excitement.

A feeling of deep sadness and despair began to wash over Frankie, leaving him almost too weak to move. Slowly, mechanically, he pushed his way past Joe and unlocked the door, and sat down heavily on the side of the bed. It was a full five minutes before he realized there was a hastily written note pinned to the door for him.

"Frankie, had to leave in a hurry. Ship leaving at five, couldn't wait for you any longer. Take care of yourself. Brian."

He glanced at his watch. *Five after. Too late to do anything about it now.* He sighed and threw the crumpled note at the wall. *Would've been nice to at least say good-bye.* No sooner had he said it, a thought popped into his head.

"I've never seen the day a ship left on time. Ever!" The last word sprang out of his mouth, setting his body into motion. He yanked open the door and stopped dead in his tracks. Only inches away from his face was the startled, somewhat bewildered-looking face of old black Joe, whose rubbery lips were babbling incoherently about why he was standing there.

"I want you to leave me alone, Joe," Frankie said, in a cold, deliberate tone. "I ain't no queer and I don't like queers, especially nigger queers!"

He'd caught Joe completely off guard and left stammering to find words to reciprocate.

"You, you little punk sonofabitch! You can't talk to me that way," he fumed.

Frankie pushed by him and walked briskly down the hallway. He wanted to run, run as fast as his legs would go, but that would have given Joe the impression he was running scared, and he wasn't. He felt no fear. His mind was totally preoccupied with getting to Brian before their lives became separated, probably forever.

The old Scotsman at the front desk greeted him cheerily. "Hello, Frankie. And what can I do for you this fine evening?"

"Scotty, I need to find a ship in a hurry. All I know is it's leaving at five. Can you help me, please?"

Scotty rummaged under the desk and brought out the New York Times, and quickly located the shipping page.

"No name or anything, Frankie?" he asked, his eyes following the progress of his finger down the page. "Here we are," he exclaimed, before Frankie could answer. "There's three leaving at five. Two Yankee boats and a Norwegian ship."

"That's it, Scotty, the Norwegian ship, that's it! Write down the information for me. Do you think three dollars is enough for a taxi?"

"Don't take a cab at rush hour, man," he cautioned, scribbling away on a piece of paper. "Here, take the subway and follow these directions."

It was ten minutes to six when he finally hit the dock gates. He stopped to catch his breath and stood for a long moment staring at the Norwegian flag flapping in a stiff wind. He blinked back the tears before stepping cautiously up the gangway. An officer, dressed in a white uniform and cap, broke off a conversation with a couple of deck hands in order to confront his arrival.

"Just stopping for a minute, sir. Didn't get to say good-bye to me mate, Brian."

"Ah, the young Englishman. Try the mess hall, second door on the right. Don't stay too long."

"Thank you, sir. I won't."

Brian sat alone at a small table facing the door, his hands caressing a mug of hot coffee in front of him. Crew members stood in small groups in animated conversation, waiting for the word to come in that the ship was ready to cast off. He glanced up when Frankie came through the door. For a fleeting moment, his brain refused to respond to the face grinning back at him. Slowly, hesitantly, his body eased itself out of the chair, his eyes fastened onto the familiar face in front of him.

"What..."

"Hi, there, you little Cockney. You didn't think I'd let you get away without saying good-bye, did you?"

The crew fell silent as they watched the two Englishmen attack each other, whooping and hollering and feigning punches to the body and the head.

"How's the coffee?"

"Horrible! Here, you can sip on mine."

They sat across from each other, Brian staring at the mug of coffee, Frankie trying to read the mystical look on his countenance. "You don't like it here, do you," he deducted.

Brian leaned closer. "Did you get a good look at the ship when you came aboard?"

"Yeah, a little rusty on the outside. Needs a good paint job."

"Well, the whole dam ship's like that, dirt and rust everywhere." He stopped and glanced around to make sure he wasn't being overheard. "Not a Norwegian among the lot, except for the officers. All foreigners, they are!"

"Do you want off?"

Brian's serious face broke into a mischievous grin, causing Frankie to chuckle with relief.

"Then what the hell are we waiting for? It's time to hit the road again!"

The gray granite building housing the Immigration Service blended with the slate gray of the threatening skies above it. A mixture of sleet and rain had fallen for much of the early morning, leaving the streets very slippery.

"Now remember, Bri. We stayed because we love America and want to be a part of this great country, okay?"

The light changed and they stepped off the curb as a car rounded the corner, sending a spray of dirty slush all over their newly pressed jeans.

"Why can't we just talk normal instead of putting on a show?" Brian protested, while Frankie shook a fist at the passing car.

"'Cause we gotta impress them. This is it. We only got one shot at it."

A uniformed officer stood waiting for the elevator when they walked through the revolving door.

"Excuse me, sir, we wanna give ourselves up," Frankie announced.

The officer looked them over with an amused smile. "You'll need the fourth floor, same as me."

He ushered them into a small office and left them alone, returning with three cups of coffee and a plate of cookies on a tray.

"Help yourselves, gentlemen, and when you feel comfortable, you can go ahead and tell me the whole story."

His disarming manner made it easy for them to open up and share their dreams, along with the hardships and disappointment they'd endured since coming to America. He listened attentively for over an hour before excusing himself and leaving the room. There was a long silence before Brian spoke.

"Seems like a decent sort of bloke, don't he?"

"Yeah, let's hope he's not leading us down the garden path to the slaughter house! I almost think we said too much, don't you?"

"No, I felt it went okay. We gotta trust somebody, sometime."

They fell silent again until the officer stuck his head in the door.

"Can you boys make it back between one and one-thirty? The judge would like to take a look at you then."

"You mean we ain't under arrest, like?" Frankie asked, a little puzzled with the easy way things were being handled.

"No, nothing like that," he laughed. "Just be sure and show up."

***

The judge entered the chamber from a side door clutching papers in the crook of his right arm, his left hand deftly buttoning up his flowing black robe. On the wall behind his elevated desk, an impressive bronze eagle stared down at him with black, piercing eyes, its sharp talons and extended wings delineating a pending battle.

"Just try to relax," the officer friend had said, when seating them in the front row of wooden, high-back chairs. He'd left right after that and never returned. It was just them and the judge now.

How can anyone relax at a time like this, Frankie thought.

After reading the report in front of him, the judge removed his glasses and settled back in his chair in a contemplative mood. He studied the two faces for a few moments then drifted back to the open pages on his desk. Finally, he sat up straight, shuffling the papers together.

"You two gentlemen seem to have made quite an impression on Captain Shoreland. His recommendation is to allow you both to stay and become productive members of these United States. Is that what you want?"

"Yes, sir!" they said in unison, their heads still nodding long after their answer.

"I have a great respect for Captain Shoreland's professional intuitive insight. Whenever there's a lack of documented information, as in this case, I tend to rely on his good judgment. Pending a fuller background check, you are now free to engage in the normal pursuits accorded a permanent resident status. Please inform this agency of any change of address and good luck to both of you.

It was such an unbelievable turn of good fortune, it staggered Frankie's imagination, as he sat rooted to his chair. What if they hadn't turned themselves in today, at the very moment Captain Shoreland stood waiting for the elevator to arrive. How different the outcome may have been on another day, with another man. On their way out, he stopped at the information counter to inquire about Captain Shoreland.

"He left a few minutes ago and won't be back today," the blonde lady said, chewing madly on a piece of gum.

"Can you give him a message for me?"

"Sure." She held the pen at the ready while he searched for something profound to say.

"Tell him 'thanks,' from Frankie and Brian."

"Just, thanks?"

"Yeah, thanks."

It was just before closing when they walked in on Gene counting the day's receipts at the open till.

"Is it too late for some of your delicious pancakes, Gene?" Brian sang out.

"I just got through cleaning my grill, you dirty limeys," he growled, without taking his eyes from the stack of bills in his hand.

"Go take a seat and I'll be with you in a sec."

He brought over two mugs of coffee and sat down.

"Pancakes'll be ready in a minute."

"I thought you just got through cleaning the grill," Brian said, wrinkling his nose at him.

"So, tonight you get clean pancakes, for Chris' sake. What are you two looking so happy about?"

"We're 'permanent aliens' now, Gene! Frankie said, his eyes and mouth wide open in mock surprise.

"I thought there was something strange about you guys. What planet?"

"I'm not paying for burnt pancakes," Brian said.

Gene jumped up and headed for the counter. "Sounds like you got some money for a change," he shot back. When he brought their pancakes and refilled their coffee mugs, he sat down again.

"Now, what's this about aliens?"

Between bites, they told him the whole fantastic story.

"I wouldn't believe it was possible in a million years," he murmured, clearing the plates away.

"Just think, Gene. We'll be able to get a real job and pay you back for all the free meals. You'll be rich!" Brian said.

"Nah, don't talk about payback to me. The moment I saw you guys on that cold New Year's morning, I knew you were just a couple of nice kids down on your luck."

"You're gonna make us cry, talking like that, Gene," Frankie said.

"Then, go do it in the street and let me close this place so I can get out of here!"

43

Kate struggled to maneuver the pram over the rippled snow that had turned rock hard during the night. Every few steps, she stopped to catch her breath and to rearrange the shopping bags that were threatening to topple over from the jarring motion. She spotted the postman coming out of the first block and hurried to catch up with him.

"Anything for me, Charlie?" she shouted, fighting for every breath. He gave her a knowing smile and wet the tips of his fingers with his tongue.

"Well, now, let's take a gander and see, Kate," he said, rummaging through the canvas shoulder bag. He knew exactly where the letter was, but he relished the suspense his stalling created.

"Ah, here's the little bugger, girl. All the way from America, no less."

Her face radiated with pleasure as she took it from his hand.

"Thank you, Charlie."

"I can give you a hand with the pram up the stairs," he called after her. But she didn't answer. She could already see herself making a nice fire and sitting in front of it with a cup of tea to read her letter.

Dear Mam,
I got your letter and I must admit it made me a bit homesick. I'm a real Yank now, Mam. Me and me mate went before a judge last week and He let us stay for good. Can you believe that? Thought we was a couple of nice lads, he said. And, that's not all. We already got a job at the swankiest hotel in America. The Waldorf Astoria. You will never believe how posh it is. It's even got gold taps in every lavatory. All day

long we take rich people and film stars up and down in the lift. It's a smashing job. I want you to be proud of me 'cause I'm doing good and I'll come home someday and buy you the biggest house in Liverpool with a maid and a butler, how does that sound?
I love you. Your son, Frankie. P.S. Notice my new address on top.

She lay her head back against the overstuffed chair and closed her eyes, wondering if she had the heart to write and tell him David was locked up in Menlove Avenue Remand Center with little brother Allen not too far behind. *No, just let him be at peace in his new land*, she thought, her mind drifting back to the memory of their last good-byes. The nagging premonition that she was seeing him for the last time was even stronger now. The warmth of the fire soothed and lulled her troubled mind into rest...

...She was running with childlike abandon through the lush green fields adorned with summer flowers; her long, dark silken hair caressing her flushed and laughing face. The sweet sounds of birds singing, carried on the warm summer breeze, drifted and eddied around her like a halo of music...

"Well, just look at the cut of this one, why don't you," Dorothy proclaimed, in playful mirth. "Like the Queen of Sheba all decked out in front of the fire."

Sarah joined her at the side of her mother's chair.

"Living a life of Riley since we left home, aren't you, Mam?" she said, trying to keep a straight face. Kate grimaced and opened her eyes.

"Was having a luvly dream until you two sods came along."

Dorothy's two year old Rachael pushed the pram around the kitchen with Sarah's one year old Paul still sitting in it, almost decapitating the poor lad beneath the heavy kitchen table. His pathetic wails filled the room as Sarah rushed to rescue him. Little Rachael soon joined in the chorus when her well-padded behind became the focus of her mother's attention. Kate took Paul from his mother and laid him on her breast, stroking him tenderly until he lay quiet. Rachel looked on with downcast eyes and quivering little mouth in a show of quiet contrition.

"There's room for you too, Rachael," Kate whispered.

Rachael broke into a big grin as she scampered to climb on Nanny's lap.

The red and blue envelope slipped to the floor by Sarah's feet and she picked it up and handed it to her mother.

"Is it from Frankie, Mam?"

"Yes, girl."

"Would you read it to us?" she asked, sitting on the arm of the chair and beckoning Dorothy to come closer. Before Kate had a chance to begin, the front door flew open and four hungry, tousle-headed kids came rushing through.

"What's for dinner, Mam?" Daisy asked, eying the empty table with suspicion while slipping the coat off her plump frame.

Anna, with her Shirley Temple ringlets and shy smile, volunteered to run down to the chippy.

"No, I've got the dinner in, girl," Kate said. "Come over by the fire and warm yourself."

"Now, let's all be quiet while me mam reads Frankie's letter from America." Dorothy insisted, beckoning Colleen and Taylor, the two youngest, to come closer.

After Kate finished reading, there was a long silence. The clock on the mantel piece sounded loud in the stillness. Daisy leaned close to her mother's ear.

"Is it time to start the dinner, Mam?" she whispered.

Kate nodded, but made no move to get up out of the chair.

"Mam, is Frankie coming back?" Anna asked.

She looked into the cherubic angel face and smiled.

"Of course, he's coming back. Be a good little girl and set the table for me."

Central Park was alive with the promise of spring. Birds chirped and fluttered among the canopy of blossoming trees and pecked beneath the budding flower beds in search of the early worm. The shrill voices of children at play echoed in the still air, while couples strolled arm in arm, their faces reflecting the inner peace and serenity that comes with the magical awakening of spring. Vendors were busy setting up their hot dog stands in anticipation of the Sunday crowds that would soon converge on the park after church services.

From a park bench, Frankie watched the activities with a mixture of pleasure and fascination. It never ceased to amaze him how very American everything was and he loved it all. Brian came back with two hot dogs and offered him one.

"Try it with mustard for a change," he said, sitting down.

"No fried onions?"

"No, they told me it was too early."

They ate in silence as they watched two teenagers throw a baseball back and forth; the hard ball making a dull thud each time it was caught in the oversized leather mitts.

"Took Douglas up on the service elevator yesterday, do you know him, Bri?"

"Yeah, fat Doug, the waiter. So what about him?"

"Offered us a job waiting tables in some Pennsylvania night club. Said he'd train us when we got there."

"Why bother with us when there's plenty of good waiters at the Waldorf to choose from?"

"Something about the new owners wanting to open with an all English crew. I guess Doug's having a tough time recruiting that many for him."

They got up and walked slowly along the dirt path, stepping aside for a couple of joggers and a stream of rowdy teenagers in a bicycle race.

"What about Kim and Maureen?" Brian asked, once the path was clear for them to resume walking.

"You're not soft on Maureen, are you?"

Brian gave his usual little chuckle. "No, not likely. When do we leave?"

"I'll race you to the stables. Last one there pays for the ponies!"

"That ain't fair and you know it! My legs are shorter!"

"I'll give you to the count of three..." Before he could finish, Brian was off and running.

They stepped off the train in Trenton, New Jersey, and stood waiting expectantly for someone to come by and claim them. Within minutes, the outdoor platform was deserted and silent, except for the hollow sound of a woodpecker nearby. A little after eight, and already the temperature had reached into the seventies under a cloudless blue sky. Frankie couldn't remember a morning more perfect than this one. The warm breeze caressed his upturned face and he inhaled deeply of the fragrance coming from the profusion of pink and white blossoms on the trees. He felt a sudden rush of well-being, a youthful vibrancy that he remembered experiencing many times as a child running free. Years of heaviness that he'd been unaware of, lifted from his shoulders and he became almost giddy from the joy that filled his chest.

"Are you alright, Scouse?"

"Never felt better in me life," he answered, still looking to something beyond the endless landscape of trees.

"Remember the Liverpool family we had dinner with in the Bronx? Came over seventeen years ago and never left New York. Can you imagine that? Coming to a country like America and settling for the Bronx! There's so much out there to see; so much I want to experience before settling anywhere. How about you?"

Before Brian could respond, an old World War II army jeep tore into the gravel parking lot, sending up a plume of fine dust as it came to an abrupt halt near the platform. Three young lads wearing sun glasses and muscle tee shirts, sat grinning back at them from the front seat, like something out of a Hollywood movie.

"Sorry we're late there, mates," the blonde driver said, more in the way of a greeting than an apology. "Been waiting long?"

"No, just a bit," Frankie responded, as he and Brian tossed the battered suitcases into the back seat and climbed in. His body was tingling with the sensation that he was about to embark on a whole new adventure that would somehow change his destiny.

"Danny's the name," the driver shouted back, while maneuvering the jeep in reverse. "Sitting next to me is Tony, from the great city of Sheffield, and next to him is Fagan, from London. Can you imagine anyone in their right bloody mind naming a baby, Fagan, for Chris' sake?"

They all laughed good-naturedly as the jeep pitched forward, hitting Highway 29 without regard to the oncoming traffic.

Over the raucous sounds of Jerry Lee Lewis' *'Great Balls O' Fire,'* which Danny had cranked up on the radio, Frankie and Brian introduced themselves.

"A Scouser and a Cockney as friends?" Fagan gasped in mock disbelief, staring from one to the other, "and no scars to show for it?"

"They're all internal," Brian quipped, throwing Frankie a sideways glance and flinching as though fearing retribution.

"Yeah, you better move, you little Cockney. If it wasn't for me, you'd be back in foggy London pushing a handcart!"

Highway 29 followed the meandering Delaware River which separates Pennsylvania and the State of New Jersey. The lushness and serenity of the country on both sides of the river was in sharp contrast to the jarring rock'n'roll music coming from the radio.

"Right over there is where George Washington crossed the river to finally beat us," Danny shouted in disgust. "But, now we're back to reclaim it, ain't that right, lads?"

A chorus of 'yeah's rang out as the front seat erupted into a frenzy of flailing arms and stomping feet. Frankie hadn't a clue as to what all the fuss was about. He tried to imagine what America would be like today if Washington hadn't succeeded. He shuddered at the thought.

They passed through the small working-class town of Lambertville and crossed a wooden bridge that spanned the Delaware River into the sleepy town of New Hope, Pennsylvania. The handful of tree-shaded streets looked so peaceful nestled there beside the river. Thick forested hills and patchwork farmland surrounded it like a beautiful painting.

On impulse, Frankie touched Danny lightly on the shoulder, "Can you pull over for a minute?"

Danny found a shady spot beneath an oak tree and glanced back. "What is it, mate?"

"You're driving too fast," he lied, as he jumped out and walked slowly back toward the bridge. He didn't really know why he needed to get out and walk. He was acting on emotions he could never begin to explain. All he knew was he wanted to experience it at close range, the incredible peace, the stillness. Whatever it was, he wanted to capture and hold on to this moment in time, when he felt truly at peace with himself and the world around him.

***

The house lights dimmed until they faded out completely, leaving the beautiful dining room bathed in soft candlelight that danced like miniature campfires atop each of the tables. The Maitre d' walked slowly down the row of waiters standing stiffly at attention. His face showed no expression, but his dark eyes were alive with movement, taking in every detail of the maroon jackets and cummerbunds, starched white shirts, black bow ties, and black slacks perfectly creased. He came face to face with Frankie and Brian, and paused. His brow furrowed slightly, as though he needed to say something, then he moved away without a word being spoken. Frankie let out a sigh of relief. He didn't want anybody changing their mind this late in the game. Doug had tried to break the news real easy to them earlier that afternoon.

"Look, you guys," he'd said, putting an arm around each of their shoulders and walking them out to the pool side. "You've done great, better than I expected, but six days just wasn't enough time to make topnotch waiters out of you two. Did you get a look at the reservations for the opening tonight? Christ, we got movie stars, Broadway actors, politicians, millionaires, even got mob bosses showing up at the door tonight!"

"What're you trying to say, Doug? We don't have a job?" Frankie had asked, removing Doug's arm from around his shoulder.

"Oh, no! The Maitre d' wants to ease you in, like. Start you off as busboys for a while, 'til you get the hang of things. We'll all pitch in a percentage of the tips so you'll make out okay."

Brian had started laughing about that time, causing Doug to look from one to the other, a little bemused, "Am I missing something, here?"

"Tell him, Frank," Brian teased.

"Tell him what?"

"Tell him we were ready to run last night because we were so bloody scared."

"Brian, we were just kidding around."

"Like hell, we were! We even started packing, 'til we realized we had no money to go anywhere with!"

It was Frankie's turn to laugh now, as he remembered the many Laurel and Hardy-like skits they'd performed for each other, depicting their inevitable failure on opening night. The wobbling trays of hot food; the rubbery legs as their feet became entangled; the extended fingers clutching after trays of food that were finding their own way toward elegant faces frozen in horrified repose! Still chuckling to himself, he lowered his head in mock contrition.

"It's true, Doug, we got to thinking of all the things that could go wrong and we started to panic."

Doug was genuinely relieved. "Hang in there. We'll make waiters out of you two in good time." he promised.

Frankie's hand trembled slightly as he reached over to fill the lady's water glass. The six people seated at the table abruptly stopped talking. He was sure they were watching every move he made. Doug came from behind and whispered urgently over his shoulder,

"Clear dirty dishes at table seven right away, and don't forget the coffee refills for table nine."

The lady put a hand on Frankie's wrist and gave it a gentle squeeze.

"Be a nice young man and tell the cocktail waitress to make mine a dry martini instead of the champagne."

"Scouse, table four's still waiting for their rolls and butter, please," Tony called out softly, as he breezed by laden with a tray of food.

"Ma'am, we got three cocktail waitresses. Do you know which one took your order?"

She looked thoughtful for a moment. "Charles, did you get a good look at our waitress?"

"Be lying like hell if I said I didn't, honey." he snickered, looking around the table for approval.

Brian grabbed Frankie's arm and pulled him aside.   "Maitre d' wants another table brought in and set up for four!"

His eyes scanned the room with a look of helpless futility. "They're packed in like sardines already! Where're we supposed to put them?"

Doug skidded by holding a large tray of food deftly on the palm of his right hand, his face flushed and damp with perspiration.

"Table seven," he announced with an incredulous stare, "it's still got dirty dishes, and I'm ready to serve them desert!"

"Well, me 'arts bleedin' fer ya, Doug," Frankie mimicked, with an exaggerated mixture of Liverpool and Cockney. "The boss just ordered another table brought in."

Doug wiped his brow with the back of his free hand. "My, God," he mumbled, as he turned and ran.

"Waiter, waiter."

"We're not waiters, sir," Frankie answered, easing himself through a narrow opening between two tables.

"Then why the hell are you dressed like that?"

"That's him, that's our waiter over there," the lady sitting next to him shouted in triumph. Frankie and Brian closed the door behind them and stood staring at the moon's reflection in the swimming pool. The din inside sounded muffled and distant in the cool night air.

"Like a madhouse in there, ain't it?" Frankie chuckled half-halfheartedly, as he put the lit match to his cigarette. "Almost lost it a few times tonight. Just not used to people ordering me about like this."

The door opened behind them and they both turned in surprise. The upper portion of the Maitre d' was poking out of it with a look of utter exasperation on his dark face.

"What are you guys doing out here?" he scowled, articulating every word.

"Where's the goddam table I asked for?"

"Right here, sir. We were looking for the best one to use," Brian lied, wiping the damp table with the palm of his hand. Frankie flicked his lit cigarette into the pool, in order to help Brian carry the table inside. Then it dawned on him what he had just done. He glanced at the Maitre d', hoping somehow he'd missed seeing it. He hadn't.

"I think I just done meself in," he whispered to Brian as he picked up his end of the table. The Maitre d' held open the door for them. His icy stare needed no interpretation.

The chorus girls in skimpy outfits gave their final bows and exited the stage. The stage lights dimmed for a moment, creating a silent expectancy in the audience. Bing Crosby's four sons bounded onto the stage, accompanied by a long drum roll that grew in intensity, along with an array of flashing, pulsating lights.

The Fountainhead Night Club erupted into a tumultuous round of applause, as people stood to their feet in a show of affection and respect for the legend of the Crosby name. There was to be no movement at all by staff during the main attraction. Frankie leaned his weary body against the back wall and watched the show, mentally preparing himself for the massive cleanup that would be needed in time for the second showing and a whole new crowd of demanding people.

46

Frankie eased himself into a sitting position on the couch and waited for the pain in his head to subside before attempting to open his eyes. A warm sun squeezed itself through the cracks in the Venetian blinds, revealing the debris scattered about the spacious living room. It was a scene that had become all too familiar since the success of the club's opening almost three months ago.

Bloody suicide, it is, he muttered, as his hand reached for a cigarette. He knew it was going to taste lousy, but he lit it anyway. Someone was moving around upstairs. A toilet flushed, a girl's muffled giggles, then silence. He took a few drags on the cigarette before crushing it into the overflowing ashtray. His elbow inadvertently knocked over an empty whiskey bottle, sending it clattering along the coffee table and into two half-empty glasses of beer. Everything landed on the carpet with a crash. He held his breath, hoping whoever was upstairs wouldn't come down to investigate the sudden racket he'd created; he didn't want to see or talk to anybody right now. All he wanted was to stop this madness; get off the merry-go-round and get back to living a normal life, whatever that was.

Must be at least three chorus girls still in the house, he thought, surveying the women's garments draped over chairs and laying on the floor. *The rest must have gone to the diner for a late breakfast.*

While taking a hot shower, he began to think about the oriental girl, Kimmi, and how she always seemed to slip away unnoticed whenever a party was in progress. Her sweet mannerisms and quiet nature intrigued him at times, though he'd never gone out of his way to get to know her better. He and the rest of the lads from the club were more enamored by the flirtatious and carefree natures of the other seven chorus girls to give Kimmi much attention. Now, he felt a little guilty for it. The more he thought about her, the more his body came alive. He bounded out of the shower and toweled himself hard and fast, humming and singing a tune by the Everly Brothers, *'Wake up little Kimmi, wake up.'*

He slipped quietly out the back door and crossed the well-manicured lawn that separated the house from the row of gray bungalows. The warm sun felt good on his revitalized body as he stood waiting for the door to open. Kimmi opened the door and immediately closed it half-way. The surprised look on her face left him wondering if this was all a big mistake.

"Morning, Kimmi. Just come by to say hello," he stammered, feeling absolutely stupid.

She managed a faint smile while her right hand gathered the front of her bathrobe in a tight little fist.

"Good morning, Frankie. Forgive me. I'm not quite together yet. Is there something I can do for you?"

Her awareness at his discomfort had prompted her to give a more friendly response. He sensed the change and returned the favor with his best impish grin learned from Brian.

"A nice cup of coffee and a little chat, girl, and I'll be on me merry way."

There was another moment's hesitation before she opened the door wide enough for him to slip through.

"I have no coffee, only tea," she said in a soothing voice.

"Blimey, girl, I haven't had a good cup of tea in ages."

She liked his cheeky, disarming nature, but still wondered if it was wise of her to be alone with him.

He watched her fill two tiny cups with what looked like pale water from a tea pot.

"I think you forgot to put the tea leaves in, Kimmi," he laughed.

"You don't like oriental tea?" she asked, feigning reproof.

"Yeah, yeah, okay, I'll give it a go," he teased, looking into the cup like it was filled with mysterious secrets.

They sat facing each other, yet neither one looking at the other. They sipped the tea and listened to the silence. The morning sun filled the small room with a warm glow.

"It's good."

"So, you like it?"

"Yeah, I like it a lot. We oughta do this more often."

She smiled and looked away to avoid his gaze, His eyes slipped from her beautiful face to the smooth softness of her rounded breasts showing through the gap in her robe.

"How come you don't like parties?"

She turned to study his face. "How come you like them so much?"

"I don't. I hate parties."

"You could have fooled me," she said, with a knowing smile.

"Yeah, I seem to fool everybody but meself. To be honest with you, I think the bloody stuff tastes horrible. Makes you do stupid things you feel bad about the next day."

"You just answered your own question better than I ever could," she laughed, picking up the dishes and walking over to the sink.

He stared after her doll-like figure, trying to visualize her without the robe.

"What is a girl like you doing...?"

She spun around, taking him completely by surprise.

"I know you mean well, but that's really not your business," she said in a firm but respectful manner.

He sat in numbed silence, wishing he could retract his stupid question and restore their friendship. He got up from the table and turned toward the door.

"I enjoy dancing. Always have, since I was a small child," she said quickly. "This is only a part of it, like training for something better."

He opened the door without looking her way.

"You make a great cup of tea, Kimmi, but you gotta try some English stuff, when I can find some meself, that is."

He closed the door quietly behind him.

For the next few days he felt moody and out of sorts. Irritable and impatient one minute, quiet and reflective the next. He found himself stopping frequently at the back door and staring across at the bungalows. In his mind, she would be sitting there in that bathrobe, her dark hair curling loosely around her delicate face, her brown eyes slightly misty with shyness. He would reach across the table and gently part the robe while she turned her head away in embarrassment.

"What are you staring at, Scouse?"

"She's doing me head in."

"I thought you were acting kinda funny lately. Let me guess which one it is."

"I don't want you poking fun, okay? This is serious stuff."

"It's the Chinese girl, Kimmi, ain't it?"

"You've been spying on me," Frankie protested, brushing him aside and heading for the front door.

"Spying, like hell! You can't take your bloody eyes off her at work! Do you want me along?"

"Only if you keep your gob shut," he shouted over his shoulder.

They always enjoyed the two-mile walk into New Hope for breakfast. The quiet country road held an abundance of wildflowers and birds, and it wasn't uncommon to see deer crossing the road or standing in a field.

"How come you didn't go see her this morning?"

"Don't want to make a bloody fool of meself, do I? I mean, what if she don't wanna see me."

"She does."

"Now, what's that supposed to mean?"

"I've seen her watching you when you weren't looking."

"Bri, don't have me on, now."

"It's true; she watches every move you make."

Frankie fell silent. There was a lightness in his step now as he picked up the pace.

"Starving! Are you, mate?"

Brian smiled his coy little smile.

***

The blue-green water in the swimming pool shimmered in the heat of the noonday sun. Tiny rays of sunlight glanced off the ripples created by two little girls sitting at the pool's edge, their small feet kicking the water in syncopated rhythm. Their delighted giggles and happy banter contrasted with the quiet surrender of the grownups around the pool.

Frankie shaded his eyes and squinted from the glare of the sun, his eyes searching beneath each brightly colored umbrella until he spotted her. Kimmi sat in a chaise lounge reading a book, a skimpy red bikini barely hiding her nakedness. He trembled at the sight of her tanned, supple body and knew he had to make it with her very soon, or put her out of his mind forever.

"I'd like some ice cream, please."

Frankie went through the motions of making an ice cream cone, but his mind was still preoccupied with thoughts of Kimmi.

"That's not chocolate, I wanted chocolate!"

For the first time, he looked down into the blue eyes of a blonde little girl with freckles all around her pert nose. "You didn't ask for chocolate the first time," he chided with an exaggerated frown.

"But, that's the only kind I like," she replied, shrugging her bare shoulders, as though he should have known that all along.

He chipped away at the frozen ice cream until he got enough together to make a scoop.

"Can I have a double-dip?"

"A double-dip? Now, what's that supposed to mean?"

"You're the ice cream man and you don't know that?" she said in awe. "Anybody knows that."

The little gleam in her eyes tipped him off that she was enjoying the banter of words.

"So, you want one dollop getting a piggy-back ride, is that it?"

She giggled and nodded her head. "Yes, that's it!"

"It won't work. The ice cream's too hard and it'll fall off."

"No, it won't, if you squish it down."

With more effort than he cared to exert, given the stifling heat, he extracted another scoop and laid it gently on top of the other. He applied a little pressure before placing it carefully into her outstretched hand. She gave him a big smile before turning to leave, her free hand cupped around the extra dollop, like she was shielding a candle from the wind. She took a few faltering steps, then abruptly stopped. Her head looked down at her feet, then over her shoulder at Frankie.

"Vanilla's all I got left."

"I don't like vanilla," she giggled, and walked on.

Brian came to join him pulling a hot dog stand behind him. They laughed at each other wearing bib aprons and a chef's bouffant hat that collapsed down one side of their faces.

"Want a hot dog?"

"I'm too young to die."

"Come on, I gotta get some practice in before I serve real people," he laughed. The laughing abruptly stopped when they spotted the Maitre d' heading straight toward them.

"What the hell are you guys doing here? I thought I fired you smart alecks a week ago."

Brian tended to the hot dog that was threatening to go up in flames, leaving Frankie to face the music alone.

"Well, that's right, sir, you did, and me and Bri, we come here every day looking for odd jobs so we can survive."

"I don't want to see either one of you within a mile of my dining room, do you hear me?"

"Yes, sir, but that's kind of hard to do, seeing the dining room's right above us."

"I think you get the drift," he hissed, narrowing his eyes and bobbing his head for emphasis.

"Yes, sir, I think we do," Frankie said, as he lowered his head in mock submission.

"That was brilliant, Scouse. He was sure pushing you hard, but you didn't blow it again!"

Frankie wasn't listening. He'd caught sight of Kimmi diving into the pool. He stood captivated by the graceful way her body moved through the water. After watching her dry herself off, he could stand it no longer.

"Hey, Chelsea! Chelsea, over here, girl." The cocktail waitress stopped in mid-stride.

"Let me borrow your pen and pad for a minute, will you?"

Chelsea was a beautiful blonde, with long, curvy legs that were accentuated by the high-heel shoes she was wearing and a silk wrap-around mini-skirt that barely concealed her rear end. She adjusted the tray of drinks on the palm of her right hand before reaching for the pen and pad in her breast pocket.

"What are you boys up to, now?"

"Long story, Chels. I'll fill you in some other time. Would you deliver a note to Kimmi for me?"

"Sure. Can I read it first?"

Frankie looked up from writing.

"Waitress found face down in swimming pool. Foul play is strongly suspected!"

"I didn't think so," she sighed, grabbing the note before he'd had a chance to fold it.

"Not even so much as a peek!" he shouted after her.

They both watched as she walked around to the other side of the pool and dropped the note into Kimmi's lap. She picked it up and read it.

Hi, Kimmi. For the next five minutes, I'll be giving away free ice cream cones to every pretty girl who asks for one. Frankie.

She put the note in the book and closed it without so much as a glance his way.

"That's it, ain't it? That finishes it for me," he said, quietly resigning himself to the obvious. "Bri, I'll take one of your hot dogs now."

"So, now you're ready to die and you'll blame my cooking. Hey, look! She's calling Chelsea over. She's giving her something!"

They stood together watching Chelsea round the pool and head their way.

"Are you gonna tell me what you wrote her, ever?"

"Bri, just stay quiet for a minute, will you?"

Chelsea slapped the note on the counter. "If you lovebirds are quite finished, I'll get back to serving drinks, okay?"

"You're just jealous, because you're secretly in love with me, yourself," Frankie grinned.

"Oh, sure. All I need is one more headache!"

He opened the note, making sure Brian was safely in front of him. Brian watched his face change from disbelief to sheer joy, in a matter of seconds.

"God, it's killing me, Scouse, you gotta let me read the bloody thing."

Frankie handed it to him without a word. Brian read it, looked up at him, and read it again.

"Is that it? She'd rather have a cup of English tea?"

"Yep. Sweetest words I ever heard."

"You still want a hot dog?"

"Hell, no! You wanna kill me or something?"

"I can make some coffee."

Frankie propped himself up with a pillow. "I thought you didn't drink coffee?"

"I don't, I bought it for you."

He looked down at her face, barely visible in the dark room.

"When did you do that?"

"After you left here that first time." She was smiling now.

"If you were so sure I was coming back, how come you didn't help me along a little bit?"

Her eyebrows went up in a question.

"Like, you know, give me the eye once in a while to show you're still interested."

She giggled now, just like the little blonde girl at the ice cream stand.

"Ladies should be discreet about those things."

"Does that mean you've been peeking on the sly?"

"Well, something like that."

She slipped from between the covers and put her robe on, all in one graceful movement. The light from the small kitchen area gave her a ghostlike transparency. At certain angles, he could make out every contour of her body beneath the robe. Coffee was the last thing on his mind when she brought it back to the bed for him. She waited until he finished his coffee before breaking the news.

"The dance troupe is leaving the *Fountainhead* after Saturday's performance."

He placed his cup down and gave her a long, confused look.

"What's going on? Why so sudden?"

"We haven't been paid for over two weeks. Our manager in New York did some checking and found the Club had filed for bankruptcy."

He eased himself out of the bed and pulled his jeans on.

"How long have you known this?"

"Since yesterday."

She followed him to the back door and out into the cool night air. He lit a cigarette and looked up at the dark blue expanse of sky filled with tiny stars.

"It don't make much sense. How can you pack them in every night and still go broke?"

"It's the oldest game in the world, Frankie. They take in the money and leave when all the bills come due. Do you want to stay the night?"

He put an arm around her shoulder. "I think I snore in my sleep."

"That's okay. I sleepwalk."

"Do you go very far?"

"No. I usually end up stubbing my toe on something."

The early October air felt damp and slightly chilly as they packed the car in sleepy silence. The distant landscape, laced with ribbons of gray mist, began to take form against the dark blue of the sky. Daybreak was no more than a heartbeat away. Frankie took one last look around the austere room before sitting down at the small wooden table to compose a thank you note to Mony.

It had been almost two months since they'd crossed the bridge into Lambertville in search of a job and a place to live. Mony was there doing the thing he loved most; restoring beat-up cars to their original beauty. He was a stocky six-foot-two bachelor with rugged good looks and a mop of unruly black hair that was in need of a good stiff brush.

"Nice car you got there," Frankie had said, as he walked around the fifty-four Dodge, with genuine admiration for its simple beauty.

Mony gave him an unpretentious smile. "You'd never know she was the same car I brought in two weeks ago. "What can I do for you boys?"

"The shopkeeper said you might have a room for rent."

"Might be a little small for two, but you're welcome to it. How does ten bucks a week sound?" He could tell from their faces they were broke. "Popcorn factory next to the railway lines is hiring. Tell 'em Mony sent you."

Frankie made popcorn by day while Brian got hired on as a night watchman for the Buck's County

Playhouse in New Hope. Within a week Mony offered
Frankie the fifty-four Dodge.
"It's yours," he'd said, with a wave of his hand. "Pay
me a little each week and you'll do just fine." He
made life seem simple and uncomplicated, like a
child.

Frankie put the note in an envelope along with a ten dollar bill for the last week's rent, and propped it between the salt and pepper shakers. He wished he could pay the fifty dollars still owed on the car, but they had just enough money to get them to Houston, Texas. At the door, he hesitated, his heart doing battle with his conscience. He walked back to the table and took the ten dollar bill from the envelope and stuck it in his pocket.

They headed southwest on Highway 202, being sure to give the large city of Philadelphia a wide berth. Once past the city, they began to relax a little and enjoy the beauty of the Pennsylvania countryside and savor the giddy sensation of the unknown yet ahead of them.

The plan was to drive in four-hour shifts during the day and a full eight hours at night to give the navigator-sandwich maker, radio station-changer, a full night's sleep in the rear seat. At least that's how it was supposed to work. By early afternoon, Frankie was fast asleep and Brian was thoroughly lost, zigzagging across half the state of Maryland trying to connect with Highway 29 into Washington, D.C. He never did find it. By the time he crossed the border into Virginia, he was a basket case in need of rest.

"Time for your little driving lesson, sleeping beauty."

"Where we at?"

Brian laid the map open on Frankie's lap. "Highway 66, Virginia, mate. Just keep going until you hit 81 South, all the way to Tennessee."

He studied the map until his mind cleared of sleep. "What happened to Washington, D.C.?"

"Damned if I know. They moved it on me. I swear it wasn't where it was supposed to be."

"You mean we don't get to see the capitol of America because some lousy little Cockney from London don't know how to read a simple map?"

"You want a bologna sandwich, or don't you?"

"Why don't you take a little nap, Bri, say for about two days."

"With or without cheese?"

"With."

***

There were no stars or moon to illuminate the landscape, only an endless curtain of darkness that refused to divulge the beauty Frankie knew was out there beyond the car's headlights. The iridescent sunset on ripened and furrowed fields and across the Appalachian Mountain Range ablaze with autumn color, was still vivid in his memory.

He squinted at his watch. Half one, or was that two? No matter. Time didn't seem important. He felt a sense of contentment sitting there in his insulated little world. Everything took on a timeless quality; the empty highway, the sleepy towns, the impenetrable darkness. He was glad for the radio, even though all he could find was country music. *Bloody sad stuff, that,* he thought.

At first, the music lulled his mind to rest, but then it began to stir up feelings of longing or missing something. He wished Brian was awake. His mind began skipping through familiar streets, calling each one by name, as thought it was a contest. *Grafton Street, Carl Street, Northummy, the dock road, yeah, the dock road! So busy, teeming with life. Vibrant. Noisy. The clickety-click of wheels over wet cobblestones, the overhead railway train vibrating and swaying on stilted steel. And the smells! Oh, God, the smells. How can anyone describe the smell of a warehouse full of brown sugar or peanuts, or the smell of a horse blanket draped over your head to ward off the early morning chill? Ah, and wafts of the pungent Mersey River mixed with diesel exhaust and chimney smoke?*

Brian snorted from the back seat and began to stir, then settled back into sleep.

Frankie tried projecting his thoughts to what lay ahead, but his mind raced back for more like a hungry child. He was truly homesick now. The very thing he tried hard to avoid, he was now enjoying.

The two-ouncy! Remember the two-ouncy?

Sure I do, he grinned, as though there were two of him. *He could see the rows of sweets in tall glass jars. Toffees, lemon drops, licorice-all-sorts. And the Park Palace across the street with fat Stagecoach guarding the entrance. Next to saggin' school, going to the Palace was his very favorite thing to do.*

Can I borry a tanner, Mam? He could hear himself say. *Only a tanner, an' I'll pay ya back, honest I will. And that pained look his mother always gave whenever she was about to disappoint him.*

Oh, I couldn't lad. I'm scrimpin' as it is to get the tea in.

Next stop, Nin's house. Nin was always good for at least thripence.

Do ye need any messages in before the shops shut, Nin? The owlish peering over two pair of glasses, looking for the real motive behind his kindly offer.

Now what yer after?

Picture money, Nin. Only need thripence more, that's all.

Go on, puddin' face, before I get me shoe off to ya.

When all else failed, there was always the 'bunk-in.' Getting by crafty old Stagecoach and under the ticket window without being caught was no easy thing. But, oh, such a feeling of pride whenever he succeeded!

The neon lights of an all-night diner penetrated the darkness up ahead. It was a welcome sight and time for him to let go of his childhood memories and get on with the real world. He was very impressed with the cute blonde smiling back at him from behind the counter.

Brian pulled Frankie to one side, leaving Darryl standing alone, pretending to look preoccupied with the dirt under his fingernails. Frankie felt weary from another fruitless job search on foot and was in no mood for game playing.

"You'll never believe it," Brian whispered. "This guy has offered to pay for the whole trip to San Francisco if we'll drive him! What do you think about that?"

"I think it stinks. The lad's a bleedin' queer," he responded coldly.

"How'd you know that?"

"He's got shifty eyes and they're set too close together."

"Well, it's true. He is a fairy. But, he isn't trying to hide the fact. When he found out we were straight, he still wanted to make the deal."

"Bri, it must be at least three or four days to San Francisco! What the hell are we gonna do with a queer all that time? We gotta sleep sometime!"

Brian became visibly agitated at Frankie's unwillingness to see any viewpoint other than his own. He walked around in a tight little circle before fixing a steady gaze back on his friend's obstinate face.

"Take a look, take a good hard look. Does he really look like a threat to you, macho man? Christ, he couldn't be more than nine stones soaking wet!"

Like an admonished child, Frankie found himself glancing over at Darryl. It was true; he was quite small and unassuming.

"So, you want us to give up after only two days here?" he asked in quiet resignation.

"You said, yourself, Houston don't feel right. Besides, we only got one more free night at the Mission."

For a few moments, Frankie's eyes looked distant, thoughtful.

Then a half-smile creased his weary face. "San Francisco," he mused. "Got a nice ring to it, don't it?"

He sauntered over to where Darryl was standing and offered his hand. "It's a deal, mate. Any hanky-panky though, and we dump you out on the highway, okay?"

Darryl grinned back and shook his hand. "Either one of you guys eaten yet?"

"Nope, not since early this morning," Brian volunteered.

"Then, let me introduce you to the best chili and beans I have ever tasted. It's just a hole-in-the-wall, but, man, is the food good!"

Frankie slipped further down in his seat and pulled the cap low over his eyes. He was feeling a little out-of-sorts sitting there next to Darryl, while Brian slept in the back seat. But, he had to admit to himself, the lad was doing a fine job of driving the car.

Can't ignore him forever, he reasoned to himself. *Ain't done or said a thing wrong so far. Damn it, it's gonna be a long trip if I don't start being a little sociable. Not too friendly, mind you. Cordial-like. Yeah, that's it. Cordial. That way, he don't get no wrong ideas and we can get along fine.*

He sat up straight, pushed the cap back on his head and cleared his throat.

"How's it going, Darryl? Need a break from driving?"

His sudden interest took Darryl by surprise, but he managed a nervous little grin.

"No, no, I'm fine, thanks. I really enjoy driving."

They immediately lapsed into an awkward silence again.

The sun peeked over the horizon, bathing everything in a warm, pink glow. They could now make out the silhouette of thousands of longhorn cattle spread across the Texas prairie. Wisps of fine mist hung suspended like miniature clouds, creating a halo effect around many of the cattle.

"Beautiful country," Frankie offered, turning toward Darryl. "What brought you to Houston?"

"I've always wanted to go away to sea. A friend of mind suggested Houston as an easy place to catch a ship out, but it wasn't. Too many people on the waiting list, just like in San Francisco."

Frankie suspected it was Darryl's small build and feminine characteristics that kept him from realizing his dream. For the first time, he felt sorry for him and a little guilty for the way he treated him.

"Well, don't feel too bad. Me and Bri back there, we drove over two thousand miles through seven states to work on the oil fields, and never got near one."

Darryl started laughing. "Why oil fields?"

"I'll be darned if I know. I think I saw Clark Gable in a film once where he got filthy rich doing something like that."

They were both laughing now. Brian popped up from the back seat looking disheveled.

"Can't sleep with you two carrying on like that, can I? How soon before we eat?"

"San Antonio's just ahead," Darryl said. "I'll treat you guys to a nice breakfast. But remember, no more food until we reach the Texas border in El Paso. That's at least an eight-hour drive from here."

"Beats the hell out of bologna sandwiches, don't it," they both agreed.

By late afternoon, they had crossed the border into New Mexico, a vast no-man's-land of desert cactus and sagebrush. Frankie glanced in his rear-view mirror at the highway patrol car that had seemingly appeared out of nowhere.

"Don't look now, guys, but we're being followed," he groaned, as though fearful of being overheard. Brian stole a quick glance over his shoulder.

"Man, he's right there, ain't he? Think he's gonna pull us over for something?"

"Don't know what for. I ain't speeding or nothing."

For the next twenty miles, the cop seemed content just to sit back there, riding on their tail.

"Maybe he's gonna escort us right through New Mexico to Arizona, to make sure we don't get into any trouble." Brian quipped, half in jest.

Around the next curve, Frankie was astonished to see two highway patrol cars strung out across the roadway, blocking his path.

"Oh, my God! They must think we're bank robbers or something. Just look at the cut of that!"

He eased the car to the side of the road and turned off the motor. In his side mirror, he could see the cop approach from the rear, his right hand resting lightly on his gun holster. The two cops in front stood with hands on hips and feet spread apart.

"Don't anybody so much as scratch their head," Frankie warned, afraid, himself, to let go of the steering wheel.

"May I see your driver's license, please?"

The cop stood just out of view, but close enough that Frankie could detect the smell of leather from his belt and holster.

"Yes, sir. Were we doing something wrong, officer?"

The cop took the license without comment.

"Registration, please."

"Registration, sir? I don't think I know what you mean."

"Does this vehicle belong to you?"

"Oh, yes, sir, it does. I bought if off me friend in New Jersey."

"Do you have any papers that would show that?"

"No, sir, I don't. Me friend never mentioned papers, like. Maybe it's because I still owed him fifty dollars. Do you think that's why?"

"You tell me!"

He made a slow tour around the car, peering into each of the windows.

"I think you'd better follow me," he said with conviction. He gave the other cops a hand signal and they immediately climbed into their vehicles and opened a path for him.

By the time they reached Silver City, the sun had gone down. The night air felt chilly, as Frankie parked the car and followed the officer into an old brownstone building with Brian and Darryl close behind.

"Empty your pockets out on the counter. Remove your belt and shoe laces." It was a casual request, spoken as though it needed no explanation.

Frankie glanced around at the drab interior, panic beginning to rise in his chest.

"Are you gonna put us in jail? We haven't done anything wrong!"

The leathery, sunburned face finally cracked a half smile. "Only for a short time. Just long enough for us to gather some information about the car you were driving. Then you can all be on your way again."

The steel door clanged shut behind them, leaving them standing rigid in the gloom. A small opening in the door gave off just enough light for them to make out the outline of mattresses lying on the floor. The smell of urine and feces was so strong, it made Frankie gag.

"Jeez, what's the matter with these people, sticking us in a place like this? Don't they ever clean it? It's not even fit for a dog!"

He squatted to get a closer look at a mattress. "Just look at that, why don't you! Piss stains from one end to the other. And sick! Somebody got sick, and it's been there so long it's crystallized! I bet they've never bothered to look inside here for months, maybe even years!"

Being locked up brought back painful memories. Frankie began pacing the floor like a caged animal.

"Relax, Scouse. I'll make you a bet they'll be back for us within an hour."

He stopped pacing. "What do you think Mony's gonna tell them? We did run off still owing for the car and the last week's rent, remember?"

"Yeah, but Mony ain't that kinda guy."

"But, what if he's mad at us? Do you think they'll hold us for that?"

"How am I supposed to know? I feel sorry for Darryl here, getting mixed up in all this."

Darryl started laughing. "Don't feel sorry for me. Before I met you guys, my life was pretty dull."

Frankie managed a smile. "You're okay, Darryl."

The three of them began pacing the floor together.

"How would you guys like to visit the Grand Canyon on the way back? It's not too far out of our way."

"Sounds great, Darryl," they both chorused.

"And, how about Las Vegas?"

"Yeah, sure."

"And Hollywood?"

"Oh, God, yeah, Hollywood."

"From there, it's a straight shot up the beautiful scenic coast highway to San Francisco."

Brian looked at Frankie, "Not a bad lad after all, is he?"

"Couldn't have said it better meself, Bri. Tell us about San Francisco, Darryl."

Darryl brought the car to a stop on top of a hill overlooking the city. His misty gaze needed no interpretation. He was happy to be home again. He stepped out of the car and motioned Frank and Brian to do the same. Before them lay the sweeping vista of a very beautiful San Francisco, basking in the mid-afternoon sun, like some jeweled Mediterranean paradise. On one side of the city stretched the deep blue of the Pacific Ocean. On the other side, the wind-swept bay kicking up white caps and filling the sails of pleasure boats bobbing in its swells. Frankie felt an instant liking for this newest discovery, and he wondered if maybe this could be the end of their journey.

"What do you think, Bri?"

"Fantastic!" he sighed, without taking his eyes from the scene. "Looks like a good place to hang out for a while."

Frankie nodded in response.

Darryl made a right turn off of Market Street onto Page Street, and parked alongside a white stucco, two-story apartment building. Frankie felt a little apprehension rise within him again, as they followed Darryl up a flight of stairs.

The three men inside the apartment looked a little puzzled when they saw Darryl walk through the door. Then all hell broke loose, as they converged on him, screaming and hollering and throwing their arms around him. He was obviously the baby in the family. Then they stood back in respectful silence, waiting for Darryl to make the introductions.

"Phillip, David, Stephen. I'd like you to meet my two good friends, Brian and Frankie. They're straight," he added quickly. "Real straight. They'll need to spend the night here, though. In the morning, I'll help them find another place to stay."

Philip, a tall, gangly man in his late thirties, reached out to shake hands first. "Welcome. I hope you guys like spaghetti. I made enough for an army." While he put the finishing touches to the spaghetti, David helped Stephen set the table. Darryl poured the wine, all the while sharing excitedly about his adventures on the road. He was much more effeminate in his mannerisms now that he was home and on familiar ground.

"I know the perfect young lady to give you guys the grand tour of the city tonight," he announced, when dinner was over.

"You do?" Frankie asked, incredulous that he would even know any girls.

"You bet. You're just going to love her, I swear to it."

His child-like enthusiasm wasn't shared by either Frankie or Brian. They couldn't imagine what kind of a girl a homosexual could possibly hook them up with.

After a short conversation, Darryl hung up the phone. "Well, guys. I've got some good news and some bad news. The bad news is Anna Marie can't make it tonight, she's washing her hair."

"Oh, that's okay, Darryl. At least you gave it a good try," Frankie said, trying to sound disappointed.

"But, the good news is, she wants to meet you guys at seven-thirty tomorrow night and she'll bring along a friend."

"Great! That settles that then, don't it?" Frankie said with forced enthusiasm. Where do we sleep tonight?"

Darryl led the way through a room that had nothing but wall to wall mattresses on the floor. The second room they entered was also empty of furnishings, except for two single mattresses.

"This is it, guys. In the morning, I'll take you to see my brother. He's promised to take care of you until you can get things going for yourselves."

There was a long, awkward silence, then Brian took a step forward and offered his hand.

"Thanks for everything, Darryl. We're gonna stay friends. Right, Scouse?"

"Yeah, you bet," Frankie exclaimed, coming forward to put an arm around his slender shoulders. "You don't get rid of us that easy, mate."

Darryl wasn't convinced, but he grinned anyway. He'd come to appreciate their English humor and offbeat mannerisms. He was glad not to be losing the friends who had accepted him for who he was.

50

Frankie took a long, deep drag on his cigarette before arcing it out into the wet street. The moment he'd been dreading had finally arrived. With a sigh of resignation, he pressed on the doorbell and stepped back to wait.

Not exactly me cup of tea, this, he mumbled under his breath. *What if the girls don't even like us, what then?* He ran nervous fingers through his thick, curly hair, reminding himself he needed a haircut. *What if we don't like them? God, what if they're fat and ugly?* He loosened his tie a little and rang the doorbell again. *Could be a disaster, mate. No more blind dates for us after this.*

She stood in the open doorway, a winsome smile playing on her beautiful, young face. Her short, blonde hair and light complexion gave her the look of a Scandinavian beauty. Frankie was riveted to the spot. Stunned. Completely captivated with her. Her soft brown eyes held his gaze, and for a brief moment, he felt a strange affinity with her. He managed a weak grin.

"Hi, I'm Frank. Me mate, Brian, is out there waiting in the car."

She opened the door wider and moved to one side, indicating for him to go inside.

"I'm Anna Marie, Frank. I love your accent."

He felt his face get flushed. *This one's really doing me head in,* he thought, stepping inside. He followed her down the short hall and into the spacious living room, all the time admiring her youthful figure and a pair of the most fantastic legs he'd ever seen on a woman.

"Laura, this is Frank. You should hear his adorable accent." Anna Marie laughed, hurrying by them to finish off her makeup in the bathroom.

He couldn't think of one thing to say to Laura, in order for her to hear his accent, but she stood there waiting, anyway.

"Luvly place, ain't it," he finally said, his eyes roaming over the living area. "Must cost a few bob to live here."

Laura was short and heavyset, but with a pretty face. She was obviously very shy, but she did manage a smile.

"Yes, Nob Hill is expensive. But, if you share the rent, it's not so bad."

Her eyes lowered and she looked away. They were quiet again until Anna Marie joined them.

"I'm supposed to show you guys around the city, right? Well, prepare to get lost," she laughed. "I know where everything is, but I'm not sure of the streets you take to get to them!"

She somehow managed to make getting lost sound like an exciting adventure.

Amid the clamor of gears, hand brakes, and the incessant clanging of its bell, the Powell Street cable car labored to negotiate the steepest and final stretch of Nob Hill, before making its descent down the other side toward the Bay and Fishermen's Wharf. As it crested the hill, the cross traffic and pedestrians hurried to get out of the way. The cable car was obviously the king of the road in this city, even when the traffic lights were against it. Frank thanked God for small favors.

After riding rather precariously, standing on its outer step and silently coaxing the old relic up every hill, he was sure it was about to quit the struggle and go sailing back down toward the neon lights of Market Street.

Anna Marie sat facing him, her knees touching and caressing his with each sway of the cable car. She studied his ruggedly handsome face and wondered if she would have a chance to know him better. He was different from any boys she had known before. Very English-looking, quiet, in a mysterious way, yet with a sense of adventure about him that left her a little breathless with anticipation. She wished he would pay her more attention.

He turned, and for a brief moment, their eyes met and held each other. He smiled and looked away, as though distracted by something, surprised at his own shyness.

Here I am with a beautiful girl on me hands and I'm acting like a silly dope, he lamented to himself. He gripped the hand rail a little tighter, as the cable car tipped forward to begin its downward journey. Her soft hand brushed his on the rail and he wondered if it was by accident. A warmth began to grow in the pit of his stomach and he wanted more than anything to touch her, hold her hand, to somehow share the pleasure with her that he was feeling inside. He wanted to communicate something beyond words, but all he could do was stand in silence, as though preoccupied with the world around him.

"That's Alcatraz!" she shouted over the noise of the cable car, pointing a finger in the direction of an island sitting out in the Bay. "And, that's the Golden Gate Bridge over there. Isn't it beautiful?" Her eyes were bright and her face flushed with excitement, as though she was discovering it all for the first time.

"Yeah, it's fantastic, Anna," he answered, his voice quiet. "It doesn't get much better than this."

The Golden Gate Bridge stood tall and majestic in the thin veil of fog that shrouded and eddied around its high masts. Its lights, like strings of jewels, flickered and winked their reflection in the dark water below.

From the bustling stalls and cafes of Fishermen's Wharf, came the sounds of music and gaiety and a multitude of voices drifting up into the night sky. He glanced back toward the contoured streets of the city, with halos of lights, then back again at the Bay.

"It's the most beautiful city in the world. I've never seen anything more beautiful."

Anna Marie stood up, as though to get a better view, but the rocking motion of the cable car forced her to sit down again. He offered her his hand and she took it, pulling herself up. He put his arm around her waist to steady her and she didn't seem to mind. His head was racing now and every nerve and muscle felt like it was doing the Irish Jig. *I'm acting like a school boy on me first date,* he thought, a little disgusted with himself.

"What are you so mad about, Bri?" Frank asked, as though he hadn't a clue.

The girls walked ahead of them threading their way through the busy stalls toward the water.

"I ain't mad. What makes you think I'm mad?"

"I don't know; you're just not your chipper self, that's all. You know what I mean?"

Brian abruptly stopped and pulled Frank around to face him. "Okay, how come it's always me ends up with the ugly one, or the fat one, or the one old enough to be my mother? Tell me, do you have some special rights that say you get to choose the best and I get whatever's left over?"

Frank found himself hard-pressed to keep from laughing.

"So, you are mad at me! You think I stole the best girl, right? Well, that ain't true. Besides, Laura ain't such a bad looking girl. She's kinda cute in her own way."

"Well, good, then that settles it. You take Laura for a bit and I'll take Anna Marie."

Brian turned abruptly and walked quickly in the direction the girls had gone.

"It's only a blind date, for Chris' sake! We probably won't even see them again after tonight," he shouted after him, but Brian wasn't listening.

Anna Marie stood at the side of the bed looking down into Frank's sleeping face. She smiled a contented smile and pulled the pink bathrobe a little tighter around her naked body to ward off the slight chill in the room. This was all new to her and she hadn't a clue as to what to do next. If she climbed back in beside him, she knew she could kiss the rest of the morning good bye, and it was such a perfect day outside. On the other hand, she wanted to be sensitive to his needs when he did wake up. After a few minutes of indecision, she could stand it no longer. Walking over to the bay windows, she threw open the heavy drapes with a flourish, filling the small bedroom with bright golden sunlight. She let out a mischievous giggle and turned back toward the bed.

"Honey, just look at this beautiful morning. It's perfect for that walk across the Golden Gate Bridge you've been promising me."

He let out an involuntary groan and shielded his eyes from the glaring onslaught.

"God, Anna, are you out of your mind? You could blind a person doing stuff like that." He squinted at the clock on the bedside table and grimaced. "Only half-seven?"

Slowly, he sat up and fluffed up his pillow, placing it behind his back. He was silent for a moment until his head cleared of sleep, glancing over to where she was standing silhouetted against the sunlit window. It was the look of an angel. *How in the world did she ever fall for me?* he wondered, throwing her a weak smile and beckoning her closer.

"How come you're so beautiful?"

"I bet you say that to all the girls," she retorted with a nervous laugh, slapping him lightly on the cheek. He grabbed her wrist and pulled her toward him, kissing her longingly on the lips. When he felt her begin to yield to him, he separated and held her at arm's length.

"And, what was all this walking across the Golden Gate Bridge bit about?" he baited, in the sexiest voice he could muster. She felt her face get hot under his gaze.

"I was merely making a suggestion," she stammered.

He kissed her again, this time more passionately. "I thought honeymoons were for making love all day long," he teased, his hands beginning to untie her robe.

"Do you think we rushed into things just a little bit?" she asked, her breathing more labored now. He slipped the robe off her slender shoulders without saying a word. "After all, we've only known each other for four months," she continued, her voice trailing off as he pulled her down beside him.

"Should have closed the drapes."

"Don't you dare move again."

When they finally left the upstairs apartment, it was almost noon. The morning sunshine had given way to cumulus clouds, but the air still had a morning freshness to it. Walking next to her, Frank felt such an overwhelming sense of joy and well-being, it was hard for him to contain it all inside. He gently squeezed her hand and she looked up at him and smiled.

"Are we gonna grow old together, mate?"

She nodded her head, still smiling. It was obvious to her what he was feeling. It was written all over his face. She was feeling it, too. She wanted this moment to go on forever.

Even before he put the key in the lock, he knew she wasn't going to be there. His hand trembled at the thought, and his mind fought back waves of nausea and despair that threatened to engulf him. The door squeaked a little as he opened it onto the darkened hallway. Only silence greeted him. He swallowed hard, still hoping against hope, and closed the door quietly behind him. He opened the bedroom door and stood motionless, breathless, his eyes penetrating the darkness, like a hawk seeking its prey. He let out a short gasp and leaned his shoulder against the door frame for support. The bed was empty. Made up like it had never been slept in. Short sobs escaped him as his body slumped to the floor. He leaned his head back against the wall and closed his eyes. It was over this time and he knew it.

***

"Frankie who? Oh, Kate's lad, in America...oh, my God! How are ya, son?...just a minute then, there's a good lad!"

Martha Ford covered the mouthpiece with her left hand and looked around her tiny shop at the line of inquisitive faces staring back at her.

"It's Katie Hawkins' lad, on the phone from America!" she announced to each and every face.

"Could someone run 'round for her!"

"His sister, Sarah, was just outside a bit ago, so hang on, and I'll have a look," volunteered a young girl from the back of the queue.

Within minutes, Sarah ran into the shop, her eyes wide with fright. "Is he alright, Martha?" she asked in a hoarse whisper. Martha handed her the phone without saying a word. A hushed silence fell on the shop as she brought the phone to her ear.

"Are you okay, Frankie?...Yes, this is your sister, Sarah...I sound funny? Well, you sound like a right bleedin' Yank! I'm the *gear,* meself. Are you looking after yourself, too, like? Yes, me mam's on her way. Somebody ran 'round for her."

Kate was hanging the wash over the railing when a young girl shouted up to her from the street.

"Mrs. Hawkins, your Frankie's on the phone in Martha Ford's, and he wants to talk to you. He's calling from America!"

For a long moment, she stared down at the girl as though she hadn't quite understood. Then panic began to rise within her. Telephone calls and telegrams in this poor part of the city were very often the bearer of bad news. She couldn't decide whether to run inside and grab her coat, or go just the way she was. She began to move toward the stairs, her hands abstractedly dropping clothes pegs as she walked. When she reached the street, she tried to run a little, but her heart was pumping too fast, making her feel dizzy.

She remembered the beautiful letter her son had written her not two weeks ago, saying he had bought the plane tickets and was coming home for a visit with his wife and three-month old son, Andrew. *Yes, that's it*, she reasoned to herself. *Probably calling to say they're on their way already, and I haven't even started putting up the new wallpaper yet!*

When she entered the shop there was hardly room enough for her to get to the phone. People kept coming in to do their shopping, but nobody was willing to leave. Not until the drama had played itself out. He was Kate's son, but he was also connected to them. He was part of the neighborhood. The one that got away. To America, no less!

"Mam, Anna's left me. She's gone for good, taking the baby with her!"

Kate tried to speak, but the words wouldn't come. She began to cry, softly at first, so as not to offend anybody. Then her heart broke and she wept openly, handing the phone back to her daughter. The silent crowd parted, allowing her to walk through them, her face buried in her hands. They each bore the pain with her, without knowing the source of the pain.

Frank hung up the phone and walked over to the bay windows. He had just turned twenty-one, but he felt old, drained of energy, adrift in a sea of pain with no lifeline to grasp and hold on to. Even the city, which had brought him so much joy and happiness, now seemed cold and indifferent in its empty pre-dawn silence. The hurting little boy within him had needed his mother; had reached out to her for comfort, only to discover she was no longer able to help. Her tears were for both of them. He wished, with all his heart, he had never made the call and broken her heart again.

He lay on the bed watching the first rays of light steal across the ceiling. Somewhere in the apartment building, a baby cried out as though in pain, then it was silent again. His mind, numbed for a short time, began to awaken with the dawning of a new day.

Where did it all go wrong, and why was I so helpless to stop it? He wondered, as his mind drifted back to the day before.

"See if you can pick me out of that mess?" Anna Marie laughed, pointing to a large group picture in her high school annual.

"I didn't know you played in the school band," Frank chuckled, genuine surprise showing on his face.

They sat on the edge of the bed, weary from the long stroll through Golden Gate Park. The baby slept peacefully in the crib, only a few feet away. He noticed handwriting on the corner of the page and began to read it out loud. "Hope you and Tim have a great future together."

He felt his body begin to tremble and he stopped reading. They sat there in silence.

"We were engaged to be married," Anna Marie said quietly, laying her hand gently on his in reassurance. He pulled away and sat in ominous silence, his eyes staring blankly at the bedroom wall.

"Don't do this, Frank," she pleaded, her voice trembling a little this time. She had seen him like this before. She could only wait now, and hope, and not move lest she upset the balance.

Anger, fueled by jealousy, crept through his body, like some sinister drug, twisting the truth and innocence into lies and distortions. He was hurting so badly he wanted to strike out at her. After all, if he didn't love her so much, he wouldn't be hurt by past boyfriends and their intimate relationships. So, it was her fault he was hurting and he had to punish her for it.

He stood to his feet and turned toward her. His face was ashen, menacing. He was two people. He was touched by the pleading in her eyes and wanted to reach out and gather her fragile body in his arms and soothe away her mounting fears. Instead, he took her by the shoulders and shook her violently, then pushed her down on the bed, all the while abusing her verbally. He felt shame for what he was doing to his beautiful little girl, yet, at the same time, deriving pleasure from the control he had over her. The

*moment he slapped her hard across the face, the
exhilaration subsided. It was like waking up from a
bad dream. He sat down on the side of the bed next
to her and watched her cry softly into her hands. He
knew, this time he had gone too far.*

*"I'm really sorry, Anna. I don't know what got into
me," he mumbled in confusion.*

*He hated leaving her like this but it was time for
him to go to work. He put on his jacket and walked
over to the baby's crib. He stroked the soft skin
gently with one finger, grateful that the commotion
hadn't disturbed him. He looked over at Anna Marie
one last time, but she refused to acknowledge him.
When he closed the door behind him, he wondered
what he would find when he returned.*

After a long, hot shower, he dressed to impress, putting on his best
gray slacks, starched white shirt and tie, cuff links, sports jacket, a
shoe shine and lots of after-shave lotion. He even hummed a tune
while checking himself out in the long mirror behind the bathroom
door. He hadn't a clue as to why he was feeling so good. Somehow,
morning had brought with it a renewed hope that if he hung in there
and gave it his best, he could win her back to him. He took a step
back from the mirror and knocked on an imaginary door and cleared
his throat a couple of times.

*..."For you, my darling," he crooned, sticking out
his hand, as though presenting her with flowers.*

*"Oh, how sweet of you, Frank, but you shouldn't
have," he mimicked, feigning modest surprise.*

*"I didn't sleep a wink last night thinking about you,
Anna."*

"Me neither, Frank. Let's just go home..."

Before getting into his car, he stood basking in the warmth of the
mid-morning sun. Across the street, a sallow-faced hippie with long,
stringy hair, sat at an open window strumming softly on a guitar and
mouthing lyrics that only he himself could hear. Normally, Frank had
nothing but disdain for the influx of 'flower children' turning Haight-
Ashbury into a carnival of clowns. But not today. He loved

everybody today. He waved in greeting and received a peace sign and a toothless grin in return.

Now, if I could only get Anna's mother to cooperate like that, he mused with a little chuckle, pointing the car in the direction of Twin Peaks and the Sunset District.

Except for a fleeting smile of greeting, Mrs. Clairborne's face revealed very little in the way of emotion. Frank responded with a perfunctory smile of his own, then held out the bouquet of flowers for her to admire.

"They're for Anna Marie, Mom. Ain't they luvly?"

She took a quick glance at them, then back at him without changing her expression.

"You shouldn't be here, you know. Anna Marie doesn't want to see you." Her words stung him and he looked away.

"I'm sorry I hurt her. More than you'll ever know," he responded humbly. When he turned his gaze back to her, there was a little more fire in his eyes.

"Anna and Andrew are all I've got. They mean everything to me. I can't just let them slip out of my life like this. This is crazy!"

Mrs. Clairborne's body stiffened slightly at his sudden show of emotion, but her face remained expressionless. She didn't want to get into a verbal confrontation with him standing there at the open door, and she wasn't about to invite him inside. She found him too unpredictable for that.

"I'm sorry, dear, but Anna Marie doesn't feel she can trust you right now; you've hurt her too many times already."

He felt the creeping sensation of anger and resentment building up within him toward this woman who had silently disapproved of him from the very beginning. He was sure she was trying to keep them apart.

"I want to see her, Mom. I want to be able to say I'm sorry, face to face. Christ, we've only been married a year! Hardly enough time to work all this stuff out, don't you think?"

Mrs. Clairborne knew it was time to close the door.

"I know you're hurting, but I'll have to call the police if you don't leave."

He stood staring at the closed door, allowing his anger to slowly subside. Anna Marie had loved him so completely and so unconditionally, he couldn't fathom the kind of inner strength that was keeping her from opening that door and falling into his arms. He turned and walked down the steps, not really sure what he should do next. Everything seemed empty and without purpose. Even the thought of getting drunk had no real appeal. He realized he still had the flowers in his hand and walked back up the steps. As he propped them against the door, he could make out the baby's muffled cries from deep within the house. He stood for a moment and listened, remembering his own traumatic childhood growing up without a father's love, and he knew then that he would do whatever it took to bring them together again. He was convinced it wasn't going to happen today or tomorrow, or even next week, for that matter. To win back her trust was going to take time, lots of time and a lot of patience.

"Divorce papers! Oh, my God, what is she thinking about!" he moaned, as he paced the living room floor in shocked disbelief. He kept reading the crisp document over and over again, while tears of anguish trickled down his cheeks. "She can't mean it. She loves me too much. What? Santa Rosa! That's fifty or sixty miles from here. My God, she's even running away from me."

He knew now only a miracle could possibly save his marriage. He couldn't give up. Not just yet. It was still too painful to even contemplate.

Later that day, he cashed in the airline tickets home to pay for Anna Marie's attorney and one for himself.

"What exactly, is it you want me to do for you, Mr. Hawkins?"

Frank gave his attorney a blank stare and shook his head.

"I don't know. They just told me to get myself an attorney, too."

"Is she an unfit mother? Do you want me to try to win custody of your son for you?"

"Hell, no, nothing like that! She's a great mother!"

"Whoa, you don't have to get upset with me! I'm just trying to find out what you want out of this divorce."

"There isn't going to be a divorce," he answered tersely.

The attorney leaned back in his chair and nodded his head in affirmation.

"I see. You feel it won't go that far, so you want to go real easy on her. Okay, I can dig that. But, just in case things don't go like you planned, let's at least nail down some respectable visitation rights. Does that sound like a good idea to you?"

The attorney was leaning forward now, his calm voice coaxing and coercing him into making some basic decisions.

"Yeah, I guess so. But, I don't wanna see her get hurt, that's all."
"You have my word on that."

Anna Marie sat in a child's rusty swing rocking herself slowly, mechanically, back and forth. Her eyes stared vacantly into the gloom of twilight and misty rain that had been falling intermittently all day. The white blouse and print skirt she wore clung to her skin, causing her to shiver in the cold night air. She wondered how long it would take before she caught pneumonia and lost the baby that was growing inside of her.

Frank awakened with a start and fumbled around for the phone. According to the clock on the night stand, he'd only been asleep for a couple of hours.

"Hello?"

"Hi, sleepyhead. Did I wake you?"

He sat bolt upright, his eyes wide with unexpected pleasure. "Anna! Is it really you?"

"Yes, of course it is," she laughed. "Which of your girls did you think it was?"

"Nah, I don't have any other girls. You're the only one for me!"

There was silence on the other end of the line. He could have bitten his tongue.

"What I really meant to say, was..."

"No, don't apologize, I know you meant well. It's just that I'm not ready for that kind of talk. Not just yet." Her voice was soft, almost melancholy.

"Why did you call? Are you okay?"

"Yes, I'm fine. I do need to see you, though. Can you make it up to Santa Rosa sometime soon?"

His heart was racing. She was the only person in the whole world that could make him feel this way.

"I could be there in an hour, if you promise to let me take you out for lunch."

There was another long silence. He held his breath, wondering if he'd blown it again.

"Okay, that sounds fine. Let's plan on having lunch together."

His trembling hand slowly hung up the phone. He was so full of joy inside, he felt like he was going to burst. "She wants to see me," he whispered, over and over, as though somehow it was all too good to be true.

Traffic on Van Ness Avenue, leading to the Golden Gate Bridge, moved at a snail's pace, due, in part, to the heavy fog that hid all but the first few cars in front of him. He grew restless, impatient, lighting one cigarette after another. He'd seen her only once in three months, a brief encounter at the divorce hearing. On orders from her attorney, he wasn't allowed to speak to her or make eye contact. All he could do was sit there with a big ache in his heart and steal glances when he thought no one was looking.

Once he crossed the Golden Gate Bridge, the fog began to dissipate, allowing the warm June sun to work its magic on the forested hills and lush, green valleys of Marin County. After finding the familiar soothing music on KABL radio, he began to relax and give some thought as to how he was going to behave when he saw her. He realized he wasn't free to go around hugging and kissing her whenever he felt like it, so that was out. And he certainly didn't want to show anger of any sort. That would only bring back painful memories of why she left him in the first place. *Just play it cool*, he reasoned to himself, *you gotta win her all over again, so you better start impressing her.*

When he drove into the Sunset trailer park, she stood next to her sister's trailer, smiling and waving him over. He took a couple of deep breaths. He'd never seen her look quite as lovely as she did just then. Her face was radiant, her short blonde hair, soft and golden, her light blue summer dress perfectly tailored to show off her youthful figure.

"Do you want to see your son before we go?"

Without waiting for his reply, she slipped inside the trailer home and reappeared holding a beautiful blonde, brown-eyed boy in her arms.

He stared at the baby as though he were seeing him for the first time. He couldn't believe how much he had changed in just three short months. He reached out to take hold of him, but Andrew clung tenaciously to his mother's breast.

"Hey, wait just a bloody minute, mate," Frank said, in a playful tease. "I'm the chap who changed your nappies and got up in the middle of the night to give you a bottle, so you gotta show some respect."

Andrew managed a little grin but refused to loosen his grip.

"You need to come up more often so the two of you can get to know each other a little better," Anna Marie said casually, as she turned to take the baby back inside.

He stood looking after her, afraid to read too much into her invitation, yet feeling a warm glow of hope at its possibilities. The glow continued as they walked together through the quiet tree-lined streets of downtown Santa Rosa, looking for a place where they could stop for lunch. He wondered what she would do if he reached out and took her hand.

"Do you like it here?"

"Yes, it's very peaceful," she answered, as though preoccupied with other thoughts. He waited, but she didn't elaborate.

"Was there something you wanted to talk to me about?"

There was a long silence before she answered.

"We're having another baby."

They stood waiting for the light to change. He took her by the shoulders and turned her slowly around to face him.

"Did you just say we're having another baby?"

She giggled at the look of absolute astonishment on his face and nodded her head in affirmation.

"It's a miracle baby," he blurted, his face beginning to break into a huge grin.

"A bloody miracle baby, that's what it is!"

He scooped her up in his arms and twirled her around, laughing and shouting, "It's a miracle baby!" He was oblivious to the onlookers, who had paused to see what all the excitement was about.

"Frank, please, put me down! Honey, you're making me dizzy!"

He finally stopped and put her down, and looked around at the faces in the crowd. They were all smiling at his show of affection toward this pretty young girl.

"It doesn't change anything, you know," she said tersely, smoothing out her now wrinkled dress. "I won't go back until I'm sure things have changed and you won't hurt me anymore."

He felt frustrated with her. One minute she's making him feel great. The next minute she's lashing out at him. But, he knew he had to stay cool. One show of anger would end the delicate balance of trust that had barely started to take root between them. He took her hand and they began to walk. She didn't try to pull away.

"What do you want this time, a boy or a girl?"

"A little sister for Andrew would be nice," she said, giving his hand a squeeze.

He said, "How about naming her Anna Marie?"

"You wouldn't dare!"

Baby Catherine came into the world screaming and hollering, and that turned out to be her favorite pastime. But she was beautiful, just like her mother, and she was the miracle child that eventually brought them back together again. They purchased a modest, ranch-style house in Santa Rosa, and for a few months, life seemed perfect.

When Frank wasn't commuting to work in San Francisco, he was working on the house, painting, putting in a lawn, making a sandbox for the kids, or building a picket fence and planting rose bushes.

On sunny days, Anna Marie would pack a picnic basket and they would take a drive through the beautiful vineyards of Sonoma County to the Russian River. They laughed a lot, were carefree, and glad they had found each other again.

"I'm pregnant again..." Her words were barely audible, but the power of emotion resounded like thunder in his heart. He withdrew his arm from around her waist. She lay motionless, her eyes staring upward through the darkness. He felt weary from working the night shift and the long drive home from the city. It was after four in the morning. Soon, it would be daybreak and he knew it would be much harder to sleep then.

"Honey, trust me, I'll take good care of you, you know that."

He searched for her hand to give it a reassuring squeeze, but she had it in a tight fist and flinched it away at his touch.

"I swear, everything will be okay. Try to get some sleep and we'll talk about it in the morning, okay?"

"I'm only twenty-one...and I'll barely be twenty-two with three babies in diapers..."

He felt at a loss. She seemed so fragile; he didn't want to say anything more for fear of saying the wrong thing. She turned her back to him and began to cry softly into her pillow. He stroked her hair until she stopped crying.

"I'm gonna pack Foster's in and find a job closer to home. How does that sound?"

She had already fallen into an exhausted sleep.

Daniel was born with lots of problems; psoriasis, asthma, allergies and constant diaper rash, all of which made for a very unhappy little boy. Catherine was so fascinated with his crying that she gave up her own crying for a while, just to listen to his. Andrew, being the mature one at two years old, decided he could help mom best by standing at the side of the cradle and poking the pacifier back into the baby's mouth, whenever he spit it out to cry. It helped a little, but it wasn't quite enough.

Alone each evening with the children, Anna Marie cried herself to sleep, then struggled to keep the children quiet during the day while Frank slept. She tried keeping her fragile emotions hidden whenever he was around, but he would catch her crying at odd times and think she was unhappy with him for somehow failing her. But, it wasn't anything he had done. When he wasn't working, he was home playing with the children or helping around the house. He loved her too much to ever want to hurt her or take the chance of losing her again.

She stood at the kitchen window staring vacantly out at the pink glow of sunset. Behind her, she could just barely make out Frank's soothing voice reading a bedtime story to the children in the next room. She hoped he would understand, but whether he did or not, she was convinced it was the only answer. For her, the struggle was over.

"I think the little buggers finally fell asleep," he chuckled, surprised at how easy it had been. He made himself a cup of coffee and sat at the kitchen table. She didn't move to join him.

"I have to leave, Frank. I have to get away for a while. I'm sorry."

Her voice was quiet, soothing; yet, there was no mistaking the finality of what she had just said.

He felt a sinking sensation in the pit of his stomach and cold hands of fear begin to grip his chest. He was losing her again and he was helpless to stop her. His body trembled as he got up and walked over to the window.

"What did I do wrong?" he asked, as he curled his arms gently around her waist. "I thought I was doing a good job."

"It's not about you. It's about me. I'm hurting. I'm in pain and I don't know why. I'm empty inside. I have to get away before I do something terrible, do you understand that?"

He turned her around to face him.

"What about the kids? What's gonna happen to them?" he asked quietly, not wanting her to feel afraid of him in her fragile state of mind.

For the first time, tears welled up in her eyes.

"I'm doing it as much for them as for myself. Sometimes I feel trapped, angry, like I want to strike out and hurt them for no other reason than their crying." She laid her head on his shoulder. "I want you to help me leave; I know you'll do fine until I get well again."

He stroked her hair gently with his hand. "Where will you go?"

"I'll stay at Mom's, and maybe go down to live with my sister in Los Angeles for a while."

They stood in silence until the last passenger boarded the Greyhound bus.

"I'd better get on now," she said, moving slowly toward the door. "I'll call you when I get to Mom's, okay?"

Frank smiled but didn't say anything. It was all still too confusing to him. Here he was saying good bye to his beautiful young wife, without any indication when she would be back, if ever. He was alone now to care for three small children until his sister, Margaret, could arrive from Liverpool to give him a hand.

Anna Marie kissed him lightly on the cheek and stepped up into the bus. He waved as the bus pulled out, but she didn't see him. She was staring straight ahead.

He lay in bed listening. Something had awakened him, but he wasn't sure what. He could hear Margaret vacuuming in the rear of the house, and distant voices of the children playing in the sand box outside. A loud knock on the front door startled him and he jumped up and grabbed for his bathrobe hanging over the bedpost.

"Telegram, sir. Just sign here, please."

Frank signed for it and closed the door and leaned against it. He didn't like telegrams. It usually meant bad news. He opened the envelope and stared at the simple typewritten message:

> YOUR MOTHER DIED
> EARLY THIS MORNING
> **STOP**
> SORRY **STOP**
> CAN YOU AND MARGARET
> MAKE IT HOME **STOP**
> UNCLE ALVIN **STOP**

He felt dizzy, nauseous. His hand flew to his mouth and his eyes searched wildly around the room, as though he were trapped and looking for a way out.

Oh, God! There must be some mistake, he moaned, as he read the telegram again. *No warning that she was sick and needs to see us? Not even a chance to say good bye? To say we love her?* The pain was almost too much for him to bear.

The noise from the vacuum cleaner stopped. He felt panic. *Jesus, what am I gonna say to her,* he wondered, stuffing the telegram quickly into his robe pocket. *How the hell am I supposed to tell her our mam died while she's over here taking care of my damn problems?*

A door opened, and he heard the sound of running water. Slowly, he walked into the kitchen and put his arms around her. She looked into his pallid face, her brow furrowed in a question.

"Margaret, there's just no easy way to tell you this. Mam died this morning."

Her body stiffened, her eyes still searching his face. From the depth of her being came a heart-rending cry of anguish.

"No! I don't believe it!" she screamed, pounding her clenched fists against his chest. He held her tight until her energy was spent, then slowly let her go, knowing she needed time to be alone to process the tragedy in her own way.

She sat in the shade of the walnut tree out back, watching the children at play in the sand box.

56

The plane's engines roared to life, sending a mixture of fear and excitement coursing through Frank's body. He had been so busy running around getting everything ready and in order for the trip back to Liverpool, he had completely forgotten about his fear of flying. Now, as the plane taxied slowly toward the take-off point, his heart began to thump wildly against his rib cage, giving him a bad case of dry mouth and sweaty palms. He glanced at Margaret, sitting prim and proper next to him, and threw her a sick little grin.

"I can't help it, girl. It just comes over me."

She chuckled at the strained look on his face. "Take a few deep breaths and let it out slowly," she said, dabbing at his wet brow with her handkerchief. "You look like you're going to die on me, lad!"

The plane shuddered and vibrated as the jet engines became a deafening, high-pitched scream. Then it began to move forward, faster and faster, until everything inside was shaking, creaking, straining. Frank had never heard such a tumultuous racket. He was sure the plane was going to disintegrate with the sheer force of power that it needed to get a lift off.

With his eyes tightly shut, he could sense the plane was off the ground and climbing, straining against gravity, sinking in mid-stride, then climbing some more, banking over the glittering skyline of San Francisco and the Bay Area. He took a peek out the window. He couldn't help it. It was beautiful; magnificent.

The *No Smoking* sign went off.

"I'm gonna live after all," he sighed, lighting up a Camel and taking a deep drag on it.

Margaret leaned her head against his shoulder and was asleep in minutes. He felt tender toward her. He remembered the shock he felt on seeing her that cold December morning four months ago, standing there at his door. The little fourteen year old that had been in his memory, was gone forever. In her place stood this lovely, slender, well-groomed, poised and self-confident young woman of twenty-one smiling back at him. Coming to America to be a nanny for her big brother had been the ultimate fantasy come true for her. Now, it may have been the ultimate sacrifice. He wondered how he could ever make it up to her.

It was raining, foggy and very cold when the plane touched down at Heathrow Airport in London. Frank looked at his watch. It was after midnight. They grabbed their luggage in silence and hurried to catch the underground train that would take them to Houston Station. From there, it would be a four or five hour train ride to Liverpool.

"We should arrive in plenty of time," he assured Margaret, as she began to pace the platform. It had been three long harrowing days since the telegram had arrived. Now that they were getting close to home, any delay, no matter how small, sent their nerves unraveling. At one-thirty, they arrived at Houston Station. It was empty! Deserted, except for a handful of dark-blue uniformed workers scattered throughout the mammoth station.

Frank put down his suitcases. "What in the world is going on here?" he wondered, looking around him in disbelief.

Row upon row of empty trains sat lifeless alongside empty platforms. Ticket windows were dark and shuttered. Margaret spotted a couple of porters loading boxes onto a trolley and marched herself over there looking like she was ready to do battle.

"Excuse me, luv. Can you tell me why there's nobody around here?"

They both stopped working and gave her a puzzled look.

"Are you looking for somebody in particular?" the younger of the two asked, his eyes beginning to appreciate what he was looking at.

She ignored his obvious display of attention.

"Look, lads, my brother and I have traveled all the way from America to bury our mother. We're tired and we need to catch a train to Liverpool. Can you help us?"

The older man took off his cap and ran his fingers through his silver hair, his craggy face deep in thought.

"I'm real sorry, Miss. The first train out isn't 'til six o'clock. Can't think of what else to tell you."

"But, that may be too late!" she gasped, her eyes brimming with tears of frustration. The older man looked away, shaking his head in a show of sympathetic understanding. She walked back to where her brother was standing and sat down on a wooden bench and closed her eyes. Frank dragged the suitcases closer to where she was sitting.

"What did they tell you?"

She opened her eyes and looked up at him.

"We're not gonna make it in time, I can just feel it. The first train out isn't 'til six."

"I'm sure everyone will wait for us to get there. They know we're on our way," he reasoned, sitting down next to her and putting an arm around her shoulder. "It'll all work out, girl."

"Hey, Guv'na. There's a mail train heading up north in a couple of minutes. Would you be wanting to take it, like?"

Frank was up and grabbing for the suitcases before the silver-haired porter had finished speaking.

"Like I said, it's only a mail train," the porter called over his shoulder as he led the way. "No water or lavatory facilities, mind you, and it might be a tad bit cold."

Except for the steady stream of white steam escaping from the underbelly of its engine, the train looked dead; foreboding. The porter opened a carriage door and helped lift their luggage into the dark passageway. Frank fumbled for his wallet and offered him a pound note. The porter shook his head. "This one's on me, Guv."

Before Frank could thank him, the door slammed shut, leaving them staring after him through the dirt-encrusted window. The train jerked a couple of times and began to move slowly through the station.

"Stay here with the bags while I scout out a good spot for us, girl."

"No, I'm coming with you," she stated, grabbing for his coattail.

Once the train cleared the station, there was no more light coming through the windows, so he struck a match to light the way. There were canvas bags of mail stacked everywhere.

"Looks like as good a place as any," he said, pointing to what used to be a passenger compartment.

They were exhausted and collapsed onto the filthy benches. But they couldn't sleep right away. They shared their favorite childhood memories, until the incessant clickety-click of the train's wheels lulled them into a fitful sleep.

Frank awakened to absolute silence. Not even the familiar sound of hissing steam or the slamming of carriage doors invaded the silence. He got up and poked his head out the window. The platform was deserted. A large sign, lit with the only light on the platform read, Stafford.

"Wherever that is," he mumbled to himself.

A portly gentleman with a ruddy complexion and thick graying sideburns and mustache, came out of a small office holding a tea pot in one hand and the lid in the other.

"Excuse me, sir. How long is the train gonna be stopped here?" Frank called out.

Glad to see another human, the man gave him a big grin. "This is the end of the line for that bugger. Where you heading to?"

"Liverpool."

The man poured the dregs of tea into a bin and took out his gold watch from a waistcoat pocket. "Be just about two hours before it passes through here. Come get yourself next to a warm fire and have a nice cup of tea with me."

"I've got my sister here with me," he said, trying hard not to show the exasperation he was feeling inside.

"Bring her along, too," he laughed, with a sweep of his arm. "There's plenty of room."

***

The train slowed to a maddening crawl as it entered the cavernous Lime Street Station. The squealing of steel sent pigeons scattering up into their lofty perches and out through broken windows in the ancient roof. Frank and Margaret looked at each other without speaking. They both knew what each was thinking and feeling. The old clock, high up on the station wall, said it was almost eleven o'clock. They picked their way quickly through the throngs of people until they reached the taxi stand outside.

"Can you take us to Upper Mann Street as fast as you can, please? It's an emergency!" Frank pleaded, as he threw the luggage in and climbed in after his sister.

"Right, mate. I'll do me best for you, and still get you there in one piece, like. Is that off Mill Street or Park Road?"

"Mill Street, then right on Northumberland Street," Frank said, wincing, as the driver sped through a red light, almost mowing down a group of people. Half-way down Harding Street, they spotted a funeral procession coming the other way.

"I'm awful sure that was Uncle Peter in the second car," Margaret shouted, wiping furiously at the steamy window, in hopes of getting a better look at the rest of the cars as they went by. But the rain never afforded a clear view.

"How sure are you?"

"I'm almost positive!" she said, choking back tears.

"Driver, can you turn around and follow that procession that just passed us by?" he shouted.

By the time the taxi made a U-turn in the busy street, the cortege had disappeared from sight. He sped half-way through town hoping to catch a glimpse, but there was no sign of it anywhere. He looked at the couple in his rear-view mirror and felt sorry for them.

"I'll take you to where I think they were heading, how's that sound to you?"

They both nodded in his direction, neither one sure of anything anymore.

At Allerton Cemetery they were told their mother would be buried there the next day.

As the taxi pulled up to the curb, children came running from all directions to see who it was. People came out of their houses and stood on landings, looking down in silent welcome. The grownups knew who the young couple was in the taxi, and why they had come home.

Margaret sped upstairs while Frank paid the driver.

"That'll be two quid, mate."

He looked at the driver in surprise. "It's gotta be more than two pound! That was a long ride!" The driver grinned back at him. "The rest is on me, then, ain't it?"

He stood at the curbside watching after the taxi, surrounded by chattering children still too curious to leave. This was the moment he had dreaded most to think about. He suddenly felt naked, vulnerable.

Everything was done, finished, nothing to hide behind, no more plans to keep his mind occupied, nothing left to stave off this inevitable moment from arriving. He picked up the suitcases and smiled at the young faces.

"Hi, how are you kids doing?"

"I told ya he was a Yank," one kid chided to his friend.

"No, he's not. He's one of us; he used to live here, a long time ago."

PHOTO CREDITS

From Liverpool Picture Book – **www.liverpoolpicturebook.com**
Used by permission of the Liverpool Records Office

1. Scallywags
2. Overhead Railway
3. Dock Road
4. Liverpool Pier Head
5. Essex Street Fire Station
6. Upper Mann Street
7. Back of Mann Street
8. Custom House Foundation
9. Collage of Liverpool Streets
10. Customs House – May Blitz 1941
11. Post Card of St. Gilbert's Boy's School
    (private collection)
12. Upper Warwick Street
13. SS Basra and British Passport
14. High Park Street
15. Collage of Albert Dock Area
16. SS Free State
17. Frank and Bella (private collection)

Martha Ford's Corner Store

PROCEEDS FROM FRANKIE BOY ARE DONATED TO AMAZIMA MINISTRIES INTERNATIONAL

At age 18 Katie Davis visited and taught Kindergarten for the summer in a Ugandan orphanage. She lost her heart to the children, and now six years later, she has adopted thirteen daughters!

In 2008, Katie established a non-profit organization called Amazima Ministries International with a sponsorship program that includes feeding 1,200 school children Monday through Friday. The ministry also provides medical care, Bible study, and general health training to the Masese community. She also initiated a self-sustaining vocational program to empower women to be self-supporting and send their children to school.

Watch Katie's Story on You Tube: "2011 Amazima Overview with Katie Davis."

Purchase her book *Kisses from Katie: A story of Relentless Love and Redemption* available on **amazon.com**.

The author has committed his heart and financial support to this ministry with all proceeds from the sale of his book *Frankie Boy*.

For more information or to become a child sponsor visit www.amazima.org.

May God bless you in your support, as He has blessed me,
–Frank J. Rossiter

ABOUT THE AUTHOR:

Frank Rossiter is a retired business owner
and the author of
Frankie Boy and *Letters from Liverpool*.
He and his wife, Bella, have been married for 53 years
and are enjoying retirement in Mesa, Arizona.

I welcome reader comments and questions,
and look forward to hearing from you at
frankrossiter97@gmail.com

If you would like to order signed copies of
Frankie Boy or *Letters from Liverpool*,
contact me at the email address above.

Frankie Boy is proudly published by:

Creative Force Press

Guiding Aspiring Authors to Release Their Dream

www.CreativeForcePress.com

Do You Have a Book in You?

36240720R00180

Made in the USA
Charleston, SC
28 November 2014